NEW
SOVIET
SCIENCE
FICTION

NEW SOVIET SCIENCE FICTION

INTRODUCTION BY
Theodore Sturgeon

TRANSLATED FROM THE RUSSIAN BY
Helen Saltz Jacobson

COLLIER BOOKS
A Division of Macmillan Publishing Co., Inc.
NEW YORK

COLLIER MACMILLAN PUBLISHERS
LONDON

Library of Congress Cataloging in Publication Data

Main entry under title:

New Soviet science fiction.
   (Macmillan's Best of Soviet science fiction)
   CONTENTS: Varshavsky, I. The violet. The duel. Plot for a novel. Escape.—Bulychev, K. Share it with me.—Bilenkin, D. Personality probe. [etc.]
   1. Science fiction, Russian—Translations into English. 2. Science fiction, English—Translations from Russian. I. Series.
PZ1.N44415 1980 [PG3276] 891.73′0876′08947
80-10790
ISBN 0-02-578220-7
ISBN 0-02-022650-0 pbk

Macmillan Publishing Co., Inc.
866 Third Avenue, New York, N.Y. 10022
Collier Macmillan Canada, Ltd.

First Collier Books Edition 1980
New Soviet Science Fiction is also published
in a hardcover edition
by Macmillan Publishing Co., Inc.
Printed in the United States of America

"A Provincial's Wings" was translated
by Alice Stone Nakhimovsky and
Alexander Nakhimovsky, the remaining
stories by Helen Saltz Jacobson.

Contents

Introduction

Here in your hands: new Soviet science fiction. Let us immediately define our terms.

New. New to me, and almost certainly to you. New, in that it is of recent genesis; new, in the sense that it is revealed to us for the first time.

Soviet. Let me pass on this for a moment. I shall return to it.

Science fiction. Ah. Know all men by these presents that no one has yet managed to define this genre in any way that does not leak, and I am not about to be trapped into trying to accomplish it. All I can do is to descend into the subjective; to tell you what it means to me. Kindly bear in mind as I do this that my definitions deal with *good* science fiction and *good* fiction.

In order to do this I must fire up my literary cyclotron and split the axioms.

Science. I am uneasy with the dictionary as a source. To define "science," as most of them do, as the discovery, arrangement, and retrieval of data is restrictive. Better to go to etymology and find that the root word *scientia* means "knowledge"—just that: knowledge, and nothing more. To me "science fiction" has always been a misnomer to the degree that "science," in its accepted sense, is restrictive of the wide spectrum and vaulting ideation possible in the field. Only poetry is its rival in wingspread, and it will not limit itself to anyone's taxonomy. Science fiction? Better it were called knowledge fiction—and even that delimits. I wish sometimes that the scientists were still named as they were in the seventeenth and eighteenth centuries—natural philosophers; for science, like mathematics, in its higher reaches approaches philosophy and extends itself through religious paradigms into something like mysticism. If you can find a term for fiction which is at home in such altitudes, remember that it must include wild humor, satire, and that most wonderful literary miracle-worker of all—fable, the "moral" of which is greater than the narrative and illuminates the human condition (or predicament). So the *scientia* in science fiction can be the knowledge of today's hard scientist or that of Joyce Carol Oates, Nabokov, Wells, Verne, Poe, Mary Shelley, Cyrano, all the way back to Lucian of Samothrace and Ezekiel the prophet; up again through Plato and Thomas More, Swift and Kipling, Orwell, Richard Hughes, Vonnegut (sorry, Kurt!) to Woody Allen. And, of course, these mad and maddening Soviets.

Fiction. One writes about people. One may not write about ideas and call it fiction. Fiction deals with the interaction between people and people, and between ideas and people. The highest achievement in fiction—rarely met—is to induce in the reader not the feeling that he has read the story, but that it has happened to him. When this occurs within the exhilarating ideation of science fiction, the resonance, the reverberations, do not stop. Fiction that goes not only into outer space, but to inner space—that much roomier and less empty volume of knowledge and self-knowledge; that goes into areas that are not present or future but just "other," whereby new perspectives can be found for society and psyche, history and hard science; that goes into xenobiology and xenopsychology, the studies of intelligences we may meet and deal with one day, aliens in every sense even though some may be our own descendants (Heavens!

there are times when we feel that way about our own children, here and now!)—fiction like this, adventuresome and seminal, abrasive and hilarious, daring and biting, has to be worth some investigation.

Soviet. Ah! again . . . yes, the stories in this book came from the Soviet Union. And yes, here and there, filtered through the most skilled and respectful translation and editing, one catches glimpses of national and cultural difference: the village that the postman reaches only on foot through woods and bogs, impassable at certain seasons; the taken-for-granted, even in cities, of three roommates rather than one and the rental (equally taken for granted) of chicken-coops and lean-tos for vacationers; the wide familiarity among working people with the great literary and political figures in their history—wide as ours with screen and gridiron celebrities. Beyond that, one is struck by the similarities herein of the people and places we know, the problems and issues we face. Boundaries and ethnic and cultural and political differences tend to blur in this métier, and one is tempted to suggest that the book's title be changed to *New Terran Science Fiction.*

Not all of these stories do all of the things suggested above. Yet the showcase is a wide one. There are highly comedic satires like Shefner's two offerings, told in a childlike cadence but with teeth and claws for the bumbling bureaucrat. Varshavsky pivots on human reactions to single stimuli, once pathos, once stupidity, once shock, once horror, in his four brief pieces. Kirill Bulychev, a fine novelist, plays here with the idea of an empathic people—people who cannot keep themselves from feeling what you feel. Gennady Gor rings yet another change to that fascinating corner of science fiction, time travel. Bakhnov, a first-order ironist if there ever was one, tells us, among other things, of a museum that specializes in forgeries, and the cataclysmic events that occur when a young man proves one of its treasures to be genuine. Dneprov's story troubles me, not so much because of its disturbing theme but because of the feeling that it should have been a novel. *Ne gustibus* . . . yet it provokes thought, and that is always good.

Three of these stories demand special attention—two because of their involvement with computers, and one for its unique merits.

Computers are with us to stay, and it is no surprise to discover that there is already a vast body of computer-oriented science fiction from every source. Increasingly the jargon of computer technology is permeating our language as its presence creeps into the other facets of our lives. All around us new careers are opening in hard- and software, and in the design and use of these astonishing devices. It is by no means the first time the science fiction writer has had to scramble to keep ahead of the technologists.

Dmitri Bilenkin has created for us a completely original use for the computer, and he presents it with a clear example of that "knowledge" quantum mentioned above. Advanced students in an institute program a computer with a vast amount of information concerning one Bulgarin, the man responsible for the persecution and ultimate destruction of the great poet Pushkin. Coupled to a holographic projection, the machine is capable of producing, in effect, a living ghost, conscious and aware, of Bulgarin. They are then able to take him to task for his actions, to let him rationalize them in any way he can, to defend himself against the facts of his biography. Bilenkin's handling of this "trial" is most dramatic, and in the process provided me—quite unexpectedly, I confess —with knowledge of Pushkin and the prerevolutionary atmosphere in which he lived and died.

Vladimir Savchenko certainly lives with and works with computers. The high degree of his sophistication concerning computers and their possibilities is matched by his intimacy with educational/scientific institutions, their administrators, and their ability to produce, along with scientific miracles, a class of self-seeking, bombastic, hypocritical and immoral bureaucrats. Savchenko takes after these creatures with savagery and high good humor; his sketches of all the people involved are mordant and memorable. Most of all, they are supranational. What he illuminates here is found everywhere.

Mikhail Emtsev and Eremei Parnov, collaborators, have already proved themselves as fine novelists. (Parnov, by the way, is chairman of the Science Fiction section of the Soviet Writers Union.) Their story here is more than an adventure into far space and the kind of nuts-and-bolts "hardcore" science so dear to the heart of the science fiction purist, for it pursues its theme smoothly into one of the most horrifying periods of recent history, the rise of Nazism and the persecution of the scientific community in Germany. The writing here has a harrowing quality of reality. Underlying this is the frightening thought that even in the distant future, with miraculous technology a commonplace, human stubbornness and stupidity (not necessarily in the political area but even in the scientific one) may ruthlessly crush a new and revolutionary concept. Overall, this remarkable story is one of the most eloquent pleas I have read anywhere for the freedom of science to do science freely.

In closing, I should like to share with you a remarkable illumination which came to me recently. Gerard O'Neill at Princeton has conceived the great dream of colonies in space—huge cities hovering in the Trojan positions between the earth and the moon. Many of us are writing about life on these colonies, and of course we deal with meteorite holes, population pressures, defective orbits, and the like.

But inevitably, in these communities there will emerge the science fiction writer—the Heinlein, the Strugatsky, the Clarke, the Savchenko of his time and place. And he will *not* be writing about meteorites and population control and decaying orbits.

What *will* he write?

When I think of that, I want to live forever.

NEW
SOVIET
SCIENCE
FICTION

The Violet

ILYA VARSHAVSKY

1

ITS EASTERN AND WESTERN BORDERS washed by the waves of two oceans, the City reached from the polar region to the equatorial zone. Beyond a forest of oil rigs sucking up oil from the bottom of the sea stood other cities, but the City was the largest of them all.

For almost two miles it descended into the bowels of the earth, and for some thirty miles rose into the heavens. Like a giant octopus it lay on the earth, its enormous pipes drooping into the water. Through these pipes flowed all the materials needed for the synthesis of food and other products essential to the life of the City.

In similar fashion purified water passed through subterranean recycling apparatus and removed heat from the planet's depths which it delivered to the City before returning to the ocean.

The roof of the City was its lungs. Here, on the boundless expanse of a reclamation bed located high above the clouds, the sun's rays broke down the expiration products of forty billion people and enriched the City's air with oxygen.

This great City, the planet's most grandiose structure, constantly interacting with the air and sea surrounding it, was like a living being, as busy and energetic as the people inhabiting it.

Beneath the earth, on the subterranean floor of this lively, bustling metropolis, factories converted raw materials into a never-ending supply of goods for the City's huge and demanding population.

Here, in the light of phosphorescent solutions, the silent and fully automated processes of synthesis continued around the clock.

High above the earth in an endless maze of apartment dwellings, as in every city on the planet, people were born, lived, dreamed, and died.

2

"Children, we are not having our regular lessons tomorrow," announced the teacher. "We are going on a field trip to a national preserve. Be sure to tell your parents that you will arrive home an hour later than usual."

"What's a preserve?" asked a little girl with a big ribbon.

The teacher smiled. "A preserve is a special place where all kinds of plants have been brought together."

"Plants? What's that?"

"Next semester I'm going to tell you all about them."

"Tell us now," pleaded a little Boy.

"Yes, yes, tell us now," shouted the children.

"We have very little time now, children, and it's something we can't possibly discuss in just a few minutes."

"Please, teacher, now!"

"Well, all right. What else can I do with you! Now, children, our planet, Donomaga, was not always the way it is now. Many centuries ago there were only small settlements."

"And no City?" asked the Boy.

"No, no big City as we have now."

"Why?"

"For many reasons. Things were badly organized then. No one knew how to produce synthetic food, and people lived on plants and animals."

"What are animals?"

"You will learn all about them in fourth grade. So, in those days, long ago, there was a lot of land that no one lived on, and people raised all kinds of plants that were used for food."

"Sweets?"

"I don't know," she smiled again. "I never tasted any. Besides, not all plants were suitable for food."

"Why did they pul . . . pl . . . them?"

"Plant?" the teacher helped the Boy find the right word.

"Yes. Plant."

"They planted only those plants which they could eat. Many plants grew by themselves."

"How did they grow, like children?"

The teacher thought she would never escape from this endless barrage of questions.

"Now, children," she said, "I told you it would be impossible to tell you everything in five minutes. They grew because they took nutritious substances from the earth and used sunlight. Tomorrow you will see it with your own eyes."

3

"Mama, we're going to a preserve tomorrow!" shouted the little Boy as he burst through the door.

"Did you hear that? Our Boy is going to the preserve."

Father shrugged his shoulders. "Is the preserve still there? I thought . . . "

"It is, it is! Our teacher told us all about it today. It has all kinds of plants. They eat something from the earth and grow! Do you understand, Papa, they grow by themselves!"

"I understand," said his mother. "I visited it, too, twenty years ago. It's all very touching and so very naive."

"I don't know about that," said his father. "To tell the truth, it never made a big impression on me. Besides, there is also bare earth in the preserve—not a particularly appetizing sight."

"I remember when grass grew there," his mother said dreamily.

"A thick carpet of green grass."

"As far as I'm concerned, I'll take our good, solid, plastic floors any time. You can have your green grass," said his father.

4

The elevator decelerated gently.

"Children, we'll have to change to another elevator here," said the teacher. "The express doesn't go any further."

For a long time they waited before a strange looking door covered with an iron grating and watched two slowly moving steel cables gliding on squeaky rollers. A box with glass doors crawled toward them. The teacher pried open the door and the children, awed by the ancient elevator, stepped into the cage silently.

Jerking lightly at every floor, the elevator descended lower and lower. The children, no longer surrounded by luminescent paneling and fragrant warm air, began to grow anxious.

The rectangular bottomless well was illuminated by glaring electric bulbs. It seemed as if the shaft's rough concrete walls were about to close in over their heads and bury them forever in this strange, joyless world.

"Much further?" asked the Boy.

"Only twenty more floors," replied the teacher. "The preserve is at the bottom because the plants must have earth."

"I want to go home!" the smallest girl in the class began to whine. "I don't like it here!"

"We'll be there in a minute," the teacher consoled her, although she, too, felt vaguely uncomfortable. "One more minute."

Down below something clanged loudly and the elevator stopped. The teacher stepped out first and the children quickly crowded out the door after her.

"Is everybody here?"

"Yes," said the Boy.

They stood quietly in the dimly lit corridor.

"Follow me, children!"

"Teacher, something is dripping from the ceiling!" the little girl with the ribbon cried out.

"Those are pipes that bring water to the preserve," the teacher reassured her. "They are so old, they leak."

"Where is the preserve?" asked the Boy.

"Here it is." She opened an iron door. "Go through one at a time."

Dazzled by their sudden exit from semi-darkness into bright sunlight, the children instinctively screwed up their eyes. It was several minutes before curiosity got the better of them. They opened their eyes cautiously and looked around.

Never before had they seen anything like it. The seemingly bottomless well was flooded with sunlight. A stream of sunlight lit up the walls of the shaft like a yellow flame; it flowed like a rainbow into the fine spray of a small fountain and raised heavy, thick fumes from the damp earth.

"This is the sun," said the teacher. "I told you about it at your science lesson. Special mirrors, set up high, catch the sun's rays and send them down to the plants."

"It's warm!" shouted the Boy, stretching out his hand. "The sun—it's warm! Look, I'm catching it in my hands!"

"Yes, it's very hot," said the teacher. "The temperature on the sun's surface reaches six thousand degrees. And inside—even more."

"No, it's not hot, it's warm," the Boy objected. "It's like the walls in our house, but quite different and much better! Why don't they give us sun in the City?"

The teacher frowned. After all, these were only children and it was very difficult for them to understand problems which even philosophers could not answer. Was it possible to explain to them that forty billion people . . . Yet, she knew that she would have to find an answer to each of their questions.

"We could not live without the sun," she explained, patting the Boy on the head. "Our entire way of life, our very lives depend on the sun. But plants use the sun's rays directly, while we put it to work for us in many other ways. As for the light the sun gives, we have no need of it. Don't our lamps give plenty of light?"

"It's not the same at all. It's cold," the Boy said stubbornly. "You can't catch it in your hands like you can the sunshine."

"You think you can, but you really can't. Next year you will study physics and you will learn that it only seems that way. Now, we'll ask the gardener to show us the plants."

He was very old and very strange. A long white beard hung below his waist. His eyes were very tiny, two slits covered by bushy gray eyebrows. And he wore a handsome white smock.

"Is he real?" asked the Boy.

"Hush!" the teacher whispered to him. "Talk less and look more."

"But I can talk and look at the same time," said the Boy. He thought the gardener had winked at him, but he wasn't sure.

"Now, here, for example," piped the gardener in an extraordinarily thin voice, "are useful grasses. Fifty stalks of wheat. They aren't ripe yet, but in a month, several ears containing seeds will appear on each stalk. Long, long ago these seeds were used for food, to make bread."

"Was it tasty?" asked the girl with the ribbon.

"No one knows," replied the little old man. "The recipe for bread was lost a long time ago."

"What do you do with the seeds?" asked the teacher.

"We save some of them to raise new wheat. Some go to replace those in the museum's archives. And the rest . . . " he threw up his hands, "the rest we have to throw away. We have so little land: all we have here is this little garden plot with wheat, two trees, a few flowers, and a tiny meadow with grass."

"May we see the flowers?" suggested the teacher.

The gardener led them to a small flower bed.

"These are violets, the only species of flowers that has survived." He bent over and straightened a twisted leaf with great care. "In those days there were still insects, pollination. . . ."

"The children haven't learned about that yet," the teacher interrupted him.

"May I touch them?" the Boy asked.

"Bend over and smell them," said the gardener. "They have a wonderful scent."

The Boy got down on his knees and inhaled deeply. A gentle fragrance mixed with the smell of damp, hot earth tickled his nostrils.

"Ah," he whispered, bending closer. "Oh, this is so ... so ... " He couldn't find the words to express his feelings.

The other children had already finished inspecting the grass and trees, but the Boy was still on his knees, his face caressing the soft, sweet-smelling petals.

"All right, children!" the teacher looked at her watch. "It's time to go. Thank the gardener for an interesting excursion."

"Thank you!" they shouted in chorus.

"Good-bye!" said the gardener. "Be sure to come again."

"We certainly shall," replied the teacher. "This trip is part of our curriculum. I'll be back next year with our new pupils."

The Boy was already at the door when a miracle occurred. Someone was tugging at his sleeve. He turned around. The gardener handed him a violet. Looking like a conspirator, the gardener put his finger to his lips.

"Is this for me??!" the Boy asked softly.

The gardener nodded.

"We're waiting for you. Hurry!" the teacher shouted to the Boy. "You're always lagging behind."

"I'm coming!" He hid the flower under his shirt and darted into the corridor.

5

That evening the Boy went to bed earlier than usual. After he turned out the light, he placed the violet next to his face on the pillow and lay wide awake for a long time.

It was already morning when his mother heard strange sounds coming from his room.

"I think he's crying," she said to her husband.

"Probably overtired from the trip," he muttered, turning over. "I noticed that he was behaving strangely last night."

"I must take a look and see what's wrong," said the mother, putting on her robe.

The Boy was sitting on his bed, weeping bitterly.

"What happened, dear?" She sat down next to him and put her arm around his shoulder.

"Look!" he opened his fist.

"What's that?"

"A violet!" In the sweaty palm of his hand lay wilted petals and a withered stem. "This is a violet. The gardener gave it to me. Oh, Mama, how it did smell!"

"Come now, silly!" his mother said. "You're crying for nothing. We have such beautiful roses right here at home."

She went into the next room and returned with a vase of flowers.

"I'll set the odorstat on 'very high.' All right?"

"No, I don't want them! I don't like those flowers!"

"But they are much, much prettier than your violet and they smell nicer."

"No, they don't, they don't!" he cried, punching his pillow. "They don't. A violet is completely different. It's . . . it's . . . " Again he began to weep because he just couldn't find the right words.

The Duel

ILYA VARSHAVSKY

1

WHEN HE REACHED THE BOTTOM of the stairs, he hopped over the railing and sprinted through the lobby, gobbling down a sandwich on the wing.

He had just enough time to reach the path and stretch out on a bench. There he would intercept that cute coed as she came from class and invite her to the soccer game. After the game they would have a snack in the student cafeteria and then . . . Well, he hadn't quite figured out the next step, but it didn't worry him; in dealing with the ladies he always relied on instinct.

Suddenly the loudspeaker boomed out:

"Freshman student Mukharinsky, phenotype 1386.16 MB, report immediately to the Dean of the Radio Technology Department!"

He had to make a split-second decision. If only he could slip beyond the range of the analyzer. It was no more than a few steps, and with a little luck he could make it. Puckering his lips, pulling out his ears, squinting with his left eye and feigning a limp, he tried to con his way past the phenotype analyzer's eagle eye.

"Stop clowning, Mukharinsky!"

It was the voice of the Dean himself.

"You are late, young man!"

Within a fraction of a second the analyzer had singled him out of ten thousand students, and now the image of his artfully distorted mug graced the T.V. screen in the Dean's office.

Mukharinsky returned his mouth and ears to their normal positions and began to rub his right knee vigorously, hoping to convince the Dean that he had suddenly been stricken with an acute attack of rheumatism.

No luck. With a deep sigh of resignation he headed for the second floor.

The Dean studied him with interest for several minutes. Mukharinsky's face had assumed an intent, mournful expression, most appropriate to the occasion, while his brain was trying to calculate how much time he would need to catch up with that cute coed.

"Tell me, Mukharinsky, is there anything you are really interested in?"

What a silly question, thought Mukharinsky. He had dozens of interests, dozens of important matters that kept him constantly occupied. Like Natasha and Musa. Or his favorite soccer team. And there was that cute coed. Oh, he could go on endlessly about his wide range of interests, but there was no point in confiding such matters to the Dean.

"Well, sir, I am very interested in engineering and radio," he replied humbly.

"Then perhaps you can explain to me why you haven't passed a single examination this semester?"

"Oh, God!" he thought to himself. "I am going to be expelled."

"Perhaps the teaching machine . . . " he began weakly.

"Three different machines have refused to work with you," interrupted the Dean. "What are you counting on to get you through?"

The wisest thing was to pretend it was a rhetorical question and let it pass.

Now deep in thought, the Dean drummed his fingers along the

edge of the desk. Mukharinsky looked out the window. Aha, there she was! Beside her strode a lanky chap in a blue T-shirt carrying a set of oars. Well, that was that. He would have to forget about his red-headed coed and give away his extra ticket to the soccer game.

"I would not want to expel you until I was absolutely convinced that it was impossible to give you an engineering education."

"I am very pleased, sir," said Mukharinsky, lowering his eyes, "that you still have faith in the possibility of my ... "

"No, Mukharinsky, if it were *your* possibilities I was concerned with, you would have been dropped from our student rolls a long time ago. I am referring to the possibilities of our teaching machines. I have a great deal of faith in them. You can be sure of that. Have you heard of the UIWFB?"

"Of course, sir. That's the ... uh ... "

"Of course you have, my boy," the Dean grinned. "I am sure that you have read all the literature produced by our Department of Teaching Machines. UIWFB stands for *Universal Instructor With Feedback*. I hope you know what 'feedback' means?"

"Well, sir, in a general sort of way," Mukharinsky replied cautiously.

"I am planning to demonstrate our UIWFB at the International Congress in Vienna. Right now we are conducting an experiment to determine its potentialities. It is teaching a control group of engineering students. Naturally, I would prefer not to lower the group's average grade, but it is my duty as a scholar and scientist to test the machine's capabilities even on students such as ... h'm ... such as you. In brief, I am now including you in the control group."

"Thank you, sir."

"I do hope it succeeds in transmitting at least some knowledge to you. Its circuitry is ... "

Mukharinsky didn't give a damn about the machine's circuitry. His thoughts flew to the soccer field where the first half of the game was probably ending and Natasha, if worst came to worst. ...

"So, during the teaching process, your brain and the teaching machine's circuitry are integrated into a single working unit involving feedback. The machine changes its tactics in relation to the student's assimilation of the material. Is that clear?"

"Yes, sir. Perfectly clear."

"Thank God! You may go now."

2

The computer scans the subject's brain for the three-hundred and forty-second time and presents its sixteenth variant of the theorem's proof. Again the blocking unit gives the signal: "Material not assimilated. Change tactics." More scanning. Then: "Proof of theorem requires elementary knowledge on a high-school level." A command: "Proceed to a review of basic principles of algebra." A second signal: "Material assimilated minimally. Shift to theorem proof." Toward the end of the proof, another signal: "Basic knowledge lost." Again a command to change tactics. More scanning. Suddenly a red light flashes on the control panel: "Overheated." Smoke belches from the transformer and the machine shuts off automatically.

Mukharinsky removed the electrodes from his head and wiped his perspiring face. Phew! What a session! He had never experienced the likes of it with the electronic lecturers. They were a lot easier to work with than this damn thing. You could sleep through a whole lecture without even bothering to answer questions. But this UIWFB wouldn't give you a moment's peace. Thank goodness its automatic defense system shut the machine off from time to time.

His ruminations were interrupted by the videophone. The Dean's face appeared on the screen.

"Why aren't you working?"

"The machine is cooling off, sir. It overheated."

To Mukharinsky's dismay the green light flashed. Back to work! Sighing, he fastened the electrodes in place again.

More scanning, and that detested equation flashed in Mukharinsky's brain for the nth time. He tried to fight the machine, to shift his thoughts to other, more interesting worlds. He thought about the possible consequences should Demetriev fail to make a goal at the end of the second half. He tried to picture that little redhead in the most seductive situations. But all in vain.

More scanning, a signal, a command, a change in tactics, another signal, more scanning. . . . Hour after hour, day after day.

3

Seven days passed and, oh, miracle of miracles! Learning didn't seem quite so agonizing anymore. The machine, too, appeared to be adapting itself to its stubborn human subject: the "overheating" signal flashed less and less frequently.

Another week went by and the loudspeaker roared through the halls of the institute:

"Freshman student Mukharinsky, phenotype 1386.16 MB, report to the Dean immediately!"

This time he did not attempt to elude the phenotype analyzer's all-seeing eye.

"Congratulations, my boy," said the Dean. "You have revealed extraordinary abilities."

For the first time in his life Mukharinsky blushed.

"I feel, sir," he replied modestly, "it would be more proper to speak of the UIWFB's extraordinary abilities. It is a truly remarkable invention."

"When I say 'abilities,' Mukharinsky, I have you, and you alone in mind. As far as the UIFWB is concerned, its two-week contact with you has not been unproductive. It is no longer a run-of-the-mill teaching machine, but a kind of Don Juan or Casanova. To put it on a level more comprehensible to you—a lady-killer. It has also become a fanatic soccer fan and has enticed the entire control group in this direction. It has become fantastically lazy. So, we are dismantling it tomorrow. Now, as far as you are concerned, you can understand that we . . ."

"Of course, sir. And I wish you every success."

He bowed deeply and started toward the door.

"Where are you going?" the Dean called after him.

"Home, of course. You've expelled me, haven't you?"

"Yes, Mukharinsky, that's true. We have expelled you from the institute. But only as a student. We have just appointed you Senior Laboratory Assistant in the Department of Teaching Machines. Henceforth not a single machine with a feedback system will leave the laboratory before it has undergone the supreme test, that is, before it has engaged in a duel with you and won. Mukharinsky, you are a real find!"

Plot for a Novel

ILYA VARSHAVSKY

I WAS REALLY HAPPY. Anyone who has experienced a painful and protracted illness and is finally restored to good health can fully appreciate my state of mind. Everything delighted me: the fact that I was not placed on disability pension but, instead, was granted an extended leave from work in order to complete my dissertation, which I had begun before my illness; the fact that I could now look forward to a rest at the sanatorium, thus relieving me of the pressure of thinking about my dissertation for the present; the comfort of the double compartment; the fact that my fellow passenger turned out to be a pleasant chap rather than some capricious female. And, to boot, I was being seen off by a charming woman whom I loved passionately and sincerely. I was flattered that such a beauty, ignoring the admiring glances of the passengers, was holding my hand like a little girl afraid of losing her father in the crowd.

"Are you going far?" she asked my fellow passenger.

"To Kislovodsk."

"Really? So, you'll be traveling together all the way."

She broke into that winning smile of hers that never fails to delight the men. "Well, then I have a special favor to ask of you. Keep a good eye on *my husband*." This was the first time since we had known each

other intimately that she had used those words, and I was struck by
the simple and natural way she had pronounced them. "He is still
convalescing," she added.

"Don't worry!" my fellow passenger smiled, "I'm almost a doctor,
you know."

"What do you mean 'almost'? Are you a student?"

"If you like . . . an eternal student with an M.D.'s diploma."

He slipped into the corridor and gently closed the door behind him
to avoid disturbing us.

"He's probably taking his Ph.D." she whispered, kissing me
good-bye.

I love to begin a journey in the daytime; to settle slowly into the
rhythm of activity around me; to observe my fellow passengers; to
unpack leisurely and get accustomed to my compartment.

Today, everything was just as I liked it, and besides, I repeat, I was
completely happy. At least I thought I was. I say *thought* because for
some reason I sensed a strange anxiety and restlessness building up
within me. One minute I would jump up from my seat and go into the
corridor; the next, after returning to my compartment, I would sort
through my suitcase rather aimlessly; or I would begin reading and
a minute later would toss the magazine aside and return to the
corridor.

I don't know why, but travelers are ready to pour out their
innermost secrets to the first stranger they encounter. Perhaps this is
an atavistic emotion, a hangover from the time when any journey
was fraught with danger and every traveler became a friend, companion, and confidant; or perhaps it can be attributed to man's
inherent need to unburden his heart to someone, and the casual
acquaintance, whom he surely will never meet again, is the most
ideal listener.

Meanwhile, dinnertime had come and my fellow passenger suggested that we go to the dining car.

At dinner I began to chatter endlessly. Even after we had finished
our meal I went on and on, although the waiter had changed the tablecloth—a gentle hint for us to leave.

My new companion was an ideal listener. His boyish, angular
figure, his greenish eyes with their sunburnt lashes, and even his

hands, amazingly expressive with their long, thin fingers, were the personification of concentrated attention. He didn't ask any questions or probe, but simply sat and listened.

I told him everything that had coursed through my mind on sleepless nights. I told him how, at the age of thirty-five, I hated my profession and knew intuitively that writing was my real calling. I told him about my attempts to write and my failures, about my new ideas and also that my stay at the sanatorium would clarify and settle many things for me. Either I would write one successful novel or I would abandon all attempts forever. I even told him the plot I had in mind. I have no idea why I suddenly blurted out my secret, which I had not entrusted even to my beloved. I suppose I was assailed by too many doubts to confide my plans to her. However, I must admit, that wasn't the real reason. The real reason was that I didn't know if I had talent and I was ashamed to be a failure in her eyes. If I were to encounter failure and disillusionment, I must suffer them alone. This, too, I confided to him.

When I had talked myself out we returned to our compartment where a reaction soon set in. I was ashamed of my loquaciousness; I felt embarrassed about having confided my still unformed thoughts to a perfect stranger. I had shown myself up as a windbag and fool.

He noticed my changed mood and asked: "Are you having misgivings about talking so freely and confiding in me, a stranger?"

"Of course!" I replied bitterly. "I chattered like a schoolboy! That's one of my weaknesses. Someone once said that anyone could be a writer if he was not hindered by either a lack of words or an overabundance of them. I'm afraid that verbosity is a major stumbling block for me. I have plenty of plots for novels, but no sooner do I sit down to write than I get hopelessly enmeshed in a web of unessential details. For instance, now . . . "

My companion drew a small box from his pocket.

"I promised your wife. . . . Here, take your pill. It's just what you need now."

That was the last straw!

Evidently, the face I made expressed my feelings.

"You are right," he said, returning the box to his pocket. "All these drugs are double-edged swords. Especially tranquilizers, although I sometimes use them myself. In that respect folk medicines are more reliable. They've been tested over the centuries. Here, we'll have a go at one of them right now!" He opened his suitcase and took out a bottle of cognac. "Armenian, the best there is! Wait, I'll get glasses from the conductor."

He scarcely resembled the accepted image of a physician, especially when he returned with a triumphant air, bearing two glasses.

"Here we are!" He poured out a few drops for me but filled his own glass nearly a third full. "Warm it first in the palms of your hands. Real connoisseurs say it adds a kick to it. Try it!"

I swallowed a drop and a pleasant warmth coursed through my esophagus to my stomach. It was so long since I had tasted cognac.

"It's strange," I said. "If you knew how many times I've had it drummed into me: 'Not a drop of alcohol!' And when I was discharged from the hospital . . . "

"Nonsense!" he waved his hand carelessly. "Medicine has a lot of formal taboos. Alcohol is a social evil. The sad consequences of its abuse gives some people an excuse to call for its prohibition. Yet, in certain situations there is no substitute for it. Look, you've taken a swallow, and all is forgotten. Right?"

He looked so serious when he said this, that I couldn't help laughing.

"True, but what about its aftereffects?"

"I won't give you any more, so don't worry about aftereffects, because nothing is going to happen from just a few drops."

With evident pleasure he took a large gulp.

"Then again, everyone reacts differently to liquor," he continued, holding his glass up to the light. Coffee gives some people insomnia and helps others to fall asleep. The human brain is a cunning mechanism. An eternal struggle goes on between excitation and inhibition. In each individual case we must know what to stimulate and how to stimulate. In your case, for example, alcohol has a soothing effect. Wouldn't you agree?"

"Yes, I suppose I would. But how the devil did you know that about me before I'd taken a single drop?"

"If I didn't I'd be an awful psychiatrist."

"Oh, so you're a psychiatrist?"

"Partly."

As I was unaccustomed to alcohol, my head was slightly woozy, and that combined with the train's gentle rocking left me feeling completely relaxed.

"What do you mean by *partly?*" I asked languidly. "A little while ago you said you were *almost* a doctor, and now you tell me that you're *partly* a psychiatrist. Exactly what are you?"

"Well, to be more specific, I am a psychophysiologist."

"What's that?"

"I can't explain it to you in two words, and there's hardly any point to going into detail. I'll try to give you a very simple example. For instance, you have just had some cognac and your psychological state has changed somehow. Correct?"

"Correct."

"That was an artificially induced change. However, there are internal factors in the human organism which influence the psyche, for example, the hormones. Between the brain and entire organism are many direct and feedback connections. All of this constitutes a kind of whole which must be examined only in its totality. In brief, psychophysiology is a science that studies the influence of the organism on the psyche, and the psyche on the organism."

"So, for example," I said, "a *bilious disposition* is evidently not a chance expression. Probably, when bile is secreted . . . "

"Exactly! Although it's all far more complicated than that. Sometimes it is difficult to separate cause from effect. What is generally accepted as effect often turns out to be the cause, and vice-versa. There's much work to be done here, and very interesting work, too."

He took another swallow and became rather pensive.

I looked out the window. You could sense that we were heading south. Instead of undergrowth and occasional patches of snow, greening fields flashed by us. And the sky, sun, and earth had a totally different quality.

"You know, I could be of help to you," my companion said

suddenly. "I have a fascinating plot for a novel. The events, which can be used as a base, actually took place. Although much of it will appear to be utterly fantastic, it is not a fabrication. Would you care to hear it?"

"Of course!" I replied. "I'd be delighted to, although to be perfectly honest with you, I'm not sure if I can, even with the best possible plot. . . . "

"Well, that's your business," he interrupted. "But I must warn you that the medical profession has a code of ethics that prevents me from releasing certain details. Names, in particular. You'll have to make up your own, and the rest . . . Well, listen.

"The story begins in the clinic of a well-known scientist. We'll call him *professor*. I'll give you a few facts and you can create his character yourself. But, for goodness sake, don't turn him into a shining hero or a maniac in some fantastic novel. This man has a very complicated and contradictory nature—a marvelous surgeon and a scholar with a broad outlook. At the same time, he is painfully ambitious and stubborn and, to boot, knows his worth darn well. Although attentive and responsive to his patients, frequently he is unjustifiably rude to his subordinates. If you wish you can add some additional traits at your own discretion. But that isn't too important.

"You can note in your novel that his work on tissue incompatibility in organ transplants has led his clinic onto a new and promising path. You will have to picture for yourself what the organ transplant section in this clinic was like. It doesn't require any technical knowledge of procedures, but you must develop a feeling for the special kind of atmosphere that pervades it. A constant state of tense expectation. A large team of medical specialists stands ready to play its role, but no one knows when the crucial experiment will take place. Perhaps in an hour, maybe in a month. But don't think they are idle during this indeterminate waiting period; at the same time important work is going on in the laboratory. Many experiments are performed on animals. Each experiment generates new plans, hopes, and, of course, disappointments.

"The professor drives relentlessly toward his goal: transplantation of a human brain. Dozens of experiments have already been performed on rats and dogs. However, all this does not happen as quickly as you might think. It takes time. Years pass. Finally, the decisive experiment: a monkey with a brain transplant lives and thrives. Then the question arises, where do we go from here? Will a similar operation be performed on a human being? You are probably aware of the cautious attitude toward transplantation in general, and here we are dealing with an experiment fraught with new moral and ethical problems. The professor presents his case to higher authorities, but no one will commit himself one way or another. They use every plausible excuse to evade a decision. In brief, his request to perform a brain transplant is neither formally rejected nor officially approved.

"Meanwhile, time passes and the clinic performs successful heart, kidney, and lung transplants while continuing to pursue the main problem in the laboratory. All this, you might say, was a prelude to the final act.

"One day the break came unexpectedly: the ambulance corps delivered two men to the clinic almost simultaneously. Both were unconscious, both had been picked up on the street. The first had no identification. His name, address, age, and profession were unknown. The diagnosis was 'massive lung hemorrhage.' The situation was practically hopeless. The second was a teacher, a bachelor, thirty years old—a victim of an unfortunate accident. An open skull trauma with brain injury. A state resembling life was maintained with heart-lung machines. However, if the second victim was unquestionably a candidate for the morgue, they could, at least, attempt to save the first one—with a lung transplant from the second. That was the decision the professor made.

"Everything was ready for the operation, but they could not begin. You cannot imagine the restrictions a physician faces in such cases. In the first place, he must get the consent of the patient or his relatives and, in any case, the consent of the donor's relatives. In the second place, the organ to be transplanted can be taken only from a dead person, and while a spark of life remains in the donor's body, the physician is obliged to do everything in his power to maintain it.

"In the third place . . . well, I could go on and on about the problems you run into here! The surgeon encounters innumerable problems at this time, but the worst of them is the tense expectation of the patient's death. The heart ceases to beat, clinical death ensues, and high-frequency charges are applied to the myocardial region; again there are barely audible pulsations followed by cardiac arrest; and this time the shocks do not help. The last resort is to open the chest and massage the heart. This last measure yields results, although not for long. However, in the case I am describing, there was one detail that closed the door to life completely. The second victim had tuberculosis.

"There are many people ill with tuberculosis who are unaware of it. Their bodies have developed certain means of holding the illness in check so it does not progress. But not a single physician will transplant an organ from a tubercular patient. In this case, you might say, the surgeons could have removed their gloves and shipped the bodies to the morgue.

"I had a good reason for focusing your attention on the professor's personality. Otherwise you would not have understood what followed.

"Another decision was made instantly: to transplant the first victim's brain to the tubercular patient. And, please note, that this was to be done without observing any formalities. There was no time to phone Moscow and ask for permission. To tell the truth, I'm not even sure the usual ethics I mentioned were observed here."

"Then what did the professor count on?" I asked.

"It's hard to say. First of all, naturally, on success. When people of this type are taken by an idea, they simply don't allow for the possibility of failure. In such situations someone must be the first to shoulder the entire responsibility for the undertaking. Besides, he evidently felt, and justifiably, that one corpse was better than two. In general, I feel that he acted more on impulse than on the basis of a rationally and carefully thought-out plan. But the patient didn't have time for debates and plans.

"You can skip the description of the operation itself. It is such an extremely delicate procedure and can hardly be of interest to the lay reader. Besides, you would probably get it all wrong. The most important thing for a writer is psychological collision, and this situation was loaded with it.

"So, the operation was performed. The following morning the donor's wife traced her husband through the information bureau and identified him at the morgue. She was told he had died of a massive lung hemorrhage, which, of course, was true. She was spared the remaining details. It would have been too much of a shock for her. He was a twenty-five-year-old journalist. They had lived together only one year and had been very much in love. Believe me, the most difficult task in the arduous practice of medicine is talking with the relatives of a dead patient. Even if he has done everything in his power to save him, he still has the feeling that he is guilty of something. Therefore, we can forgive the professor for not speaking to her himself, but assigning an assistant to the task. Sometimes the boldest people are fainthearted. Besides, one must not forget that there was still a second victim to consider, and the professor not only felt a responsibility to society for him, but to his own conscience, too.

"Now, what had they learned from previous experiments with brain transplants in animals? That animals with brain transplants recovered their motor functions and their sense of balance comparatively quickly; that most of the conditioned reflexes developed in the donor's lifetime disappeared after a transplant but were restored more rapidly than those developed from scratch in a control group; that subjects with brain transplants were fully capable of functioning. That was all they knew. This was hardly enough information to predict the behavior of a human being after such an operation. There are many, many factors here that can't be verified in animals. What remains in the brain? What is completely erased? What is driven into the subconscious for a long time or, perhaps, forever? Finally, there is the matter of speech. It is also a product of training. Personality? I have already said that the activity of the brain cannot be studied apart from the total organism. There are innumerable paths of interaction, most of which are still a puzzle to us. In brief, a man with a brain transplant cannot be considered a symbiont, with one individual's personality in another's body. What you get is a completely new individual. As you can see, there are more unknowns than knowns.

"However, the operation was performed. On the bed now lay a man, a man who breathed, reacted to light and took liquid nourishment. His gastrointestinal system and kidneys functioned, and that was about it. Weeks and months passed and he was taught to walk. He even learned a few words. What next? There remained only the hope that time would take care of the rest. Time passed. He made some progress. He talked with difficulty, but he did talk. He learned to read. He couldn't remember his past. A year went by. He spoke, read, and wrote without difficulty. He displayed an interest in his surroundings. Everything but the memory of his past had been restored. All attempts to awaken it were futile. He was told he had suffered a severe brain trauma which had caused total amnesia. He understood and accepted this. More time passed and he began to grow weary of the hospital setting.

"The question arose: what should they do with him? According to his documents, he was a teacher, but you can understand that his professional fitness in this field was now out of the question. Nothing remained of the journalist in him either. Start afresh, learn something new? It was still too early to think in those terms. Put him on a disability pension? You know what that would have meant for him. Besides, it would have been necessary to terminate a unique experiment at its most critical stage. He had to be given the opportunity to meet people, to go to the theater, the movies, while keeping him under the vigilant observation of specialists.

"I forgot to mention that this teacher had had a sweetheart. When she learned about the accident and operation, she constantly pressed for permission to visit him. She even appealed to the Board of Health, but the professor categorically banned all visitors. At that time it could only have had a harmful effect. But now the situation was different. So, she was permitted to visit him. He did not recognize her, but the appearance of a new face from the inaccessible world outside made him happy. Besides, he liked her. She was a beautiful, charming woman.

"She was permitted to visit him every day and they would talk for hours. She told him about his past life and the poor devil even thought he was beginning to remember some things. Finally, she requested permission to take him home with her. The professor agreed.

"At first everything went well. She did not doubt that she had taken in someone very dear to her who had suffered a great misfortune. Financial problems were not anticipated as the teacher had had savings, and the clinic could maintain him on the sick list for a lengthy, indefinite period. A change of environment was simply a necessity for him. As far as the moral aspects of this story are concerned, one doesn't cry over a few hairs when a head has been removed. The more so when both of them were unquestionably very happy together. It was now a matter of 'wait and see.'

"Unfortunately, things didn't continue to go well. Either his memory had begun to revive, or something from his past as a journalist had been pushed into his subconscious. At any rate, he began to leave the house regularly and stand by the hour on the staircase of the apartment where the journalist had once lived. Naturally, his sweetheart became alarmed. She sought the professor's advice, but what could he tell her? Apparently, something inevitable had entered the picture, and in this situation it was hardly possible to change anything.

"Finally it happened. He met the wife of the journalist.

"I've already mentioned that the journalist and his wife had been very much in love. Ah, love! How many volumes have been written about it, and yet how little it has been studied. Oh, the hell with it!" He interrupted his story and reached for the bottle. "We won't be prigs about it. One more swallow won't hurt you. After all, you are, so to speak, under the watchful eye of a doctor."

"Where did you hear this story?" I asked.

"I . . . " he stammered, "well, I was called in several times as a consultant on the case. Shall I continue?"

"Please!"

"So they met. He was overwhelmed. Evidently her image still remained somewhere in the recesses of his memory, and what he thought was love at first sight was simply a subconscious reaction."

"And what about her?"

"What about her? He was no more than a stranger to her, evidently, not to her taste, and besides, she had not yet recovered from the shock of her husband's death. So she paid no attention to him. He began to pursue her. He would wait outside her apartment by the hour, or strike up a conversation with her on the subway. If a man is persistent enough, then sooner or later ... In short, everything followed the classic pattern. Don't judge her too harshly. She was still quite a young woman and painfully lonely. Besides, she sensed something of the man she had once loved in this determined suitor. Naturally, not in his physical appearance, but in his personality, his way of talking, in the dozens of petty details that make one individual so different from the next."

"But what about the woman who had taken him from the clinic?" I asked. "Did he leave her?"

"That's just the point—he didn't. He loved her too. You will have to be very tactful when you describe their relationship. You must understand his psychology. This was not a vulgar love triangle. It is difficult to explain. . . . Just as there were two men in him, so both women . . . No, that's not it! Ah, I have it now. The two women merged into a single image for him which he could not separate. Perhaps a specialist would find the seeds of mental illness here, but how many of our literary heroes, strictly speaking, were in sound mental health? Raskolnikov, the Karamazovs, and others?"

He took out his little box and swallowed a pill. He looked awful; his eyes darted about wildly, and his forehead was covered with sweat. It appeared that we would have to reverse our roles and I would have to soothe him. However, I became more and more interested in his story, and I began to have suspicions about a few things.

"Tell me," I probed, "this second fellow, the teacher—what did he teach?"

"What difference does it make?! Let it be anything you wish, even physiology. I'm giving you the plot and not ... "

"Please continue," I broke in. "It's really a fascinating plot. "

"All right! So, there were these two women, and neither of them would accept this situation. Both were young, beautiful, and ambitious in a feminine way. Each looked upon him as her own. The last act of this tragedy, in which the principal players did not know their true roles, was played out. I purposely told you about the seeds of mental illness. The brain, you see, has defense mechanisms. When a situation becomes intolerable, one often retreats into an imaginary world, and reality is replaced by delirium. Specialists have a name for this condition, but you can use the term 'insanity'. When an individual imagines himself to be someone else, it takes a special form. And so, at the end of your novel, you can, if you wish, include a mental institution."

"An unhappy ending," I said. "I must admit I expected something other than lifelong confinement in a mental institution."

"Why lifelong?" he objected. "The medical profession is well equipped to treat such diseases. You can always cure them if you can remove the cause, and that is the most difficult part. You can, of course, remove the patient temporarily from the conflict situation. But you understand that in this case it was, at best, a temporary measure. Sooner or later they would meet again, and everything would begin anew. There is a more radical approach: tell the patient the truth so he understands the cause of his illness and can examine his problem more objectively. He might even find himself telling someone all about it some time. Excuse me, I can't continue. It's terribly smoky in here. I'm going into the corridor."

I waited until the door had closed behind him, poured out half a glass of cognac and drained it in one gulp because. . . .

My God, how could I have forgotten that boyish figure in the white smock with those attentive greenish eyes and sunburnt eyelashes leaning over my bed at the clinic when they were teaching me to talk, and then through the haze of delirium. . . .

Much became clear to me now. So much. I could start anew. The most important thing to me now was that *she* had really called me her husband.

Nothing else mattered, even the three-month stay ahead of me at the tuberculosis sanatorium.

Escape

ILYA VARSHAVSKY

1

"ONE, TWO, THREE HOIST! One, two, three, HOIST!"

A primitive device—a board and two ropes, plus some muscle, and the heavy rocks clattered into the truck.

"Come on, get going!"

It was an average load, but the little fellow in striped fatigues, trying desperately to move his pile of rocks into the truck, couldn't budge them.

"Come on, come on!"

One of the prisoners tried to give him a hand. Too late: the overseer was on his way.

"What's going on here?"

"Nothing, sir."

"Then get going!"

The little fellow made another unsuccessful attempt to move his load. He broke into a fit of coughing and covered his mouth with his hand.

The overseer waited patiently for the attack to subside.

"Let's see your hand."

The outstretched palm was bloody.

"OK, knock off!"

The overseer jotted down the number stamped on the prisoner's jacket.

"Go to the infirmary!"

Another prisoner quickly filled the sick man's place.

"Excuse me, sir," pleaded the little fellow, "but can't I ... "

"I thought I told you to go to the infirmary. Get going!"

As the stooped figure moved off, he rechecked the number in his notebook: △ □ 15/13264. Well, it was all quite clear: the triangle meant he was a deserter; the rectangle—life imprisonment. From the looks of him, this chap's sentence didn't have long to run. It was the cotton fields for him.

"One, two, three, HOIST!"

2

The tired, gray eyes of the doctor peered carefully through thick lenses. Here, in Meden's subterranean camps, human life was very valuable. And for good reason! The planet desperately needed uranium in the fierce struggle to maintain its dominant position over other planets.

"Get dressed!"

The prisoner's long, thin arms pulled his jacket quickly around his emaciated body.

"Stand over there!"

A light press on the pedal and the prisoner's number was blocked out by a large red cross. Henceforth, prisoner △ □ 15/13264 would be known once more as Arp Zumbi. A humanitarian gesture toward those condemned to labor in the cotton fields.

The cotton fields. The prisoners knew little about them except that one never returned from them. It was rumored that the intensely hot, dry climate shriveled the body into dry brushwood—excellent fuel for the crematorium's ovens.

"You are excused from any further work in this camp. Here is your certificate. You may go."

Arp Zumbi showed the barracks sentry his certificate. A familiar

acrid smell of disinfectant stung his nostrils. With its Dutch tile and
overpowering odor of disinfectant, the barracks resembled a public
toilet. Its white walls were broken only by a large poster proclaiming
"Death by torture for escapees."

A structure like an enormous honeycomb ran along one of the
walls. These were the prisoners' quarters, cubicles separated by solid
partitions to prevent communication between their occupants.
Comfortable and hygienic.

Since it was forbidden to enter one's cubicle during working
hours, Arp passed the time away on a bench. His thoughts turned to
the cotton fields. Every two weeks a new lot of prisoners, collected
from a number of camps, was transported to the fields; and two days
after each shipment, a new group of prisoners would be delivered to
Arp's camp. The last group had arrived five days ago, and one of the
new arrivals had been placed in the cubicle next to Arp's. Some kind
of nut. Yesterday at dinner he had given Arp half his bread ration.
"Here, take it," he had insisted, "or you won't hold up your pants
much longer." Who ever heard of giving away bread?! This guy was
probably a psycho.

Arp's thoughts returned to the cotton fields. He knew it was the
end of the line for him but, for some reason, he wasn't too upset. After
ten years in the mines, one grew accustomed to the idea of death. Yet,
he wondered what it was really like in the cotton fields.

This was the first day he had not worked during his ten years in the
labor camp. No wonder time passed so slowly.

Toward evening Arp's fellow prisoners returned from the mines,
and the smell of barracks disinfectant fused with the sweetish odor
of decontamination fluid. Those who worked with uranium had to
take prophylactic showers. It was one of the measures taken to
extend the work-life of the prisoners.

Arp took his place in line and marched off to dinner.

At meals, the guards tended to be lax about the "no talking" rule.
After all, how much could one say with a mouth full of food?

Arp finished his portion in silence and waited for the command to
rise.

"Here, take it!" Again that psycho offered him half his ration.

"No, thanks."

The guard bellowed the command to rise and fall in. Arp noticed that all eyes were focused on him. Probably, he thought, because of the red cross on his back. Doomed men always arouse curiosity.

"Step lively!"

This was directed at Arp's neighbor. His row had fallen in, but he had remained seated. Then, he and Arp rose together and, as he walked toward his place in line, Arp barely caught the words:

"There's a way to escape."

Arp pretended not to hear; the camp was crawling with informers and the prospect of death by torture certainly did not appeal to him. Better the cotton fields.

3

The voice rose and fell, alternating between screeching and barely audible whispering which compelled its captive audience to strain its ears. It poured from a loudspeaker fastened to the head of each prisoner's bed. This was the regular brainwashing session.

It was impossible to escape the voice that pounded its messages into the prisoners three times a day: before sleep, during sleep, and before reveille. Like the shouting of the overseers, it could not be blocked from one's consciousness. It was an eternal reminder to all that this was a penal colony and not a health resort.

Arp lay there with his eyes closed, trying to think about the cotton fields. The brainwashing session was over, but he was disturbed by a rhythmic tapping coming from the other side of the partition. That psycho again, he thought.

"What the hell do you want!?" Arp yelled through his cupped hand pressed against the partition.

"Meet me in the latrine."

Without thinking, Arp slid off his bunk and walked toward the gurgling sound of water.

It was hot in the latrine, so damn hot that two minutes in that sweatbox was more than a man could take. Arp was dripping wet before the newcomer appeared.

"Do you want to escape?"

"Go to hell!" whispered Arp hoarsely. As a veteran of camp life, he was very familiar with the tricks of these informers.

"Don't be afraid," he tried to reassure Arp. "I'm from the Liberation Committee. Tomorrow we're going to try to move the first group out of here and get them to a safe place. You have nothing to lose. You will receive a poison capsule. In case the escape fails . . . "

"Then what?"

"You'll take the capsule. It's a lot better than death in the cotton fields. Right?"

Arp found himself nodding in agreement.

"You will receive instructions in the morning, in your bread. Be careful!"

Arp nodded again and left.

For the first time in ten years he was so deeply lost in dreams, dreams of hope and freedom, that the second and third brainwashing sessions were completely blocked out.

4

At breakfast Arp Zumbi stood at the end of the serving line because the idle were the last to receive their rations.

The gangling prisoner distributing bread looked carefully at Arp and, grinning faintly, tossed him a chunk of bread set apart from the rest. After gulping down his porridge, Arp crumpled the bread gently. It was there! He hid the tiny wad of paper in his cheek.

Now he must wait until the column left for work.

The command to rise rang out. Bringing up the rear of the column, Arp marched from the mess hall and, reaching the gallery, turned left while the others marched straight ahead.

Here, beyond the bend, Arp was relatively safe. Since the barracks clean-up detail was still busily at work, it was too early for the sentries to take their posts.

The instructions were very brief. Arp read them three times and crumpled the note into a wad and swallowed it after he was certain that he had memorized it thoroughly.

Now that the moment had arrived for him to begin his flight to freedom he was seized by fear. He hesitated. Death in the cotton fields seemed preferable to death by torture.

"The poison!" he remembered, and the thought of it calmed his nerves. After all, what did he have to lose?

Fear gripped him once again as he handed his medical certificate to the sentry at the border zone.

"Where are you going?"

"To the doctor."

"OK, go on."

Trudging slowly along the gallery, Arp's legs felt like cotton as he sensed danger lurking behind him. Any moment he expected to hear shouts, followed by a burst of machine gun fire. Fugitives were always shot in the legs; in that way the penalty for escaping, death by torture, could be properly executed. Prisoners must not be deprived of such an instructive spectacle.

Turn here!

Arp turned the corner and rested against the wall. His heart pounded wildly and he was covered with sweat. His teeth chattered like the drumbeat at an execution.

An eternity passed before he decided to push on. Somewhere in the vicinity he should find a recess in the ground, the site of the garbage tanks. Arp recalled the instructions, and once more was assailed by doubts. Suppose it was a put-up job? The instant he crawled into one of the tanks he'd be nabbed! And he hadn't received the poison yet. Fool! Blockhead! He shouldn't have agreed until he had the stuff. Arp was ready to beat his head against the wall. Some informer had really hooked him!

Ah, ha! Here were the tanks. Someone had left paint brushes by the left one, just as the note had said. Arp hesitated. Maybe he should turn back?

Suddenly he heard loud voices and dogs barking. Rounds! No time to think. With surprising agility he leaped onto a sawhorse and dived into a tank.

The voices came closer. He heard the yelping of a dog straining at the leash and the pounding of hobnailed boots.

"Zip! Gar!"

"Someone's in the tank."

"Probably rats. The place is full of them."

"No, Gar doesn't bark like that at rats."

"Rubbish! Let's get going. And calm your hound."

"Easy there, Gar!"

The footsteps died down.

Now Arp could inspect his refuge. The tank was one-quarter full. No point trying to get out: it was a good twelve feet to the top. Arp ran his hand along the wall and felt the two small holes described in the note. They were in the embossed sign, "Labor Camp," which circled the tank. Arp would have to breathe through these two openings when the covers were slammed shut.

When the covers were slammed shut! What a trap! How would this wild adventure end? What was this Liberation Committee? He had never heard any mention of it in camp. Perhaps it was composed of those same lads who had helped him desert from the army ten years ago? Oh, how stupid he had been! He had disobeyed them and visited his mother, where he was caught. If he hadn't been such a damn fool how differently things would have turned out.

He heard voices again and the scraping of wheels. Arp pressed his eye against one of the holes and relaxed. Two prisoners were hauling a bucket of garbage. Probably the clean-up detail. They were taking their time. Sitting down leisurely in the cart, they took turns smoking a butt discarded by one of the guards. Arp's mouth watered as he watched the pale puffs of smoke. Lucky dogs!

They dragged all they could from the butt. The bucket crawled upward and the cable pulling it was thrown across the pulley above Arp's head. He covered his head with his hands as the contents of the bucket slurped over him.

Only now, after the prisoners had gone, was he conscious of the foul odor in his refuge. The breathing holes were at eye level, so he had to pile garbage under his feet to raise himself.

He must be vigilant now. Garbage collection usually ended at ten o'clock; then the tanks were covered, raised, and hauled to the dump.

5

Where the rough, wide board had come from was a mystery. One end rested against the wall at the bottom of the tank; the other end lay against the tank's opposite wall, extending slightly above Arp's head. Like the sawhorse, it was evidence of someone's concern for the fate of this fugitive. Arp was especially aware of it when a sharp metal rod poked through the thick refuse and bumped against the board. If not for the board . . .

The inspection of the tank seemed endless.

"Well, what'cha got there?" asked a hoarse voice.

"Nothing, just an old board."

"OK, slam the cover on. Now, heave!"

A light jolt, the rattle of a gate, and the tank, rocking, moved up the shaft. As it ascended it banged against the sides of the shaft, and Arp's face, pressed to the wall, felt sharp blows.

After the last and worst blow, the cover opened with a loud noise. Once more the rod poked through the rubbish, and again the lifesaving board concealed the trembling man hiding beneath it.

Now the breathing holes faced a concrete enclosure, and Arp's visual world consisted of a rough, gray surface. But it was a world full of long forgotten sounds: the whirring of automobile tires, the voices of pedestrians, and even the chirping of sparrows. How close and dear freedom seemed to him now.

Suddenly, a new sound: a rhythmic, persistent tapping on the cover of the tank. Arp froze. The tapping grew more frequent, more persistent, more terrifying. And then it dawned on him. "Of course," he laughed to himself, "it's raining."

6

It was a long, harrowing night for Arp. From the moment he was tossed from the tank into the rat-infested garbage dump his exhausted body found no rest. Somewhere nearby he could hear automobiles speeding along a highway. Every now and then their headlights would illuminate the mound of garbage behind which Arp was hiding. The rats would scurry into the darkness squealing, scratch his face with their sharp claws, and bite him if he tried to push them away.

Arp was sure that his escape had been discovered by now and he tried to picture what was happening at the camp. Suppose the dogs picked up his scent leading to the garbage tanks?

Two bright beams of light struck him like a hammer blow, and he jumped up. The headlights went off and a small light went on inside the truck. It was a military van, the kind used to transport military supplies. The driver motioned to Arp to come closer.

Arp breathed a sigh of relief. The door opened and Arp grasped someone's outstretched hand. Once more he found himself in darkness.

The van was stuffy. Seated on the floor, Arp heard heavy breathing and felt the pressure of bodies surrounding him. Gently rocking on its springs, the van rolled silently through the dark night.

Arp was awakened by a light shining in his face. Something was wrong! The rocking motion that had lulled him to sleep had ceased.

"Take a break!" said the man with the flashlight. "You can go out for five minutes."

Arp had no desire to leave the van, but the press of bodies behind him left him no choice and he had to jump out with the rest of them.

Everyone crowded around the cab of the truck; no one would risk wandering away from the van.

"Hey, boys!" said their rescuer, shining his flashlight on the figures in prison garb. "So far everything has gone well, but anything could happen before we deliver you to your destination. Do you know what the penalty for escaping is?"

Silence.

"Yes, I'm sure you do. Therefore, the Committee offers you poison. One capsule per person. It works instantaneously. Take it only as a last resort. Is that clear?"

Arp received a capsule wrapped in silver foil and climbed into the van.

The capsule clutched in his fist gave him a feeling of control over his own destiny. Now his jailors could not hurt him. With this comforting thought, he fell asleep.

Trouble! It could be sensed in everything around him: in the motionless van, in the white faces of the fugitives illuminated by a shaft of light coming through the cab's rear window, in the loud wrangling coming from the road.

Arp started to rise, but dozens of hands signaled to him to sit still.

"Military vehicles are not subject to inspection," came the voice of the driver.

"And I'm telling you that I have an order. This evening . . . "

The engine suddenly roared and the van shot ahead in a hail of machine-gun fire. Chips flew from the roof of the van.

When Arp finally raised his head, he found himself clutching someone's tiny hand. Dark eyes looked up at him from beneath a shaven forehead. Prisoner's garb could not conceal the feminine curves of the figure beside him. On the left sleeve was a green star, symbol of the lowest caste.

Instinctively Arp unclasped his hand and rubbed it on his trousers. Contact with Meden's lowest caste was prohibited by Meden's laws.

"They won't catch us, will they?"

The trembling voice sounded so pathetic that Arp, ignoring the law, shook his head in response to reassure her.

"What's your name?"

"Arp."

"Mine's Jetta."

Arp dropped his head onto his chest and pretended to doze. He wondered how his rescuers at his final destination might react to such contact.

The van turned off the highway and bounced along a road full of potholes. Arp was hungry and began to feel ill from the jostling ride. Afraid of disturbing the others, he tried to suppress a cough, but this only made matters worse. He was doubled over and suddenly broke into a wracking, bloody cough. So exhausting was the attack that Arp was too weak to push aside the arm with the green star that was wiping his perspiring forehead.

7

The warm night air was filled with the fragrance of exotic flowers and the chirping of cicadas.

Their prison garb had been discarded. An ankle-length unbleached linen shirt cooled his body pleasantly. He had just come from a steam bath. Arp carefully spooned the last bits of porridge from his bowl.

At one end of the dining hall, three people stood next to a dais constructed of old kegs and boards: a tall man with gray hair and the sunburned face of a farmer—evidently the leader; a handsome chap in the uniform of Meden's army—the van driver; and a short woman in a white smock, with a thick red braid wound around her head.

They were waiting for the fugitives to finish their supper.

When the rattle of spoons died down, the leader leaped nimbly to the dais.

"Welcome, friends!"

In response to this unusual greeting, a joyful murmur swept through the hall.

"First of all, I must tell you that you are completely safe here. The location of our evacuation point is not known to the authorities."

The haggard, gray faces radiated happiness.

"You will spend five to ten days at the evacuation center. The exact period will be determined by the doctor, because you will have a long, difficult journey ahead of you. The place we are taking you to is, of course, no paradise. You will have to work there. We win every inch of earth for our settlements from the jungle. However, you will be free there. You can raise a family and work for your own welfare. At the beginning you will live in quarters prepared for you by those who preceded you there. That is our tradition. Now, I am ready for your questions."

During the question period Arp tried to summon up the courage to ask if one could marry a girl of lower caste in these settlements. By the time he raised his hand timidly, the tall man had already left the dais.

The woman in the white smock addressed the fugitives in a soft, melodious voice, and Arp had to strain his ears to catch her instructions.

She asked everyone to go to their quarters, to go to sleep and await their physical examinations.

Arp found his bunk with his name on it, lay down on the cool, crisp sheets and fell asleep quickly.

While asleep he had the sensation of being turned onto his side and felt the cold touch of a stethoscope. Opening his eyes, he saw a short woman with a red braid writing something in a notebook.

"So, you woke up?" she smiled, revealing her dazzling, white, even teeth.

Arp nodded.

"You are very weak. Your lungs aren't too good either. You will sleep for seven days and when you wake up you will feel much better. We'll put you to sleep now."

She pushed several buttons on a white console near his bed and a strange hum whirred in Arp's head.

"Sleep!" came a very distant, melodious voice, and Arp fell asleep.

8

Arp had an amazing dream, full of sunlight and happiness.

Only in a dream was such entrancing slow motion possible; only in a dream could one experience such weightlessness, could one soar through the air like a bird.

An enormous meadow was covered with dazzling white flowers. In the distance Arp saw a high tower, shining with all the colors of the rainbow. He was irresistibly drawn to the shining tower from which emanated an inexplicable air of bliss.

Arp was not alone. From all directions people were streaming toward the mysterious tower. Like him, they were dressed in long, flowing white gowns. And Jetta was among them, too, with a skirtful of white blossoms.

"What is that?" she asked Arp, pointing to the tower.

"The pillar of freedom. Come, let's go to it!"

Holding hands, they floated together through the sun-filled air.
"Wait!"

Arp stopped to pick a skirtful of white blossoms and they continued on their way.

At the foot of the tower they emptied their skirts, heaping the
blossoms in a huge pile.

"Who can pick the most?" shouted Jetta as she flitted among the
gray stalks. "Come on, friends, try and outpick us!"

Their example fired the others. Within a short time the entire base
of the tower was overflowing with white blossoms.

Then bonfires were lit, and huge chunks of meat strung on long,
thin skewers were roasted. The delightful smell of shashlik together
with the scent of burning twigs revived very old and pleasant
memories.

After quenching their thirst, they lay on the ground by the fire,
gazing at the stars, enormous, strange stars in an ink-black sky.

When Arp fell asleep by the dying fire, a tiny hand was resting in
his.

When the fires went out, varicolored lights circling the tower
went on. Below, at ground level, a door opened and two huge
mechanical paws shoveled the cotton inside.

In a glass-enclosed cupola an old man with a sunburned face
looked at the arrow on the scale.

"Wow! They picked five times more than all the preceding
groups," he announced, turning off the conveyer. "I'm afraid they
won't last a week at such a mad pace."

"I'll bet you two bottles of vodka," the handsome chap in military
dress grinned, "that they last the usual twenty days. Hypnosis is a
marvelous technique! You could have died laughing, watching them
devour those baked turnips as if they were shashlik. You can get them
to do anything under hypnosis. Right, Doctor?"

The short woman with the thick red braid was slow to reply. She
walked over to the window, turned on the floodlights and looked
down carefully at their faces which, with their tightly drawn skins,
resembled skulls.

"You are overestimating the possibilities of electro-hypnosis," she smiled. "The powerful radiation of the psi-field can do no more than impart a rhythm to their work. The most basic factor in their conditioning is preliminary psychological tuning. The fabricated escape, the contrived dangers—all this created a sense of freedom won at a terrible cost. It is difficult to foresee what colossal reserves can be released in the human organism by lofty aspirations and goals."

Share It with Me

KIRILL BULYCHEV

How I long to go back, but I know it can never be. I know I'll be consumed by envy for the rest of my life. . . .

At the time I suspected nothing. The elevator doors clicked and buzzed, and I walked down a steep ramp onto the spaceport's brightly colored walkway and paused, trying to determine who among the waiting crowd had been assigned to meet me—my hosts had been informed of my arrival well in advance.

The man who approached me was tall and wiry. His long fingers stained green from constant contact with herselium told me at once that he was my colleague.

"How was the flight?" he asked as our car passed through the spaceport's gates.

"Fine, thanks," I replied. "Uneventful."

Actually my words contained a polite lie: it had been a tiresome journey with layovers for connecting flights in uncomfortable, stinking, cargo ports; on top of everything else I had almost blacked out from the G forces which had absolutely no effect on passengers native to this section of the galaxy, and now I had a splitting headache.

My host didn't answer but only frowned as if he were suffering from a chronic toothache and anticipating the next wave of pain. Some three minutes passed before he spoke.

"I guess the G forces on our ship were pretty hard to take. You're probably not used to such an overload."

"No, I'm not."

"Do you have a headache?"

Seeing that the pain had struck him again, I didn't answer.

"Do you have a headache?" he repeated, then added almost apologetically: "Unfortunately, your ships rarely come this way."

It was only after the spaceport was several kilometers behind us that I felt myself in a foreign land. Until then I had seen only the spaceport, and if you've seen one, you've seen them all. Like all stations—train, plane, or astrodisk—they are uniformly impersonal and tasteless.

The further we rode, the more distinctive became our surroundings; here, outside the center of the city that had succumbed to the latest galactic fashions, everything had developed in its own unique way. Only minor details brought to mind what I had seen elsewhere. But, as usual, it was the minor details that caught the eye.

It was fascinating. I even forgot about the headache and nausea that had been bothering me since I landed. My mood had improved, and the fresh, fragrant air flowing through the window promised a warm welcome.

At the edge of the city, amid low buildings surrounded by gardens, my companion slowed down.

"I hope you're feeling better," he said.

"Thanks, much better. I like your planet. Reading about a place or seeing pictures of it is no substitute for the real thing. You've got to experience colors, scents, and distance to get a feeling for new surroundings."

"That's very true," he stated with a grimace. "By the way, you'll be staying at my house. You'll find it more comfortable than a hotel."

"Oh, no. I wouldn't want to put you to any trouble."

"It's no trouble at all."

The car turned into a driveway which skirted a steep hill. Seconds later we drove up to a two-story house set deep inside a garden.

"Wait for me here," said my companion. "I'll be back in a minute."

While I waited I studied the flowers and trees. I felt rather uncomfortable; I sensed that I had intruded, that my presence was superfluous.

A window on the second floor flew open and a slim young woman looked out. After looking me over briefly but attentively, she nodded in agreement to someone standing behind her. Then she moved away from the window.

Suddenly I felt at ease. Something in the girl's expression, in the way she opened the window, in her fleeting glance, banished into the depths of my consciousness the tribulations of my journey, the disappointment at my host's somewhat cool reception, and the disturbing prospect of having to live in a strange world two or three months before I could return home.

I was sure the girl would come downstairs to greet me, and my expectation was quickly realized. Suddenly she emerged from a mass of foliage.

"Hello there! Bored yet?" she asked, smiling.

"Not in the least. I'm in no hurry. And your garden is marvelous."

The girl was lightly dressed, and her movements were abrupt and awkward.

"My name is Lena. Come, I'll show you your room. Dad is awfully busy, with Grandma being so sick."

"Then you must excuse me for intruding. Your father didn't mention it. Look, I'll go to a hotel—"

"You'll do nothing of the sort," objected Lena. Her eyes were a strange color, like old silver. "You'd be miserable there with no one to look after you. Don't worry, you won't be in the way. Dad asked me to take care of you while he stays with Grandma."

I probably should have insisted on going to a hotel. But I was powerless: somehow I felt that I had known Lena and this house and garden for a long, long time, that I belonged to the household. Every fiber of my being resisted any suggestion of abandoning it to live alone in some hotel's impersonal indifference.

"Well then, it's settled," said Lena. "Come on, we'll go inside."

Lena showed me the room where I would be staying and helped me unpack. Then she took me to the warm, bubbling swimming pool obscured by a dense arch of trees.

From there we went up to the roof to visit her noisy menagerie. It boasted striped talking grasshoppers, six-winged birds, tiny blue fish dozing in flowers, and the most ordinary terrestrial cat, that is, ordinary to me, but extremely rare to them. The cat ignored me. Lena was disappointed.

"I was sure she'd be delighted to see you. What a letdown!"

Lena stayed with me all day, and I hardly saw anyone but her. Every now and then she would excuse herself and run off. "You're probably terribly busy," I would say. "Please, don't pay any attention to me." But each time I was left by myself the loneliness and physical discomfort would return. I would wander over to the bookshelves, pull out a volume, and quickly put it back. Then I would go out to the garden and return to the house again, all the while listening carefully for her footsteps. Lena would come running, touch me lightly and ask:

"Get bored?"

"A little," I would reply.

Once I even summoned up the courage to tell her that all my ailments vanished in her presence. Lena smiled; her brother, she said, would return by suppertime with medicine to relieve my post-flight distress.

"By morning you'll feel like new. All your symptoms will vanish."

"And you?"

"Me? What about me?"

"Will you vanish too? Like the Good Fairy?"

"Don't worry," said Lena firmly. "I'll still be here tomorrow."

At supper the entire family, except Grandma, gathered around a long table. I was surprised to learn that no fewer than ten people lived in this seemingly deserted house. The head of the household, pale and tired, sat next to me and saw to it that I downed all the medicine brought by his son, a medical student. It was miserable stuff, just what medicine is supposed to be, but I took it obediently;

and I told no one that the only sure cure was Lena herself. Lena sympathized with my plight, frowning when I had to down a particularly bitter pill.

My host announced that his mother was feeling better, that she had fallen asleep. Despite his fatigue and pallor he talked and laughed a lot, presenting quite a contrast to the morose man who had met me at the spaceport. Then, he had been upset about his mother's condition. But now . . .

"She's awake," my host announced suddenly.

My ears perked up. I hadn't heard the slightest sound: neither a cough nor a sigh had broken the dead silence.

"You're tired, Dad," said my host's son. "I'll go up to her."

"Nothing doing!" objected his father. "You have school tomorrow."

"What about you—don't you have to go to work?"

"All right. We'll go together," said his father. "Please excuse us."

After dinner Lena escorted me to my room.

"I hope you don't have trouble falling asleep," she said.

"I'm sure I won't, especially if one of those tablets was a sleeping pill."

"Of course one was," said Lena. "Good night. Sleep well."

Sure enough, I fell asleep immediately.

I woke up the next morning completely recovered. I hurried out to the garden, hoping to find Lena there. She was waiting for me by the pool. I was about to tell her how soundly I had slept, how delighted I was with the beautiful morning, and how pleased I was to see her, but I didn't get a chance to open my mouth.

"I'm so glad," she said as if she had read my thoughts. "Grandma's feeling better too. Dad will take you to the institute now. I'll be waiting for you this evening. I'm anxious to hear all about your work and what you've seen."

"Oh, I'm sure you'll be able to figure that out yourself."

"What do you mean?"

"You can read people's thoughts."

"That's not true!"

"I know I'm right. For example, you didn't even wait for me to tell you myself how I felt. And yesterday your father left the table because your grandmother woke up. Yet there wasn't a sound in the house. He couldn't have heard anything."

"It's still not true," insisted Lena. "Why should I read people's thoughts? Including yours."

"I suppose you wouldn't have any reason to do that." I was mildly disappointed by Lena's lack of interest in my flattering thoughts about her.

"Good morning," Lena's father greeted me as he stepped into the garden. "You're in fine shape today. I'm glad."

"You see, I'm right," I whispered to Lena before following her father to the car.

"Why would I have to read your thoughts?" she repeated. "Your face is an open book. It's all there."

"All?"

"Too much, I'd say."

Several days passed. I worked at the institute during the day, evenings were spent wandering about the city, hiking through fields and woods, or strolling along the shores of a large salt lake teeming with armor fish. Sometimes I went alone, sometimes with Lena. I grew accustomed to my hosts and met two or three other engineers. Yet, as ordinary as my daily existence was, the feeling never left me that the people around me were far from ordinary. I was almost convinced that they possessed telepathic abilities.

At times I felt uncomfortable with Lena because I caught myself thinking thoughts that I wouldn't want to share with her. It seemed as if she was hearing the soundless words and was laughing at me.

One day I was walking along a street, green and winding, like most of the city's streets. Ahead of me some boys were kicking a ball. As I walked behind them I struggled with an impulse to catch up and take a crack at it.

I didn't notice a protruding root; I tripped and fell, injuring my knee on a rock. The pain was so sudden and sharp that I let out a yell. As if struck by my shout, the kids stopped dead in their tracks. The ball rolled on, down a slope. Ignoring it, the kids turned to me. I tried to smile and wave them away. "Go on, boys, go chase your ball. It's nothing. It doesn't hurt a bit." But they stood there and watched me.

I raised myself a little but couldn't get to my feet. It was clear that I had strained a ligament. The boys ran up to me. One, a little older than the others, asked:

"Does it hurt a lot, mister?"

"No, not so much."

"I'll get a doctor," said another.

"Hurry!" said the older boy. "We'll wait here till you get back."

"Never mind, boys," I said. "It's nothing serious. Just a strained ligament. I'll be OK in a few minutes."

"Of course you will," replied the older boy.

As if obeying a command, the pain subsided and then vanished. The boys stood there silently, watching me with concern. But the youngest suddenly burst into tears. The older boy told him to run home, which he did.

The doctor arrived. It turned out that he lived in the next building. He examined my leg, gave me a shot, and the kids disappeared immediately. Only the distant sound of a bouncing ball reminded me of their so recent presence.

The doctor helped me back to the house, even though I kept insisting that I could make it on my own.

"The pain is gone, doctor. It hurt only the first minute or so. The kids can tell you that."

"Are you new here?" asked the doctor.

"Yes, I am."

"H'm, then it adds up."

Although it was still early, the entire household had gathered. Grandmother had taken a turn for the worse and had to be rushed to the hospital for surgery.

I went over to Lena. Dark circles showed beneath her eyes and her face was pale and tense.

"Don't worry, everything will turn out all right," I said.

She didn't quite catch my words at first and glanced around with a puzzled expression.

"Everything will turn out all right," I repeated.

"Thanks. Oh, did you fall?"

"Nothing serious. It doesn't hurt anymore."

"Grandma is in terrible pain."

"Why don't they give her a shot? It worked for me right away."

"They can't. Nothing helps anymore."

"I'd like to do something to help."

"Then just go away for a while," she said gently, trying not to offend me. In an even, flat voice, as though she were asking for a glass of water. "You're in the way."

I went out to the garden. I tried to be understanding. After all, it was hard on her, and on the rest of the family. I watched them leave. Alone now, I went upstairs to the menagerie. The cat recognized me, pattered over to the screening and rubbed up against it, curling its tail. Where I came from cats didn't live in cages, but here they were rare, exotic animals. I, too, was a rare animal who could neither understand what was happening nor hope to understand. Yet, I felt that a warm friendship had sprung up between my hosts and myself. At a most inappropriate time some sort of mysterious defect or gap in my make-up had surfaced. Utterly baffled, I realized that I would have to visit the hospital to find the answer. There I would learn something very important. Although I hadn't been invited, and most likely my presence would be undesirable, I felt compelled to go.

No one stopped me at the entrance. The girl at the desk asked if she could help me. I gave her Grandma's name and was escorted to the elevator.

I walked down a long corridor that didn't look as if it belonged in a hospital. Chairs jammed against each other lined the walls. People were sitting in them. Completely healthy people. Silently they were enduring great pain.

I saw my friends near the frosted-glass door of the operating room. Lena, her father, her brothers. In adjoining chairs sat mutual friends, coworkers, and neighbors. Lena glanced at me. Her eyes, filled with pain, slid over my face.

I slipped into an empty chair. It was uncomfortable watching people so totally oblivious to my existence. But now I knew what had been a mystery to me only an hour ago.

I didn't have to wait very long. Suddenly, as if an invisible sorcerer had waved his hand over them, Grandma's visitors brightened and revived. Someone remarked: "She's under anesthesia now." Among themselves they arranged for some to remain and keep vigil and for others to return after the operation, when the anesthesia wore off.

Lena came over to me. I stood up.

"Please forgive me," she said. "I'm awfully sorry, but I'm sure you understand. . . . "

"Of course I do. How can I be angry at a time like this? I'm just sorry I'm an outsider."

"Please don't be. It's certainly not your fault."

"You know, when I fell today, kids came running over to me and stayed with me until the doctor arrived."

"That doesn't surprise me."

Her father joined us.

"Thanks for coming," he said. "Take Lena with you. We'll manage here without her. The doctor assured me that the operation would be successful."

"I'm staying, Dad," said Lena.

"Whatever you want."

"Please try to understand," said Lena after her father had gone. "It would have been very difficult to explain everything to you at the very beginning. It's as natural for us as eating, drinking, and sleeping. Children are taught as soon as they come into the world."

"Has it always been this way?"

"No. We learned several generations ago. But the potential was always there. You probably have it, too, but buried somewhere deep in your brain. I'm sure any intelligent being would want to have the ability. Don't you think so?"

"Yes, I suppose you're right." I said. "If someone near you is suffering, especially if it's someone you love, you'd want to share the pain."

"Not only the pain," replied Lena. "The joy, too. Remember your first day, when you arrived? You felt awful. Dad could do little to help you. The main burden of Grandma's pain fell on his shoulders, as her son. Even when he met you at the spaceport, he had to help

Grandma. The greater the distance between you and the person you're trying to help, the harder it is to help. You thought Dad was rude. Didn't you?"

"Well, not quite, but—"

"As if Grandma's misery wasn't enough, he had to take on yours, too. After all, you were our guest and you had a headache."

"An awful one, too."

"Sometimes I wonder how Dad made it home. As soon as he arrived he relieved me at Grandma's bedside. I saw you through the window and I liked you. So I stayed with you all day, and because of you I had a splitting headache all day."

"I'm sorry," I said. "I didn't know."

"It was better that way. Imagine how upset you would have been if you'd known."

"I would have left."

"I know. I'm glad you didn't. Please go home now. When I return in the morning I'll knock on your door. We'll finish talking about it then."

Again I passed through the long hospital corridor where relatives and friends of the sick were sitting. They had come together to share the suffering. And it wasn't a question of mind reading: people simply knew they needed each other.

I walked home. My leg ached a little but I tried to ignore the pain. At times it would flare up and threaten to overwhelm me. The pedestrians who passed closest to me glanced around and looked at me, and instantly I felt better. But I quickened my pace to avoid troubling these good people. On the way I encountered a group of young women carrying flowers. They were chattering and laughing. No sooner did they notice my glum expression, than they boosted my spirits with their radiance. A happiness not my own flowed through me. From an old man on a park bench I received another gift—serenity. These things had happened to me before, but I hadn't noticed the connection between my own and other people's feelings.

Life is both easier and harder for them than for us. They can give and receive joy and grief; rather, I should say, they *must* share their happiness and pain. It is impossible for them to turn away from their fellowmen: where we see human tears, they feel them. And the heart is more sensitive than the eye.

That day I became an envious man. Yes, I envy them; at times I even feel something akin to hostility toward them. To them I'll always be an outsider, like a beggar among munificent rich men. I can receive gifts but am incapable of giving them.

The day arrived for my return to Earth. As prearranged, only Lena accompanied me to the spaceport; I had said good-bye to the others in the city.

"I'd like to go back with you," said Lena.

"You can't, and you know it. Life on Earth would be very hard on you. You couldn't share only my joy or my pain, could you?"

"You're right, I couldn't," agreed Lena. "It's a shame."

"And I couldn't live with you knowing that you were lonely and I couldn't help you when you needed it most."

"Then maybe you could stay with us? Here? With me?" A note of doubt crept into her voice.

"Do you remember the day your Grandma was operated on?" I said. "I went to the hospital, but I was like a blind man among the sighted. No, I can't stay."

Our conversation had been rehearsed for days. We were merely repeating our lines, knowing how it would end. But we couldn't help ourselves. We were hoping against hope for a compromise, for a way out of our dilemma, for anything that would keep us together.

When we reached the ramp, Lena drew so close to me that I could see the dark flecks in her silvery eyes.

"Try to remember me as I am now," she said.

Overwhelmed by my own and her emotions, I began to feel dizzy. I grabbed her arm for support. But not one of the passengers boarding the ship came to my assistance; not one attempted to share my anguish. Yes, there are times when the impulse to help another must be restrained.

Then came the lift-off, the G forces, and the jolting. Layovers for connecting flights in uncomfortable, stinking cargo ports, nights in impersonal hotels, lousy food at identical shiny counters. But mentally and physically I was in great shape. And I knew why. Millions of kilometers away Lena was sitting in her second-story bedroom, suffering from a splitting headache. I was angry at her. "Forget about me, my love. Leave me at least my pain. . . ."

How I want to go back, but I know it can never be.

Personality Probe

DMITRI BILENKIN

VOICES COMING FROM BEHIND THE DOOR attracted Pospelov's attention. He halted. Evenings at the boarding school were not particularly noted for their silence, so it wasn't the noise drifting from the history office that stirred his curiosity, nor the fact that students appeared to be involved in an activity closed to faculty. They were fully entitled to their privacy. But who was the owner of that high-pitched, breaking voice? It was obviously an old man, and judging from the intonation, he was an awfully frightened one.

"Have mercy on me. It is all foul slander circulated by my enemies, malicious spite of the envious. . . ."

What a strange vocabulary! Oh, well, it was the history office and anything could be going on there.

"No, Faddey Venediktovich," came a voice from behind the door. "Please answer our question."

Faddey Venediktovich? Pospelov knitted his brows. What an unusual name! Yet, it had a familiar ring. Faddey Venediktovich. . . . "Of course! Bulgarin!" gasped Pospelov. "The Russian journalist who was notorious as spy and informer for the secret police during the reign of Nicholas I back in the nineteenth century . . . Pushkin . . . persecutions . . . denunciations. . . . What the devil is going on in there?!"

The days had long since passed when students behind closed doors were suspected of engaging in unwholesome activities, nor were their teachers now considered unwelcome guests. Without further ado, Pospelov pushed the door open, entered, and closed the door gently behind him.

The seven boys and girls didn't notice his unobtrusive entrance. So immersed were they in their project that even an invasion from outer space would not have distracted them. The questions on the tip of Pospelov's tongue remained there. And no wonder! The room in which he found himself was the most ordinary school office, steeped in semi-darkness, and occupied by the most ordinary twenty-first century teenagers whom Pospelov knew personally: barefoot, sleeveless, very excited, and displaying their customary self-discipline. But just as authentic was the contiguous reality evoked by the massive simulated furniture—a huge stove with a tiled opening, a writing desk with randomly scattered manuscripts written with quill pens, a cupboard containing dark bound volumes, a high, narrow window through which gloomy daylight filtered—obviously from St. Petersburg, because the steeple of Peter and Paul's Cathedral was visible in the distance over the rooftops. Yet this part of the room was not physically separated from the reality of the twenty-first century: two steps from where the students sat an akmolith floor ended abruptly as if it had been sliced off by a knife, and polished parquet began at once from that point. Then, too, the light from the window, illuminating the figure at the desk, did not penetrate the boundary, although there was no visible barrier in the air.

Pospelov wasn't the least bit startled by this strange but so real scene—the joining of two time periods. As a physicist, he knew very well that everything, so vivid and visible beyond the boundary, was actually a phantomatic production woven by a computer hologram and indistinguishable from a real model of the past. A paradox. The reverse of the phenomenon produced by the rapid spinning of a wheel: the steel spokes, retaining their physical characteristics, blur into a phantom, and now, in the eyes of the beholder, a transparent nothingness had been transformed into an illusion of solid matter. One could even cross the boundary into this nineteenth century setting and touch objects, only to be convinced of the illusory nature of the desk, the massive scrolled wardrobe and the carved armchairs, all as penetrable to a wave of the hand as the most ordinary shadow. Nor was the presence of Faddey Venediktovich Bulgarin's sweat-glazed face in this illusory setting an extraordinary phenomenon. Like the rest of this scene, the computer had modeled him from drawings, notes, and memoirs of that period, and reconstructed his appearance, psyche, and way of thinking. As far as possible it had endowed the apparition with the independent existence of an authentic Faddey Venediktovich, so that the figure at the desk could listen, think, speak, and feel like Bulgarin himself. There was nothing new here for Pospelov. Not too long ago, as a student, he had been spurred by a mad urge for justice to reconstruct Lobachevsky, using a similar technique, so that the great man could hear posterity's expression of gratitude for his work—even though it would only be his specter. During his lifetime Lobachevsky had not received one word of recognition, not even a simple understanding of his work. However, the blind old man had interrupted Pospelov's effusive praise. "Thank you, sir, but I always knew that my own concepts of geometry would be needed one day."

Now his attention was captured by a strange, puzzling conversation, and the whole point of that youthful venture slipped away from Pospelov.

"I repeat the question, Faddey Venediktovich. Did you understand Pushkin's significance in literature?"

Pospelov recognized the speaker. Of course, it was Igor, and he was in charge!

"I understood, sir. I understood very well, Your . . ."

"May I remind you, no titles, please!"

"Very good, sir." Bulgarin gave the impression of bowing slightly at each word, but this impression was created by his dipping, breathy voice. Actually he bore himself with humble dignity.

"If you understood Pushkin's importance, why did you hound him?"

"Lies, spread by scandalmongers and base slanderers! I . . . I hounded him?! Dear Lord above, as I stand before you . . . I always wished Aleksandr Sergeevich only good. I was delighted to publish his poetry. His letters to me were most amicable. Why, I've even saved them all. As sacred objects. . . . I can show them to you. . . ."

Bulgarin's hand moved toward the desk.

"That won't be necessary," a squeamish note appeared in Igor's voice. "We are very familiar with those letters from the twenties. We'd rather you told us what you wrote about Pushkin, for example, in March and August of 1830."

"I wrote those letters. I don't deny it!" exclaimed Bulgarin hastily and not entirely without enthusiasm. "It happened that I had reproached Aleksandr Sergeevich and bid him, in some manner, to serve his tsar and country worthily. My counsel was misunderstood. I was insulted with epigrams and my literary works were reviled. There was an indecent hint about my former wife, but, God forbid, I bore him no malice and printed that epigram myself. And I cried at Aleksandr Sergeevich's untimely end. . . . The deceased was arrogant, rejected good advice, and lost favor as a poet. Thus do we all, we sinners, err! Oh, Lord, forgive him his transgressions as I have forgiven him. . . ."

Overwhelmed by his emotions, Bulgarin grimaced and wiped away a tear in embarrassment.

A rustle of indignation coursed through the room. One girl jumped up, ready to rush at Bulgarin and discharge her seething anger. The others managed to remain calm, but all eyes turned at once toward Igor. Halting, the girl sat down. Igor's lips were tightly compressed. "Yes," thought Pospelov sympathetically, "dear boys and girls, this is a form of demagogy you have never encountered. This chap is a past master of the art, so don't expect to snare him barehanded. I wonder what you hope to accomplish by this little venture?"

"So, you say you only wished him good?" continued Igor. "Then how do you reconcile that with the written and oral denunciations of Pushkin that you secretly communicated to Benkendorf, the chief of the secret police?"

Gripping the edge of the desk, Bulgarin leaned forward, as if trying to hear better. His eyes, glazed with tears, blinked like an old dog's, but he did not make a sound.

"Have you forgotten? Perhaps you need to be refreshed about some of your reports? This one, for example: 'I am enclosing copies of Pushkin's verse, circulating secretly in manuscript form, the content of which unquestionably reveals the dangerous bent of his thoughts. . . .' "

"Oho!" Pospelov was surprised. "I wonder where they found that document. It's probably an artifact, or it would have been in our text books. H'm. . . . Aha, of course! No such document was preserved. A paleontologist can reconstruct a skeleton on the basis of a single bone. In the same way the central computer—to which the students were undoubtedly hooked up—can reconstruct a lost text on the basis of known facts and notes. Well, not literally. But even the real Bulgarin would hardly remember what he had written that long ago. . . . It was a gamble, but those kids hit the nail on the head."

"Give us the exact date you wrote this," persisted Igor.

No response. Bulgarin's lips, whispering something, turned white. He staggered and collapsed into a nearby chair.

"Protective impulse!!!" shouted Igor, enraged. "Why the hell didn't you warn me?"

"Take it easy," came the cracking bass response from a teenager seated second from the end. His short fingers nimbly flipped something on the remote controls resting on his knees. The dial's rapid flashing lit up his face. "It's not a heart attack. Not even a fainting spell. He's scared stiff and is playing his own version of 'Let's Pretend'."

"Did you, at least, balance his tonicity?"

"And how! Let him sit a while, rest and think. . . ."

"What about feedback?"

"It's off. He can't see or hear us now. You can raise Cain if you want to."

Pospelov hastily withdrew into the shadow, for the students had leaped to their feet and a commotion had erupted. Everyone talked and shouted at once.

"What a character!!! Mess with a creep like that and you'll be puking for a year."

"Aw, come on, Igor, what's the matter with you? Why keep harping on Pushkin? You've got to cover the whole spectrum—and slow and easy, too. But you—bang!...I transmeditated to you. Didn't you receive?"

"Listen, imagine what it was like for Pushkin! The guy has just finished 'The Prophet,' and the lines are still ringing in his head. Then this Bulgarin character, in his editorial office, comes out to greet Pushkin, all smiles. And Pushkin has to exchange bows with this lousy informer and shake hands with him."

"Naturally he had to. But in his letters, Pushkin called him the 'scum of our country's literature'...."

"Yeah, that was in letters! But there was no escaping Bulgarin in everyday life."

"Lenka, did you notice Bulgarin's eyes? How awfully sad they became?"

"That's what I said! He had a rotten life. Maybe he's not so guilty...."

"Who?! Who isn't guilty...Bulgarin??!"

"Oh, come on, what are you saying? We should look into this more carefully ... and get at the truth."

"Hey, did you hear that?! She feels sorry for him!!!"

"And why not? In all fairness, you must—"

"Was he fair to anyone?"

"OK, that was his style! Do you want to be that way, too?"

"What did you say? Come again, please!"

"I didn't say anything—only that there were Bulgarin types later, too. Much, much later."

"You watch, he'll probably repent now. You can't fight that. It's even boring."

"Quiet, please!" Igor raised his hand. "He's coming to. To your places. Step lively! Petya, set up contact, and think before you dish out advice...."

Everything was quiet now. All signs of the recent commotion, the shouting and wrangling, vanished instantly as their customary re-straint took over. Although relaxed and at ease, they sat in their places with poise and dignity. Judges? No. Neither were they spectators. Nor children. But scientists, conducting research. Meditation phono-clips in their ears supplied feedback to Igor: he caught unspoken suggestions and selected the best of them. In effect, thinking became a collective effort, although only one person conducted the conversation. Pospelov couldn't help admiring the familiar faces that reflected so clearly the intensity of their intellectual effort and emotions. It was pointless to interfere. Whatever goal they may have set for themselves, they had prepared for it very seriously, with the sense of responsibility and inner freedom so vital to civic consciousness.

Bulgarin's eyelids fluttered. Surreptitiously he cast a rapid, fearful glance, then froze for an instant. His limp hand made the sign of the cross. Somehow his face relaxed suddenly; he rose heavily, shuffled forward like an old man and straightened up with humble dignity.

"Be seated if you don't feel well," said Igor quickly.

"It's not weakness that bows me down," his words rustled softly through the room. Bulgarin's lips quivered pathetically. "I am crushed and prostrated by the slander I am encountering here, too. . . ."

"Do you mean that you never wrote reports denouncing Pushkin?"

"Denunciations—never! Those reports were the cry of conscience, a loyal subject's service, for which I suffered and suffered. No one . . . no one understands me!" Bulgarin's voice cracked, and his arms spread wide, entreatingly. "My innermost soul, oh Lord, most Gracious One, is bared to you. I beg you to judge it fairly!"

His voice fell and flagged. A chill ran down Pospelov's spine. What Pospelov had vaguely suspected, but his confused brain had refused to accept, struck him now with frightening clarity after hearing Bulgarin's pleading words. "What or whom does Bulgarin think these young people are?! A diabolical delusion?! Hallucination? Divine justice?!"

Any of these assumptions would be more credible to Bulgarin than the truth. No matter that this wasn't the real Bulgarin. The apparition created by holography and computer technology behaved and felt exactly as a live Faddey Venediktovich would have in the same situation. Undoubtedly the students had suggested to him (or even had inserted this knowledge in him beforehand) that his descendants were conversing with him. But the psyche, even that of a simulation, is guided by the concepts indigenous to its time and milieu. It meant that the phantom could think. . . .

Pospelov glanced at the students in bewilderment. Did they feel even an ounce of the horror that gripped him? Apparently not. For Pospelov's generation the phantomatic was a totally new experience, but for these youngsters it was an ordinary tool. Anything unreal or alien that at one time boggled the mind was no more than a sentence in a textbook for them, an impersonal fact from the distant past. And when dealing with the past, one had to consider such facts rationally. That's all there was to it. Igor leaned casually toward Petya and inquired in a whisper: "That appeal to God . . . was that on the level?"

Petya shrugged his shoulders. "According to the emotionalizer, it certainly was."

"OK, thanks."

"So, Faddey Venediktovich," continued Igor calmly, "your actions were motivated by concern for the public welfare?"

"Precisely! I believe you will be convinced—"

"We are already. However, please explain how your reports, your denunciations to the secret police furthered the development of your country's literature?"

"They were submitted every day. Yes, every day. Although they were not always appreciated, they did have a beneficial effect. What would have happened to Pushkin and other writers if ignorance had prevented the authorities from noticing something unwholesome in their work and, therefore, forestalling the consequences, gently, with a paternal, guiding hand? It is frightening to think of the drastic measures a neglected illness would have required! My duty lay there: to attract attention and sound the alarm before it was too late. I did the best I could and, I hope, succeeded."

"You were so successful, Faddey Venediktovich, that your efforts to serve were appreciated by posterity."

"Ah!" Bulgarin's plump cheeks flushed, and his eyes sparkled with emotion; he seemed ready to jump up and embrace his interrogator. "Yes, I wrote His Excellency Dubbelt, Leonty Vasilevich: 'There is God and posterity. Perhaps they will reward me for my efforts.' I am happy that I have been vindicated!"

Bulgarin raised his index finger toward heaven meaningfully.

"Ye–es, Faddey Venediktovich," drawled Igor. "We understand you completely. You served faithfully, sincerely, zealously, and were poorly rewarded. Worse than that, you suffered insults."

"Yes, I suffered. Oh, how I suffered." Bulgarin latched on eagerly to Igor's words. I was even arrested for my opinion of Zagoskin's novel, which displeased His Majesty!"

"Not only were you arrested . . . the gendarmes dragged you by the ears, like a child, into a corner and forced you to your knees. You, a writer, known throughout the land! Remember?"

"Did that actually happen?" wondered Pospelov. Unfamiliar with documents of that period, he reacted with disbelief and surprise, but his doubts were quickly dispelled by Bulgarin's sagging face.

"I was slandered by all kinds of people." Bulgarin's voice grew hoarse. "And because I even suffered cruelly at the hands of Their Excellencies, I placed my hopes on posterity!"

"You have our sympathy, Faddey Venediktovich. What a miserable life you must have had. Imagine being upbraided not simply for expressing an opinion, but for offering the most exalted praise to the powers that be. Is that the way it was?"

"God's truth, it was! Once, when I had cursed the Petersburg climate in my newspaper, a complaint was lodged against me: 'How dare you curse the climate of the Tsar's capital!' Or, all I had to do was give due credit to government measures, and that would displease them. They would say to me: 'We don't need your praise. . . .' "

"Still, you continued to serve the authorities who humiliated you. Aside from the question of your self-respect, why did you praise a system that had pushed you into a corner and forced you to your knees for some minor offense?"

"I did not serve for personal gain! I had contempt for those who abused me."

"And for Dubbelt?"

"For him in particular!"

"Then why did you address him in letters: 'Father and Commander'?"

"A Russian custom. . . ."

"The master metes out punishment to his slave, and the slave still kisses his hand. Correct?"

"Again I am misunderstood?" exclaimed Bulgarin bitterly. "I was committed to an idea, not to rotten lackeys. And for that I endured. . . ."

"Yes, of course! You wrote in your memoirs: 'It is better to unleash a hungry tiger or hyena than remove the yoke of obedience to authority and the law from the people. . . . All efforts of the educated class must be directed toward educating the people in respect to their duties to God, legal authorities and the law. . . . Whoever does otherwise, violates human laws. . . .' So, is that the ideal for which you suffered humiliation and labored so earnestly?"

"Yes, sir! Rebels threatened to cut off my head for my devotion to God, the Tsar, and the law!"

"Let's say that initially you formed very strong ties with the revolutionary Decembrists although it was no secret to you that they wanted 'to violate human laws.'"

"Yes, I am guilty of that, but it was a youthful transgression. I repented immediately and thereafter proved my loyalty by my actions!"

"You certainly did. Right after the Decembrist uprising you presented a proposal for improving censorship and began to work for the secret police. Let's leave that for the moment. Would it be incorrect to say that Nicholas I and his administration pursued the same idea as you did?"

"It would not be! How could I do otherwise?"

"A good idea, properly implemented, should benefit the people. Do you agree?"

"I do."

"Then explain your own memorandum about the state of affairs in Russia: 'The practice of concealing evil-doing and the fear of accounting to one individual for all, has generated a terrifying system of despotism on the part of the ministers and the whole satrapy of governor-generals. . . . ' "

"That referred specifically to the Tsar's evil servants and to shortcomings in need of correction!"

"Your evil servants turned out to be ministers, governor-generals, the chief of the secret police himself; and shortcomings—only the general system of arbitrariness and lies. According to your own words that is what flourished in the glow of your idea! Whom were you really serving? Perhaps not your idea at all. Nor the Tsar. Nor the State. But you yourself?"

"That is not true! Everything has been falsely interpreted!"

"Why protest so, Faddey Venediktovich! There are facts and there is logic. You are convinced, I believe, that even the darkest secrets about you are known to us. Would it not be better for you to tell the truth?"

Bulgarin was a pitiful sight: he looked as if ice water had been poured over him suddenly, just when he was beginning to feel the warmth of understanding. He shriveled, faded, and appeared speechless. But in his hounded eyes flickered evil sparks, wholly incompatible with his pitiful, bewildered expression.

"I shall speak the whole truth, sir," he managed to force out in a muffled tone. "I have carried my belief in goodness and truth through misfortunes, but have been hounded by circumstances, entangled by them like a prisoner by a net, and . . . and . . ."

"And?"

"And I stumbled. . . . Man is weak; I didn't wish anyone evil, but was surrounded by swine, by envious people; I was compelled to struggle. Even saints are not without sin."

"Who compelled you to befriend these swine? At the beginning of the twenties Russia's finest people were well-disposed toward you."

"They understood my real worth! If Griboedov were alive. . . . When he departed for Persia, he entrusted me, his best friend, with the manuscript of his comedy."

"Which you promptly sold for several thousand rubles. You even betrayed your Decembrist friends. Don't tell us that it was inspired by high-minded principles. You also betrayed your powerful benefactor, Shishkov."

"For God's sake, try to understand me! A publisher and writer in Russia was like a lamb among wolves."

"I beg your pardon! Not a single writer whose books stand on our shelves served the secret police. They did not inform on their fellow writers, although they lived under the same conditions as you did."

"Oh, no, their situation was not comparable to mine! I am not ashamed of my past, but in the eyes of the authorities—"

"You aren't ashamed of your past?"

"I fought bravely against Bonaparte at Friedland and was wounded for the glory of Russian arms."

"Then for the glory of French arms you fought against Spanish peasants. And later in the Great Patriotic War of 1812, you fought against Russian soldiers."

"Even a biased commission acquitted me!"

"From which you concealed a few details. And Benkendorf put in a word for you. Your masters loathed you, but needed you. It's all very clear. And so is the reason that compelled you to go over to Napoleon's side."

"My regimental commander did me an injustice. My resignation and dire poverty forced me to—"

"Yes, yes, we know how you stood holding out your hand in Revel, begging alms . . . and in fine literary style. Sometimes even in verse."

Bulgarin's plump figure jerked like a frog hit by an electric current.

"That never happened!!!"

It was like the cry of a wounded man. Everyone shuddered.

"It did!" Igor, turning pale, insisted. His words cut through the air like a scalpel. "It did, Faddey Venediktovich. Are you ashamed of such petty stuff? And you drank hard, stole an officer's overcoat . . . . All of this happened."

Gasping for breath, Bulgarin staggered, and the pain he felt was felt by everyone. It sparked a desire to recoil, to shield themselves from their bitter, reluctant, oppressive sympathy for him, and even more, from their intense, hypnotic, despicable curiosity for the involuntarily bared depths of a soul scorched by cynicism. In his confusion, even the operator forgot about his switches, although it seemed that Bulgarin was about to have a genuine fainting spell. Everyone had touched, as it were, the terminal of a high and dangerous psychological voltage, and was ready to shout: "Turn it off!"

But Bulgarin did not come crashing down to the floor. On the contrary, his voice acquired strength.

"It's all true." He quickly licked his parched lips. "I fell as low as one can fall and begged for help. Neither God nor man responded. You cannot imagine what I had to take from people! Thus did I come to understand the kind of world I lived in. Then I wanted to forget the past and clear myself, which is why I sought to befriend Russia's finest citizens. But the gendarmes knew about my sullied past. What is a man to them? A speck, an empty sound. . . . Life is fine for those with a stainless past! Where could I go with this millstone around my neck? Back to poverty? To the bottom? Shoot myself after a drunken orgy? Oh, no, sir! My talent lay concealed. God himself has ordered everyone to guard their gifts. I began to strengthen myself and to bait my ill-wishers. Thus did I bring glory to Russian literature with my *Ivan the Rogue* and many other works!"

Even Igor, prepared for anything, appeared bewildered by this unexpected turn, by Bulgarin's touching words, breathing sincerity.

"He'll squirm out of it!" thought Pospelov in dismay, yet with unconscious admiration. Suddenly conscious of his reaction, he felt pangs of disgust for himself.

Igor recovered his balance. "Do you consider your books to be a contribution to Russian literature?"

"It would be immodest of me to reply with a quotation from Pushkin's works: 'Unto myself I reared a monument/Not created by human hands...' However, few books have achieved the success that my *Rogue* did. Even my slanderer, that liberal Belinsky, admitted it."

"True, you had some success. But, despite loud publicity, official support and eulogies arranged by you, readers quickly cooled toward *Rogue* and your other works. Didn't you wonder why?"

"The heavens would tremble were I to enumerate all the intrigues of troublemakers who, by praising the latest literary fads, spoiled the public's taste and turned it away from truly patriotic examples of literature! But everything will assume its rightful place again. Everything."

"I think we understand your patriotism quite well, Faddey Venediktovich. Now, let's discuss the circumstances that compelled you to slander and inform. Ugh, Faddey Venediktovich, even lying has its limits! Now then, your circumstances. . . . You grew wealthy very quickly. You could have abandoned your affairs quietly and written novels on your estate. Please, don't tell us that the secret police would not release you from service! You stubbornly continued your activity. You enriched yourself without any qualms about the means to this end. There wasn't a talented writer, artist, or actor whom you didn't malign in print at least once. Your newspaper even ran down Lobachevsky's geometry . . . without, of course, giving him the right to reply. For decades you fired away at everything decent, talented, progressive that arose in Russia. We want you to tell us why."

Bulgarin's bloodless lips compressed to a fine line. He did not reply.

"First of all, deep down you understood very well that you and your literary works would have gotten absolutely nowhere without support from the authorities and your cooperation with the secret police. Only by ingratiating yourself, by behaving like a scoundrel, by pleasing the authorities, could you build your reputation and enrich yourself."

"Good heavens, where is justice?! Yes, I made money. Is that such a sin? That isn't why I sought influence. By gaining the authorities' complete trust, I hoped to incline them toward improving conditions and lightening the yoke on our people! My memoranda to the government, which you have already touched upon, and my projects prove—"

"That even you suffered in the total absence of civil rights in

Russia! We can believe that. But you made matters even worse. Wasn't it you who proposed the organization of a new criminal investigation department to be administered, on your recommendation, by the most vicious brute imaginable? No, Faddey Venediktovich, the mask of secret liberalism doesn't fit you at all. Unfortunately, everything is far more simple. Let's review the logic of your actions. Up to a certain time, you didn't touch Pushkin. You even published his work, bowing and scraping to him in the process. Then, suddenly you began to dash off reports, denouncing him. In the press you hinted that he was a plagiarizer, thereby provoking the Tsar's displeasure with him. How do you account for the abrupt change? What happened? Only this: Pushkin and his friends founded a newspaper which could have become a dangerous competitor to your *Northern Bee*."

"Slander! You have no documents to prove that—yet you can say anything you wish!"

"There is the logic of facts. Although your *Northern Bee* was considered by everyone to be a wretched paper, it had quite a few subscribers. It was Russia's only daily paper, so its subscribers had no other choice. Obviously, subscribers mean income. You certainly didn't want to lose that monopoly! A rumor circulated—only a rumor!—that Pushkin's friend Vyazemsky wanted to publish a paper. Immediately you rushed a report to the authorities, accusing Vyazemsky of immoral conduct. Do you want to hear more such facts or is that enough? Enough. Also, you tried to discredit talented writers because their works constituted competition and could drive yours from the market—which of course happened. That was the source of your hatred for all talent! And you had a need to denigrate others because their honesty and decency bothered you. You would have been far more comfortable if everyone around you bootlicked and informed. Even the Tsar, even the gendarmes loathed you. . . . Your life was certainly not an envious one!"

Bulgarin began to pant and wheeze. Until this moment neither fright nor the most degrading servility affected the determined expression on his face. He had been ready to take on anything. Now, in a flash, his face underwent a remarkable change. It went blank. No expression. Utterly blank. Except for the external signs of old age: sagging cheeks, purplish-blue sclerotic veins beneath flabby skin, flaccid parted lips with a bead of saliva drooling from them. The sight of this pitiful, worthless bead suddenly overwhelmed Pospelov with such horror that he almost shouted to the whole room: "What the devil are you doing?! Bulgarin has been dead a long time. This can't touch him. You're dealing with an apparition, a phantom. Whom do you think you're tormenting? And why?!!"

Pospelov's protest against this turn of events was nipped in the bud by Bulgarin's abrupt recovery. He looked as if he had acquired a second wind. The decrepitude vanished: a burst of energy erased the vacant expression, and the eyes glittered with hatred as a completely unexpected tirade rang out angrily and distinctly.

"Your verdict is more than absurd. The facts? Murder, too, is rewarded when committed on the battlefield. Laws determine who is guilty! They are created by people and applied by earthly sovereigns. My own actions were encouraged by the Emperor himself. If I am guilty before the highest law, what law is it, may I ask? It is impossible to observe a secret law, since it is unknown to us. The Holy Church oversees the observance of known laws; yet it, too, never regarded me as a grave sinner. Before the laws of our State and divine law, I am pure! But what laws do you observe? None! Or the devil's! But hear this: I am not under his jurisdiction. And since I have not violated God's laws, He is on my side!"

His voice died down on a note of triumph, and the insulted sanctity looked down on his judges and reveled in their obvious confusion. It didn't matter who these judges might be: descendants, gendarmes, devils, angels . . . as long as he could deflect some yet unidentified punishment hovering over him. Any means would do in the terrifying, unprecedented situation in which he was trapped. After all, hadn't his entire life been a battle of wits? He could adapt himself to any situation and always emerge victorious.

Pospelov trembled with humiliation and rage to think that such evil had triumphed over his boys and girls. No longer could he hold his tongue; he had not the right to remain silent. Feverishly, but in vain, he sought the words that would rescue the bewildered youths from this crushing rout and the shame of defeat. There were no arguments. He also felt that the students had involved themselves in a worthless game of cat and mouse. Although he was neither a historian nor psychologist, it seemed incredible to him that in the twenty-first century even an adult like himself, an ordinary teacher, was incapable of refuting a monstrous sophistry of lies. And to think of all the wasted years studying subjects so useless to him now, when he should have . . .

Bulgarin's lips were twisted in a defiant sneer: his well-oiled instinct had correctly evaluated the significance of so long and painful a silence. But suddenly—Pospelov didn't understand the reason immediately—the arch-demagogue's eyelids flickered warily. He had noticed—everyone had noticed!—an almost imperceptible sad and, perhaps, indulgent smile on Igor's face. Pospelov stepped forward impatiently. Bulgarin and his distant descendant stared at each other. Unable to maintain his direct gaze, Bulgarin averted his eyes.

"Why are you afraid to look me in the eye?" asked Igor softly, his smile vanishing.

With a haughty gesture, Bulgarin tossed his head back defiantly.

"What are you afraid of, Faddey Venediktovich, if truth, the law, and God are on your side? By the way, doesn't it seem strange to you that even in your time good deeds required neither excuses nor self-justification, while evil ones required both? By trying to justify your actions, you have accepted our judgment."

"Sophistry!" Bulgarin shrugged his shoulders contemptuously. "I wanted to affirm the truth and nothing more. If you accuse me of trying to justify myself, then it behooves you to know that villains more often appear innocent in the eyes of others than the reverse. Or, perhaps you are not familiar with this phenomenon? Aha, I see you are not."

"Then enlighten us, Faddey Venediktovich. Did we understand you correctly, that before the law an innocent will appear to be a villain, and a villain an innocent?"

"Just so! Just so!"

"In that case the law's goodwill toward you, which you keep stressing, is meaningless."

Bulgarin became confused, but instantly recovered his balance.

"Neither does it prove the reverse!" he exclaimed heatedly. "You can interpret it this way and that—that's philosophy. . . . But what have I actually asserted? The truth alone. Only the truth have I spoken."

"Which of three, Faddey Venediktovich? First, you presented yourself as a fighter for an idea, but that didn't turn out to be the truth. Then you blamed all your reprehensible acts on the relentless pressure of circumstances. Even that turned out to contain little truth. Finally, the third, and I hope, the last truth: you acted with the blessing of the law, meaning 'my life was a model of civic virtue.' "

"Even your all-knowing, prejudiced court of alleged descendants did not refute that!"

"He's squared it away: if you're not caught, you're not a thief," thought Pospelov wearily. "But here he's caught and exposed and he's still not a thief. . . . There appears to be only one way out of this. I see it, but do the students?" The proceedings had drained him; all he wanted to do was bury his head in something soft and cool. And Bulgarin was as fresh as a daisy. . . ." Don't lose your grip, Igor boy. Hang in there!" Pospelov prayed.

"If your actions, Faddey Venediktovich, were completely compatible with human laws and norms and were motivated by them, you have nothing to hide. Why, then, did you conceal your work with the secret police from everyone?"

His response was a condescending sneer.

"As you will learn, the highest interests of the State require the utmost secrecy in that type of work."

"Did society consider your work moral or was it merely accepted as an unavoidable evil?"

"Only troublemakers could speak out against such service to the State!"

"So, for example, your denunciation of Turgenev, for which he was imprisoned, was moral. He wrote an article that displeased you. Therefore, in your opinion, he had acted immorally."

"As the law judges, thus does it stand."

"Suppose the law punishes in some cases, but in other cases encourages a criminal. What is such a law worth?"

"That is casuistry, for which, thank God, I lack the gift."

"Really? How often did you take bribes?"

"I?! Bribes??!"

"Yes, you. Bribes."

"Slander, false rumors."

"Enough, Faddey Venediktovich! I see you still refuse to believe that we know everything about you."

"They looked like bribes, but really weren't. They were simply friendly gifts, tokens of appreciation."

"You're lying! Show us where, when, and from whom you took bribes for publishing various notices in your paper? Tell us the names of those mill owners, booksellers, actors. Incidentally, all this was very well known to the secret police."

"Good Lord, who in Russia doesn't take bribes?! It's a custom, you might say. Everyone takes them, and took them from me as well. You can't draw any conclusions from that. Each offense must be weighed individually and judged accordingly."

"In other words, it's not the act that counts, but how it is judged. Turgenev angered the authorities—therefore he is a criminal. But you are an informer and bribe-taker, an exemplary patriot. So, there is no law, but only the benevolence of higher authority."

"As it has always been and will always be."

"Judge the past, and not the future. You know nothing about it."

"You speak the truth. In my time it was as impossible to practice morality as spend the winter without a fur coat."

"Was that the law of life?"

"Indeed it was! But did I create it? I observed it as did everyone else. Even people in the very highest positions. . . ."

"Everyone was equally corrupt? Right?"

"Whoever touched power. Yes. All of them."

"And if all were guilty, no one was. That appears to be your fourth truth. But even here, Faddey Venediktovich, there is a discrepancy.

Most of your contemporaries detested this business of informing. They did not accept bribes! They did not tolerate lies and servility! Didn't public opinion have contempt for you because you were the living embodiment of all these wretched practices?"

"Gracious, what do I have to do with such matters? I only followed orders from above. If a shepherd leads his flock astray, is the lamb to blame?"

"But you were a watchdog. Intellectually you can't deny that you understood a great deal; but personal gain was the most important thing in life for you."

"What is wrong with that? Only the righteous are disinterested in profit; and when God created people, he put few righteous ones among us. Was my guilt so great? I did not avoid temptation. Of that I am guilty. The Tsar himself lied about events surrounding the Decembrist uprising. I am not holier than the Tsar. Informing was encouraged: If I hadn't informed, someone else would have.... What was permitted, I did; what was not permitted, I did not do. Bribes were taken all around me, and I took them, too. So, I am very sinful! But then, I didn't live in idleness, like many others did. I had ideas; I respected work; wrote ten volumes. Doesn't that tip the scales? Saint Peter betrayed Christ three times, repented, and became the head of the Church. My repentance is certainly no weaker."

"Faddey Venediktovich, somehow it doesn't impress us as genuine. Your repentance sounds more like an attempt to justify your actions and strike a bargain."

"I swear, that was not in my mind!" His voice suddenly sounded desperate. He looked around wildly. "How can I prove my sincerity?!"

"When you worked for the secret police you didn't bother searching your soul, did you?" Igor smiled ironically.

"Scarcely!" shouted Bulgarin, staring at Igor's sneering face. "I must with all my heart, in our Christian way ... " He broke off and doubled over. Before anyone realized what was happening, he was on his knees.

"I stand before you like an errant child!"

The students were stunned. One let out a muffled cry and covered his face with his hands. More revolting and disgraceful than the sight of the old man on his knees pleading with trembling hands, was the speed of his about-face. No one had foreseen the possibility of such an outcome. But the frightening logic was all there: behind it stood the long experience of a slave, whose keen senses catch the harsh cry; he knows precisely when he can argue and when he must bow down to be stepped upon.

The scene was so disgusting, and the thought of their guilt so unbearable, that Igor, his face pale with horror, was the first to rush to the controls and tear them from his comrade's paralyzed hands. Everything ended with a click that echoed through the room like a pistol shot. The nineteenth century setting vanished and with it, Bulgarin. Once more alone in their own century, no one spoke nor dared raise his eyes, for fear the ghastly phantom might still be there.

Theocrates' Blue Window

GENNADY GOR

1

WE COULD SEE THE RIVER from our window. A little man kept hopping from stone to stone, and once he slipped and almost fell in.

Whenever I wandered over to the window, the same scene greeted me: the river with its rounded stones and that little man hopping from one to the other.

"How long has he been doing that?" I asked my father.

"Ten years, son," my father replied. "For ten years he's been trying to cross the river, but he can't. Something keeps holding him back."

"What holds him back, Papa?"

"Well, son, it's like this. I do know and I don't know. No one really does. We have different physical laws operating in the river. He has fallen into a decelerated time field."

At this point I must interrupt the narrative I have just begun to avoid disturbing the mysterious little man hopping from stone to stone. As you will learn later on, there is a secret link between my story and his activity.

Even now, as I write this, he continues to hop, trying to cross from the left bank to the right bank, but time flows differently for him than it does for you; he has fallen into a decelerated time field.

The blue window was a part of my early childhood. It is still there, by the river; but now I am here, in a large, sprawling city. The world of my childhood was not unusual, but rather ordinary, even humdrum.

My dreams? For dreams I went to school where dreams made it possible for us to pass from century to century. Those amazing and very graphic lessons were called "Dream Studies."

How well I remember being led to the doors marked "CAUTION! XIX CENTURY."

One day those doors opened. Venturing a few steps beyond them, we found ourselves in the suburbs of Hartford, Connecticut, on Nook Farm, the home of Samuel Clemens, known the world over as Mark Twain.

We were greeted by Mr. Clemens himself, a kindly middle-aged man with drooping mustaches and a polite but puzzled smile on his intelligent face.

"Who are you?" he asked. "Where are you from?"

"We are students, sir, and I am their history teacher," stammered our teacher, somewhat embarrassed. "We . . . we come from the future."

"What future?"

"The future. We, sir, are from the twenty-second century."

"Come now, you want me to believe that humbug?" said the great writer.

Suddenly he noticed that our clothing was distinctly different from his.

"Do you think," he asked as he studied our teacher's semi-transparent jacket, "that people of the future will be so stupid as to make a display of their wretched looking bodies?"

Our teacher blushed; as a sportsman he prided himself on his handsome physique. Instead of replying that he knew precisely how people dressed in his, the twenty-second century, he mumbled:

"Yes, I think so, sir."

"Well, then," said Mr. Clemens, "it seems I've a far better opinion of our future generations than you do."

"But you don't know them, sir," our teacher began to argue.

"And you do?"

"Yes, sir."

Mr. Clemens began to bombard him with questions.

Our teacher attempted to reply but became so rattled that all he could do was mutter some disconnected phrases.

Mr. Clemens listened and shook his head.

"A likely story. So, all you had to do was open a door and—PRESTO!—you found yourself at my doorstep. Tell me, young man, why is it that I've never found myself in some other century? And I've opened many doors in my lifetime. Perhaps I don't know how to open doors properly?"

Our teacher's response was quite irrelevant; he reminded Mr. Clemens of his book *A Connecticut Yankee in King Arthur's Court.*

"What are you trying to tell me, young man?" Mr. Clemens was getting more and more irritated. "*A Connecticut Yankee in King Arthur's Court* is a novel and NOT a history book. Come now, out with it! Tell me why you arranged this stupid masquerade!"

"Sir, this is no masquerade," replied our teacher who, by this time, was thoroughly confused and bewildered.

"Then what the hell is it?!"

"It's a history lesson. We don't study the past from textbooks but try to establish personal contact with historical figures."

"Personal contact instead of cramming? H'm, rather amusing," said Mr. Clemens. "But do you always appear so informally, without forewarning? Without even knocking?"

"We deliberately use this approach," explained our teacher, to approximate dream conditions. You know—noiseless, soundless, and a complete absence of logic."

"Who the hell is doing the dreaming now?" shouted Mr. Clemens. "You or I?"

"Well, sir, it works both ways. You are dreaming of us, and we of you," replied our teacher evasively. "But, have it as you wish."

"I'd prefer to wake up. I don't care for this dream. Now, get the hell out of here!" he roared as he slammed the door.

2

Our school boasted many other doors. By slipping through them one could journey whither one's heart desired: to ancient Greece and Egypt, to yet undiscovered Mexico, to the Neolithic, Mesolithic and Paleolithic periods.

Ah, yes, we had skeptics among our schoolmates, but I was not one of them. I was a true believer. Not for a moment did I ever doubt our meeting with Mark Twain in the twentieth century. But, to tell the truth, I was not too enthusiastic about excursions into the past. Should something go wrong—with the timer, for example—we could be stranded forever in another age, never to return to our beloved families and friends.

I frequently worried about such a possibility and was not especially overjoyed when I learned that our next lesson would involve a personal meeting with Ivan the Terrible or, should we fail to contact him, with some great conqueror like Batu or Attila the Hun.

My worst fears were realized. Something did go wrong. Our class, led by the teacher, visited Batu but was stranded in the thirteenth century owing to the carelessness of our technicians and malfunctioning apparatus.

Fortunately, I had been ill that day and could not go on this field trip.

From time to time I would question my parents:

"Mama, will they return, or be stranded there forever?"

Mama was optimistic. "When they get sick and tired of Batu, they'll come back. You'll see."

Father was cautious and evasive: "Maybe yes, maybe no. They could be stuck in another age, you know, like an elevator jammed between two floors."

As a result of this incident our school was closed temporarily. With some difficulty the director managed to establish intercentury contact with the stranded history class.

"How are you and the children?" was his very first question.

"We're in excellent shape. Khan Batu has taken us for God's

assistants. We sleep in nomadic tents, drink koumiss and arrack, ride wild horses, and are studying their customs and culture."

The director was infuriated by the history teacher's nonchalance. "The equipment has been repaired," he exploded. "Get back here at once! An extended visit will wreck our entire academic schedule and upset the teachers and parents as well."

"May we have your permission to extend the lesson a few more days to avoid irritating the khan?" pleaded the teacher.

Suddenly the connection went dead.

3

Like most of the city's inhabitants, my father was a scientist. He wrote about ancient cultures and was quite partial, perhaps too partial, to the Hellenic writer Achilles Tatius.

You will hear about Tatius shortly because a discussion of this writer is not only relevant to ancient history, but to our family as well.

Mother was also a scientist and was writing a dissertation on extinct animals—whales. Whales had become extinct in the twentieth century; rather, I should say, had been exterminated. To see a live whale, one had to use doors that led into the nineteenth and twentieth centuries.

Like all paleontologists, mother frequently went on expeditions into the past and left the present for rather lengthy periods. It took a long time before father became reconciled to these separations from mother. Time and time again mother would disappear. She went off on expeditions or with tourist groups to every conceivable period and place: to ancient Egypt, Mesopotamia, ancient Rome and Greece.

It was in Alexandria that she met Achilles Tatius, the Hellenic novelist to whom father had devoted an entire chapter of his work on antiquity.

Achilles Tatius fell in love with mother and tried to persuade her to remain in ancient Alexandria. Father was furious with Tatius but managed to retain his objectivity in his writings about him.

One of mother's hypocritical friends, Aphrodite Kapronycheva, circulated a false rumor that I was the son of the ancient Greek novelist. But who could believe such an incredible charge? Besides, I was the spitting image of my father, who bore not the slightest resemblance to Tatius.

In a constant effort to maintain contact with her numerous friends scattered about in various centuries, mother traveled almost continuously. She counted many of these people among her closest and dearest friends.

"My dear friend Titian," she would say in her very rapid speech, "is waiting impatiently for me. He had barely begun my portrait when I had to fly off somewhere. I must return as soon as possible."

With the ease and grace of a butterfly she would glide through the centuries and through the windows of the most famous personages. Like Velázquez, and even the gloomy El Greco.

Mother was an eternal tourist, touching a thousand years with her pale, beautiful, sensitive hands. Her research on those extinct sea animals, whales, was written up carelessly, in great haste, in some intercentury pension or hotel and was far from being a brilliant success. Specialists found not only petty inaccuracies in her dissertation, but gross factual errors.

So, disillusioned with paleontology, mother was soon attracted to classical antiquity and began to write a novel on life in Hellenic society. Actually, it was a good excuse for lengthy expeditions into the past, for meetings with Achilles Tatius who had remained where she had left him, at his home in ancient Alexandria.

However, scientific ethics prevented father from curbing mother's expeditions and her meetings with the classical novelist; but, oh, how he suffered during her absences, which sometimes lasted for years.

4

Finally our school reopened. The doors to the past had been repaired and my classmates and our teacher made a hasty exit from Batu's khandom.

Oh, how my classmates gloated! While I had been at home, ill, they had galloped through the Siberian steppe on wild horses, drunk koumiss, and hunted with bows.

Vainly trying to conceal my envy, I waited impatiently for the next lesson on world history. My desire to take the risk and find myself in some other century or millennium was not stronger than my fear of the unknown. When the bell rang and class began, the history teacher announced, "Today we are going to visit the twentieth century."

Having heard so many fascinating stories about the twentieth century, I was delighted.

The teacher led us to the door which separated us from the past. Suddenly we found ourselves in a small provincial town in Russia. It was 1915. Its inhabitants took us for a troupe of young actors who had just arrived from South America. After they had settled us in a hotel, we went out to see the town.

We dropped into a small shop that smelled of soap, kolbasa, and cheap candy. As we left it we heard the sounds of music coming from a park in the center of town. It was here, in the park, that I met Tonya, a pretty girl with a long thick braid and large green eyes.

"What's your name?" she smiled.

"Theocrates," I answered softly.

"Theocrates? I've heard that name somewhere before," she laughed. "Oh, now I remember; it was last year in my classical Greek class. So, you're from ancient Greece?"

"Oh, no," I replied, "I'm from the future. But I don't think you'll believe me."

"Suppose I do?" she teased.

Suddenly her green eyes turned blue, as blue as my blue window.

"You do resemble the ancient Greeks in a vague sort of way," she continued. "Of course it's rather obvious that you don't want to be one. I could tell that from the expression on your face."

"Then you've guessed," I said. "Some nasty gossips say that my father was an ancient Alexandrian, Achilles Tatius."

"Say, you're quite a tease. Do you know anything about ancient Greece? My father teaches Greek at the boys' high school. Watch out before he quizzes you. Anyway, until I find out for sure who you really are, let's take a walk around the park."

The orchestra was playing slow dance music.

"Say, who are you, really?" Tonya asked. "I think I know," she continued. "In town they're saying you and your friends are a Lilliputian troupe."

"What are Lilliputians?"

"Freaks—dwarfs who stopped growing in childhood because of some dreadful disease."

She laughed loudly.

"Don't be offended. You're no Lilliputian freak; you're just a boy."

She paused and said tenderly:

"You're an ordinary boy who accidentally fell into this group of Lilliputian dwarfs. You're too big and handsome to be a Lilliputian. Besides, I think you're a conjurer. Aren't you?"

"Yes, and maybe even a magician."

"Then show me a trick. Well, don't wait for me to insist."

We walked and kidded each other. Time passed so quickly. And I told Tonya about the little man hopping from stone to stone.

"Is that supposed to be funny or sad?" she asked.

"I'd say both. But he doesn't seem unhappy."

"Where is this going on?" asked Tonya. "South America?"

"No, in the twenty-second century."

"But the twenty-second century isn't here yet. This is only the twentieth century."

"I won't argue with you. OK, it's the twentieth. But I live in the twenty-second century."

"Impossible!" said Tonya.

" 'Tisn't," I objected.

"How I'd like to believe you."

"Why can't you?"

"Because it's impossible."

"Well, believe it anyway."

"I can't."

"Why not?"

"I don't know. I guess I'm too grown up for fairy tales."

"Believe it anyway. I beg you, please do!"

"You're a strange one," she said quietly. "Very strange. Why are you trying to convince me that you're from the twenty-second century?"

"Because it's the truth."

"Then how did you get here?"

"Through a door. Through the door to the past."

"What kind of door is it? And where is it?"

"It's where we live, in the twenty-second century. In our school. But we use it only at history lessons. Our teacher takes us into different historical periods according to the schedule in our school's curriculum. Our class visited Batu recently. Then Karl XII, Ivan the Terrible, Catherine II, and Winston Churchill."

"Winston Churchill? Who's that? We never learned about him."

"You will, later on. When he becomes prime minister. He hasn't become known yet and gone down in history. You have much less history to remember than we do. We can, if we wish, meet any historical figure."

"Very interesting." She laughed. "You've cast a spell over me and for a moment I almost believed in your door and that you were from the twenty-second century. But, unfortunately, it's impossible."

"I'll prove to you that it isn't."

"When?"

"Not right now. When we return to our own century. We'll disappear—and forever."

"Forever?" she asked.

"Yes, forever. That's the way our school's history program works. Once we've studied something, we never repeat it."

"Don't you want to repeat it?"

"Repeat what?"

"This lesson, that's going on right now."

"I wish this lesson would never end. But we don't have lessons like that. All this will end and we'll return to our century, our school, our teachers, our parents, and our work."

"You'll return, but what about me? Will I remain here? In my own century?"

"Yes. You don't have a door to the past. It hasn't been invented yet. It won't be for a long time. Not for two more centuries."

"I don't believe you. I don't believe such a strange, fantastic door will ever be invented. We have lots of doors. But they're all very ordinary doors. Nothing unusual behind them. You open them and see what you saw yesterday and will see tomorrow. Isn't it that way where you come from?"

"Sure it is. But I'm talking about a special kind of door. To the past. But don't think they're very reliable. Sometimes they get stuck."

"Then aren't you afraid it might happen this time and you'd be stranded here with us, in our little town?"

"Oh, I don't know. It could happen. But then I'd see you every day."

We began to make dates and write notes, leaving them in the hollow of a spreading weeping willow on the river bank near Tonya's house.

Days later when we met again Tonya said:

"I see the lesson is still on."

"What lesson?" I asked.

"The history lesson, of course! Don't you remember? You came through the door to the past. You're from the twenty-second century, and I'm from the twentieth. Although my head doesn't believe it, my heart tells me it's true. I've a feeling that your lesson is about to end and you will disappear. Please don't, Theocrates. I beg you."

"I would like to stay," I said, "but our teacher is not allowed to return without me. And I don't want to get him into trouble. He's a good chap even if he does get things all mixed up sometimes. When we visited Mr. Clemens—he called himself Mark Twain—our teacher became so flustered he said all the wrong things. Mr. Clemens scoffed at us and sent us packing."

"How could you have seen Mark Twain? He's been dead a long time."

"And so have you," I blurted out, "but all the same, you and I are talking. Even laughing."

I caught myself and regretted what I had said, but it was too late.
"I'm dead?" asked Tonya. "When did I die?"

"Many years from now," I replied, flustered. "I . . . I really don't
know and am only supposing you will. I'm sure you'll live a long time.
But not until the twenty-second century, of course. I've come to you
from there."

"That means I'm dead?"

"Oh, no! You're alive! In the whole wide world there isn't a girl
more alive than you. You're more alive than anyone from the past,
present, or future. Honest to goodness!"

"I believe you! Yes, I do!" said Tonya. "But let's talk about
something more cheerful, not about death. You told me last time
about a little man who keeps hopping from stone to stone in your
river. Is he still doing it?"

"I don't know. Probably he is. After all, he did fall into a
decelerated time field."

"What's that?"

"You'll have to ask a butterfly or our physicists. They have
transformed seconds into years."

"Is that good or bad, Theocrates?"

"I don't know, Tonya. Maybe it's necessary. We do live in a very
mobile age; we can penetrate easily into any millennium. But in the
decelerated time field everything is different. I kept wanting to ask
that little man about it, but never succeeded. When I get back to my
century I'll be sure to ask him."

"How will I find out about it?" asked Tonya.

I paused. After a long silence I said, "Won't we ever meet again?"
Tonya was silent, too. Then she said, "How can we? I'll be dead."

"From what?"

"From nothing. What everyone dies from."

"What does everyone die from?"

"Time. Once you return to the twenty-second century, I won't exist
anymore. You'll get back to your century in an instant, won't you?"

"Yes," I replied, "within a few seconds."

"Then I don't understand anything at all," Tonya said. "It means that within those few seconds I shall become an adult, then grow old and die. Isn't that true? Please, Theocrates, explain it to me."

"It's not worth explaining."

"Why not?"

"Because it isn't going to happen. I'm staying here. I don't want to return."

"What about your teacher?" she asked. "He'll get into lots of trouble if you don't go back."

"He'll think of something. He can say that I was trampled by a horse or that some criminal robbed and killed me. Your newspapers have a lot of that."

"But they'll demand some sort of proof, a clipping from the newspaper or something else. . . ."

"Everyone knows that your century was a violent one and lives were lost easily."

While I tried to convince Tonya that I would remain in her century, I was also trying to convince myself. I was torn by two conflicting emotions: a desire to see Tonya every day and a desire to see my parents, classmates, and the blue window of my childhood, all of which was so very far away now.

Tonya seemed to divine my thoughts.

After my meeting with Tonya I returned to the hotel to find my teacher and classmates very upset.

"Where did you disappear to?" my teacher asked sternly. "Our lesson is almost over and everyone must be in his place. Now we shall return to the future, to our century."

Not for an instant did he take his eyes off me. And then . . . then the curtain of time separated Tonya from me.

5

I kept a snapshot of Tonya in my pocket. It had been taken by a provincial photographer. Wretched as it was, it conveyed all the charm of her smile and her large mocking eyes.

Tonya had remained in the past, in another, distant century; and

I was here. And the words "here" and "now" seemed like an impenetrable barrier separating me from her, from her "there" and "long ago." Would I ever see her again? Meet her? If I did, it would not be during a history lesson. They were never repeated. This was forbidden. But I could not go on living without Tonya, without her smile, without her mocking and melancholy words. I told my parents about her. For some time they had observed that I had been secretly grieving over something and losing a great deal of weight.

"You must find a girl in your own century," said mother sternly. "Have we so few of them?"

Father took my adolescent feelings more seriously. He understood that mine was a genuine, powerful, and pure love. I showed him her picture, which confirmed her uniqueness. My father understood at once and did not try to persuade me to forget Tonya or to find someone like her among my contemporaries.

"But what can you do about it, son?" he asked sympathetically.

"What can I do, Papa?" I replied. "I can return to the twentieth century to see her. We never had a chance to really talk to each other. Time went by so quickly. And our teacher was afraid to linger for a single hour. The Batu lesson was still too fresh in his memory."

"The door was out of order then," said father.

"But this time it worked perfectly. Before I could blink an eye, there we were, back in our classroom. Sometimes I think it was all a dream. Yet, this dream is stronger and more real than reality."

"Try to imagine, Theocrates, that is was a beautiful dream."

"But, Papa, it wasn't. You know that as well as I do. The door to the past exists. I want to go back to Tonya, to the very spot where I left her. She is waiting. I'm sure she is. She's waiting and hoping. And I've deceived her."

"Did you promise her something?"

"Yes, I promised to stay. But I have deceived her, and I'm afraid she's dead now."

"Of course she is," said father. "This is the twenty-second century, and you left her in the twentieth, over two hundred years ago."

"But I shall try to return to that very moment when she was

walking toward the tree to meet me. I don't want to keep her waiting a single minute."

"For that, Theocrates, you must wait," said father. "You are not old enough to travel alone as an intercentury tourist. You are still a minor."

"Oh, Papa, must I wait?"

"You have no choice. Wait, be patient, Theocrates."

So, I began to wait. My life consisted of waiting, of thinking of nothing else but my reunion with Tonya. I counted the days, weeks, and months. They drifted by slowly, as if I were hopping from stone to stone in our river's decelerated time field.

I wrote letters to Tonya. But with whom could I send them? No one wanted to return to 1915, when Tsar Nicholas II ruled Russia. So, the letters filled my desk drawer.

In one of them I had written:

"Dearest Tonya! There are doors to you, but for the time being they are closed to me. Wait, my darling, a few more years, and I shall see you. . . ."

6

Finally that day arrived. At last the door opened, and there I was in the little town where Tonya lived.

I recognized the hotel. Church bells were ringing. Once again I breathed the air of a remote provincial decade.

The sultry scent of hay tickled my nostrils. Suckling pigs squealed in the marketplace. I bought a pickle from a baba, a peasant woman, sitting next to a barrel and consumed it on the spot.

Then I walked down to the river where Tonya's house stood. I walked as if in a dream, as if each step were separating me more and more from the goal I was trying so desperately to reach.

After walking for about half an hour, I saw her.

There she lay, in a baby carriage, sucking a pacifier. She was six months old. Next to the carriage stood a stout, angry-looking wet-nurse. The nurse glared at me as if I were a thief.

The instant I saw the nurse, carriage and baby, I realized what had happened. The door's timer had not functioned properly. Instead of 1915, I had popped in on 1899. Everything in town looked pretty much the same: the houses, trees, people. But not Tonya. She had not learned to talk yet and only gazed at the world with her lovely green eyes.

"Tonya," I said tenderly, bending over the carriage. "Tonya! Don't you know me?"

"You silly young man! How can she recognize you when she scarcely recognizes her own mother?" said the nurse.

I lingered by the carriage, thus further arousing nurse's suspicions.

I visited this section of town every day at the same hour, when the nurse appeared with her charge. I would go over to the carriage and gaze at the baby with intense emotion, hoping that this tiny thing sucking a pacifier suddenly would turn into the girl I had left behind. But the baby went on sucking her pacifier and looked at me as merely another object in the big world around her.

One day her nurse started up a conversation with me. "Young man, you shouldn't come here so often," she warned.

"Why not?"

"Never mind. You are a gentleman, and I am only a poor, simple country girl. People will talk."

"Why?"

"Because I'm only a wet-nurse. My master and mistress are fine people, but if they catch wind of this they will be furious."

"If they learn who I am they won't be."

"Who are you? Where do you come from?"

"I come from the future. From the twenty-second century."

She stared at me with a puzzled expression. "How's that again? From the future? H'm, you are odd at that. I can see, for example, that you are overly fond of babies."

Such was my first attempt to see Tonya. Every day I would return to the same spot as if I had fallen into a decelerated time field.

Sometimes a thought flashed through my mind: "Stay and wait patiently for Tonya to grow up!" But in the end I decided to return to my own century.

7

My next attempt to see Tonya was even less successful. This time I arrived too late. Tonya was surrounded by grandchildren.

She recognized me and was stunned by my youthful appearance. Of course I mentioned nothing of my having seen her in a baby carriage during my first attempt to find her.

Ah, yes, she was an old woman, hale and hearty, but some forty years stood between us like an impenetrable barrier.

"A dear old friend," she said, introducing me to her children and grandchildren. "We haven't seen each other in over forty years."

How everyone gaped at me! As if I were an actor who had forgotten to remove his make-up.

Valentina, Tonya's daughter, who closely resembled her mother, studied me carefully. "For one of Mama's contemporaries, you look incredibly young. Tell us who you really are," she insisted.

"A magician," I replied. "A wizard. I belong to the Wizards and Magicians Union. With the permission of our local trade union committee, I halted the process of my own aging."

What else could I say?

Hoping they would eventually grow accustomed to me, I began to visit Tonya's noisy and hospitable household frequently.

One day we were alone.

"I shall make another attempt to meet you," I mumbled.

"But you *have* met me. What more do you want? We have no power over our own time, Theocrates. Do you blame me for growing old?"

"Well, then who is to blame?" I asked.

"No one. The years."

"But I have not let time overpower me; I have remained as you knew me."

"Why, Theocrates?"

"Because I loved you so; and for the sake of meeting you again I didn't want to change."

"Loved? You're using the past tense. You no longer love me?"

"I don't know. *You* don't exist. Instead, I see an old woman with gray hair and a wrinkled face. Oh, Tonya darling, where are you?"

"I am here, Theocrates, in front of you."

"Yes, *you* are. But *you* aren't Tonya."

"Then who am I?"

"I don't know. Only your name hasn't changed, and something elusive in your eyes. I wait for hours to catch that expression, if only for an instant. It plays hide and seek with me. Somewhere inside you lurks the charming young girl I once knew. For me this is unbearable."

I returned the following day. We talked for a long time, exchanging words as if words could return us to the past, to that moment when we stood in the park, listening to the music.

Was there ever really such a moment?

Yes, there was. But it could never be repeated.

"So, you find that I've changed a great deal?" Tonya asked me. "The horror of it all is that we don't notice how we change. That is the frightening thing about life. How did you manage to keep your youth? You might be playing a trick on me. Maybe you aren't *you*."

"Who else could I be?"

"The son of the Theocrates I met in 1915. I thought about him often, but he never returned. I wondered why. I thought he had died. Later, I married. Tell me the truth: are you his son?"

"No, I am he. And I have come to you."

"From where?"

"From the future."

"He said the same thing."

"It wasn't *he* that said it."

"Who did?"

"I did."

I showed her the snapshot she had given me forty years ago.

"Don't you recognize yourself?" I asked.

"I do."

"Why can't you—why won't you recognize me?" I asked.

My question remained unanswered.

I heard weeping.

Last time it was the crying of a little baby girl in a carriage. Now it was the weeping of an old, withered woman.

I left without saying good-bye. It was more like an escape than a departure. I never returned.

8

The door opened and I took one step, an ordinary, human step, but it was equivalent to almost a century.

This time I found myself in the twenty-first century, in a large university lecture hall where a discussion of "Reality and the Modern World" was in full swing.

On the rostrum stood a man with unusually cheerful and kindly eyes.

"Reality kills," he said quietly, as if he were talking about a river that was growing shallow. "Everything becomes as illusionary as a dream. Here is an example of what the invention of the door to the past has wrought. Through those doors I recently visited Rembrandt's studio. The great artist was deeply engrossed in thought. Before him, waiting, stood his wife in her nightclothes. I felt extremely uncomfortable. Indeed, I had invaded someone's personal life. Finally, the great Dutch artist emerged from his thoughts and noticed me. He became enraged and waved his brush at me. . . . But what interests me at this time is the purely physical aspect of the problem rather than moral or ethical questions. Did or didn't this happen? A direct and precise answer to this question will not be forthcoming from either technologists or sociologists. Everyone will reply most politely and ambiguously: 'It did and it didn't.' What does that mean? Does it not mean that we are dealing not with reality itself but only with its substitute? For the past two centuries we have been substituting everything: we have been transplanting skin, trees, nature, hearts, and other organs. In this case we also have a substitution. But the essence of this substitution evades us. Are you a spectator or an actor? Were you daydreaming or did you exist in another time? We cannot give you the answer to this. They say the experts are working on it. But I want to know: did I see the real Rembrandt or his ghost? I shall not rest until I find the answer."

He was followed by another speaker, a man who bore a strange resemblance to everyman: to Darwin, Newton, even to Oscar Wilde.

"I have just returned from the nineteenth century," he began. "I spent several hours chatting with Dostoevsky. Afterward he portrayed me as the devil conversing with Ivan Karamazov. But did or didn't it happen? It would appear to my advantage to say 'yes.' But it is my opinion that it did not. I only thought it did. I do not believe that a door actually opened into the past. The past doesn't exist; there is only a present. I was a victim of illusion. I agree with the previous speaker. Reality kills. It is growing ever smaller in this excessively plastic world in which people know a great deal but don't know what knowledge itself is. I propose that we close the door to the past. It is highly unethical to appear where you are not expected. I can understand Rembrandt's fury at the previous speaker. I would have reacted as did the artist. For the past to become reality, the doors must be shut."

The third speaker was a very tall man with a stentorian voice. It seemed capable of penetrating centuries as well as walls.

"Reality kills," he said. "I agree. We have less and less of it as time passes. It is the tempo, the pace, that is to blame. Speed! Speed! We are burning up with speed. Within minutes we can go anywhere: to Mars, the Paleolith, the Mesolith, to the bottom of the Pacific Ocean. But we don't have enough free time to experience the simple joy of living. Therefore, I propose the creation of a decelerated time field. By entering this field, one could be alone with one's self, with one's leisurely thoughts and feelings. One could dream and reminisce to one's heart's content."

I sent the speaker a note, received a reply and soon became acquainted with him and his work on decelerated time fields.

He persuaded me to participate in his experiment. I agreed to be a subject.

9

Tonya was standing next to the tree where I had left her several years ago.

"Hello," I said. "Have you been waiting long?"

She laughed. "What are you saying? You haven't left me for an instant. Why are you suddenly greeting me? We've been standing here together ever so long and I hadn't noticed that we'd separated."

"It only seemed that way to you," I said.

"I don't think so. If it seemed that way, it was you, not I, who thought so. You imagine a lot of things. What doesn't exist, what never did exist and never will, you accept as truth."

"What are you talking about?"

"About what you just finished telling me. You were telling me about the twenty-second century. About doors to the past. About Achilles Tatius. About a little man who keeps hopping from stone to stone."

"And didn't I tell you that I saw you in a baby carriage and as an old woman, too?"

"No, you didn't. And I can guess why."

"Why?"

"Because you won't see me as an old woman before you yourself are an old man. Nor did you or will you ever push me in a baby carriage. Theocrates, we are the same age. We've been lucky enough to have been born at the same time. And that's why we're standing next to each other, not separated by decades or centuries."

"Are you sure of that?"

"Of course. Aren't you?"

"No, I'm not. There is a door through which I passed to get here. Really, Tonya, I've come from the future."

"Yes, you've tried so many times to convince me of that. I almost believed you, but everything was so mixed up. I don't believe any of it now."

"Then how did I get here? Where is my past? Who am I?"

"Who are you? A boy. That's all I know about you. The Lilliputian troupe left town and you stayed behind. You stayed because of me. The illusionist in charge of the troupe was furious. And desperate. He valued his talent as a visionary and wizard. You hid on the river outside the city. You were hopping from stone to stone—in dense fog. It never occurred to anyone to look for you there. But why am I telling you this, Theocrates? You know about it better than I do. What are you going to do now? Alone, without the troupe and that illusionist who pretended to be a history teacher? And I'd like to ask you something, Theocrates."

"About what?"

"About the blue window of your childhood. Where did you leave that unusual window?"

"In the future. In the twenty-second century."

"The future cannot be the past, Theocrates. I want to know the truth. Prove to me that you are from the twenty-second century."

"How can I?"

"Very simply. Show me something that does not exist now but will exist in two hundred years.

I slipped a talking pen from my pocket and handed it to Tonya.

"Sit down on the bench," I said, "and try to write with it. Do you have paper? Ah, here's a piece. Now, write something!"

Tonya took the pen. Suddenly it began to speak Tonya's thoughts in Tonya's voice: "Theocrates, do help me to understand what this is all about. Indeed, this pen resembles nothing that exists today in Russia. A pen! A talking pen! It speaks for me, divining, reading, repeating my very own thoughts. But maybe this pen isn't real? Maybe I only think it is. After all, you are an illusionist."

"Perhaps I, too, am only an illusion?" I asked.

"No, you aren't. But everything is so strange. I suppose if such an unusual object exists, so does the door to the past. You've told me about it so many times."

"It does exist."

"And you won't leave me and return to the future?"

I did not reply. I myself did not know what would become of me.

There I was, standing by a tree on a river bank, in a long past century, and next to me stood a girl—cheerful, intelligent, lively. So very real!

The moment grew longer. I had fallen into a decelerated time field, into a field of youth and love. The moment stretched out, as if transformed into eternity. And the pen began to speak again:

"Theocrates, this simply hasn't happened and couldn't. You invented the whole thing—didn't you?—that you came from another century and that your mother was in ancient Alexandria? You did it just to prove you loved me. Isn't that true?"

"What about the talking pen?" I asked. "Doesn't that prove . . ."

Tonya laughed and threw the pen into the river.

"Well, and now? Now there isn't any proof," she said. "And I don't need it. Theocrates, all that matters is that you are with me. You are, aren't you?"

"I'm with you," I said softly, scarcely believing myself.

Cheap Sale

VLADEN BAKHNOV

I GREW FOND OF THIS LITTLE CAFÉ. Maybe because the juke box didn't blast my ears off. Or because I didn't want to run into any of my old friends. No, sir, no worries about that here: they wouldn't so much as poke their noses into a place like this.

I used to come here every evening and take a corner table from where, thank God, the T.V. screen wasn't visible. I'd nurse my drink while contemplating measures to improve my deteriorating financial situation.

I would arrive in a lousy mood because I couldn't see any solution to my problem, but I'd leave full of confidence, inspired by an exciting premonition that some incredible brainstorm, my salvation, was about to strike.

The transition from one mood to another was not abrupt, but could be decelerated and accelerated at will. With the help of whiskey I learned how to control this process. Oh, hell, how I love that divine, sublime state! What a pity I can't make it stick permanently, that I have to work my way up to it from scratch every evening.

Sometimes, to divert myself when I was down in the dumps, I'd take to studying the café's patrons. Most would come in, gulp down a jigger or two, and disappear. Some were happy and carefree, others, sad and depressed. But I envied them all because they were always rushing off somewhere, while I had no reason to do anything but stay put.

There were a few steadies like myself who hung around all evening. For some time a neatly dressed elderly man had caught my eye. I noticed him because he was always alone. He didn't read the papers, wasn't interested in T.V., and generally appeared oblivious to his surroundings.

He would sit there with half-closed eyes as if he were deeply engrossed in something. Evidently his thoughts were not as gloomy as mine, because from time to time he would smile happily as if recalling some pleasant memory. Occasionally his smile would fade into a confused expression and he would shake his head sadly, perhaps regretting some past deed.

One day we collided in the doorway. He glanced at me absent-mindedly and apologized. Then he studied me more carefully and with an expression of surprise. Since that time I had often caught his eye on me, and even when I turned my back on him I could sense that I was being observed.

This irritated me no end. I even thought of looking for another café. Then I became infuriated. Sometimes I get that way.

"Listen," I said, marching up to his table, "I keep having the feeling you're looking me over, and I don't like it one bit!"

The polite gentleman reddened and sputtered apologies. Then he urged me to join him at his table or vice versa so he could explain everything to me.

I said that either way was all right with me as long as we kept the conversation brief. He began to thank me and would have thanked me for another half hour if I hadn't interrupted him and asked him to get down to business.

"I beg you to forgive me for annoying you," he said, "but I have the feeling I know you, and very well, too. At the same time your face eludes me, although sometimes I'm certain we've met somewhere. Perhaps you're a movie star? Maybe I've seen you in make-up and that's why I can't recognize you now?"

"No, I'm not an actor. But I have a marvelous visual memory," I replied. "Believe me, we have never met."

"H'm, strange. You insist we've never met. Yet your speech has such a familiar ring. Amazing, isn't it?"

I shrugged my shoulders.

"Maybe it's just coincidence. . . ."

"Pardon me, my dear sir, but it definitely is not. Until I understand why I feel that I know you, I shall not be able to rest."

"Well, now . . . I've been living in this city for many years. You could have seen me somewhere."

"No, that's not it! Now, look here, I have the feeling I know you *very* well. Perhaps we met in some business connection?"

"I doubt it," I grinned. "And what do you do?"

"Oh, what haven't I done!" he said proudly. "If you have no objections, we might as well introduce ourselves. I'm Rage Over."

"Glad to know you. I'm James Nobody," I said, uttering the first name that came to mind.

"Pleased to know you, Mr. Nobody. Nobody? H'm, your name does sound familiar. Where do I know you from?" He paused briefly. "May I ask what you do for a living?"

"I'm an astronaut," I lied.

"Strange as it may seem, I have never left Earth. So, we could not possibly have met on your spaceship. Have you been flying long?"

"Almost all my life."

"Everyone is dashing off into space these days. And what for? I am convinced that you can still make out well on Earth if you know how to use your head. All you need is a little luck and money!"

"Pretty tough conditions!" I replied.

"I won't argue with you about that. For a start I did have money, and plenty of it. Inherited it from my father. His invention of a very ingenious and amusing device, a Mood Battery, made him a wealthy man."

"A Mood Battery?" I asked in amazement.

"They are no longer in use," he explained, "but at one time they were very popular. This bulky piece of apparatus (bulky by our present standards) was about the size of a pen and fit easily into a jacket pocket or lady's pocketbook. If, for some reason, you were upset, overstimulated, or enraged—in short, if you weren't yourself, the excess psychic energy was channeled into the battery and your normalcy was restored. If you were excessively overjoyed, the same process took place: the battery absorbed the excess. Then, when you felt depressed or lethargic, the battery returned the accumulated energy to pep you up."

"Very interesting," I said, determined to listen to my new friend's story to the very end. "And then what happened to the batteries?"

"Nothing. Father made a pile of money. Then Emotion Stabilizers became popular and Mood Batteries went out of style. Shortly thereafter Father died, and I began to think about my future.

"I could have invested my inheritance in some solid enterprise, but that didn't interest me. You see, I am a born entrepreneur. I've spent my whole life discovering new ideas for exploitation. Whenever a successful competitor appeared and squeezed me out, I would look around for some new venture. . . .

"I'm not complaining. But I must honestly admit that my ability to discover new ideas is a good deal stronger than my ability to derive profit from them.

"So, I realized that in our day and age only one promising area remained for exploitation: the human brain. You have probably heard that certain positive emotions can be elicited by stimulating specific parts of the brain. For instance, satisfaction, joy, tranquility, pleasant tastes and smells, and so forth.

"Well, I organized a company—General Emotions. We could elicit any emotion a client ordered. Moreover, my firm created for its clients the rarest, subtlest, most delicate feelings. Our clients could experience what no other individual had ever experienced. And although our services were expensive, very expensive, we had an ever-growing clientele. I was about to open branches in other cities and countries when suddenly competitors appeared. Evidently they knew more about psychology than I did. They devised schemes which, unfortunately, never occurred to me.

"As I've already explained to you, my clients could experience only positive emotions. My competitors, however, by stimulating other portions of the brain, induced negative emotions in their clients—longing, fear, horror. Then these emotions were erased, and these individuals immediately felt enormous relief and a *joie de vivre.* This feeling of relief was the positive emotion for which clients willingly paid good money. This might appear strange to you. But don't forget that we were dealing with people who were looking for intense sensations. Our clients had tried everything, from wine to narcotics, and they had tired of all of them.

"Look, for example, suppose your teeth *don't* hurt. Does that make you happy? No! But you experience sweet bliss when a miserable toothache vanishes. Or if you walk about in shoes that don't pinch—does that fill you with joy? No! But if you drag around in tight shoes for just one hour and then remove them, what intense pleasure you feel. Nothing can compare to that moment!

"Therefore, positive emotions elicited via negative ones are more effective than positive ones alone. My competitors' fees were much lower than mine because they did not require the complex apparatus that my firm did. Finally, after losing a lot of money, I liquidated General Emotions.

"By that time a wonderful new idea had taken shape in my mind. It was so simple and promising that I was amazed that it hadn't occurred to me before.

"Everyone is aware of inspiration, even if he himself hasn't experienced it personally. But the precise mechanism is unknown to us. All we know is that people fired by it have produced immortal works, made brilliant discoveries, and have solved problems in unbelievably short periods that humanity has vainly labored over for centuries.

"We have not yet mastered the art of producing inspiration on demand. But we do know that inspiration is often experienced under certain conditions. For example, when a person falls in love. And it is fully within our power to create such conditions artificially.

"So, I organized a new company—Inspiration. I had to maintain a vast network of secret agents who worked in various laboratories and institutions. Through them I received information indicating that such-and-such scientist in such-and-such laboratory had been given an unusually difficult assignment. Then I would meet with the scientist's chief in complete confidence and explain to him that his scientist could complete his task in one-tenth the normal time if the services of my company were engaged.

"Usually the chief would agree and the scientist would be sent to us, ostensibly for a medical check-up. The whole process took half an hour. But the scientist would leave the premises totally unaware of the fact that he was about to fall wildly in love with one of his co-workers. (You understand, of course, that this could not be done without hypnosis, and the apparatus for the production of such instantaneous inspiration had been custom-made for my firm.)

"As a result, the scientist, inspired by love, acquired exceptional gifts for a brief interval of time and, working at peak capacity, produced a miracle. The contract was fulfilled and my company received its fee.

"We were inundated with clients. Orders poured in from every corner of our planet. I was preparing to open branches in other cities and countries when competitors began to appear. What do you think these unscrupulous creatures did? They hired their own agents and shadowed everyone entering our facilities. They tapped our phones and intercepted our mail. Why? I'll tell you why. All my competitors had to do was to get wind of the fact that scientist X had visited our offices and had fallen in love with Miss Y. Then, by means foul or fair they enticed the unfortunate Miss Y to their offices and under hypnosis forced her to fall in love with scientist X. Do you follow?

"Petrarch, hopelessly in love with the already wedded Laura, wrote sonnets about her all his life. But in my case, figuratively speaking, barely had my Petrarch written half of his first sonnet, than Laura herself came to him, suitcase in hand, and declared her intention of living with him forever after. Could Petrarch have composed sonnets after that? I don't think so.

"Now you can see what insidious methods my competitors resorted to. I issued huge refunds to my clients. Eventually, after losing most of my money, I was compelled to liquidate Inspiration.

"But I didn't throw in the towel. I thought and thought and finally arrived at a perfect solution.

"I decided to become a memory salesman. I don't know if you are familiar with this technique, but the memories of one individual can be implanted artificially into the memory of another. The implantee will actually believe that he had personally experienced these memories.

"For example, imagine that you once had a million dollars. You had drunken orgies or lost on the stock market, spent money on women, or, like me, were an entrepreneur. In brief, nothing remained of your million except some pleasant memories. Such memories are very interesting, but to lose a million dollars for them is rather expensive, I would say. Right? Now, suppose you could acquire those memories for one hundred dollars? For only one hundred dollars you could remember all your life how you squandered a million! Can you picture that? So, I organized a new company called You Had a Million.

"You could take your pick of recollections of how you lost your million: you could reminisce endlessly about Bacchanalian revelries or gambling that ruined you, about government coups or the nationalization of your factories. Moreover, my company implanted genuine recollections, never fictitious ones. My agents searched all over the world for recently bankrupt millionaires. They sold our firm their memories down to the last detail for very substantial fees. In keeping with our contract they would recollect images of their past life while special apparatus received and fixed these images. Then they were implanted in our clients. I paid original sources more than one hundred thousand dollars for their memories alone. Expensive, but in this manner my company, You Had a Million, accumulated a huge inventory of all kinds of unquestionably genuine recollections.

"My firm guaranteed that our recollections, purged of all depressing thoughts, would not spoil one's disposition and would retain their charm and freshness. They were guaranteed for a lifetime. Once implanted, a client would never realize they were not his own.

"Everything went beautifully. We had clients galore. I was about to open branches in other cities and countries, but, again, competitors appeared. This time their methods were absolutely brazen. They didn't bother to look for ruined millionaires and pay them huge sums for their recollections. No, my competitor, Fond Memories, didn't need expensive originals; it was satisfied with cheap copies. Thus it could sell and resell the very same memories five times cheaper than I could. And that was it! I was ruined. But this time, for good. . . . Oh, by the way, have you ever visited our firm?"

"Your firm? No," I replied and, unable to restrain myself any longer, burst out laughing.

This was so unexpected that Rage Over was rather offended.

"I see nothing amusing in my story," he said drily and, stumbling against the table, walked toward the exit.

"Do you know that man?" I asked the elderly waiter.

"Of course. That's Rage Over. He has a little tobacco shop not far from here."

"For long?"

"Yes, I'd say about thirty years. His father left the shop to him."

The café closed for the night. It was drizzling outside.

How could this poor devil have known, I mused, as I headed for home, that he had been recounting my own memories to me all evening. Memories sold to competitors who had ruined me! As an exception, they had payed me as much for them as I myself at one time had paid ex-millionaires. My competitors were very pleased to purchase from me my very last piece of goods.

But . . . but, could I, too, be living with someone else's memories?

Beware of the Ahs!

VLADEN BAKHNOV

NO MORE DEBATES, theories, or speculation about Planet Sigma Z. It is now an accepted fact that a very advanced civilization had once flourished there and the distant ancestors of its present primitive inhabitants had possessed a body of knowledge that these descendants will acquire only after many thousands of years.

The ancient Sigmans had preserved all sorts of historical documents in hermetically sealed steel capsules sunk deep into the earth. No sooner were they discovered than all debate ceased and the amazing history of Sigma's rise and fall unfolded before us.

It has always been assumed that catastrophe precedes the sudden decline of a civilization: a cosmic disaster, floods, glacial movements, or war.

But nothing of the sort happened on Sigma Z. Its disintegration began with a petty, ridiculous lawsuit. If the court action brought by the plaintiff hadn't been so incredible and pitiful, even the most wretched newspaper would not have devoted a single line to it.

The suit originated in the following manner.

On the Street of Blue Roses in Foneytown, Sigma's capital, stood a most unique institution, the National Museum of Forgeries. Only forged works were exhibited in its galleries, unique forgeries of very rare ancient works, counterfeit coins from various periods and countries, and superb imitations of precious stones. Its most valuable holdings were its brilliant forgeries of the great works of art, the paintings of the masters. Many forgeries achieved notoriety before they appeared in the museum's collection.

The museum was popular with Sigmans. They loved to gaze at counterfeit coins and canvases, to listen to the guide's stories about swindled collectors; and while shocked by the enormous sums paid for forgeries, their admiration for the forger exceeded their sympathy for his poor victim.

Experts, too, visited the museum, not only to admire the skill with which these forged masterpieces were produced, but to reassure themselves that their expertise could distinguish between an original and a copy.

Then, one day, an obscure young man by the name of Dave Davis accused the museum of exhibiting an original work rather than a forgery. The original, "Food of the Gods," had been painted by the renowned Strutsel. The museum, he charged, was deceiving the public. He demanded that the court expose this shameful fact and order the museum's owner to pay him damages: the price of the ticket to the museum, the round-trip taxi fare, and compensation for undermining his faith in the honesty and integrity of his fellow Sigmans.

The museum's owner, Louis Ellington, was not concerned about the paltry sum demanded by Davis, but he was disturbed about damage to the museum's reputation. So he decided to fight it out in court.

The judge proposed that the two parties settle the affair amicably, but both sides stubbornly rejected his suggestion. Thereupon, the court requested an opinion from experts. Following a careful examination of the painting in court, a committee of three experts declared it a forgery. Davis refused to accept the experts' opinion and requested the High Court to appoint another, more competent commission of experts. Davis was prepared to assume court costs if he lost the case.

This time the experts labored for six months, subjecting the canvas, paints, oil, and priming to chemical analysis and x-rays; they photographed and enlarged every inch of it, even studying the artist's signature. After collecting all the necessary evidence, Sigma's leading experts on Strutsel's works had to admit that the painting in question was an original created by the hand of the immortal master himself.

Truth had triumphed! Davis was awarded damages and Louis Ellington, the unsuccessful defendant, now possessed an extremely rare masterpiece. He sold it immediately for four hundred fifty thousand dollars which helped to soften the blow of his defeat.

The trial had generated universal excitement. Strutsel specialists pleaded with Davis to explain how he had determined that the canvas was an original. Day and night he was besieged by journalists. Finally, he decided to reveal his secret at a press conference.

The capital's largest auditorium was packed to the rafters. Reporters from every corner of Sigma Z were present, and radio and television networks offered full coverage of the event.

"As you probably have surmised," began Davis, "I did not sue the museum merely to extract a few paltry bucks from Mr. Ellington. If he has not yet been reconciled to his loss, let him say the word and I shall return the money cheerfully.

"I needed this case for one purpose," continued Davis. "To attract attention to my humble self. You see, I am an inventor, and I know how difficult it is for an unknown inventor to publicize his invention. As a matter of fact, if not for this court case, you would not have attended this press conference, which, hopefully, will serve as my vehicle for publicity. First of all, you want to know how I determined the originality of this painting. I shall tell you my secret: I determined it with the aid of a device I invented, an 'ahmeter.' "

Davis held up a round object that resembled a compass and demonstrated it to the audience.

Television networks magnified the device for home viewers so they could easily distinguish the ahmeter's dial face, which was divided into degrees. Next to the degree markings stood numbers, and a freely swinging dial was fastened to the center of the meter.

"Undoubtedly you are curious. You want to know what this instrument is and how it is used. I shall try to explain it to you. All of you have observed, I am sure, that a genuine work of art elicits involuntary exclamations of delight: 'Ah, how beautiful!' or 'Ah, how superb!'

"Why do we utter this 'Ah'? Because the work we are viewing has an emotional impact on us. In fact, every work of art carries a specific emotional charge and, as we know, any charge can be measured. So, my ahmeter's function is to measure the magnitude of an emotional charge.

"The unit of measurement is the 'ah.' Some works carry a charge of one hundred ah, others, thousands, while still others carry no more than ten.

"Naturally, not every work of a particular artist carries the same number of ahs. However, after visiting every museum on Sigma Z and recording ahmeter readings for the works of eminent artists, I arrived at the conclusion that each artist has his own individual ah range. For example, all of Trentel's canvases fall within the 3500 to 3650 range; the paintings of that remarkable artist, Veidim Seidur, produce from 4900 to 5000 ahs, while Zaigel-Zweigel's cover a range of 3970 to 4135 ahs. And so it goes.

"A talented forger can, in every respect, reproduce the hand of the original artist, his methods, and all his stylistic peculiarities.

"But it is impossible for a forgery to duplicate precisely the emotional charge of an original work. It will be less than that of a given original. Or, in an exceptional case, it will be greater if the forger is more gifted than the painter of the original. But even if the copy is superior to the original, it remains an imitation. An airplane is superior to an automobile; nevertheless, it is not an automobile.

"However, let us return to Strutsel. I knew from my research that his range was 3770–3850 ahs. So, when I toured the Museum of Forgeries and discovered that 'Food of the Gods' registered 3810 ahs, I did not doubt for an instant that I was standing before an original Strutsel. And, as you know, the ahmeter did not deceive me.

"What are my plans for the future? I am certain that every museum and private collector possessing an ahmeter will have excellent protection against the acquisition of forgeries. Therefore, the potential market for ahmeters is very attractive. But I am not interested in producing them myself. I would like to sell my invention, and at this time would like to announce that I am open to offers from anyone who wishes to acquire production rights."

Following his statement to the press, Davis spent the next two hours answering a barrage of questions from reporters: How was an ahmeter constructed? How old was the inventor? Whom would he marry should he divorce his wife? and so on in the same vein.

Enough said about the press conference. Or Davis's haggling with potential buyers. Or what sum he eventually received for the rights to his invention.

Ahmeters were finally put on the market; initially at a very high price, but the price dropped as volume sales increased.

We shall note further that, as a result of the ahmeter's widespread use, so many forgeries were exposed in art galleries and private collections that the Museum of Forgeries lost its claim to uniqueness.

Sigmans began to visit galleries with increasing frequency, not to become acquainted with famous works of art but solely for the purpose of detecting forgeries. They were gripped by hunting fever. After a superficial inspection of a work for its aesthetic interest, they would check its ah charge and compare it with the amount listed in the catalog.

These people were, to use a newly coined expression, antitreasure hunters. The discovery of a brilliant original elicited far less excitement than the discovery of a genuine forgery.

All important works of art were measured for their ah charge. To be considered a cultured Sigman it was only necessary to know that Marinelli's "Madonna" registered 6500 ahs, while Flower's landscapes registered an average of 3400. To do well on examinations, art students had only to possess a precise knowledge of ah ranges. In any discussion of art, the first consideration was not visual images, not ideas, but statistics.

Before long the ahmeter was adapted to measure the emotional charge in literary and musical works. But here it must be pointed out that it was no easy matter to apply the ahmeter to literature. Many famous poems and novels could not be measured accurately with standard ahmeters, and supersensitive devices had to be developed.

An extremely advanced technology overcame such obstacles and unique devices were created which could measure ahs in tenths, hundredths, and even ten thousandths. As a result, literary works could now be measured with the same accuracy as other works.

Numbers had always been worshipped on Sigma Z, and it was believed that anything could be subjected to mathematical analysis. The classical proof of human existence, "I think, therefore I am," had been modified long before the advent of the ahmeter to conform to their love of numbers: "I analyze, therefore I am." Anything that could not be expressed in numbers aroused suspicion, skepticism, and even total disbelief.

Perhaps this infatuation with numbers explains the Sigmans' unbounded enthusiasm for the ahmeter. The opportunity to make ahmeter measurements gave literary and art critics precise criteria for judging a work. So precise that the need for professional critics eventually died out. Anyone equipped with a ahmeter could now evaluate a work of art with complete accuracy.

For several years Sigman life followed an uneventful course until a new trend surfaced: it began with novelists and rapidly involved all literary genres as well as other art forms.

A certain prolific author, one Johann Damm, whose novels generated eight to ten ahs, announced one day at a press conference that he deliberately wrote low-ah novels. It was easier, he explained, for the average reader to absorb ten ten-ah novels than a single one-hundred-ah novel. Therefore, low-ah novels were superior to high ones. And furthermore, it was his opinion that a writer was obliged, first and foremost, to consider the benefits his work would bring to his readers.

A debate erupted, but gradually more and more writers and artists agreed that low-ah works sold faster and were absorbed better than high-ah works. Psychiatrists, who by now had replaced all professional critics on Sigma Z, confirmed after numerous experiments that, from a medical point of view, it was better for a reader or spectator to utilize the energy of a work in small doses—in quantums—rather than gorge himself on large ones. Low-ah works completely satisfied this requirement.

In this manner did quantum literature make its appearance on Sigma Z. Writers tried their best to produce enormous quantities of low-ah works.

If a writer produced a powerful literary work it was considered a sign of creative weakness rather than strength, and it indicated a total indifference to the health of his readers. The public simply ceased reading authors who stubbornly refused to write low-ah books. What reader would willingly undermine his health?

Almost simultaneously with the appearance of quantum literature, quantum music and art began to develop. But as far as we can determine from our examination of historical documents, not a single Sigman displayed the slightest anxiety about the future of his planet. If science and technology, they reasoned, had produced such unprecedented triumphs, why worry? Nothing was impossible for Sigmans.

So, when a provincial pharmacist, Bidl Baridl, was inspired by an exciting but technically complicated idea, the hand of omnipotent science stepped in to guide him.

Baridl's idea was based on the following reasoning.

It is an accepted fact that literature and art enrich our lives. But many hours are spent reading a book; a film requires some three hours of our time; and a whole hour is killed listening to a symphony. If people did not have an innate need for ahs, they would not devote so much time to these activities. Therefore, why not develop a process that would permit the consumer to receive the ahs he needs through some other medium? Why must it be in the form of a book, film, or musical work? Why not, he reasoned, in the form of ahspirin tablets? For example, instead of watching a thirty-ah film for three hours, you take an ahspirin of equivalent strength. Thus, by absorbing the same emotional charge you would normally receive from a time-consuming film, you have actually saved time. And time is money!

Moreover, different kinds of ahspirins could be produced which not only differed in ah strength but in the type of emotional effect they would have on the individual consuming them: the ingredients of one type would produce the same emotions as a specific film, the ingredients of another type—a symphony, and so on.

Thus, each variety of ahspirin would be labeled according to the particular work it was replacing. For example, an adventure tablet might bear the label "Tarzan," a comedy tablet, "Horsefeathers."

This, in brief, was the idea introduced by pharmacist Baridl. Although he hadn't the vaguest notion of how to produce ahs in the laboratory, he did know that he could make his fortune on them. And so, I repeat, despite seemingly insurmountable obstacles, ahspirin, unfortunately, was finally synthesized and sold everywhere on Sigma Z.

Sigmans were extraordinarily successful in their attempts to prepare music ahspirins. After the production of the first, very primitive tablets, which were capable of eliciting only a single mood, either cheerful or sad, a complex type appeared on the market. These tiny tablets consisted of several different emotion-laden layers and were constructed somewhat like our time-release capsules or spansules. While some layers dissolved and were digested rapidly for faster action, others were absorbed slowly. The fantastic possibility of four-part ahspirin symphony became a reality. As the first layer (allegro) dissolved, it induced a sensation of lightness, airiness, and elation. The second layer (andante) evoked leisurely lyrical contemplation. The third (vivace) elicited a lively mood, and, the fourth, in keeping with an ahspirin symphony's optimistic finale, evoked in its consumer an ecstatic joyfulness and belief in the ultimate triumph of good.

A close working relationship developed between composers and ahspirin producers, so that new musical works and tablet substitutes of the same name appeared on the market simultaneously. Later, when composers themselves mastered the art of composing prescriptions for music tablets to match their own musical works, they also began to create original compositions in tablet form, thus bypassing the process of writing lengthy musical pieces. Full-length productions quickly became obsolete. Often one would stumble upon young lovebirds in a park who, having found a secluded spot and having swallowed some concerto for piano and orchestra, would be sitting side by side, holding hands and happily digesting the inspiring music.

Everyone took ahspirins.

There were even addicts who gulped music, art, and literature tablets at one sitting. And there were charlatans in the medical profession who advised their patients to take ahspirins before meals as an aid to digestion.

One eminent scientist discovered that cows doubled milk production when music tablets were mixed in their daily feed. If, in some cases, the new feed formula failed to yield predicted results, this scientist would insist that the idea was perfectly sound but that composers were at fault for their failure to produce the kind of music cows required.

It should be noted that the events outlined here occurred over a long period of time: some two generations passed between the invention of the first ahmeter and the appearance of the first ahspirin. After the passage of another three generations, Sigmans could scarcely imagine a time when music and literature ahspirins did not exist, when time-consuming, full-length artistic productions were the cultural norm.

The art of conversation and the exchange of ideas suffered severely. Since the Sigmans were so busy popping pills, little time was left for talk, and besides, their mouths were too full. And there weren't many ideas left to exchange. The stomach, where ahspirins were digested, now played a dominant role in their intellectual lives.

From the course of events one would be led to expect an eventual total degeneration of these once intelligent beings. For one simple reason that should have been foreseen, this did not occur. The sinking Sigmans were rescued from irreversible degeneration by the process of degeneration itself. This is not as paradoxical as it sounds! Because they were going downhill so rapidly they lost the secret of ahspirin production along with the vast store of knowledge they had accumulated over the centuries.

Deprived of ahspirin, the primitivized Sigmans began to recover their senses after the passage of several centuries.

Hundreds of years passed until one day, lo and behold, a caveman scratched an image of a hunter on the wall of a cave. His fellow cavemen uttered an exclamation of delight: "Ah!"

In another cave a savage, in some completely incomprehensible fashion, composed a legend about a brave hunter named Or. When he finished his tale, his audience emitted a thunderous "ah!" and demanded an encore.

Slowly Sigma's inhabitants began to tread the narrow path of progress.

As I dig through these historic documents I wonder if we ought to divulge the whole truth to the Sigmans as soon as they are capable of understanding what we have to tell them. Would it be worthwhile? Would it help them?

Very likely it would. Without such knowledge of their past, the cycle could repeat itself, and this time nothing, not even their own degeneration might save them.

Formula for Immortality

ANATOLY DNEPROV

1

IT ALL BEGAN THE DAY ALBERT RETURNED from Europe. He had just reached his father's villa and was paying the driver when a ball flew over the fence and bounced along the asphalt drive.

"Would you please pass the ball to me?" called a girl's voice.

A fair-haired girl wearing a string of pearls around her slender, graceful neck peered at him over the fence.

"Hello there. Who are you?" asked Albert, handing her the ball.

"And who are you? Why do you want to know who I am?"

"Well, young lady, this happens to be my home, and *you* are playing in *my* garden."

The girl looked at Albert in surprise, ducked behind the fence again, and disappeared in the garden.

He found his father in the study. Albert sensed that he wasn't particularly overjoyed about his son's arrival but attributed it to fatigue. After several questions about life abroad and the work of some of Europe's leading laboratories, he suddenly announced:

"You know, Albert, I got so sick and tired of it all I decided to leave the institute. Professor Birkhoff agreed that I could remain as a consultant."

Albert was shocked; as recently as a month ago there had been no hint of retirement.

"But, Dad, you aren't that old yet!"

"Age has nothing to do with it, Al. Forty years in the lab is a long time, especially when you consider how hectic those years were. One scientific revolution after another!"

Unconvinced by his father's explanation, Albert merely shrugged his shoulders. Perhaps he was right. Albert knew him to be a tireless worker who never spared himself. After his wife's death he had thrown himself into his work with a frenzy. For days he would not leave the laboratory and literally drove himself and his research assistants to the point of exhaustion. A long time ago, some twenty years back, his group had been working on the structure of nucleic acids and the deciphering of the genetic code. They developed an interesting method of controlling the sequence of nucleotides in deoxyribonucleic acid chains through the action of mutagens on the primary material. It generated a great deal of discussion everywhere, and sensational headlines appeared in the press: "Key to Biological Code Found," "The Riddle of Life—in Four Symbols" and so on. . . .

"I hope that Professor Birkhoff will appoint you in my place after a trial period."

"Dad, that's too much to expect. I haven't done a thousandth of what you have."

"You know everything I've done, and you must pick it up and go on from there. I'm sure you can do it."

Albert glanced out the window. "Who is that delightful child?"

"Oh, I forgot to tell you. She's the daughter of an old friend, Elvin Shawley. The poor thing's an orphan," said the professor softly. "But she hasn't been told yet, and musn't be."

"What happened?"

"Elvin and his wife died in a plane crash over the Atlantic. I was so upset by their deaths that I invited the girl to stay with us. I told her that her parents had gone on an expedition to Australia for several years."

"She'll learn the truth sooner or later."

"Of course she will. But the longer it can be kept from her, the better. . . . Her name is Mijee. She's thirteen."

"Strange name."

"Yes, I suppose it is a bit strange. Ah, here she is!"

As Mijee dashed through the door, she paused for an instant. Smiling shyly, she curtsied.

"Good evening, Professor. Good evening, Mr. Albert."

"Good evening, dear," said the professor, kissing her on the forehead. "I hope you and Albert will be friends."

"We already are. Where's your racquet, Mijee?"

"Oh, I don't play tennis often. I'd rather read. But it was so nice out today. . . ."

"You should spend more time outdoors." Albert sounded like an older brother. "I hope you'll let me join you. I like tennis, too."

The girl blushed.

"I'd love that, Mr. Albert."

"OK, enough of this 'mister' business. Just call me Al. And I'll call you Mij. All right?"

She nodded, took the professor's arm, and they went down to the dining room.

2

When Albert returned to the laboratory, Professor Birkhoff suggested he analyze the structure of x and y chromosomes, the sex determinants. Although this was a complex problem, certain related facts had already been established. The principal tools in this research continued to be artificial mutations produced in genetic material with the aid of chemical mutagens of the acridine class. Mutants were then controlled in an artificial "biological nursery" where the future organism's sex could be determined after ten to twenty cell divisions. A tremendous number of mutations had to be produced.

Tackling the problem, Albert estimated how long its solution would take, and the figures stunned him. Given the most ideal circumstances, an entire lifetime would not suffice!

"Discuss it with your father," suggested Birkhoff. "Maybe he has some ideas."

When Albert entered his father's study that evening, Mijee was there too. The professor was sitting in a rocker with closed eyes, listening to Mijee reading Byron in a low voice.

"Oh, it's you Al." His father raised his head and looked at him dreamily. "When Mijee reads, it brings back memories."

"Dad, I envy you. You probably have plenty to remember. But you've hardly ever spoken to me about your youth."

Closing the book, the girl left the room quietly. Albert sat down near his father.

"Too bad you left the institute, Dad. Without you I'm like a blind kitten. I'm afraid I'm going to bother you. I've lots of questions."

He told his father about the problems he faced in his new job at the lab. The more he spoke, the harsher grew the expression on his father's face. Finally his father rose abruptly.

"That's enough, Albert. I know it's a completely hopeless task and there's no point wasting time and energy on it."

"But all the other chromosomes have been deciphered," objected Albert.

"That's a different matter. They have the same structures. Unravel the formula of the initiator and the rest falls in line. For the x and y chromosomes there is no such formula. For them you have a uniform sequence of nucleotides. . . ."

Suddenly he broke off. A silence filled the room. Through the window wide open to the park drifted the faint rustle of chestnut leaves, the barely audible droning of nocturnal insects and . . . singing. The song was very simple, melodious, and familiar. For some reason it reminded Albert of a scene from his childhood: a tall flower bed, densely overgrown with azaleas, a very small boy, and someone singing this song behind the flower bed. He runs around the flower bed, searching for the source of the voice, but she runs away from him and interrupts her song occasionally to call out in her sweet, gentle voice:

"Albie, try and catch me!"

As he runs and runs, the colored flowers streak past him. He cannot catch up with that elusive, marvelous voice. Then he flings himself on the flower bed, crawls through the jungle of flowers, and cries out . . .

"Who's singing?" he asked his father, barely moving his lips.

"Oh? Can't you guess?" He sat down heavily in the rocker.

"No."

"It's Mijee."

For several minutes no one spoke. Why was his father's breathing so labored? His pale hands clutched the edge of the table nervously. Noticing his son's anxiety he said with deliberate indifference:

"The girl has a lovely voice, hasn't she? By the way, Al, you can pass on my opinion about the x and y chromosomes to Professor Birkhoff. Tell him it's a hopeless task. I can't see any sense in working on it."

"No sense in working on it?" Albert was stunned. "Coming from you, Dad, that sounds strange. You've spent a lifetime working only on that. You've studied the molecular structure of genetic material in detail. And now . . ."

His father interrupted him with a sharp wave of his hand.

"There is research that absolutely cannot be justified . . . from an ethical and moral point of view. Albert, I'm very tired. I'd like to sleep."

As he was leaving the study Albert noticed his father take a vial of medicine from his pocket and put it to his lips. It seemed his father must be very ill but was trying to hide it. It was also clear to Albert that for some incomprehensible reason his father did not want him to continue his research on the chemical nature of x and y chromosomes.

Albert went to the park and wandered slowly along the path, dark and wet with evening dew; he headed for the source of Mijee's singing. She was sitting on a stone bench before a small pond.

"Oh!" she exclaimed at Albert's sudden appearance. "Gosh, you frightened me! That's not a very nice thing to do to someone, Al."

He sat down beside her and they were silent for a long time.

"Mijee, are you happy here with us?" asked Albert.

"Oh, yes. I like it here. Even better than my own home."

"Where is your home?"

"In Cable. One hundred kilometers north of here. But I don't like Cable. When Mom and Dad went to Australia I felt awfully lonely there. It was so good of your father to take me in."

"Cable, Cable . . ." Albert vaguely remembered the name; he thought he had heard it mentioned at home.

"Mij, I know this is a pretty strange question, but do you love your father and mother?"

She paused for a while, apparently confused by this unexpected question.

"Do you have to love your parents?" Her voice had a bitter edge. Suddenly she laughed.

"It's strange, but I've never really thought about whether I loved them. Now I understand. I suppose I stopped loving my parents after Mr. Korsh became a frequent visitor."

"Who is Mr. Korsh?"

"An awful man. He looks like a doctor. He probably is one, too. Because whenever he came to see us he examined me, and sometimes he took blood for tests although I wasn't sick at all. I felt very hurt that my parents let him do that. . . . It almost seemed as if they didn't care what Mr. Korsh was doing. They would walk out of the room and leave me alone with him. He's a very unpleasant doctor, especially when he smiles."

Albert felt sorry for the girl and gently placed his arm around her shoulders. Like a small child she pressed herself to him trustingly and murmured:

"It's chilly, Al, isn't it?"

"Yes, dear, it is."

She wound her thin little arms around his neck and buried her face in his chest.

3

Albert did not mention his conversation with his father to Professor Birkhoff. The complex study of the x and y chromosomes offered him the opportunity to prove his worth as a research biophysicist. He refurbished his father's laboratory. Under his direction a proton gun was constructed that could bombard any nucleotide in the DNA and RNA molecules with protons.

Much attention had to be devoted to the preparation of the "biological nursery." a miniature quartz cuvette where protein synthesis would take place in synthetic cytoplasm and artificial ribosomes.

When the apparatus was ready, work in the laboratory began in earnest. As the research expanded, Professor Birkhoff gradually transferred to Albert all the research assistants who had once worked for his father.

They were a fine energetic team. Some of them, in particular Klemper, a physicist, and Gust, a mathematician, part philosophers, part cynics, were working on a theory of the continuous transition of inanimate matter to animate. They viewed living organisms as enormous molecules, all of whose functions could be described in terms of energy exchanges between different states. Klemper called their quest a "search for a needle in a haystack." Their initial experiments had convinced them that sex is not encoded at the nucleotide level, but somewhat deeper, perhaps in the sequences of atoms in the sugar and phosphate chains. Although on several occasions they had succeeded by mutation in transforming an x chromosome into a y chromosome, that is, to alter sex, no one really understood the basic mechanism involved.

Before long the work assumed a routine pattern: experiments were performed, data was gathered, and, in general, nothing particularly significant occurred. Albert felt that new ideas were needed which neither he nor his colleagues could supply.

He stopped consulting his father. It was very evident that he was putting up a kind of passive resistance to his son's research. Not only was he disinterested in his son's work, but whenever Albert wanted to ask him something, he apparently surmised his intentions and deliberately diverted their conversation or sent him from the study.

Albert's diagnosis of passive resistance was correct: his father willingly received individuals and entire delegations from various pacifist organizations.

Albert had never suspected that his father was interested in political questions; he had always been a model university professor, standing aloof from all ideological struggles. Now, though tired and ill, his father suddenly underwent a complete transformation in the presence of visitors, discussing political questions that scientists usually brushed aside.

"You're a scientist, not a politician," said Albert bitterly one day as he placed a compress on his father's chest.

"No, Al. First of all I am a man. The mask of phoney neutrality should have been torn from our scientists long ago. They use their prestigious positions as a shield, feigning innocence when it suddenly turns out that the results of their research are being used to destroy millions of people. They feign the innocence of fools who are incapable of foreseeing a simple thing—the consequences of their research and discoveries. They resort to any excuse, to any loophole to avert incrimination in these crimes. And they shift the blame onto misguided politicians. If I give a madman a weapon, I alone must be responsible for his actions. . . ."

After this tirade Albert realized that his father considered research on the x and y chromosomes a threat to humanity.

One overcast autumn day Albert returned home earlier than usual. It was cold and raw, and drizzling.

As he approached the door he noticed it swing open, and from it Mijee, coatless, dashed headlong into the park.

"Mijee, Mijee!" he shouted.

But she did not hear him. Albert caught up with her at the end of the garden where she huddled like a hunted animal.

"Mijee, dear, what's the matter?" he panted.

"Oh, Al, it's you! I'm so glad you've come!"

"What happened?" Albert threw his raincoat over her trembling shoulders.

"He wants to take me away."

"Who?"

"Mr. Korsh. He's here now and talking with your father."

"But why?"

"I don't know. He says for medical research."

"Let's go home now. I won't let anybody take you away."

She followed him submissively.

"Mij, stay right here." Albert led her into his study on the first floor. "I'm going upstairs now to find out what this is all about."

Through the slightly open door of the study came the professor's voice and the harsh and grating voice of a stranger. Albert paused for a moment.

"Listen, my friend, this is absolutely insane! I've told you my views many times. Sure scientific discovery is a great thing. But there are times when deliberate retreat from discovery is even greater."

"I can't do otherwise," replied a shrill voice. "I can't understand how you can throw a lifetime's work into the trash can. We had a completely different view of everything then."

"We were stupid and naive. That's not the way . . . "

"No, damn it, it's the only way! You're simply a coward! A naive pacifist. If not for Solveig . . . "

Albert flung open the door and entered. His father, deathly pale, sat in his rocker and beside him stood a tall, sallow-faced man with high cheekbones and a shock of auburn hair. Apparently he had been gesticulating wildly for he was frozen into a comical pose when Albert appeared.

"How many times have I told you to knock before . . . " began his father.

At that instant Korsh sprang toward Albert and grabbed his arm.

Suddenly he produced a phonendoscope, frontal mirror, and magnifying glass; instantaneously he was transformed into a man possessed.

"Only a tiny drop of blood. Only one," he mumbled, taking a sharp instrument from his pocket.

Recovering from the initial shock, Albert gave the crazed doctor a powerful shove. He flew the length of the study and would have kept going if a desk hadn't blocked his flight. Bent over, he grasped the edge of the desk and looked at Albert with a repulsive smile. And with curiosity, too.

"So, that's what you're like, eh?" he whispered, straightening up to his full height.

"What's going on here? Who is this man?" demanded Albert. His father was deathly pale and his eyes were closed.

"Oh, Al, this is Mr. Korsh, my old pupil and friend. I know how you feel, but I beg you not to be angry at him."

"Sorry, Dad, but your friend has vile manners."

Korsh dropped down tiredly into a chair and laughed. His eyes were riveted on Albert.

"Lord, what I'd give for one drop of blood from our Al," he muttered, fiddling with the needle in his hand.

"For God's sake, Korsh, shut up! You'll kill me yet," groaned Albert's father.

Korsh's reference to "our Al" triggered a storm. Albert ran over to Korsh, grabbed him by the lapels, raised him to his feet, and dragged him from the study. At the door Korsh straightened up to his full height and shouted hoarsely:

"But the girl is all mine! Give me back the kid!"

Then he disappeared.

Recovering his equilibrium, Albert returned to his father. The professor lay slumped in an awkward position with closed eyes.

Albert grabbed his hands. They were as cold as ice.

4

A month after his father's death Albert delivered a paper on the results of his research. They were rather discouraging.

"What are your plans now?" asked Dr. Seat after the meeting.

Albert shrugged his shoulders. Besides the methodology that his father had passed on to him, he could not contribute anything new to this research. His failure to demonstrate any special gift for research was evident in Dr. Seat's comment.

"Your group needs a good consultant," mumbled the withered, bent old man.

"Whom would you suggest, Doctor?"

"One of Professor Olfry's old students. I remember one particularly talented young fellow. I've forgotten his name. Something like Kirsh, Kursh . . . "

"Korsh!" cried Albert.

"Yes, that's it. He was a very talented chap. If we could find him...."

Albert became taut as a spring. Dr. Seat continued:

"I remember several brilliant discoveries he made when research on the genetic code was in its infancy. For example—the feedback between RNA in the cell nucleus and amino acids in the cytoplasm. ... Also, Korsh and Olfry jointly worked out a transcription of the genetic code.... A very talented scientist. But we don't know where he is now."

Albert hurried home before the meeting ended. He decided to pay a visit to Korsh; he had to find out Korsh's connection to himself and Mijee, the substance of Korsh's disagreement with his father, and the kind of man he was. To obtain this information he would even stoop to apologizing to this disgusting creature for his outburst....

Albert entered the dining room.

"Where's Mijee?" he asked the housekeeper.

"Probably in the park. She went there this morning."

He scoured the park, hoping to find her deep in a book in some secluded spot. No luck. He called out her name several times. Suddenly he spied something white through the break in the stone wall. On closer observation it turned out to be a volume of Byron. Then his glance fell on the shrubs in front of the gap in the wall. They were bent and broken as if something heavy had been dragged through them. He dashed to the gap and found Mijee's blue ribbon.

His first impulse was to call the police. But remembering Korsh, he was pricked by a terrible suspicion.

Within minutes his car zoomed out of the garage and sped toward Cable. Toward Mijee's parents' home, where Korsh had often visited her.

Through his mind flashed images of his first meeting with Mijee, then their discussion of Korsh and his meeting with him. How strange that his father had never spoken to him about his most talented pupil and collaborator.

Only now did Albert realize that his father had failed to tell him many things. Moreover, he had persistently concealed from his son something of great significance in his life and scientific work. This vital something was linked in some mysterious manner with Mijee's disappearance and Korsh. Why did Korsh need Mijee?

When Albert entered the village of Cable, it was completely deserted and he could not find a living soul to ask for directions to Mijee's home.

He drove up to a gate and entered the courtyard of a small, red brick Catholic church. It was dusk and a quivering orange light streamed through its windows. Albert was met by a stout, elderly priest who seemed to be occupied with household chores.

"What can I do for you, young man?"

"Perhaps you can tell me where the Shawley residence is? They have a daughter, Mijee."

"Mijee?" The priest seemed surprised.

"That's right."

"Please come in," said the priest after a brief pause.

They passed through a dark corridor, skirted the altar, and came to a tiny room lit by a kerosene lamp.

"So, you're interested in the girl, Mijee?" asked the priest.

"Yes, and in her parents, too."

"H'm, strange. May I ask who you are to her?"

"A distant relative."

"That's odd."

"Why?"

"Because the girl's a foundling."

"What?" exclaimed Albert. "But she told me herself that she had parents and that they had gone to Australia, and that ... "

"Unfortunately," declared the priest, "that isn't so. Naturally, the girl considers the Shawleys her parents. Actually she was brought here as a newborn infant by two young gentlemen and left with the Shawleys to raise. . . . If my memory doesn't deceive me, that was some thirteen years ago. I remember that day very well. A rumor circulated through our village that a baby had appeared in the Shawley household. So I hurried there to baptize the infant, but ... "

"But what?"

"A visitor in the house at the time told me it wasn't necessary. I was shocked and asked why. He replied . . . ah, yes, now I recall his exact words: 'Baptism is for those who come from God. She comes from man.' To this day I don't understand what he meant."

"But all of us are born of man," said Albert hoarsely.

"Naturally. And man was created by God. But the child was never baptized."

"How long did Mijee live with the Shawleys?"

"Six months ago an important looking gentleman came for her and took her away. . . ."

"She never returned?"

"Never."

"Does the Shawley family live here?"

"No, they went to Australia. They say on the money they received for raising the girl."

"A dead end," thought Albert. One last question remained.

"Do you know a Mr. Korsh?"

"His soul be damned!"

"Oh, so you know him?"

"I certainly do! He was the one who forbade the child's baptism."

"Do you know where he lives?"

"Not far from here, in Sendik."

A few minutes later Albert's car was bouncing along a miserable road in Sendik. It was very dark and drizzling.

5

The Korsh residence was an enormous, gloomy two-storied brick building in antique style, surrounded by a dilapidated iron fence.

The car stopped among the trees, opposite the entrance. Albert entered the courtyard, walked along a stone-paved path and went up to the door. It was deathly quiet and not a single light was visible in the windows.

He pressed the bell. Again. A third time. He decided that no one was home. The door was locked, so Albert began to circle the house slowly, looking up at the high windows.

A roof projected over the rear entrance, and above it was a small oval window.

Albert returned to the car for a flashlight and screwdriver. He climbed onto the porch roof easily, pried the locked window with the screwdriver, broke the latch, and entered the library.

It smelled of book bindings, old paper, and formalin. Later he noticed that the entire building was permeated by the formalin odor.

The spacious library's crammed shelves reached to the ceiling. Books overflowed into piles scattered around the room. Aiming the beam randomly at one of the shelves, Albert found stacks of back numbers of *Biophysics*. Another shelf held books on information theory, and below them was a collection on cybernetics.

Strewn about the floor were old textbooks, monographs, collections of articles on physics, chemistry, number theory, and topology. Apparently the library's owner had a very broad range of interests.

A door led from the library to a short corridor. Descending a narrow, creaking staircase to the first floor, Albert reached a tiny foyer opposite the front entrance. It was furnished with a narrow leather sofa and a mirror in the corner. There were three doors: two on the right, one on the left. One right hand door led to the kitchen, which was directly opposite the dining room. The other door on the right was locked. Albert stepped back several feet, bent over and lunged at the door with his shoulder. It opened with a loud crash, and he flew into a spacious room. As the beam from his flashlight leaped along the objects filling it, he realized that this was a laboratory. And what a laboratory! With its super-centrifuges, electron microscope, chromatographic prisms and measuring devices, it was far better equipped than the institute's laboratories. Wandering around the lab, he imagined the interesting research one could undertake with such equipment. On the table next to the window he found a miniature proton gun, similar to the one he had ordered for his genetic research. But compared to this one his looked like the skeleton of some antediluvian animal.

A large executive desk was covered with a thick plate of clear plastic. Beneath it lay papers covered with notes, formulas, and tables. Albert noticed a snapshot under one corner of the plastic, and when he brought his flashlight closer he was stunned.

It was a photograph of his mother. With trembling fingers he removed it and studied it closely.

No, it was no mistake. . . . A beautiful young woman with slightly slanted eyes and thick fair hair gazed at him with a kindly, almost mocking smile. He could not have confused this photograph with any other: an identical one lay on his father's desk. . . .

What was it doing here? Was it possible that the two men, Korsh and his father, had been deeply in love with his mother? Perhaps by choosing his father she had destroyed the collaboration between teacher and pupil? Here was some sort of secret which left Albert completely mystified.

Suddenly oblivious to his surroundings, he sank into a chair near the desk, clasping tightly in his hands the photograph of someone dear to him whom he dimly remembered. He wondered why his father had told him so little about his mother. To all his questions about her he had always received the same reply: "Al, she was a good woman. Yes, Solveig was a beautiful person."

For some time past Albert had sensed that Mijee bore a strong resemblance to his mother. He persistently tried to drive this thought from his mind. Confused and exhausted, he was finally overcome by sleep.

6

It was morning when he awakened. The sun's bright rays coming through the window fell directly on Albert's face. It took him a while to realize where he was.

The laboratory confronted him in all its splendor. Such a remarkable biophysics laboratory could be the envy of the finest research centers.

As he walked around the section devoted to chemistry he noticed a strange glass and nickel structure in the corner, which he could not identify immediately. In its center, on a small porcelain stand, rested a small oval vessel to which were attached numerous glass and rubber tubes, pipes, and capillaries coming from all directions. Around the central vessel on a latticed structure of stainless steel stood many quartz and frosted-glass flasks; and beneath the stand in special housings were fastened two nickel cylinders, one with oxygen, the other with carbon dioxide. A complex system of thin glass tubes wound around the central vessel and inside it, forming a single network for heating and thermostatic devices; this could be deduced from the labyrinth of tubes that began and ended in a metal tank into which an electric stove and thermoregulator had been built. Several thermometers projected from various parts of the apparatus; with the aid of thermoelectric transmitters, data were recorded by a potentiometer.

The glass flasks were labeled "Nutriments," "Enzymes," "Ribonucleic acid," "Adenosine triphosphate."

Immediately everything became clear.

Anyone who has ever been involved in the artificial breeding of living creatures under laboratory conditions could only dream of possessing such equipment! It was precisely for this purpose that it had been constructed.

Albert began to study its design. There was no question about it: it was, as scientists called it, "a biological nursery"—an intricate and ingenious system that imitated the system created by nature in living creatures. Everything known to science about embryology and the physiology of higher animals was incorporated in this apparatus. It had been designed as a self-regulatory system: the future development of a single cell from a living organism placed in a nutrient medium would determine the integrated operation of all the installation's units.

The equipment was in superb condition. However, from the stains and barely visible traces of residue in the thinnest tubes, Albert surmised that it probably had been used many times. But for what? What sort of organism was bred in this marvelous system?

Had his glance not fallen on a small metal box standing in the corner of the room, he might never have answered his own questions. At first he assumed it was a piece of equipment, but when he clasped the handle and lifted the lid, it proved to be an ordinary box for storing papers. Albert glanced inside at a thick green notebook and was about to close the box when he noticed a small white label in the upper right hand corner of the book. "Solveig, variant 5" was printed in large black letters.

"Solveig! What the hell is this?! Why Solveig?"

With trembling fingers he lifted the notebook from the box.

He opened the first page and stared at the writing. Then, leafing through it, he was confronted on page after page with rows of figures. They were arranged in two lines. In the upper, only two were repeated—0 and 1; and in the lower line four numbers appeared in various combinations: 2, 3, 4 and 5. It looked like this:

$$1 \quad 0 \quad 1 \quad 00 \quad 111 \quad 01 \quad 0001 \quad 0 \quad 11 \quad 10...$$
$$4 \quad 4 \quad 2 \quad 34 \quad 224 \quad 52 \quad 5433 \quad 4 \quad 22 \quad 43...$$

"The code! The genetic code!" flashed through his brain. 1 and 0 were the sugar and phosphate chains. 2, 3, 4 and 5 were the nitrous bases—guanine, adenine, cytosine and thymine.

Fifty pages were covered only with figures. In one place he discovered a small group of figures circled in red ink. Above them appeared a notation: "Lethality?"

The question mark was repeated several times and underlined heavily. "Lethality?" That means death . . . What could these figures mean? Whose code was recorded in this notebook?

Mystified by the puzzling rows of figures, Albert put aside the notebook and opened the box again. Besides papers covered with the same rows of figures, he found a small plastic box which he couldn't open for a long time. A strange excitement gripped him, as though he was about to uncover a terrible secret. . . .

The box was filled with photographs.

The first was a microphotograph of a single cell. Then the cell divided in two. Further divisions were followed by differentiation.

Now the cells formed a clump. The clump developed. Here was a large fetus. His hands shook as he flipped through the pictures feverishly, skipping a few now and then until, finally, he saw the photograph of a child. Tiny. Larger. Now smiling. Then staring wide-eyed. Now grown up.

Suddenly Albert stopped, unable to bear the tension of wading through the entire series. Clenching his teeth, he dropped his hand to the bottom of the box and pulled out the very last photograph. It was a picture of a coffin. The coffin was smothered in flowers, leaving visible only the face of a dead woman. Albert grabbed the preceding photograph and screamed.

His hands held a picture of his mother.

He didn't remember how he left Korsh's estate or Cable, or his wild ride home. He forgot everything—himself, Korsh, Mijee. Only one image remained fixed before his eyes: the image of his mother.

When he reached home he threw himself on his bed. His brain was in a turmoil, teeming with muddled images of figures, flasks, and photographs.

From time to time he lost consciousness, and during his lucid intervals he realized he was lying in bed and various people were hovering over him: his housekeeper, Professor Birkhoff, his colleagues from the lab, doctors in white smocks. . . .

He dimly remembered tearing himself from someone's arms and running somewhere. Upstairs, he thought, to his father's study, where he ripped papers and photographs to shreds until he was seized and put to bed.

This fit of insanity, lasting several days, was followed by total apathy. He lay there by the hour, staring up at the ceiling. The world had become gray and colorless. Albert felt utterly crushed.

7

While he was convalescing, two of his colleagues from the lab visited. Victor Klemper and Antoine Gust entered the bedroom noisily, exuding the cheer and optimism usually affected for the seriously ill.

"You gave us one helluva scare, Al!" exclaimed Klemper, shaking his hand. "We thought you'd never pull out of it and we'd have to hand you over to Professor Kuzano for his experiments."

Kuzano was director of the Biochemistry Laboratory of Higher Nervous Activity. Lately he had been engaged in research on physicochemical processes occurring in the brains of mentally ill patients.

"He observed you, you know. He decided that an entire mescaline factory had gone haywire somewhere inside you. You had a violent form of schizophrenic intoxication."

"Listen, friends," began Albert, "has it ever occurred to you that turning a person inside out, for example, as you or Dr. Kuzano or some biochemists are doing, is a rather heinous business?"

They exchanged puzzled glances.

"When a person is young and healthy and full of energy, sure he flirts with death from time to time. Or he jokes about its inevitability. But as far as the last stage of your earthly existence being a particularly attractive thing to look forward to, that's bullshit. Except in exceptional cases. . . ."

"Look, Al, if you're not feeling too well yet . . . "

"No, fellows, I'm absolutely OK, and what I'm telling you now comes after a lot of thinking."

"Then explain what you have in mind. Is it yourself? We can assure you that you're out of danger. You had an ordinary nervous breakdown. Dr. Kuzano demonstrated the chemical morphology of your blood at a university lecture. He showed that cases like yours are accompanied by sharp rises in the concentration of adrenaline and its derivatives. That's why we began talking about mescaline. You know, of course, that . . ."

Distressed that his illness was public knowledge, he gestured impatiently. His friends fell silent, searching for another topic of conversation. After a long pause Victor announced:

"While you were lying around here, we deciphered the molecular structure of the x and y chromosomes."

"Really? And?"

"Well, now couples can have a balanced family. Also, when

necessary, say, like in wartime, the government can maintain a balanced population. Neat, eh?"

Albert shrugged his shoulders. It was a minor discovery compared to what he had learned. Beneath their casual announcement he sensed the pride and vanity of scientists who have made another step into the unknown.

"That's how complicity in crime begins," thought Albert. "When should my fellow scientists and I be tried for a crime against humanity: before the x and y chromosomes are decoded or afterward? Or when the government is given the key to producing a balanced population in wartime? Or when the war has begun and it is too late to change anything?"

"Listen Victor, Antoine—why the hell do we need all this? This research in human molecular genetics, this probing into the hidden mechanisms of man's mysterious essence will take all the charm out of life, all its inexpressible beauty. We'll just be a bunch of anatomical models."

Albert felt that he wasn't saying what should be said. Of course sooner or later the results of his father's and Korsh's work would be reproduced throughout the world. Then what? Decent, sensible people would not create chemical combinations to produce custom-made individuals. No, this would never happen. Yet it was entirely possible that secret enterprises would flourish underground, with the same bloodthirsty aims. He wanted to shout to his friends at the top of his voice: "Stop, for God's sake! Open your eyes and try to imagine what could happen if . . ."

He recalled a remark made by his father before his death about the heroism of deliberate retreat when one is on the brink of a great discovery. He bit his lip hard.

"Al, what do you propose? That we stop? Shut down science? Return to primitive ignorance? So far we've heard only the negative side from you. What about the positives? The advances in medicine and agriculture? What about the progress man has made in adapting to his environment? The advances in treating hereditary diseases? And what about the genetic approach to the cancer problem?"

"That's all very true. . . . But I'm afraid that the excitement of expectant parenthood will soon disappear, because babies will be produced in test tubes according to a predetermined program."

"I suppose we can't discount that possibility. I, for one, can't see anything objectionable in that. In fact, experiments in that direction are very encouraging.... Hey, Al, what's the matter? You're awfully pale. Are you tired?"

Klemper and Gust rose. Albert was bursting to tell them everything, but he restrained himself; he knew they would rush to reproduce Korsh's experiment and, like men possessed, like medieval Fausts, would manufacture people in the institute's laboratories.

Only now did he fully realize how correct his father had been when he spoke about the scientist's responsibility for the applications of his discovery.

8

Following his complete recovery, Albert spent day after day in his father's study reading philosophy books. Never before had he noticed how many philosophy books filled the library, how many works his father had read on death and immortality. Now, reading one book after another, he seemed to be treading the same path.

One day, while Albert was busy reading, Korsh, stooped and considerably aged, entered the study. For an instant Albert even felt pity for him.

"Have a seat," said Albert.

Korsh nodded and sat down. For some time they were silent.

"Well, Korsh, what's on your mind?"

He raised his head.

"Al, why did you do it?" he finally asked.

"What?"

"You destroyed my life's work. And not only mine, but your father's."

"And what right did you have to perform such an inhuman experiment? What right did you have to create a human being, damn you?!"

"What right? What right? . . . What right did people have to invent gunpowder? What right did they have to create atomic and hydrogen bombs? You tell me, Al. And airplanes? And rockets? And deadly viruses? It all adds up to death, Al. Death. What right you ask? If you want to know, our right (and I'm speaking for your father, too), our right was based on an overwhelming desire to neutralize science's mad rush toward the development of devices that would destroy all forms of life."

Albert stared at Korsh in amazement; he was totally unprepared for such a response.

"Don't be shocked, Al. If you're interested in the moral reasons for our research, that's what they were. Many years ago your father and I swore to make man immortal, as a foil against the schemes of the misanthropes and madmen."

"How?"

"You know, of course, the story of the Dead Sea scrolls. A Jordanian shepherd found a roll of parchment that had lain in a cave more than two thousand years. Notes of ancient legends and laws were preserved in the scrolls. Contemporary scholars deciphered them, and now we can look into the distant past through the eyes of the ancients. The world had been beset by wars, natural catastrophes, disasters. One civilization gave way to another, and the scrolls awaited their hour. As did the Mayan inscriptions, and the Sumerian clay tablets. . . ."

"What has that got to do with your work?"

"Everything, Al. When your father was younger we decided to leave behind us invaluable records, the most sacred inscriptions ever made by man. We swore to create a golden book and record the results of our work in it."

"What exactly did you intend to record in this book?"

"What? The formula of man, of course."

"The formula of man?!"

"Yes, the same one you saw in my laboratory. And a description of the apparatus in which this formula could be synthesized. Be honest with yourself, Al. Isn't this the solution to the problem of immortality? Besides the formula the book was to contain a detailed description of the process employed in synthesis. All the instructions: how to begin, when to finish, what to do with the new baby, and so on. Finally, when we had arrived at an exact chemical formula for man's genetic material, we even began to consider the possibility of automating the entire process, entrusting it to a cybernetic device. It would be easy to develop such apparatus. We wanted to do it and record that, too, in the golden book. Can you imagine, Al, what that would mean? Immortality in the full sense of the word. The book could be placed in a space projectile and rocketed into the universe. It could travel for millions of years and fall into the hands of intelligent creatures who might be different from us. They could easily recreate a human being! And here on Earth? You, Al, myself—anyone could be immortalized to appear again and again on Earth and observe the eternal evolution of our planet. ..."

Korsh's weary face became animated; he began to speak ecstatically, oblivious of Albert, recounting the fantastic possibilities that the formula of man could open to humanity. Albert suddenly felt that the man seated before him was mentally unbalanced.

"It's a beautiful, but absolutely absurd idea." Albert tried to halt this insane raving.

"After your father married Solveig and you were born, he said the very same thing. ..."

Albert started at the name of his mother.

Korsh continued. "Nature is arranged far more simply than we think. Everything boils down to a small group of substances that initiate cyclical reactions. These are substances that begin a closed sequence of chemical reactions whose final stage is the new synthesis of the initiating molecule. You know, Al, what kind of substances these are. Primarily genetic material: deoxyribonucleic acids, DNA ... And that's all."

"Go on."

"Then we analyzed and synthesized man's genetic material."

"Well ... "

"We succeeded in breeding several children from the same formula. Solveig was the fifth."

"And the others?"

"Either they died as embryos or soon after . . . after birth."

"Why?"

"We couldn't find a complete answer to this question. The problem is that a group of DNA molecules determines an individual's viability. We discovered this group and tried to rearrange their nitrous bases in every possible way. . . . We managed to attain a life span of thirty years for Solveig. But that's too short. We had wanted to record in the golden book the formula for an individual with a very long life span."

"Then what?"

"Solveig developed into a beautiful girl. She was raised by the Shawleys . . ."

"The same family that raised Mijee?"

Korsh nodded.

"Your father fell in love with her. I was absolutely opposed to their marriage. But nothing would change his mind. And Solveig loved him too. And then . . ."

"My God!" shouted Albert, unable to control himself.

Korsh winced and his voice broke. "It's strange and therefore seems unnatural. But people will become used to it before long."

"You mean when the synthesis of people is described in textbooks?"

"Yes. Sooner or later it will be."

"All right, continue. What happened then?"

"After the wedding your father stopped all his research in this field. He transferred to the Institute of Genetics and Cytology. He said that a golden book was unnecessary and man's immortality must be attained by other means. You know what kind. He was a member of every commission on earth for the protection of humanity against nuclear warfare. I don't think it was a very clever approach. . . ."

Albert crossed over to Korsh.

"Listen, you son of a bitch, don't you talk about my father like that. After all, you were only his pupil. It's not for you to judge what is or isn't smart. I think he was damned right to reject this idiot scheme of yours. Why the hell did you come to see me anyway?!"

He looked at Albert with pleading eyes.

"Al, for God's sake, calm down. . . . Promise me that you will behave sensibly."

"What do you want?"

"Two things. . . . Try to find scraps at least of the notebooks you took from me, and then . . . then all I want is one drop of your blood for analysis."

Albert extended his right hand to him and observed with revulsion Korsh's trembling hands fumbling in his pockets for a cotton swab and bottle of ether. A light prick with a pointed instrument, and a drop of blood appeared on Albert's finger. Korsh touched a snakelike tube to it and quickly sucked the blood into a pipette.

"Why do you need it?"

"It will tell me if you will live longer than your mother. I want to know what occurred in the structure of the DNA that determines lethality. . . . And now, if you please, the notebook. . . ."

Albert rang and the housekeeper appeared in the study. She received her orders and withdrew.

A terrifying thought tormented Albert, but he was afraid to put the question to Korsh. Korsh remained silent, as if he had guessed what was gnawing at Albert.

The housekeeper returned promptly with a large file containing a pile of papers.

"Here you are, Mr. Albert, all that's left."

Korsh quickly took the box from her hands and began to straighten out the scraps of rumpled papers covered with rows of figures.

"Yes, some of it is still here, thank God. The rest can be reconstructed. Yes, here it is—the most important stuff. Lethality . . . Now we'll try something else. . . ."

Finally he tore his eyes from the sheaves of papers and looked radiantly at Albert. "Did you examine the photographs? It's really an amazing model of human history. From a single cell to death itself."

Albert remained silent. Green and violet circles swam before his eyes, blocking out Korsh's face.

"Did you notice Mijee's resemblance to Solveig?" continued Korsh.

Unable to restrain himself any longer, Albert asked:

"Is Mijee my sister?"

"Come now, Al. Of course not! She's a sixth variant."

9

The piercing hysterical cry still rang in his ears. And before his eyes swam Korsh's pale face. Then came the pain, the pain in his head, chest, and legs. Evidently he had been beaten as they tried to tear him away from Korsh's writhing body. He had cried like a little boy, and the tears had rolled down his cheeks and fallen on the unshaven chin of the lifeless Korsh. Then he had been bound and placed in a straitjacket. And finally in the prison cell. . . .

"The death sentence for murder can be changed to lifelong exile, if you present a sufficiently convincing reason for your crime," said a familiar voice that sounded like his father's old lawyer.

"Death sentence? Lethality? Did Korsh succeed in analyzing my blood?" asked Albert as if he had just emerged from a trance.

"For God's sake, Albert, pull yourself together. Try to think. Tomorrow's the trial."

"Can you tell me, my dear sir, if there are laws by which people can be tried for creating human beings who are obviously doomed to die prematurely?"

"Albert, what are you saying?!"

"The time of your death is inscribed in your DNA."

"For God's sake, don't feign insanity! The doctors have established that your crime was committed in a state of temporary insanity. And no more. Otherwise you're perfectly healthy."

"Ah, yes, normal. Healthy. How strange all that sounds now. As if you know my formula. No one knows it. And no one will. It won't be recorded in the golden book of immortality. Because I'm not long for this world."

Success Algorithm

VLADIMIR SAVCHENKO

All talented people write differently. The mediocre write alike, and
even their handwritings are similar.

I. Ilf. "Notebooks"

1

Two Conversations with the Director

ON MARCH 25, at the day's tail end, two engineers from the computer technology section, skinny, carrot-topped Volodya Kaimenov
and heavy-set, imperturbable, chubby-faced Sergei Malyshev,
marched resolutely into the office of Valentin Georgievich Pantaleev, director of the Institute of Computer Technology and
corresponding member of the Academy of Sciences. The timing of
their visit, the end of a workday, was deliberate and dictated by an
ulterior motive. After an exhausting day as an administrator, Pantaleev, if not mellowed, would at least be an easier target for his
callers.

"Valentin Georgievich, we have a special request to make. We'd
like to place this package in your custody," said Kaimenov, his green
eyes focused intently on the director.

Hefting the thick blue envelope, Pantaleev eyed it rather coldly.

"And with sealing wax, no less!" He studied it carefully.
"H'm . . .

Number thirty-four, from the computer room. Why give it to me?
Why not to Section One?"

The engineers were caught off balance. Kaimenov glanced at
Malyshev. Malyshev shrugged his broad shoulders as if to say, "Hell,
it was all your brilliant idea, so you squirm your way out."

"H'm ... well, you see, Valentin Georgievich, this thing is a secret.
But it has absolutely nothing to do with our work."

"A secret?" Pantaleev looked at the engineers with amused
interest. "What sort of secret do you have in here?"

"Some documents . . . which . . . well . . . Listen, Valentin
Georgievich, we'll explain the whole thing later. Better than
that: you will personally break open the seal and examine its
contents."

"A secret ... Well, what do you know!" Pantaleev leaned back in
his chair. This was like a fresh breeze after an exhausting round of
reports, announcements, abstracts, articles, and conferences. "Do I
have to take an oath?"

"No, what for?" replied Malyshev. "Just put today's date and your
signature on the package. That's enough."

"All right." The director wrote "25 March 19 . . . " on the
envelope, signed it with a flourish, and got the safe key from his
pocket. "OK, let it stay here. I must confess, comrades, I have a
weakness for secrets!"

Relieved, the engineers left.

The second conversation between Valentin Georgievich and
Kaimenov took place ten days later, on April 4. On this occasion
Kaimenov was hauled into the office by Zochka, the director's
secretary. Pantaleev was pacing the room in a rage.

"Listen ... uh ... uh ... Vladimir Mikhailovich, what kind of
rubbish were you dishing out at the Inter-Institute Seminar? I'm
referring to your report, 'The Organization of Scientific Research.'
Before you start blowing your horn, you must get your idea off the
boards."

"All I did in my report was formulate the problem. Nothing
more."

"I heard how you 'formulated' it—as if the 'electronic organizer' algorithm was almost in routine use at our institute! Now, get this: I don't want to upset you, but if you pull anything like this again, neither your youth nor worldly inexperience will influence my view of the matter. You were entrusted with a very important task, as risky as any social experiment. Premature announcements have jeopardized many fine scientific ideas. . . . It's absolutely taboo! Simply impermissible."

Kaimenov opened his mouth to say something, but the director didn't give him a chance to get a word in edgewise.

"And another thing—you can't seem to get to work on time! Here, take a look at this." Valentin Georgievich took out Kaimenov's time card. "Four red dates in the past two months! One more and you'll be called on the carpet. That would be a great example for a man planning to organize the work of other scientists. Yes, just great!"

"But . . . but . . . "

"Then there's your relations with Pavel Nikolaevich. It's not enough that Academician Feofan Stepanovich Mezozoisky has been giving me dirty looks since the last conference, where you had the pleasure of expressing your opinion on his report. You didn't stop there: in the presence of your fellow scientists, you had the gall to question not only the expediency of having Pavel Nikolaevich as my deputy, but even his very presence at our institute! Don't you realize that a Science Council, administration, and lastly, yours truly, exist to handle such problems? Pavel Nikolaevich Shishkin, Ph.D. candidate in Technical Science, is chief of your section. You are undoubtedly a talented fellow, but still, this sort of behavior . . ."

"Yes, sir!" said Kaimenov. "Pavel Nikolaevich is my section chief! OK, I understand. Now, Valentin Georgievich, would you mind opening the package we placed in your custody?"

"Package? Oh, yes . . . But what does your sealed secret have to do with this discussion? Well, all right."

The safe door rumbled. The director broke the seal on the

package. A batch of tapes covered with typed figures and a folded sheet of paper dropped out.

"Please read the first paragraph."

Valentin Georgievich changed his glasses. In the round-rimmed black frames he was the classical picture of a prerevolutionary intellectual.

"'During a period extending from the second to the sixth of April, P. N. Shishkin will in . . . inform . . . ' " Pantaleev frowned, " 'on Kaimenov to Valentin Georgievich about the following: 1) his frequent lateness to work; 2) his provocative behavior; 3) his "self-advertising" speech at the seminar; 4) the questionable social reference in his personnel file. . . .' Very interesting!"

The director squinted at his desk calendar, then at the date he had written on the package.

"Very interesting. Paragraph two. 'Roughly during this period, P. N. Shishkin will try to persuade Valentin Georgievich to exclude functions involving housing allocation, bonuses, and staff changes from the "electronic organizer" algorithm. Should these functions become too burdensome for V. G., he, Shishkin, is prepared to assume them. His arguments for the latter: 1) resourceful management of these functions improves the operation of the system (the Institute's); and 2) Kaimenov lacks civic and administrative experience and could program these functions on the computer incorrectly . . . ' Now look here!" Pantaleev looked up at Kaimenov and sighed noisily. "That conversation took place behind closed doors! . . . H'm. But you're not a very good eavesdropper: the dates are wrong . . . and besides, the first argument wasn't presented. Pavel Nikolaevich gave the second one you've described and also said that . . ."

"That what?"

"That programming these functions incorrectly could be interpreted as an attempt to quietly replace our organization with a computer. . . ."

"What did you say?" Kaimenov pressed him.

"That ours is not an ordinary organization, but a scientific one. If Kaimenov can't handle the programming properly, it can always be adjusted. After all, this is only an experiment . . . Hold on!" The director suddenly remembered his position. "I'm the one to be asking questions, not you. Now, what's this all about?"

"It's only a little overtime work . . . in line with the Institute's, and it won't cost a kopeck extra." Kaimenov began to inch sideways toward the door, but withered by Pantaleev's glaring expression, he pressed his hands to his breast. "Valentin Georgievich," he pleaded, "the only thing I can tell you now is that none of this will affect my work on the 'electronic organizer.' Believe me! . . . Oh, by the way, was anything said about my references?"

"Plenty!" replied the director angrily. "Now, look here: if you're planning to give me any more packages like this, please don't use the verb 'inform'!"

Malyshev was waiting in the corridor. Seeing Kaimenov looking as if he had just emerged from a Turkish bath, he asked sympathetically:

"Did he give you the works?"

"And how! . . . It's a good thing I asked him to open the package in time. Give me a cigarette."

"So, what happened?"

"Look, a coincidence is a coincidence, but there's a lot we're failing to take into consideration. Pavel Nikolaevich is a sharp operator. . . ."

2

The Birth of PANSH-2 *

The two preceding conversations were the sequel to an episode in the director's office which culminated in the birth of *Project 'Electronic Organizer' Algorithm.*

One morning, at the end of January, Valentin Georgievich had invited all the programmers to his office. The meeting was called for ten o'clock, and naturally no one was late.

Until 10:25 Pantaleev had a stormy phone conversation with the manager of the Main Office for Marketing Products of the Non-

*Pavel Nikolaevich Shishkin—the second

ferrous Metallurgy Trust. Judging from the decibels coming from the other end of the line, it seemed that the manager was demanding a top-priority time slot for the Trust's computer problems, and he threatened to complain to the National Control Committee.

At 10:26 a representative from the Soviet Academy's Presidium arrived to coordinate research plans. The coordinating process continued piecemeal until eleven o'clock, interrupted by phone conversations with various administrators, unions, ministers from three different republics, inspection commissions, science and popular science magazine editors, and two private parties on urgent business.

At 11:00 Comrade Ofitsersky, chief of personnel, barged in yelling "Valentin Georgievich, Gosplan° is breathing down our necks for next year's staff schedule."

At 11:30 the patient programmers began to grumble. Pantaleev quickly rounded off his conversation with the chief of personnel, locked the door behind him, disconnected the phone, which had begun to ring again, and addressed the engineers:

"So, you don't like it? Neither do I.... I just wanted you to observe how a once rather well-qualified mathematician has turned into a good old-fashioned bureaucrat and bungler. I moved that Nonf... momf... "

"Mompnonf,"°° someone prompted him.

"Thanks. I moved them up four places on the computer schedule. What do you expect me to do? Of course I could prove to Naconcom°°° that the significance of the trust's computer jobs are in inverse proportion to their manager's nagging, but imagine the time and effort that would require! Then, for the sake of form, the Academy representative and I threw together a coordinated plan of research. And we put together the staff schedule in a hurry because Gosplan was really breathing down our necks. Later we'll have to see them to wheedle permission for a few additions to our staff.... What

---

°State Planning Committee

°° Main Office for Marketing Products of the *Non-f*errous Metallurgy Trust

°°°National Control Committee

I'm trying to tell you is that it's time to put a stop to this piecemeal administration of our affairs!" Valentin Georgievich shook his head decisively. "We do a pretty good job of solving organizational problems for others, but we're like a shoemaker without shoes. So, let's cull the problems that drain our resources, that divert us from the creative work so dear to our hearts, and turn them over to computers...."

He paused long enough to allow his listeners to digest his proposal. "Let's take the first problem: efficient scheduling of work orders. The orders arrive continuously. Some are important to society and beneficial to the Institute; others are neither so important nor so beneficial; and a third category are neither fish nor fowl. It's ridiculous to arrange them like a queue of customers in a shop. Wouldn't it be better to do it this way? The director or Science Council would assign a number rating to each problem according to a prearranged scale. This scale plus the feasibility of solving a specific problem would be fed into the computer. The latter would include the work load of computers and repair shops, which specialists are doing what, who is in the field, on vacation, or on sick leave. The computer would compose an optimal plan and schedule for filling the orders: deadlines, number and qualifications of required specialists, computer time, orders for repair shops and supply department. Everything.

"A similar approach could be used in planning future research. It is absolutely unnecessary to wait until the end of the year to implement a favorable and important result obtained at the beginning of the year—or conversely, why delay shelving work that turns out to be hopeless in the second quarter. Here the management and Science Council would also assign a scale for rating the importance of results. The computer's task would be to plan efficiently the redistribution of labor and funds between successful and unsuccessful research....

"I would also like you to think about using computers for various internal problems. For example, the allocation of housing. We all know that the number of apartments and rooms allotted to us by the City Council is always well below our needs. Also, we are very

familiar with the carefully thought-out directives and rules which
determine how and to whom housing is to be assigned. Our union has
a comprehensive list of personnel needing apartments. Nevertheless, as you know, friction develops whenever allocations are made:
people are hurt, passed over, and there are hard feelings. . . . There
is no reason why an algorithm to solve this problem cannot be
designed.

"Another step worth considering is the automation of staff
changes. We all know each other rather well, and besides, we are
mathematicians. So, the scientific and efficiency capacities of each
individual, of one's contributions, and experience, should not be
limited to carefully worded descriptions, but also could be expressed
in numbers; and one's inclinations and ideas could be converted into
logical systems. . . . These are some of the problems which I feel are
ready for computer programming. Of course you can keep adding
problems to the list; we've no shortage of them." For an instant
Pantaleev's enthusiasm flagged; then he raised his finger. "Naturally,
the administration and the science collective have the final say in all
cases. But our institute is a large and complex system. Computers
will help us develop its maximum potential.

"Therefore, I am announcing an in-house competition for the
most constructive—and I mean constructive!—idea for an 'electronic
organizer' algorithm," concluded Pantaleev solemnly. "You have
one week to come up with something. Think about it and prepare
your proposals."

"Valentin Georgievich, aren't you afraid," asked Kaimenov, "that
your administrative functions will be transferred to a computer, and
one fine day . . . "

". . . an 'electronic director' will plot against a human being?"
Pantaleev completed his thought. "No, an intelligent man (and I,
with your permission, consider myself one) has no reason to fear
computers. To be stronger than computers, you must use them. That,
precisely, is our task. That's all! We'll meet again in a week." With
that, Valentin Georgievich plugged in the phone, which began to
ring at once, as if it had been anticipating this moment.

"That guy is a dreamer," sighed Malyshev when he and Kaimenov left the office. "Mathematicians are all alike. Everything is so crystal clear on paper."

"A dreamer, all right," agreed Kaimenov cheerfully. "But dreamers are 'in' these days. Haven't you noticed that?"

A week later Kaimenov submitted a detailed plan for an "electronic organizer" algorithm, and it was accepted. The M-117, a brand new transistorized computer, was assigned to him to develop the algorithm.

At this point in our story, it is appropriate to mention how, when, and under what circumstances V. M. Kaimenov called Shishkin "a damn fool."

The purple dusk deepened outside the computer room's glass windows, which occupied an entire wall. Air conditioners hissed above "Lightning-5" 's six gray exhaust hoods. The L-5 was the Institute's oldest computer; it still used vacuum tubes. Rows of neon lights flashed on and off on the control panel that Sergei Malyshev was operating. On the right a print-out device nervously clicked off numbers.

The light and airy strains of violin music intermingled with the air conditioners' hissing. This was Kaimenov's doing. Sitting back-to-back with his friend, next to his M-117—a small, compact unit no larger than a T.V. stand, but far more powerful than "ol' man Lightning"—he was checking out the new computer's capabilities. It read out the notes, translated them into binary digits, analyzed and synthesized them in the logic units, then converted them into a sequence of sound impulses. In brief, the computer sight read Mozart's C-Minor Symphony.

How incongruous the music sounded here, music that evoked visions of maids of honor, carriages, plumes, tallow candles, harpsichords and Jesuits—but it made no impression on the engineers. It was all in a day's work.

Malyshev fed a punch-tape with a new program between the rollers of Lightning's input, initiated a read-out, then recorded the job's number and title in a journal. Meanwhile Kaimenov turned off the M-117. Since the music had checked out OK, he concluded that all systems were in order. He rose and stretched. That was all for today.

"The formulation of an optimal schedule for shipping organic dye-stuffs on southern and southwestern roads," Kaimenov read from Malyshev's journal, leaning over his shoulder and cursing under his breath. "Well, Shishkin, old boy, you've got it made! Got yourself a nice feed box for the rest of your life. Optimal route for shipping pasteurized milk, optimal schedule for shipping bread, optimal schedule for shipping perishable hot-house cucumbers. And, finally, an unprecedented flight of cybernetic imagination: an optimal schedule for shipping dye-stuffs. . . . Hey, wait a minute . . . why does it have to be organic dye-stuffs? Why not hand-painted trinket boxes? Aha, I get it: keep in tune with the times, man!"

"OK, so you get it." Sergei raised his eyebrows, tilted back his head slightly and pursed his lips. "Anyway, it expands the computer's potential applications."

"Oh sure, of course! Science is a strange business! Now, if this happened in a factory, they would have caught on long ago that the man is planning the very same component in various sizes. But here . . . we call it 'expanding potential applications'—ha!"

"Listen, lay off," snapped Malyshev. "As a matter of fact I told Shishkin that it was time to find a general solution to the shipping problem on all major highways."

"What did he say?"

"That individual problems had top priority."

"Then what did you say?"

"I asked permission to work out this problem on the computer on my own time."

"And he said?"

"Ugh! I shouldn't have opened my big mouth about 'my own time'! Right then and there Shishkin handed me two more shipping folders. It even included one on laundry soap."

"So, what did you say?"

"Oh, cut it out! Shove off, will you!" Malyshev fumed. "It's OK for you to talk. You're working on one of Pantaleev's jobs. . . ."

The row of Lightning's neons blinked: the computer was processing a series of subprograms and awaiting further commands from its operator. Sergei, as usual, flicked the switches, then introduced a verification command. Kaimenov put away his chair next to M-117, took off his lab coat and hung it in a locker.

"Be finished soon, Sergei?"

"In about twenty minutes."

"Let's go for a spin on my cycle."

Kaimenov wandered around the room. Near the window he got a brainstorm. Not an unusual occurrence for him. And if he had an audience, he willingly shared his ideas. Right now he had one. He returned to Lightning, waited for Malyshev to finish playing with the switches and keyboard, and then launched his scheme.

"By the way, about computers' potential applications! . . . Why hasn't it ever occurred to anyone to apply cybernetics to the organization of an individual's personal affairs. For example, hasn't it happened that you suddenly remember something you did and start moaning and groaning. If only, you curse yourself, you had behaved more intelligently and honestly. But you hadn't thought of it in time. Or you did something really stupid. It certainly has happened to me. . . . Life is complicated: hundreds of things to do, plans, problems, actions, events—and everything must be considered, even trifles. The list is infinite: how to divide the hours so you have enough time to see your girl, take in a show, relax, have interesting discussions? How to meet the right people and avoid those whom you don't need? How to get to work on time, and how to make each paycheck stretch until next payday? How to get along with your relatives? Which ideas are worth implementing; which should be discarded? How to get your pension? How to arrange your daily affairs in this city? Or maybe they aren't worth arranging; it might be better to chuck everything and take off. . . ."

"To Rio!" chuckled Malyshev, examining the digit-covered solution tape.

"Not necessarily. . . . Why not the Pacific Ocean, or Kobelyaki, or virgin territory? We live empirically, don't you see? But life's tempo keeps increasing: the radio, long distance phones, jet planes. . . .

The flight from here to Moscow is so short, you don't even have time to think about your business there. That's the way it is with everything. Our sluggish brain can't interpret and compare facts quickly enough; from thousands of variants, it can't select the best one. And the variant it does choose is your life, man!"

Kaimenov's voice had a pensive timber.

"The paths that we choose . . . Bah! We don't choose a damn one of them. We live how we can, grab whatever is at hand, whatever comes our way. Then, later, a feeling of discontent gnaws at us. You've noticed how life seems more interesting in books, movies—good ones, of course; it seems more vivid, more logical than it actually is. The people in them do the same things we do—work, fall in love, fight, suffer, make friends, think up new ideas—but somehow everything turns out neater for them, more perfect."

"Well, yes, I've noticed that," nodded Malyshev.

"Do you know why? Because writers have time to think through their heroes' actions and deeds. It might take a year to write a book describing the events of one day. Or a movie that runs for half an hour could even take more than a year to film. But we don't have that kind of time to deliberate our own affairs. We've got to live each day and each hour; we barely have time to turn around. We struggle through a jungle of pressing everyday trivia and don't have the time or energy, or the desire, for the most important things in life: for creative work, real love, genuine friendship. We're left with an aftertaste; we don't feel exactly unhappy, but we're not very happy either. . . . Well, if you transfer all the crap, the everyday trivia to computers," Kaimenov snapped his fingers, "you can arrange a great life! If your mind is not occupied with trifles, you can live each day to the hilt, even brilliantly. Better than in books!"

Sergei looked up at his friends blazing eyes. "You're loaded with ideas, Volodya, but they're way out. OK, so what do you think a computer hour costs, say, for my Lightning?"

"About three hundred rubles. . . ."

"Three hundred and forty. A problem of average difficulty is processed in eight to ten minutes. Who is going to shell out fifty rubles just to find out why he's ten rubles short until payday?"

"Sure, costs will be high initially," Kaimenov dismissed it with a wave of his hand, "until the system is well established! Aluminum used to cost more than gold—and now pots are made out of it. If microelectronics is developed and the stuff produced on the assembly line, in ten years cybernetic devices won't be any larger or cost any more than radios. By that time algorithms for the masses will be a real necessity, so that cybernetics can become an integral part of everyone's daily life. So that each day can be lived brilliantly," he repeated elegantly. "Yes, now is the time to think about this. . . ."

The print-out device clicked, disgorging another digit-covered paper tape from its metal jaws. Sergei ripped off the tape and began entering the figures in his journal. Kaimenov strolled around the room, whistling.

At that moment, the door above opened, and in walked Pavel Nikolaevich Shishkin. His appearance was clean-cut and unpretentious. He had straight dark hair, a straight nose, a square, resolute chin, perfect posture, and a direct gaze beneath straight eyebrows. Why he had appeared after hours was a mystery. Pavel Nikolaevich descended into the room and looked approvingly at Malyshev, who was bent over the control board in a very businesslike manner. Then he noticed Kaimenov's idle figure.

Sparks flew. "Why aren't you working, and what are you doing here?"

"You mean me? I am working. . . . I'm thinking."

"You're thinking?!" Shishkin straightened up irately. "May I ask you not to do your thinking in the work area!"

Head down, Kaimenov halted, like a goat about to charge. For several seconds he studied Shishkin intently. Then a gleam came into his eyes, and he asked in a most amicable tone:

"Listen, Pavel Nikolaevich, has anyone ever told you that you're a damn fool?"

"N-no. . . ." Caught off balance, Shishkin's energetic face sagged for an instant, then turned purple. "Wh-what? You dare talk to me like that? You—to me?!" He slapped his hand against the breast pocket of his jacket.

Kaimenov had nothing more to lose now. His eyes narrowed.

"If you want to hear a real nice sound, try hitting your head instead
... you hack!"

Although stunned by this turn of events, Malyshev noticed that
Shishkin looked more bewildered than angered. Shishkin panted:

"I'll get even with you! I'll ... I'll ... f-fire you ... in twenty-four
hours!"

Pavel Nikolaevich dashed to the stairs and almost tore the door off
its hinges as he flew out of the room.

"Wow! You sure gave it to him!" Malyshev leaned back in his chair
and slapped his knees. "What on earth possessed you to say that? Oh,
man, you've made yourself an enemy. Congratulations!"

"But he is a damn fool. How could I have failed to realize it
before?"

"Well, do you know what 'fool' means?" Malyshev arched his
eyebrows. "It's a relative concept. . . . By the way, I don't consider
Shishkin a fool. You can't hold such a position without brains.
Besides, he's educated, has a degree."

"Don't confuse the issue!" Kaimenov fumed. "It is certainly not a
relative concept. It's as absolute as can be. College education—ha!
Education doesn't make an intelligent man out of a fool; he just
knows more. Look, I know he's not a genuine idiot; those are easy to
distinguish. But ... oh, you know damn well what I mean!"

The print-out device clicked again, but Malyshev ignored it and
turned to Kaimenov. "OK, let's assume you're right. But you can't
close your eyes to the fact that this guy Shishkin did get where he is.
So he must have something on the ball. You've got to face facts and
not fight them . . . like that nut battling windmills."

Kaimenov ignored the dig. He sat down, leaning his elbows on his
knees and sinking his fists into his cheeks.

"Yeah, that's the most interesting thing. He made it. How? Why?
It doesn't add up. Look, take Valentin Georgievich—he should be
able to see right through Shishkin and realize that he doesn't have a
shred of talent, intelligence, or decency. And kick him out. Instead,
he does the reverse: forms even closer ties with him, promotes him
... it doesn't make sense!"

"Why not?" Malyshev shrugged his shoulders indulgently. "Shishkin willingly takes on all Valentin Georgievich's dirty work, like doling out assignments, arranging staff schedules, settling all sorts of ticklish internal disputes. Valentin Georgievich's mind operates on too high a level to get involved in that petty stuff; he detests it!"

"But your reasoning is not very scientific," Kaimenov shook his head. "Look, we're conquering space; soon we'll know how to control thermonuclear fusion. But often we are as helpless as kittens when we're faced with ordinary stupidity and meanness. Why isn't there a scientific approach to this? Is this problem so much more difficult than others? Maybe no one has ever bothered trying."

"So why don't you?" Malyshev grinned.

Kaimenov lit a cigarette, blew a stream of smoke beneath the air conditioner's hood, and began thinking out loud.

"Suppose we analyze how Shishkin and his kind succeed? In the first place, they have an extremely limited goal: to promote their own welfare at any price. Grab what you can. If you need a degree—get it. If you want to be in the boss's good graces, go ahead and boot lick if you have to. A little political pull? Sure, use it! Use anything that comes in handy. They can't be bothered with searching for the meaning of life, or analyzing their own or others' experiences, or thinking about universal human problems. They utterly lack intellectual curiosity. Their logic is oversimplified and directed toward one goal. And therefore... therefore, their behavior is to a great extent predictable. Right?"

"Right!" agreed Malyshev, shutting his journal with pleasure. He rose and limbered up a bit. "I'll predict, for example, that Pavel Nikolaevich will have something pretty special in store for you."

"Very likely!" Kaimenov grew animated. "That's the whole point, get it? They have very specific behavior algorithms. 'You scratch my back, I'll scratch yours'; 'an eye for an eye, a tooth for a tooth,' or even better, a whole jaw for a tooth; 'smart people take the easy way out'; 'since we didn't make the rules, we can't change them'; 'arguing with your boss is like spitting into the wind'; 'divide and rule'; 'each man for himself'.... You know, these commonplace algorithms have their own distinct, logical structure. Since they are unambiguous, they can be converted into mathematical symbols and even programmed. Look, 'you scratch my back, I scratch yours' is a typical circuit with positive feedback. 'An eye for an eye' is a circuit with negative feedback. 'Slow and steady wins the race'—a delay circuit. 'Smart people take the easy way out' (smart people don't look for trouble, but ...) is a 'not-or' circuit, a universal logical element. But 'divide and rule' involves the principle of subdividing information into simple binary units that are easy to process. Listen, Sergei," Kaimenov leaped to his feet, "let's develop a computer analog of Shishkin. How about it?"

"Watch out that he doesn't make a computer analog of you," replied Malyshev coldly.

He walked over to the control panel and turned two switches. Lightning's lights went out and the air conditioners went off. The room grew unusually quiet. Sergei removed his lab coat, put on his coat and beret and handed Kaimenov his leather jacket.

"Come on, let's go.... Say, that's a neat jacket. What did you pay for it?"

With a flourish Kaimenov set the jacket on the floor. It stood upright like a bell.

"Listen," he said slowly, "you peddler, you soap transport specialist! I'm dead serious. Let's simulate Pavel Nikolaevich's behavior on M-117. Now's the time to do it. We won't get another chance...."

"You know, I think I'll take a bus home," Sergei headed for the stairs. "Talking to you in an empty room is a real pain in the ass, but if you're offering me a lift on your cycle, I'm your humble servant."

"Boy, working on those shipping problems has really turned you into a birdbrain. Get your coat off and sit down, I'm going to teach you a thing or two.... Have you heard about the Brain Institute's data?"

"Sure," Malyshev began, bored. "Only some ten million of several billion nerve cells in the brain are active, even in a gifted individual. And in mediocre people, it's less—millions or even hundreds of thousands. . . . So what? Still, that's a helluva lot more than your M-117 has. Besides, they aren't the same as human nerve cells."

"Correct. Now listen to this. That million cells in Shishkin's brain processes all the information he gets from his sense organs in so-called raw form. But instead, we're going to feed semi-processed material into the computer: information coded in binary digits and logical circuits. That way we take a heavy load off Shishkin's computer brain. OK—next point. We're not going to simulate all his behavior, but only his behavior at work—from ten to five. So, we eliminate domestic affairs, health problems, childhood memories—a large chunk of information. And work information, to a great extent, is subject to the rules of logic rather than the emotions. Valentin Georgievich demonstrated that theoretically. Third point: this information also must be stripped of superfluous detail—like my facial expression when I had a friendly chat with him, the kind of type used for the guidelines on preparing papers and articles, and so on. We retain only the essentials. M-117's twenty-eight thousand magnetic cells will certainly ingest all this, and its storage memory is enormous."

"OK, let's assume it can handle it," agreed Malyshev. "But where do we get the necessary information about the entire work set-up at the Institute? And remember, it must be coded too."

"There it is, in the cabinet," Kaimenov gestured casually. "It's all ready to feed into the computer's memory."

"Where?!" Malyshev rose.

"In six folders. Don't tell me you've forgotten. Remember, I'm preparing the 'electronic organizer' algorithm! Take off your coat, you're stewing. . . . Look, I'm telling you, there won't be another opportunity like this. First of all, we have all the written information in hand, about the Institute's set-up, its staff, diagrams of inter-relations with other organizations, guidelines for everything—from bonuses to housing. Secondly, you and I are in the know; we have unwritten information for operative storage at our disposal. Third point: we have a conflict, that is, a dramatic situation where a man's true character comes out. Fourth, we have a fine computer at our disposal . . ."

"Did you say 'our'?" Malyshev's eyebrows rose. "But it's government property."

"Right, that's the point. My job now, before I simulate the 'electronic organizer,' is to process that same class of problems on the computer. It's included in my proposal, don't you see?"

"Kaimenov, you are a schemer," Malyshev looked at him thoughtfully. "An out-and-out schemer. And you're getting me involved too. . . . It's crazy, unheard of—simulating your boss's behavior! Well, OK, show me the folders." He unbuttoned his coat.

Kaimenov stuck his hand in his pocket. "Here's the key, and there's your cabinet. Meanwhile I'm going to run down to the store and get us something to eat."

"Don't forget cigarettes," Sergei reminded him as he opened the cabinet.

Kaimenov had produced a truly superb piece of work. It was all there: information about scientific papers, bookkeeping, and personnel data, the local trade union committee, requests for research data, the Institute's administrative and scientific organization, interrelations of scientific organizations, programs, Union and Republic decrees. Everything was ranked on a scale of relative values and plotted in the form of logical diagrams.

"Staff scale values," read Sergei. "Director—nine hundred, assistant director—four hundred and fifty, section chief—three hundred and sixty . . . and so forth . . . chief engineer—one hundred and sixty, senior engineer—one hundred and thirty . . . Aha, oh payroll, I recognize you! . . . H'm, values for scientific degrees and titles . . . well, that's clear, too. Scale for administrative measures: promotion—one thousand, bonuses—seven hundred to two hundred, official letter of thanks—ten, and zilch for ordinary employees. . . ." Malyshev smiled faintly. "Well, that makes mathematical sense. If the scale covers positive and negative numbers, there has to be a zero. . . . Reprimand—minus fifty, reprimand plus bonus deprivation—from minus one hundred to minus six hundred . . . discharge—minus fifteen hundred. . . . Volodya oversimplified that one; you can get fired for various reasons. But it will do for now."

He removed a page from another folder: "Table of Organization." Director and assistant director were boxed off; lines extended from them to circled section chiefs; from the latter, lines branched to project leaders; then to the workers executing the projects. Also, from assistant director Shishkin's box, lines branched to the personnel section, the section he supervised, to procurement, repair shops, and the security service. Correct, so far. Then a diagram of intra-institute relationships: director–Science Council–sections–project teams–project executors. . . .

Kaimenov returned and unloaded sandwiches, cigarettes, and two cans of beer from his jacket pockets.

"Say, what are those dotted lines?" asked Malyshev.

"Where?"

"Here . . . from executors to section chiefs to the Science Council. . . ."

"Feedback. People who carry out assignments also come up with ideas. Initiative from the rank and file, so to speak."

"Throw it out! Don't confuse the computer. Shishkin supporting initiative from the rank and file? Ha . . . ridiculous!"

"But remember, this wasn't written with Shishkin in mind. Anyway, how does the whole thing shape up to you?" Kaimenov looked hopefully at his friend.

"In general . . . it's correct. At any rate, it's plausible. But for our task it should be simplified. There's no reason to insert everything into the memory . . . all the sections, all employees, all research papers. Only you two are involved in the conflict, let's say three—it won't work without Valentin Georgievich. And me, too, as an involuntary witness. So, four characters . . . four main computer addresses."

Malyshev wrote on a clean sheet of paper:

P. N. Shishkin–001
V. G. Pantaleev–010
V. M. Kaimenov–011
S. A. Malyshev–100

"All information will be distributed to these four addresses. OK? If it's favorable for a given addressee, it gets a 'plus' digit. If not–a 'minus.' "

"Correct, Comrade 'one-zero-zero'!"

They sat down opposite each other at the table and began to work. Kaimenov programmed Shishkin's algorithms. Malyshev simplified and coded the diagrams prepared by Kaimenov. Malyshev was an engineer. Skeptical as he might have been of Kaimenov's wild idea, once he decided to join the venture, he committed himself all the way. And no nonsense. The room was quiet and gloomy. Only Kaimenov's tense muttering broke the silence.

". . . 'Divide and rule,' h'm . . . Aha, the transfer of information and commands comes only through addressee 001, through Shishkin. . . . 'An eye for an eye'–reciprocal subtraction program. The lowest digit is the first to turn into zero. . . ."

"Hold on!" Malyshev put down his pencil. "Don't you think you're being rather unfair to Shishkin?"

"What are you talking about?"

"The algorithms you concocted. What proof do you have that he operates in line with 'divide and rule,' 'an eye for an eye'? . . . "

"Naturally I haven't probed his brain . . . but it seems very obvious to me."

"Nothing's obvious in mathematics. We should not prescribe a behavior analog; rather, we should study the analog's behavior! It's very possible that PANSH-2's algorithms are not as simple as sayings and proverbs. . . ."

"Hey, you're right!" Kaimenov exclaimed excitedly. "You're brilliant! Who needs algorithms? The hell with them! We'll feed the computer information about the set-up and the purpose and let it figure it out for itself and select the optimal behavior variant. Less work for us!" He tore up the sheet. "Sergei, you're a genius!"

In half an hour the information was assigned to each addressee and coded. As they consumed the sandwiches and beer, they wondered if they had skipped anything. Apparently not. After depositing the remains of their supper in a trash can outside the room, they lit cigarettes.

"Listen, Volodya," said Malyshev, "we're setting a dangerous precedent."

"What kind?"

"Cybernetic interference in a man's personal life."

"Well, hel-lo!" Kaimenov stared at him in amazement. "What do you mean 'interference'? We're not pushing Shishkin into doing anything, are we?"

"No, but . . . still, it amounts to a kind of spying on him with the aid of an electronic device."

"Stop worrying! Nothing's going to happen. And suppose he doesn't turn out what he seems to be . . ." Volodya turned on M-117, sat down at the controls and placed his fingers on the input keyboard. "OK, start dictating!"

The quivering orange light coming from the neon signals on the control panel assumed quaint shapes. The electron ray on the control screen alternately drew a steady green line and shattered it into a series of impulses.

The switches of the magnetic drum's motors clicked dully. An electronic creature was now settling into M-117's gray plastic parallelepiped. Silently and speedily it switched the transistors, sent streams of electrons across the diodes, and spattered the impulses of the magnetic field in ferrite rings. Electric signals sped along its wire nerves, amplifying or destroying each other.

Ten minutes later the blinking of the neon lights on the control panel ceased.

"OK, that's that. . . . " Volodya doused his cigarette butt. "Now we can ask questions. For a starter let's ask about 'zero-one-zero.' *Dear PANSH-2, how do you feel about Valentin Georgievich?*"

He flipped three switches on the panel, two clockwise, one counterclockwise. Instantly the digital print-out system responded with a crackling noise, and a tongue of white paper tape slid from its rectangular brass jaws. The engineers bent over it.

"Address 010, subaddress 'electronic organizer,' " Malyshev translated the figures. "Subtraction symbols, digits. . . . Get the reference table. We can't decipher this without it. Well, well. . . . He plans to subtract functions 14, 21, and 35 from the 'electronic organizer'..."

Kaimenov consulted the table. "Distribution of bonuses, staff changes, and housing allocation."

"... and take on the jobs himself. Oho! And look what we have following Pavel Nikolaevich's newly acquired functions: additional direct lines in the administrative and scientific diagrams. And even some feedback lines...."

"Why not? That adds up too." Kaimenov placed his fingers on the switches again.

"Find out about single transport problems," said Malyshev quietly. "Let him confess why he's so partial to them. Why does he ignore a general solution?"

"I'm asking."

M-117 rattled off a new piece of tape. Kaimenov scanned it quickly.

"Address 100, subaddress 'transport.' Wait a minute ... he has a different scale of values for these problems...." Malyshev hung over him, practically breathing in his ear. "Aha, here it is! Single problems yield one publishable paper per problem. General problem—only one paper.... It figures. The number of published scientific papers is the most reliable criterion in science. See, this guy is no dope!"

"He doesn't understand a damn thing," said Malyshev crossly.

"Wait, that's not all of it.... There's a few more lines about the general problem. H'm, some gibberish. Random numbers ... Ah! Well, now everything's clear: he doesn't know how to approach the general problem of freight transport."

"So that's it!"

"OK," Kaimenov turned to the control panel. "Now let's ask about ourselves."

But this time the crackling of the print-out device's type had a suprisingly monotonous quality. Malyshev tore off the tape and looked at it.

"What the hell is this?! Only zeros. Even your address isn't on it...." He looked up at his friend. "Listen, Volodya, he's wiped you out. In fact ... he's killed you."

3
A Killer Changes the Program

Kaimenov looked at the tape, then at the computer glistening from the signal lights, and made a wry face.

"Gross! I probably got what was coming to me. Let's check working storage. . . ." He pressed several buttons on the control panel.

Not a single light blinked. Kaimenov swore and pressed a few white keys.

"Well I'll be a son of a gun! The information about me is stored only in permanent storage, and the computer has no control over it. An obituary! That's a nice kettle of fish!"

"Pavel Nikolaevich is a pretty strong guy," remarked Malyshev. "If he waits for you with a brick in some dark alley, the problem of 'zero-one-zero' will be definitively solved."

Kaimenov stared through him absentmindedly.

"Wait, I think I have it. We have to feed the computer a comparative scale of dangers. Of course! We've scared the poor computer to death. I've no intention of depriving Pavel Nikolaevich of his life, hands, feet, or even his health. . . ." He walked over to the table and began jotting figures on a sheet of paper. "Life–ten thousand; serious disability . . . crippling . . . How much?"

"Five thousand."

"Serious illness–three thousand; mild illness–one thousand. But, I ask you, compared to that what's a mere one hundred for unpleasant incidents at work? For a measly one hundred is it worth wiping out a nice guy like me?" He sat down at the control panel and lay the sheet in front of him.

Three minutes later the fading neon lights confirmed that the computer had digested the new information.

"Let's try now." Kaimenov flipped the switches to '011.'

The print-out device cut through the silence like a burst from a machine gun. The tape was covered with rows of zeros.

"What do you say to that?!" Kaimenov looked at the computer indignantly. "That's some optimal variant!"

Malyshev settled down more comfortably and stretched his legs.

"When you write your will, leave me your cycle and jacket. I'll ride it and remember you with kind words."

"Sergei, a joke's a joke, but you know the first solutions were fully plausible. Almost for sure. . . . And then—if he does have such aggressive intentions, why shouldn't he try to knock off Valentin Georgievich, so he could take over his job? I'm just small fry."

"For Pantaleev he doesn't have enough digits. . . ."

An image of Pavel Nikolaevich, tie askew, shoulders shaking vigorously as he strangles Kaimenov, rose before Malyshev's eyes. He frowned.

"No, he's not that stupid. . . ."

Suddenly Kaimenov stood stock still in the center of the room.

"Boy, are we idiots!"

"Speak for yourself. Why 'we'?"

"Who the hell else? Look, we fed everything into the computer: diagrams, scales, instructions, decrees. . . . But not the Criminal Code. Get it? What time is it? Ten-thirty. OK. At this late and terrible hour only one person can save my neck."

Kaimenov dialed a number.

"Klava? It's me. Listen carefully. Go upstairs to Mikhail Nikolaevich and borrow his Criminal Code. Take a cab and step on it. I'll meet you at the entrance. What do you mean 'it's late'? . . . Mikhail Nikolaevich has everything. . . . Come on, Klava, be a good girl. I can't tell you everything now, but a premeditated murder is in the offing and we want to prevent it. . . . I'll wait for you! . . . Yes! And Klava, borrow Mikhail's Labor Code too. Don't forget!"

He hung up and looked at the computer triumphantly. "Let it know that it's not that easy to get rid of me!"

They left the Institute past midnight. Klava, Kaimenov's wife, was waiting for him astride a motorcycle glistening in the moonlight: she didn't have enough money to take a cab back. Kaimenov revved up the engine, bid Malyshev good night, and off they sped into the fragrant spring night.

Malyshev headed for the bus stop. The city lay below. Rows of fluorescent lights cast a pattern of phosphorescent blue lines. Brilliant blue flashes generated by current collectors on streetcar and trolley-bus lines illuminated low-lying clouds. A bit of moon peeked out from behind the grayish-green phosphorescent edge of a cloud. The asphalt roadway, rolled smooth by traffic, glistened coldly.

At the bus stop a large tin poster, inspired by the advent of spring, appeared on a hexagonal concrete column:

Attention Citizens!

Vegetable plots within the nuclear reactor's boundaries are *prohibited!* Such gardens will be plowed under.

DIRECTOR OF THE NUCLEAR INSTITUTE

"Ah, the atomic age!" smiled Malyshev, leaping onto a trolley-bus as it rolled up to the curb.

4

A Test Conversation

Readers tend to identify an author's position with his hero's attitudes. "All the author's sympathies lie on the side of...", write the critics, disclosing their unique discovery. But, dear readers, what does sympathy or antipathy have to do with my story? Not a damn thing! This author is conducting an objective literary study of a specific situation. That, and nothing more. Frankly, if anything, he's far from enthusiastic about Kaimenov's and Malyshev's venture. The idea of simulating an individual on a computer recalls an incident that occurred long ago, when this writer was a student. During an exam on accident prevention the instructor had asked a student to draw a schematic of a human being. The co-ed burst into tears: the idea of substituting a schematic for a person—a human being!—was monstrous to her. Naturally she was kicked right out of the exam room because such a schematic actually exists in safety engineering. It is a complex of inductances and resistances which determines how much current passes through a person plugged into a 380-volt, 50-hertz industrial frequency. But from a human standpoint, you can understand the girl's reaction.

However, that happened a long time ago, long before the great mathematical obsession of our time appeared on the scene—cybernetics, allegedly capable of performing any feat.

Any? If you consider what nonsense they came up with, using their fully transistorized M-117—as if their failure to feed the Criminal Code into the computer would prevent Pavel Nikolaevich from killing Kaimenov! Without the computer-digested Criminal Code, Shishkin would axe down his adversaries left and right.... But Pavel Nikolaevich wouldn't have the stomach for such bloody deeds. Besides, he lacks experience in that line of work! After all, his specialty is discrete mathematics.

Naturally, the computer itself, like Caesar's wife, is above suspicion; but the interpretations Kaimenov and Malyshev gave its digits were apparently rather biased. Academic objectivity is probably colored by some powerful emotions—the kind subordinates experience toward superiors who are their intellectual inferiors. Since Kaimenov and Malyshev were such subordinates, their research with computer analog PANSH-2 should be viewed rather critically.

The scientific talents of these two friends were expressed in different ways. Everyone knew that Volodya Kaimenov was an able scientist; everyone from Corresponding Member of the Academy of Sciences Pantaleev down to the lowliest, sixty-ruble-a-month lab assistant, unversed in computer science. Almost no one, except Malyshev himself, and perhaps Kaimenov, was aware of his abilities. Malyshev couldn't attract attention or spout ideas, but he was a genuine thinker. Tenaciously, unhurriedly, thoroughly, he would pursue a problem that intrigued him, for months on end. For the past few months he had been considering the very general problem of cybernetic transport. It seemed so clear and simple now; he could sit right down and program it for the computer. And, as usual, it seemed strange to Malyshev that anyone could fail to understand the problem.

The following afternoon Sergei Malyshev proceeded to Pavel Nikolaevich's office to conduct a test conversation. On even days Pantaleev usually gave lectures at the Physical-Technical Institute, and Shishkin would occupy his office. When Malyshev crossed the threshold he was surprised to see how everything had changed.

The partly drawn silk drapes lent an air of gloom and intense isolation to the room and its furnishings. Objects that normally went unnoticed in Valentin Georgievich's presence, now hit you square in the eyes. The crimson carpet runner zeroed in toward the polished desk like a landing strip. The mother-of-pearl telephone complex glistened impatiently, anxious to emit the crucial ring. A rather small blackboard, from which formulas had been erased, hung unobtrusively on the wall. Portraits eyed the room's occupants sternly. The air was charged with a sense of urgency; this wasn't a place to simply sit and grind out work, but a springboard for action.

Pavel Nikolaevich blended perfectly into this setting. Shoulders thrust back, he sat to the left of the telephone complex reading documents. His face was set in expression No. 2.

Mathematicians are inclined to classify anything and everything. Therefore, the Institute's wits had reduced to a logical matrix (a chart) those typical facial expressions which, in their opinion, Shishkin tried on each morning together with his tie and then wore through his working day (with a break for dinner from one until two).

Expression No. 1 (reserved for conversations with colleagues ranking above him in scientific and administrative functions, important commissions, foreign delegations, and correspondents from major newspapers): courtesy; attentiveness; readiness to agree, also to applaud and laugh at good (naturally they were all good!) jokes.

Expression No. 2 (for conversations with subordinates): the eyes focused slightly above and beyond his inferior, appearing to see something inaccessible to said subordinate; a sullen concern about affairs of greater importance than the subject under discussion; a rhythmic nodding of the head, which means he is maddeningly familiar with everything being said to him.

Expression No. 3 (for seminars, scientific councils, conferences): indulgent attention; bored air of comprehension of what speaker is saying and plans to say; weary satisfaction with his own abundant accomplishments.

Expression No. 4 (for meetings at the local trade union committee,

Party Bureau, Presidium, and for speeches): a steady gaze, reflecting his sound ideology, glum determination, concern, and willingness to deal with the collective's problems and affairs.

All this came through particularly vividly to Malyshev. He hadn't come here simply to chat with his subject, but to study him.

"Neat little place he's got here!" he thought, treading on the crimson runner. When Malyshev was close enough, he stole a glance at the folder Pavel Nikolaevich was leafing through and was immensely pleased—naturally from a purely scientific viewpoint—with what he saw: "Personal file of Kaimenov, Vladimir Mikhailovich."

Catching sight of a witness to yesterday's incident, the assistant director frowned and pushed the folder away quickly. Malyshev didn't blink an eyelid. He had business to attend to with Pavel Nikolaevich.

Pavel Nikolaevich squared his shoulders. Did Pavel Nikolaevich feel, suggested Malyshev, that the results of their work on the design of an optimal schedule for the transport of organic dye-stuffs could now be written up by them as co-authors? Actually a rough draft was ready. Here it was. All it needed was discussion of a few points and some polishing.

Pavel Nikolaevich's expression shifted, falling between No. 1 and No. 2. The tilt of his head and a faint smile indicated his readiness to discuss and polish.

In the course of fifteen minutes both parties demonstrated to each other a passionate interest in the problem of organic dye-stuff transport.

"Right here we must insert a paragraph about the significance of optimal scheduling of organic dye-stuff transport," remarked Pavel Nikolaevich.

"Yes, of course," agreed Malyshev. "I overlooked that."

"And this should be worded more carefully. Instead of 'it is proposed that . . .', say 'the possibility is indicated.' You know . . . scientific caution. . . ."

"Yes, I think you're right."

"And here Valentin Georgievich's role should be emphasized and his ideas noted. . . ."

"And a reference to his monograph, too?"

"Absolutely. Ab-so-lute-ly!"

Finally, Shishkin could restrain himself no longer.

"And that . . . what's his name?" Shishkin even rubbed his forehead, trying to recall Kaimenov's surname, although Malyshev knew damn well that it was flashing through his brain like a neon sign. "That . . ." Pavel Nikolaevich pulled the folder to him. "Kaimenov . . . How's he progressing with his algorithm for the 'electronic organizer'?"

Malyshev decided to play it cool and dissociate himself from Kaimenov. "I don't know. We usually work different shifts."

"Is that so? . . . Well, work up a nice little article in line with our discussion . . . and we'll submit it to *Chemical Industry.*"

"But, Pavel Nikolaevich, that journal doesn't specialize in cybernetics!" Malyshev couldn't restrain himself.

Shishkin looked at him with a gleam in his eye. "The cybernetic journals have plenty without us! But for the chemists, we really have something special to offer . . . chemistry plus cybernetics. . . . "

"Plus transport? This guy's no fool," noted Malyshev with admiration. "Far from it. Volodya was really off the beam. . . ."

"Yes. Wait, you've given me an idea. We can also submit it to *Railroad Affairs.* We'll hold that in reserve."

Shishkin paused, frowning worriedly.

"This Kaimenov . . . do you know him well?"

"How should I put it?" Malyshev pricked up his ears: round two had begun for the algorithm *You scratch my back, I'll scratch yours.* "We studied in the same department."

"Did he have a reputation then for similar . . . uh . . . escapades?"

"Not actually for that kind, but . . ."

Shishkin latched on to the "but."

"Yes, he's terribly undisciplined and has an exalted opinion of himself. And the reference from the Institute was certainly not flattering. Here, listen to this: 'Tactless with his fellow students, participated little in community activity. . . .' Everybody knows how liberal these references can be—you can be sure he didn't participate at all and insulted people with his nasty mouth, and so forth. But still they write a favorable reference. They don't want to ruin a student's career. As a result, this is what we get. . . ."

"Here it comes," guessed Malyshev, "about his being late to work."

"And discipline on the job?! Late four times so far this year! . . ."

"He lives very far away," Malyshev was about to remark, but caught himself in time. He must not deviate from the algorithm.

"And to top it off there's yesterday's incident," fumed Pavel Nikolaevich. "Today he calls me names, tomorrow—Valentin Georgievich, the day after tomorrow. . . ." He broke off, undecided about who would be Kaimenov's next victim. "To think we entrust such a person with scientific work! Eh?"

Malyshev decided that the time was ripe to inject the next algorithm into the conversation: *Slow and steady wins the race.* He turned on his evasive-deadpan expression.

Shishkin fell silent. Then, with a saccharine smile he looked up at Malyshev.

"What else is on your mind, Sergei . . . Alekseevich?"

"Well, I think the time has come for us to tackle the general problem of designing optimal transport routings. You see, the single cases are one-day jobs. . . ." Shishkin's face switched to expression No. 2, but it didn't disturb Sergei. "Computers are in use now at major rail junctions and storage terminals. Soon they'll be everywhere. Standard programs can be designed that apply to any load, and a general algorithm can be developed to coordinate the operation of all the computers in the country. Of course it's more complicated than figuring out an optimal schedule for milk delivery in the city, but imagine what scientific significance such an algorithm would have! And the economic impact? Freight shipments will go faster; no bottlenecks; goods won't spoil. Millions of rubles will be saved!"

Malyshev himself was carried away by his enthusiasm for his proposal; sparing no arguments, he layed it on thick. Pavel Nikolaevich nodded rhythmically. "Doesn't look as if he's buying it," thought Malyshev. He raised his head and met Shishkin's gaze, noticing a glitter in it that defied scientific classification.

Immediately Shishkin's expression returned to Number 2.

"Interesting, of course. Yes, interesting. . . . But it still requires a great deal of thought," drawled Pavel Nikolaevich. "Very thorough study. . . ."

Sergei recalled that yesterday evening M-117 had resorted to similar tactics: it repeatedly fed this information through the delay line before digesting it in the logic units.

"Yes, very thorough study so that everything is well grounded and carefully considered. . . . We'll return to this problem again. . . ."

"He didn't digest it; it went into passive storage," Malyshev thought, as he rose and took his leave.

After this test conversation Malyshev and Kaimenov had delivered the first package to Valentin Georgievich.

During the evening of that same day they had fed additional information for analog PANSH-2 into M-117. Its behavior was computed for the next two weeks. Combinations of digits and commands predicted the following:

1) Pavel Nikolaevich will order Kaimenov to sharply reduce the time allotted for his development of the "electronic organizer" algorithm.

2) He will refuse to hire Kaimenov's choice for his team.

3) He will try to pass off Malyshev's idea for a universal transport algorithm as his own creation.

"Ugh, how dull!" exclaimed Kaimenov disappointedly, as he packed pieces of tape, marked with the computer's predicted digits, and translation sheets into an envelope. "No divine sparks, no conspiracies! Only once did villainy rear its ugly head, and even that was due to an oversight. . . ."

The first two predictions were borne out during the first week. Once, toward evening, Kaimenov dashed into the computer room waving a piece of paper.

"Sergei, this is it! Take a look! 'Rejected because applicant's specialty is inappropriate. P. Shishkin, 10 April 19. . . . exactly what the computer predicted."

Malyshev took the application and scanned it. "I would like to apply for a position in the computer technology department as a..."

"Maybe he doesn't have the necessary qualifications. Well, you know!... Formally, he doesn't. His diploma says 'radio engineer.' But two thirds of the Institute's employees could be discharged for the same reason. After all, we took degrees when cybernetics was still considered a pseudo-science. I'm a radio engineer, too, and you're an electrical engineer. . . . Suppose this radio engineer, Vlasyuk, actually supervised a team that repaired computers like our M-117? See what I'm driving at?"

"Is he good?"

"Very good... with plenty of ideas. He invented two devices at his plant." Kaimenov's face darkened as he tucked the application into his pocket.

"Maybe you ought to speak to Pantaleev?"

"What the hell are you saying?!" Kaimenov stared at him in amazement. "We'll ruin the whole thing if we do. It can't be helped. Science requires sacrifices."

"Take care that you're not one of them. . . ."

The following day Shishkin appeared in the computer room. He poked around, stopping at the engineers' work places. After chiding computer specialist Lidochka Chainik for sloppy journal entries, he went over to Kaimenov. Itching to eavesdrop, Malyshev edged a little closer to the bookcase and began burrowing into reference books.

"Well, Vladimir Mikhailovich, how's your... ahem ... 'electronic director' coming along?"

"An 'electronic director' is not included in my project, but the 'electronic assistant director' may be ready for programming very soon," replied Kaimenov cheerfully.

"Aha ... h'm ..." Pavel Nikolaevich's face darkened imperceptibly. "Well, then, I'm delighted that everything is progressing so nicely and that you're moving ahead of schedule. So, by May Day you'll have the 'electronic organizer' in operation?"

"By May Day?" Kaimenov looked at his boss with curiosity. "But

... according to the schedule, the first trial run is set for the end of May! There's still a lot of data I don't have."

"But you just told me that you can program ... this ... this assistant director. What are you up to with this shilly-shallying? From the way you crowed about your 'electronic organizer' at the inter-institute seminars, everyone thought your computer was already replacing the administration and the science collective. But, actually, you're backing off. Get it done by May. Without fail!"

Kaimenov flushed crimson at the mention of the seminar.

"By May Day? That happy holiday of the laboring masses?"

"Yes, I mean that holiday of the laboring masses!" said Pavel Nikolaevich in a most dignified manner. "Any objections?"

"Should I be jumping for joy? Now you pull this, after you refused to hire Vlasyuk?!" With a dramatic gesture Kaimenov shoved a sheet of paper and a pen toward Shishkin. "Please put it down in writing. So that I'm not the one to be called on the carpet if this turns out awkwardly."

Staring at the sheet, Pavel Nikolaevich began to have second thoughts. Realizing there was no retreat, he sat down at the desk.

"Another strike for our side!" said Kaimenov jubilantly after Shishkin had left the room. 'To Chief Engineer Kaimenov, V. M. Inasmuch as you have informed us that your assignment to develop an 'electronic organizer' algorithm is progressing so well, I feel that the work should be completed in a much shorter period in order to meet the Institute's needs more rapidly. I suggest that you prepare experimental programs for the computer and have a trial run before 1 May of this year. Section Chief CTS° P. Shishkin.' Signature, date ... it's very simple: if the time and effort I put into this job are cut back, either the work will be done on a smaller scale or it will fail altogether. With a complicated problem like this—an electronic analog of the entire Institute—such a possibility exists. Get it?"

"Yeah, he's got the screws on you," Malyshev turned his head. "Listen, you'll never finish it by May!"

"Maybe not the 'electronic organizer.' But the 'electronic assis-

°Ph.D. Candidate in Technical Science

tant director'? ... Who knows? Either I'll finish it, or it will finish me."

5

Sergei Hits the Bull's-eye

The third prediction for the analog was borne out the following Monday at a seminar in Pantaleev's office. Under discussion was the work schedule for the second half of the year. Pantaleev berated the chief of the automation laboratory for his petty projects. ("Leave such odd jobs to the repair shop. Valery Semyonovich, try to remember that you are in charge of a team of scientists!") Following Valery Semyonovich's incoherent excuses and assurances, Shishkin took the floor.

"In our section we shall set as our task for the second half of the year 'the development of general programs for freight transport, using computers at rail junctions and wholesale terminals....' " He continued to elaborate the work plan for this task, scarcely deviating from the ideas outlined by Malyshev a week earlier.

The seminar participants listened to him attentively. Pantaleev, his thick lenses glittering, remarked:

"Comrades, this is an important task! And an algorithm can be worked out for it once the problem is well formulated. Whom do you have in mind for the job?"

"I think we'll assign it to ..." Pavel Nikolaevich swung his head in Malyshev's direction, "... Comrade Malyshev. He has already acquired sufficient experience in solving individual transport problems and will be able to handle this. Sergei ... Alekseevich needs to develop. And if he can't handle it, we'll help him."

Although Malyshev had foreseen such a turn of events, he hadn't expected to be chosen so calmly and brazenly. Stunned, he turned to look at his colleagues and saw around him only clear-eyed, attentive, intelligent faces. ... How completely natural it must appear to everyone that doctoral candidate Pavel Nikolaevich Shishkin was the author of this very promising idea, and he, engineer Malyshev, was merely its executor, a young man in need of an enriching growth experience. That it is the way it must be. How could it be otherwise? And now he, like the frog in Garshin's tale, would be plopped into a pond were he to cry out: "I'm the one. . . ." Malyshev glanced helplessly at Kaimenov who sat there without saying a word and gazed steadily at Shishkin.

In his hoarse, honest voice, Pantaleev was now thanking Shishkin and the other speakers and asking them not to delay formulation of their plans.

The seminar was over.

Kaimenov and Malyshev remained behind in the office. Pantaleev, who had begun at once to ponder some calculations on the blackboard, looked at them questioningly.

"Valentin Georgievich," said Kaimenov, "at the risk of sounding like a broken record, may I ask you, please, to open package No.4?"

"Ah, yes, that secret of yours!" The director grinned for an instant, put down the chalk, removed the package from the safe, and handed it to Kaimenov. "Be my guest."

Kaimenov broke the seal and removed one sheet.

"Please read it."

"Between the tenth and the fifteenth of April, P. N. Shishkin will outline a proposal for the design of a universal algorithm for the establishment of optimal freight transport routes. . . ." Valentin Georgievich put down the page and looked at the engineers. "All this is quite correct. A valuable idea. So, what's the problem?"

"So what's the problem?" Kaimenov was stunned. "Didn't you notice the date?"

"I certainly did. Your package is dated the sixth of April and today is the fifteenth. That's correct too. It's quite natural for someone to come up with an idea and express it later. The reverse would be rather strange."

"The fact is that Sergei Malyshev expressed and suggested the idea to Shishkin." Kaimenov was furious.

"Really?" Pantaleev looked at Malyshev with interest. Malyshev remained silent and stared off into a corner of the room. "H'm . . . Pavel Nikolaevich, Comrade Malyshev and you work together. Right? It's quite natural that you exchange views on the job, formulate problems, express ideas. Sometimes an idea occurs simultaneously to several scientists; sometimes it's simply in the air. . . . Why make a big fuss about it?" Valentin Georgievich began to get angry, and he looked at the blackboard impatiently. "And besides, Vladimir Mikhailovich, if you knew that Comrade Malyshev, and not Pavel Nikolaevich, was the author of this idea, why didn't you speak up at the seminar? Why did you find it more convenient . . . to . . . how did you yourself put it? . . . to 'inform' me about this in strict confidence?"

Kaimenov was bewildered by this unexpected blow.

"Excuse me, Valentin Georgievich," Malyshev couldn't contain himself, "we didn't intend . . . well, personally, I'm not complaining about Pavel Nikolaevich. Let's go, Volodya!"

"One minute," Pantaleev stopped them. "Listen, I suspect that you have cooked up some sort of game, probably involving cybernetics. I don't feel I have the right to interfere without your consent, since I understand that ideas may occur to you that don't fit in with the Institute's program. Every scientist has a right to pursue independent research. . . . But since you chose me . . . h'm . . . as your middleman or, rather, as your 'mailbox' in your little game, I would like to hope that it won't lead to intrigue. Nothing is more detestable than intrigue. Nothing wastes the mind so much as intrigue. . . ." For another five minutes Valentin Georgievich continued in the same vein.

Malyshev and Kaimenov left the office, their cheeks burning with humiliation.

In the corridor Kaimenov placed his hand on Malyshev's shoulder.

"Don't take it too hard, Sergei! We'll get even with him in the most literal sense of the word. Let's get together this evening to discuss it. OK?"

Sergei jerked his shoulder to throw off his friend's hand, but before he had a chance to open his mouth, Shishkin came toward them up the stairs.

"... I've had it with dreams and starry-eyed idealism. Look how it turned out—I gave it away with my own two hands. Just like that!

Three months of hard mental labor. But when something worked out right, I was on cloud nine. And now ... it's all kaput! Even if I refuse to work on this project, Shishkin will find another engineer and spill the whole thing to him. This idea is a lot easier to understand than create. I won't prove anything that way.... It's clear that everything will remain as it is. You won't trap Shishkin with your bare mathematics, so there's no use wasting your time on the computer with such nonsense."

Malyshev sat alone in the room at Lightning's controls. The breeze from the air conditioner ruffled his hair.

... Trains speeding along shiny rails, trucks roaring as they round turns, ships plowing the seas, rivers, and oceans. They carry freight: grain, coal, machine tools, ore, oil, cloth, toys, apples. At shunting yards, storage terminals, and ports, electronic devices switch over the points, control automatic loaders and cranes, light up circuits for optimal routes on dispatchers' signal panels—and without bottlenecks or stoppages. In time, transportation will be automated too: chauffeurs, drivers, dispatchers, conductors will be occupied with other tasks. Mathematical devices will become the heart of our country's circulatory system.

And even if he executed this great feat, it would not be his. "Under the leadership of Pavel Nikolaevich Shishkin, candidate for a Ph.D. in Technical Science, an algorithm was developed at the Institute of Computer Technology," the press, choked with emotion, will begin its story. What about the guy who does the work? Who ever writes about him?! Visualizing Shishkin's utterly smug face on the front page, Malyshev's stomach began to churn.

At that same hour Pavel Nikolaevich was threading his way homeward among silent buildings and trees bathed in grayish-green moonlight. He had lingered at the Institute until quite late, to avoid running into Malyshev and Kaimenov. And now he cursed himself. At the seminar Malyshev had given him a dirty look, and that bandit, Kaimenov, had mouthed some nasty word silently. Although Pavel Nikolaevich convinced himself that he hadn't caught that word, he began to feel jittery. And then there were the words he had caught on the stairs: "We'll get even with him. . . . Let's get together this evening to discuss it. . . ." What had they cooked up?

Suddenly he heard firm footsteps echoing through the deserted lane. Now Shishkin almost ran, and the moon leaped after him over the rooftops.

. . . A brief digression.

There's something in this story, now approaching its happy conclusion, that doesn't add up. Cybernetics, electronics—great stuff, but even the nervous system of a lowly garden caterpillar is far more complex than a computer. And man? Forget it! Twenty-eight thousand cells of that infamous M-117, if translated into neurons, would occupy an area not much larger than a typographical point (.254 mm).

Yet the computer does predict Pavel Nikolaevich's behavior. Of course, without the details. But it does predict his *actions*. And, after all, it is an individual's actions that define his character and personality.

But Pavel Nikolaevich is a man, not a caterpillar. A man! Granted, neither talented nor clever, but far from stupid. For example, long ago, while still a college student, he caught on that science was the kind of subject where you understood only what you did yourself. He quickly mastered the algorithm for getting a degree: publishing papers was more important than writing them; his dissertation? . . . compiled from his graduation thesis and lab reports . . . and twenty minutes of shame defending it. . . . When he started working at the Institute of Computer Technology, he sniffed out the kinds of jobs and duties which, when carried out, might give him a reputation as a reliable worker, and even push him up the ladder of success. He carried a lot of weight, was respected—and even respected himself.

Pavel Nikolaevich, the man, has a wife; his daughter is a student at a Leningrad institute; his elderly parents live in Zaporozhe; he has many friends. And not one of them questions his reputation. He shaves each morning, was recently down with the flu, spent the summer on the Caucasus' tourist trails, wears a 41 (7) shoe (and, by the way, his left leg is a little shorter, so that even now, rushing homeward, he is limping imperceptibly, although he isn't conscious of it), drinks in moderation, prefers cognac and dry Caucasian wines, has twenty-four years' work experience, fourteen published papers, has been abroad a number of times, didn't serve, wasn't subject to military service.... A mass of detail not considered by the computer! Likes good songs, sometimes sings in a group. Is subject to emotional outbursts, has hopes and disappointments, definite political views and moral values. Not that he doesn't lie occasionally, either aloud or by his silence; and if you really analyze it, maybe he doesn't lie deliberately, but doesn't know where to draw the line. Human relations...he is very sensitive to injustice—especially when number one is the target. No smirking, please! None of us is perfect in that respect. In fact, it even has a cybernetic explanation.... Oh, hell, what a ridiculous position the computer has put the heroes and author in! Imagine, having to prove that a man is a man!

But you can't ignore the experimental facts: the computer does predict. And, incidentally, those zeros with which M-117 gunned down Kaimenov in the first round—is that for real? Is Pavel Nikolaevich truly capable of killing a man for the sake of some trivial material comforts? Well, not with his own hands, but some other way, certainly not in cold blood. But is he capable of such an act?

What's it all about? How is it, that an area no larger than a typo point controls man? Man, a world in itself, as infinite and wondrous as the universe. What sort of point is this? And why does Shishkin behave as he does?

Maybe because Pavel Nikolaevich experiences fear too often. Somehow, anything new, be it a person, an idea, a problem—anything, immediately puts him on guard. He feared anything he didn't understand, that he couldn't preview, and he was afraid that others would notice his fear. Sometimes, he would become terrified when Valentin Georgievich outlined new ideas to him with enthusiasm: suppose his chief broke off in the middle of his explanation and shouted angrily, "Why the hell are you nodding? I'm only pulling your leg. I'm inventing a lot of rubbish! ... " He was afraid to suggest ideas: suppose they turned out badly? He was afraid not to suggest ideas: suppose people noticed that he didn't have any?

... These fears drained him more than hard physical labor.

Now, homeward bound, he was terrified by the inpenetrable dark shadows of buildings and kiosks, the damp odors seeping from doorways. "They won't prove anything. I'm entirely in the right," he tried hard to convince himself. "But if they really are going to get together somewhere to discuss it? Where, I wonder? ... There are two of them, they're young and strong, and they are vicious. Especially that Kaimenov. His kind is capable of anything. ..."

Only a few more blocks to his home. The street was silent and deserted. "Do they really mean to beat me up?!" thought Pavel Nikolaevich, avoiding the shadows. The idea that he, an intelligent man, still on the young side and appealing to women, would be beaten up, was too humiliating and terrible to contemplate.

Nevertheless, these fears were not the reason for Pavel Nikolaevich's actions. They were more likely a consequence of something or other. But, of what? ...

Malyshev stood by the window, gazing at the moon. "Hell, it's obvious, if you don't watch out for yourself, no one else will. Oh, of course I'll do my job. A job's a job. But it doesn't pay to forget number one. Otherwise I'll spend my whole life working for Shishkin. ... But what if? ... Damn it, why didn't I think of it before! I'm always messing with computers, planning all sorts of unloading and transport jobs; and I'm helping Volodya simulate Shishkin for kicks. But what the devil am I doing for myself?!"

Malyshev was an engineer. A fresh technical idea whetted his appetite and boosted his spirits. "Who said that only Shishkin could be simulated on the computer? Why can't S. A. Malyshev's situation and goals be programmed?" He turned on M-117, found the coding tables in Kaimenov's desk, and sat down to work. "So, additional information: I agree to work under Shishkin; I shall not subtract his digits, but want ... h'm, what do I want? First, a Ph.D.; second, an apartment. ... Why not?"

Defiantly he cast a sidelong glance at the dancing orange lights on the control panel. "You, dear lady, have been provided with a superb air-conditioned room and service. Now, it's time to think about myself!"

The computer had acquired experience and no longer ran through all the variants. A minute later the solution tape leaped from its jaws. Malyshev scanned the digits grouped near addresses 001, 011, and 100, and smiled for an instant.

"Well, what do you know! It could be interpreted that way too. . . ."

As Pavel Nikolaevich ascended the lighted staircase toward his apartment, he grew calmer with each step. Everything was all right. Why had he gotten so upset? "After all, they are decent people. . . ."

He unlocked the door and entered the dark, silent foyer. The apartment, three rooms, was new and still smelled of recent construction. The darkness was a bit frightening (Shishkin rarely stayed late at the Institute, and now, too, his wife was away in Riga, buying furniture), but these were cozy, domestic fears. As he crossed the threshold, he began groping for the switch on the wall. His eyes, unaccustomed to the darkness, could distinguish nothing.

Suddenly, something creaked next to him, and a ghastly grayish-green face with black holes for eyes and a dark bandage over its chin, leered with a twisted grimace and began to move slowly toward Pavel Nikolaevich.

"A-a-a-a!" screamed Pavel Nikolaevich hysterically, and, in a panic, he lashed out wildly with hands and feet.

The tinkling of a shattered mirror broke the silence. The little door on the cupboard flew back sharply, then slammed shut with a bang.

Pavel Nikolaevich crawled along the parquet floor and picked up the pieces. And the moon's mocking face peeked through the window as if nothing had happened.

Sergei Malyshev also returned to his dorm room at a late hour. His three roommates were sound asleep. To unwind, he smoked a cigarette, blowing the smoke out the window into the humid night. He went to the bookshelves that held all their books. He started to reach for a small green volume of Kuprin, then lowered his hand. "The gradual degradation of the human mind is more terrifying than all the executions and barricades in the world," Malyshev recalled from a story of Kuprin's he had read long ago. He looked at the shelf hesitantly. The orange volumes of Ilf and Petrov; the white

jackets on Gorky's works ("What can I do for people?!" exclaimed
Danko. . . .); Mark Twain's blue volumes; Chapek, Aleksey, Tolstoy,
Mayakovsky, Yesenin; Pushkin ("I do not envy the fate of villains
or fools who commit foul deeds."); Jack London, Remarque,
Gogol. . . .

Inside their covers, like hidden danger, lurked the ideas, love, and
anger of many people; their joy and anguish; their smiles and
sorrows; their strength and gentleness; and their deeds, so convincing in their graphic folly—life itself, amplified a thousandfold
through art.

Malyshev had the strange feeling that the books were studying
him intently and sternly, rather than he the books. "The devil with
it; I must be a machine now!" He made up his bed, turned out the
light, and lay down to sleep.

What can I do for people?! The words of Gorky's hero flashed
through his brain. "Ha! These days Danko would simply be fined for
violating fire safety rules in the forest!"

Consoled by the witty cynicism of this thought, he quickly fell
asleep.

The next day Malyshev marched into Shishkin's office. Pavel
Nikolaevich greeted him rather coldly and nervously. After the
events of the previous day the chief appeared somewhat haggard.

Malyshev sat down in the leather armchair reserved for visitors
and fired away.

"Pavel Nikolaevich, I want to gather material for my doctoral
dissertation. How do you feel about that? And, I would like to know
what the prospects are for getting an apartment."

Shishkin got his bearings with unusual speed. In ten seconds flat.

"Well, Sergei . . . Alekseevich, you'll have to check with
Kaimenov," he began fussily. "He can program it on the 'electronic
organizer' for either of you."

"I don't think he's ready for that," said Malyshev distinctly.

"Yes, I would agree with you." Pavel Nikolaevich's face assumed expression No. 2. "And I've explained that to Valentin
Georgievich. . . . I'm very glad. . . . " Shishkin didn't bother clarifying
exactly what he was so glad about. "About your dissertation—let me

say 'welcome.' It's about time. It will be a pleasure to be your sponsor. . . ."

Within the next fifteen minutes the algorithms flew hard and fast, back and forth, interweaving, alternating: "I scratch your back. . . ."; "An eye for an eye. . . ." and so on. In the end Pavel Nikolaevich accompanied Malyshev right to the door.

That day Malyshev had to work with Lightning on the second shift: Shishkin had loaded the computers to the limit because of the approaching holidays. When Malyshev descended into the room, Kaimenov rushed toward him with a tape.

"Hey, did you feed a situation change and additional goals into M-117's input?"

"Yeah, I did."

"OK, so here's the analog's solution: if you speak up against address 011, that is, against me, on all points, PANSH-2 will undertake to guarantee your scientific career and an apartment to boot. Sergei, we've got to verify this!"

"I have already."

"And?"

"It's all correct."

"That's great!" Kaimenov whirled around on one leg. "Soon we'll be able to predict Shishkin's behavior in complete detail!"

Grinning, Malyshev followed him.

"Would you like me to predict one more detail? In two days an institute staff meeting will be held at which Shishkin will make mincemeat out of address 001. That's you, brother! He's going to deliver a report on discipline and the status of our projects."

"Is that so?" The smile on Kaimenov's face faded. "H'm. . . . Listen, suppose we figure out Shishkin's report . . . we can do it on M-117. That would be a package of dynamite, all right! Eh? But . . . no, it won't work. It's too complicated. OK, we have enough material without it. All we have to do is figure out a good way to present it."

"Not 'we'," Malyshev shook his head. "After yesterday, I've had it. Count me out."

Suddenly Kaimenov began to put two and two together. He turned pale.

"Sergei, you don't really mean it?"

"I do."

"Was your conversation with Shishkin on the level? Listen, you won't say anything at the meeting about that incident, will you?"

"Well, after all, it happened, didn't it?"

"And you're doing this for an apartment and a degree?"

"Oh, cut the dramatics!" Malyshev barely managed to control himself. This wasn't an easy conversation for him. "You mean, have I betrayed you? Yes, I have. But for a good price. That's not to comfort you, but simply to clarify matters. The apartment plus a degree is worth a helluva lot more than your juvenile pranks. And, brother, you can shove that up your M-117."

Kaimenov lit a cigarette and glanced thoughtfully at Malyshev.

"So, address 100, you couldn't hold out."

Malyshev blew up.

"You mean you couldn't! All you could do was shoot your big mouth off and call Shishkin a 'damn fool.' And now you regret it. . . . What about the rest? You didn't go to Pantaleev or the Party Bureau to stand up for the fellow that Shishkin turned down. You latched onto his 'rejected,' and that was that! When Pavel Nikolaevich gave you an impossible deadline, you didn't raise a stink about it, but insured your own neck with a piece of paper. You passed the buck on to him. And at the seminar. . . . You know, Pantaleev was right: if you knew, why the hell didn't you speak up?"

"Listen, we were conducting an experiment! We would have ruined everything."

"An experiment! . . . What the hell will we prove with it? Sure, we'll lay out our packages, and then? Again Valentin Georgievich will say 'so what?'. I'm afraid you're barking up the wrong tree. You picked the wrong situation to replace a man with a computer."

Volodya slumped dejectedly into a chair.

"Ugh, why do things always turn out wrong for me?" Bewildered, he shrugged his shoulders.

"Do you want some good advice?" said Malyshev condescendingly. "Feed the computer—and play it straight—your circumstances and goals. Then check the optimal variant. Maybe you can still manage to rescue your digits."

"I see you're overflowing with good advice." Kaimenov looked at him sharply. "My goals? I'd have too much to translate into binary digits, Sergei. I love research, yes, research, and not any benefits connected with it; I want our science to help people live better, more interesting, more honest lives; I can and love to dream up ideas; I don't want to lose my self-respect by making concessions to the Shishkins; and I feel sorry for you. I'm afraid I can't select either logical circuits or standard programs for all this. So, what will be, will be."

He rose and slipped off his lab coat.

"Calm down! Nothing much is going to happen," Malyshev tried to reassure him. "You're a talented fellow and everyone knows and appreciates it. The worst that can happen is that you'll be reprimanded and transferred to another section. And that's all."

Pulling on his jacket, Kaimenov looked at him with interest.

"I'm not afraid of that. . . . You know damn well I'm not. You simply need to pull me down . . . to your level, so it eases your conscience. And another thing, Sergei. Now even you can be simulated on the computer. Why do you think it was relatively simple to program Shishkin? I'll tell you—because he lives like a worm and not like a man. So, there you are. . . . Good luck!"

Kaimenov left. Malyshev paced the room for a long time. Behind the latticed housing of Lightning's parallelepipeds, a rectangle of vacuum tubes glimmered warmly, and rows of neon lights twinkled seductively on the control panel, but Malyshev continued pacing, smoking, thinking. Finally he shook his head, put a stack of paper on his desk, and sat down to work.

He left the Institute after midnight.

A few other windows on the Institute's second floor remained lit up unusually long that evening: Shishkin sat in Valentin Georgievich's office, preparing his report. His face was set in a very meaningful expression.

How shall I describe the meeting? I can still muster up sufficient prose to tell you how the steady murmur of voices died down in the filled conference room; how the Workers' Presidium took its place on the platform next to a long table; how the chairman of the local trade union committee opened the meeting and gave Pavel Nikolaevich the floor for his report on "Improving labor discipline, increasing productivity, and our tasks"; how the faces of the audience reflected resignation to its fate.

But when Pavel Nikolaevich climbed to the podium, beneath the slogan "There are no shortcuts in science"; when his face, wearing expression No. 4, reflected concern, determination, dedication to science and all higher authority, and pure grief for heroes fallen in battles in which he, Shishkin, did not have occasion to participate, and the satisfaction of knowing that these sacrifices were not made in vain.... When, in a powerful voice, vibrating imperceptibly with tension, he said: "Comrades, during the preceding period our collective . . ."

. . . No, I cannot go on. Words fail me!

Actually, it was an ordinary report. Nothing unusual about it. It discussed the need to expand the role of cybernetics in the light of the last Plenum's decisions, and to participate in the struggle to implement those decisions. And it called for an end to shortages. Kaimenov's name was mentioned three times: in connection with the incident at the conference where he expressed his opinion about Academician Feofan Stepanovich Mezozoisky; in connection with his frequent lateness to work and disruption of labor discipline; and toward the end, Shishkin referred to the country's Kaimenovs.

Kaimenov sat toward the front, his face displaying a mixture of arrogance and disbelief. From time to time subdued conversations arose here and there and papers rustled in the rows. Valentin Georgievich, in the Presidium, was looking through papers and nodding rhythmically to the speaker. Suddenly he removed his glasses and peered almost sullenly at Shishkin. Then he returned to his papers. Sergei Malyshev pulled out a package of cigarettes and cast a sidelong glance at the door. He was dying for a smoke.

The speaker received scattered applause. Now the floor was open for discussion. Doctoral candidate "Smiley" Alper-Sidorov ascended the podium and rumpled the hair around his bald spot in embarrassment.

"Naturally new trends should be welcomed . . . and Pavel Nikolaevich's initiative as well—that is, his decision to distribute the text of his report before the meeting. This saves time and gives the staff the opportunity to plan its speeches—and all that sort of thing. . . . But, evidently, this time there was a regrettable lack of coordination. Pavel Nikolaevich, I would like to ask why, in view of its prior distribution, the report had to be read to us?"

"What are you talking about?" Stunned, Shishkin stared at him. "I did not distribute it."

"What do you mean, you didn't distribute it?" Alper-Sidorov smiled gently and drew several folded pages from the breast pocket of his lab coat. "I have the text, and it's all in here: about improving labor discipline in the light of problems related to the development of cybernetics; about Vladimir Mikhailovich Kaimenov . . . and even a reference to our country's Kaimenovs, and all that sort of thing. And about the fresh upsurge of creative activity, and the unprecedented enthusiasm for work—it's all here!"

Pavel Nikolaevich's face slowly turned ashen, and a deathly hush fell over the room.

"With your permission, I can clarify the situation!" Valentin Georgievich rose. "The fact is that the text just shown to you by Semyon Borisovich Alper-Sidorov was composed without Pavel Nikolaevich's knowledge and independently of him on an electronic simulation discrete action computer—the M-117." The dead silence exploded into an uproar.

"I have the data," Pantaleev waved a package of papers, "about a very original independent experiment, conducted by two members of the computer operations section, Vladimir Mikhailovich Kaimenov and Sergei Alekseevich Malyshev. Here are input tables, programs, output data, decoded results. . . . Using M-117 for one month, they predicted the actions of the subject of their research—Pavel Nikolaevich Shishkin. With your permission I, as the experimenters' involuntary timekeeper, shall acquaint you with this data. Since Pavel Nikolaevich is my assistant director and I am familiar with most of his administrative and scientific functions, it is all the more appropriate for me to do this. . . ."

While Valentin Georgievich read and commented on the contents of the packages, hushed silence and explosions of laughter alternated in the auditorium. Kaimenov and Malyshev were poked in the ribs and slapped on the back. "Great going! You sure gave it to him!"

"I can understand your surprise," continued the director. "We are scientists, working in cybernetics. Although, with our research papers and occasional hasty statements, we supply the press with grist for the mill, for their 'machine replaces man' twaddle, we ourselves understand that to replace a man (and particularly to simulate him) with a computer, is an unrealistic task today. I personally feel that this task will remain beyond our reach for a long time hence; and the task of simulating any person, any individual, appears insoluble. So, how did they succeed? Let's try to analyze it. As you know, three main factors determine the intelligent behavior of a system: knowledge of the setting, the existence of a goal, and the potential for achieving it. To code the setting, the experimenters used objective data prepared by Vladimir Mikhailovich Kaimenov for the 'electronic organizer' algorithm. In view of the computer's limited capabilities, naturally another factor was added: the simulated subject was incapable of producing creative solutions. But the main thing," Pantaleev raised his hand, "was that the experimenters figured out the subject's basic goal, which subordinated everything else: personal success at any price!"

(At that moment Pavel Nikolaevich's face was a dead giveaway: even without M-117 it was obvious that he was capable of an awful lot of things. The way he glared at Pantaleev, Kaimenov, and Malyshev, and everyone! If looks could kill . . . I certainly would have hated to witness that man's feelings translated into action. . . .)

"I'm sure you all remember Professor Walter Ross Ashby's brilliant paper, in which he demonstrated that knowledge of a goal increases a thousandfold the possibility of predicting the behavior of a system accurately—because a system consisting of innumerable possible behavior variants realizes only those that lead to goal fulfillment." Pantaleev paused. "Man is the most complex of systems. He might have many goals. But when, for example, one goal, particularly a goal like this, subordinates everything to itself, then...."

Valentin Georgievich smiled in Kaimenov's direction.

"You told me, Vladimir Mikhailovich, that you fed the computer fairly calculated scales, carefully considered instructions, objective information about society, and even information about Party decisions that determine the life of our science and our country. Still, the computer cranked out solutions of very limited application. I will go even further: if you had fed M-117 works of the great thinkers, the music of Mozart and Beethoven, the works of the brilliant poets—that same goal would have dominated everything. No stone would have been left unturned to achieve his goal—personal success. That's a terrifying goal, comrades! It ravages the mind and plays havoc with our emotions, turning everything to dust: generosity is calculated to win attention and esteem; love is sought with an ulterior motive; loyalty is given not to duty, but to whomever is the most powerful at a given moment.... And if such an individual does not commit vile deeds, it is not because he is repulsed by villainy, but only because he fears entrapment. To describe such a situation cybernetically, you would say that the individual is impoverishing himself in terms of information. Incidentally, you might think about the reason for this phenomenon: such impoverishment could be due to the fact that in many people only a very insignificant fraction of neurons and ganglions function. All the rest do not work toward that narrow utilitarian goal—and, consequently, are unproductive. What happens in the end, unfortunately, is that *the individual descends to the level of the computer*, rather than the computer rising to the individual's level. I am terribly sorry to say that the extremely offensive representations of Pavel Nikolaevich Shishkin's personal goals and their fulfillment potential were fully confirmed by the experiment...."

All eyes followed Pantaleev as he shifted his gaze toward Shishkin's seat. It was vacant....

After the meeting Malyshev and Kaimenov headed for the computer room. Today was their turn on the night shift. In the corridor Kaimenov, breathing heavily, shoved Malyshev in the chest. Malyshev flew toward the wall, breathless. With a determined expression, Kaimenov struck Malyshev twice in the ribs and then aimed for his face.

Malyshev turned in time.

"What the hell are you doing?! Watch out. . . . I can clobber you too!"

"Damn you, you ruined everything! How could you?! Do you think this was the last time we were planning to try this sort of thing? After this, how can I trust you?"

"Well it's like this. . . ." Malyshev fidgeted with his jacket. "What's wrong with trying some new behavior variants?"

"There are variants that you don't try on yourself. Damn, can't you get a simple point through your thick skull? We must not doubt each other. Never, not under any circumstances! You and your 'behavior variants'!"

They passed through the echoing corridors, unlocked the door and descended into the darkened computer room. Moonlight streamed through the window and bathed the room in a watery green glow. Malyshev turned the switches on the panel. Rows of fluorescent ceiling lights flashed on and the air conditioners began to purr.

"OK," Kaimenov was calmer now, "show me how you programmed Shishkin's report. How did you pull that off? I was dead sure that M-117 couldn't handle such a problem."

Sergei threw the switches on Lightning's control panel.

"I'm afraid I have a lot of apologizing to do to Valentin Georgievich," he grinned. "I misled the old man. . . . You see, you're right: it is an impossible task for M-117. I simply sat down and wrote that report. In two evenings."

Stunned, Kaimenov sank into a chair.

"We went completely overboard with our computer analog," continued Malyshev. "Even you yourself remarked that its solutions were surprisingly banal. Shishkin really operated in line with the algorithms you predicted: 'I scratch your back, you scratch mine'; 'Smart people take the easy way out', ... 'An eye for an eye'. . . .

Everything was correct. . . . In brief, you don't necessarily need cybernetics to figure out people like Pavel Nikolaevich. You can figure them out yourself."

For a long time Kaimenov said nothing. His eyes darkened and narrowed.

"What the hell did I knock myself out for?" he exclaimed.

The Pale
Neptune Equation

MIKHAIL EMTSEV and EREMEI PARNOV

MARK WAS ORPHANED AT FOUR when his parents were killed during a stellar flight. The triple role of father, teacher, and nursemaid was undertaken by his uncle, the querulous and pedantic scientist Professor Kranovsky, whose tall, gaunt figure recalled Don Quixote.

When the child began to make friends with the neighborhood children, the professor's ego was hurt: his nephew preferred the company of screeching little devils to quiet evenings of leisurely conversation with his uncle.

Hoping to discipline the youngster's curious and impressionable mind, the professor began to teach him Latin, against the advice of teachers from the grade school Mark was scheduled to enter in the fall. One fine day, to the professor's dismay, Mark gleefully spouted *Eenie meenie minee mo* instead of reciting Cicero's famous oration *O tempora! o mores!*

"Ninka taught it to me!" said the boy, catching his breath.

The professor managed to conceal his keen disappointment. He tried to recall his own childhood, but it was veiled by something hazy and elusive, like a forgotten fragrance. Always trying to restrain his emotions, he did not shower the boy with expressions of affection or stuff him with sweets. But when Mark fell asleep, Kranovsky would tiptoe to his bedside and carefully touch his dry lips to the hot little forehead.

His nephew's entire future was precisely mapped out in the professor's mind: he visualized Mark in a lecture hall among his fellow students; or he saw him as his assistant, a dream that had never faded since the day he began to feel the years catching up with him. Kranovsky even pictured himself as a stooped, white-haired old man, solemnly transferring his chair to a young energetic successor. But everything turned out quite differently.

Mark would never be a university professor: he had chosen a different path. Perhaps a better one. At any rate, a different one.

The old professor was sitting in his study. It was evening, but he didn't turn on the lights. Almost two weeks had passed since Mark's return to Earth, but he still hadn't found the time to visit his uncle. Twice he had videophoned; his face flashed on the screen briefly and disappeared. From the embarrassment and anxiety the professor detected on Mark's face, he realized that something was wrong.

"Strange," thought the old man. "Oh, well," he quickly dismissed it, "he probably feels guilty."

Mark had been away for seven years. When Kranovsky had seen his nephew off to Fomalhaut, he told himself that they were parting forever. "Forty-six light years," he had thought bitterly. "Mark will have aged slightly and I will have passed on."

Of course Kranovsky was familiar with Bruno Reich's new theory, but he was an inveterate classicist, steeped in the teachings of Einstein and Heisenberg. Reich's time paradox, based on the deceleration of a body in its own gravitational field, impressed the professor as nothing more than a brilliant exercise in abstract mathematical formulation.

But Reich was right: a still youthful Mark returned to find his uncle a very old man.

"People have outwitted time, and I must retire. I might as well face it," brooded Kranovsky, "I've grown old. Yes, turned into an old fogey, and before I know it I'll probably lose contact with my students. Well, that's life for you."

As Kranovsky stared through the black window at the brightly lit speeding cars and the violet sparks flying from power distributors, images of days long past flared up from the dark reaches of memory. Flared up and vanished in a motionless black pool of depressing senescent thoughts.

An opening door jingled. Kranovsky didn't stir from his seat or reach for the light. Resignedly he stroked his sparse white hair. As the door opened wider his heart skipped a beat; his whole being filled with a symphony of joy. Mark—Mark was home at last.

"Has the cat got your tongue, my boy?" Kranovsky asked cheerily.

"Uncle, I hardly know where to begin," Mark stammered and fell silent.

His nephew's hesitation was puzzling; Mark had always been so open and direct, with a frankness verging on rudeness.

"What's the matter? Afraid of giving me some bad news?"

"Bad news? About what?" Mark appeared genuinely surprised.

"All right. Then let's hear it—all of it!"

"We haven't seen each other for so long, Uncle."

"Well, let's get the greetings over with and get on with your story."

Mark smiled and gulped hard. "You know, Uncle, our choice of Fomalhaut was no accident. It's a star that—"

"Alpha Piscis Austrini. Luminosity—sixteen suns. Spectral class—A3. Seven planets," Kranovsky interrupted his nephew. "I know all that! Spare me the unnecessary details. At my age it clogs the brain. So, get to the point."

"OK, Uncle," agreed Mark, "but please don't interrupt me. And don't get angry. I know what I have to tell you. Listen carefully!

"The purpose of our mission was to test the graviconcentrators and establish Reich's parameters. Fomalhaut was a deliberate choice. It's not that far from our Solar System, and at the same time the round trip is forty-six light years. A wholly adequate journey to verify the transient effect of causal relativity theory.

"We flew at a constant acceleration, roughly the same as gravity.

As soon as we passed out of the Solar System we tripled our acceleration and turned on the concentrators. The circular gravitational field generated by the stellar ship elongated, concentrating on our path. So we had to constantly overcome our own gravity. The ship's instruments registered the effect immediately, but we couldn't know how terrestrial clocks were going; so, only after we returned to Earth and saw familiar faces did we realize that our experiment was successful. But that isn't the main thing, Uncle. Especially since you know all that from the psi-transmitter's bulletins."

Mark fell silent and stared vacantly out the window. The devil knows what ghosts he was seeing. Kranovsky waited a bit.

"Well, Mark, what is the main thing? Haven't you done enough already? You've made a great contribution to mankind. What could be more important than that?"

Mark's pale cheeks flushed as his heart began to pound; not a trace remained of his initial confusion and reluctance to talk. Rising abruptly, he began to pace the study and then halted behind Kranovsky's back.

"Uncle, don't think I'm crazy. I'm going to tell you something so far out. . . . Nobody—not a soul knows about it yet."

Mark paused again, as if to collect his thoughts.

Kranovsky smiled to himself. He wanted to thank his nephew for his trust in him but controlled the impulse.

"So," Mark began again, "for almost three years, according to our clocks up there, we headed toward Fomalhaut. When its pull was very distinct, equivalent to three solar masses, Alik Vrevsky, our commander, ordered me to cut the graviconcentrators' voltage. Then we switched on the engines. In this weightless state we equalized our field with the isograms of the nearest planet. We studied all seven planets. Five of them resembled Jupiter. Dense, gaseous spheres, lashed by electromagnetic storms. The outermost planet resembled the moon: a cold astronomical body, almost devoid of atmosphere. Only a pale green planet, fourth from the star, seemed more or less interesting.

"When we went into circular orbit, it seemed to us that the

planet's entire surface was covered by a greenish ocean.

"Our instruments registered a 190°–200° temperature range for Pale Neptune—that was what we named the planet. Water cannot exist in a liquid state at that temperature. Therefore we presumed, quite naturally, that the ocean consisted of some kind of liquefied gas. Spectral analysis confirmed that waves of liquid nitrogen were raging and foaming below us.

"On the seventeenth or eighteenth orbit around Pale Neptune we made out a very large island. A lead-colored plateau, completely level, probably two or three times the size of Greenland. I suggested we land and investigate the island, but the captain felt there was nothing to gain from it. He would permit us to descend only slightly. Basically he was right, and I didn't protest. We approached the nitrogenous ocean, dropping within some forty kilometers of its surface. Then I noticed that the island's coastline emitted a ghastly yellowish-green glow.

"The captain decided to send out a reconnaissance rocket. I took it out alone.

"White needlelike flakes whisked through the air. I didn't know what they were—frozen water, methane, carbon dioxide, or hydrocarbons. Only the strange phosphorescence interested me. Four kilometers from the island's surface, a soft ring sounded. The computer told me that the P-V-T had been calculated and the glow's spectrum analyzed. I pressed a button and another frelon tape with figures popped out. Nothing spectacular. At the boundaries between the solid and liquid nitrogen here, physical conditions were identical to those that are present when the density of liquid nitrogen becomes equal to the density of gaseous nitrogen. The difference between the phases disappeared, the surface tension dropped to zero, and a critical state with opalescence followed.

"I was disappointed. So, after recording the nitrogenous sea and the island on the cinemem, I returned to the ship."

Again Mark lapsed into silence. Kranovsky listened to his story without turning his head, although it was irritating to have the narrator behind him rather than facing him. Taking advantage of the pause, he swung around and asked: "Well, then what happened?"

Sensing his uncle's irritation, Mark dropped into a chair.

"We headed for home." Mark fell silent again.

"And then?"

"That was it. Nothing happened after that. Except here, on Earth, when I was preparing a report for the Physics and Mathematics Section of the Academy of Sciences and developing a few stills from the cinemem recording."

Again Kranovsky sensed that Mark was engaged in a painful struggle with himself.

"Listen, Mark. Listen, my boy, to an old man. If it's too difficult for you to tell me the truth—don't. I won't be offended. But if you've decided to share your secret with me, then . . . well, you know I'll always understand you."

To avoid revealing the painful emotions that had accumulated over the long years of loneliness and waiting, Kranovsky held himself in check and fell silent.

"I know that, Uncle," said Mark softly, "but . . . well it happened when my reconnorocket was returning to the ship. I was feeling great and was whistling some snappy tune. . . . Then, zzing! It was a narrow beam of some sort of radiant energy. It came from somewhere in space—not from Pale Neptune's surface. I'm sure of that. The cinemem motor began to drone softly. The cybers had switched it on automatically. They're programmed to deal with any unexpected situation. Then followed a chain of the most stupid mistakes and ridiculous accidents. Either I was too thoughtless or—I still don't understand why—that strange beam just didn't excite me. I figured it had as simple a physical explanation as the critical nitrogen's opalescence. I don't know. But that was my big mistake. Since I had decided that the energy ray was some sort of meteoric phenomenon in Pale Neptune's atmosphere, I didn't analyze its spectrum, and, most important of all, I didn't run off the cinemem reels until I was back on Earth. You can't imagine what was on them! The formula alone is a fantastic find. It's transcribed in our own mathematical symbols! It's puzzling. Part of it we know, part we don't. The first term is the same as in the Dirac-Heisenberg equation. Here, take a look yourself."

Whisking several photographs from his pocket, he handed them to Kranovsky.

Stunned by the meaning of Mark's words, the professor was speechless. Since Mark himself had experienced a similar shock, he could understand his uncle's reaction.

"You know, Uncle." he said affectionately, "it would be better if you examined the pictures alone. Relax and look them over, and I'll be back tomorrow morning."

Mark made such a hasty exit that Kranovsky couldn't have detained him even if he had wanted to.

The professor had been studying the prints for four hours, shots of crumpled sheets of paper covered with mathematical formulas. The last formula was circled. It was probably the final form of an equation.

$$\sum_{\gamma=1}^{4} \gamma_\nu \frac{\partial \psi}{\partial X_\nu} + K \left(\frac{\partial R_1}{\partial R_2} \right)_T \psi + \lambda \psi^3 = 0$$

Only three formulas similar to this one existed. Kranovsky didn't need reference books or computers to help him recall them; he could write them out blindfolded. After writing them out on separate sheets of paper, he placed them alongside Mark's prints.

A gust of wind swung open a vent, filling the study with March's cool, fresh breath. But Kranovsky was oblivious to everything around him: the past had taken over. Swirling through invisible layers of memory, it tore through his brain like a hurricane.

As he concentrated on the equation, he chewed the plastic tip of his pen and reasoned aloud, a habit acquired during his years of solitude.

"First of all we have Dirac's linear equation, which describes the behavior of de Broglie's electron spinor ψ waves. All right, here we have it:

$$\sum_{\gamma=1}^{4} \gamma_\nu \frac{\partial \psi}{\partial X_\nu} + \frac{2\pi mc}{h} \psi = 0$$

Now, the first term in this equation and the mysterious formula coincide. In 1938 Ivanenko used Dirac's equation to describe primary matter. The new variant differed from its predecessor by the addition of a nonlinear term:

"So, on the second sheet we have:

$$\sum_{\gamma=1}^{4}\chi_v\frac{\partial\psi}{\partial X_v}+\frac{2\pi mc}{h}\,\psi+\lambda\psi^3=0$$

"This variant is even closer to the formula from Pale Neptune. Both equations are identical relative to the wave function ψ. Only in the second term do they differ.

"Finally, we have one more nonlinear equation: the Heisenberg equation:

$$\sum_{\gamma=1}^{4}\chi_v\frac{\partial\psi}{\partial X_v}+\lambda\psi^3=0$$

"Here the second term is discarded. But the first and third terms match those in the equation on the photograph. That's all I know about the equation from Pale Neptune. Damn it, if this isn't some sort of hoax or ridiculous mistake, I don't know what it is! How the devil could an equation that could have originated only on Earth, yet is unknown to our scientists, end up in another solar system? No, this is utterly impossible! It boggles the mind."

Kranovsky rose slowly from his desk and paced the study. Unable to make any headway, he returned to his seat. After two more futile hours he pulled the videophone toward him and dialed the Physics Department. The plump, rosy face of Volodya Volkov, a graduate student, flashed on the screen.

"Hello, Volodya! How are you?"

The young man smiled and greeted the professor.

"Volodya, I don't feel well today and can't attend the seminar. Please ask Alexander Maximovich to take my place. Oh, and something else. I'm going to give you a little formula. Take it to the computer center and have it encoded immediately. Then go to Central Information and give them the code and algorithms."

Volodya nodded and assured Kranovsky that his instructions would be carried out to the letter.

"Professor Kranovsky," he stammered, "have you had a chance to look at my thesis abstract?"

"I'm sorry, Volodya, I haven't read it yet. But it's on top of my desk and I'll certainly get to it this week. And Volodya, as soon as you get a response from Central Information, call me. Is that clear?"

Kranovsky wrote down the formula quickly on a white frelon sheet and placed it against the screen. A minute later he switched off the machine, took some drops, and lay down to rest on the sofa.

The sound of a bell tore sharply into a muddled dream. For a second Kranovsky was dazed, until a second ring helped him cross the harrowing border between nightmare and reality.

Kranovsky opened his eyes. How dreary and dull his room was; the windows were bathed in the watery blue of an autumn evening. Crossing over to the videophone, he turned it on. It was Volodya calling; he had just received a processed card in Central Information, a reply to the professor's inquiry about the formula from Pale Neptune. But Volodya's words fell on deaf ears: the professor's eyes were riveted on the white tape with perforated edges which was in his student's hand. Kranovsky sharpened the focus. Names he had known since youth instantly caught his eye.

"Yes . . . yes . . ." he whispered. "Nineteen twenty-five. Louis de Broglie hypothesized that primary matter must be spinor and possess a spin of 1/2."

This was old, familiar territory: Dirac, Ivanenko, Brodsky, Mirianashvili, Kurdgelaidze, Werner Heisenberg. After 1958 nothing new had been done.

Blank lines leaped across the screen. The professor sighed with disappointment. Suddenly annotations to his inquiry flashed the familiar names of authors of the world's geometrical unity: Weyl, Eddington, Cartan, Kalyutsa. . . . Finally, Einstein, Fok, and Markov.

More names, data, and bibliography followed. As Kranovsky's initial tension subsided he skimmed through the long list calmly, hoping it would end soon.

"Aha, at last!" he mumbled.

Suddenly he detected an unfamiliar name amidst the fine print.

Victor Mandelblat, 1938, no publications (indicated by a hole punched on the third line), source: personal archives of Charles Cronford, Professor of History, Oxford University, London, Bloomsbury 6/12.

That was all.

Volodya's smiling face reappeared on the screen.

"Volodya! Get me a ticket to London. I can leave . . . well, even tomorrow morning. . . . Yes, in the morning. Thanks, Volodya!"

Turning off the videophone, Kranovsky sank into a chair and began to drum his fingers on the desk. He didn't turn on the light: it was easier to think in the dark. And he had a lot to think about. First of all, he still had mixed feelings about the mysterious formula. But he had to face this problem squarely right now. He had only to answer one question unequivocally: did he believe Mark's incredible story? Yes or no?

He took a sheet of paper and drew a line down the middle of it. On the left side he wrote "for," on the right "against."

As he was about to set down the first argument, he realized that his deep affection for his nephew might influence his conclusions about the formula.

"Damn it! How can I believe his story? I can't. But that would mean I doubt Mark . . . and his relationship to me."

Suddenly it occurred to him that Mark hadn't shared his discovery with the rest of the crew. Why hadn't he told Alexander Vrevsky? Or Shubenko, the navigator? That would have been a normal reaction, and the proper thing to do. No question about it! He must discuss this with Mark. Then he would see.

Still, why hadn't Mark told them anything? Or had he? Of course, something could have prevented him. Maybe Vrevsky got sick and was laid up on the Moon? Yes, he would have to get this straightened out.

Breathing a sigh of relief, Kranovsky turned on the lights and brought the photographs closer to his face for another thorough inspection.

It was late evening when Mark returned, very tired but more confident and determined than he had been earlier. Kranovsky caught himself ready to pounce on his nephew, as if to trap him in a lie.

"Getting ready for bed, Uncle?" asked Mark as he entered the study.

"Not yet, Mark. I must have a talk with you."

Mark crossed over to a chair.

"Tell me, Mark," began Kranoysky as soon as the young man sat down, "what does the rest of the crew think about all this?"

Shrugging his shoulders vaguely Mark mumbled with some embarrassment: "Alik became very ill as soon as we returned to our System. We left him with Waters at Lunar Spaceport No. 8. But I'll certainly tell him about it as soon as he's feeling better."

"And Shubenko?"

"I talked to him . . . day before yesterday."

"Well?"

"The whole thing is pretty complicated, Uncle. It's hard for me to explain it to you. None of it makes any sense. With Shubenko . . . well, I don't know how to put it."

Kranovsky sensed that Mark was struggling with himself, debating whether or not to reveal something very distasteful to him.

"With Shubenko it's completely different," he continued, now jabbering as if he had leaped over an invisible obstacle. "It's awfully complicated."

"I don't follow you," said Kranovsky drily. His irritation was growing, but Mark stopped him with a gesture before he could resort to stronger language.

"Shubenko doesn't want to have anything to do with it," Mark fumed. "If only Alik were well! Shubenko is a slippery character. . . . You know, Uncle, he was very interested in everything, looked at everything, and asked a lot of questions. Then he said we'd better forget about the whole thing—at least for a while."

"But why?" Kranovsky was utterly mystified now.

"Oh, Uncle! Why, why? And do you really believe this stuff? You,

Uncle? Even Shubenko says its senseless to raise suspicions about the great experiment we performed to verify the Reichian effect. No one would believe us. You just can't believe it. It's impossible. And there's no proof!"

"No proof? What the devil is all this?" He pointed to the pile of photographs.

Mark gestured helplessly. "The pictures—they're no proof.... The cinemem's assembly wasn't sealed."

"What do you mean?" Kranovsky was startled. "Oh, Lord," he thought, "things are going from bad to worse."

"Mark, I know that cinemems are sealed before lift-off and only authorized personnel of the Academy of Sciences can remove the seal. And then only on Earth."

"Well, there was a whole series of ridiculous accidents," continued Mark. I can't account for it. But Alik was careless and got hit by radiation."

"How did that happen?"

"I don't know. I was on duty at the graviconcentrators and was very busy. When I returned to the lounge, I found Alik lying on the floor with a bloody head. The cinemem was smashed, practically in splinters. Shubenko was in his seventh day of ambiosis. I got him up. Alik came to only once. And not for long. Told me he had been blinded suddenly and fallen. I asked him what he was doing before he fell. He said he was going to put the cinemem in the rigid container where he had just placed the reels."

"Why was he doing that?"

"That's always done when you approach the System. Who knows what can happen. Documents must survive any disaster.... Where was I?"

"Alik was blinded suddenly when he was standing by the cinemem, and he fell."

"Oh, yes! I asked him where he was when the radiation hit."

"What makes you think it was radiation?"

"I examined the fundus of his eye. An analysis of latent changes indicated a recent momentary radiation strike."

"Neutrons?"

"No, more likely rho mesons. We wondered where this could have happened. Alik couldn't remember anything. He had stepped into space only once, when I was in the reconnorocket over Pale Neptune. Said he wanted to grab a breath of 'fresh air.' Since he was wearing a superprotective spacesuit, it was a perfectly safe thing to do. Suddenly, when he was directly over the island, he felt an instantaneous flash and sharp pain in his eyes. But since everything passed immediately, he didn't pay any attention to it."

"But you said he was wearing a superprotective suit!"

"It will protect you against everything except rho mesons. You don't get them in natural decay, so why bother with a filter? That's really a mystery too: where would rho-rays come from on that damn island? I'm beginning to think Alik was hit by the same radiant energy beam that gave us that strange formula."

"Yes, indeed, a remarkable coincidence. . . . Then what happened?"

"Alik lost consciousness again. We left him on the Moon. Waters says he's recovering and will be fit as a fiddle again. But it will take at least a year."

"All right, let's assume that Alik smashed the equipment when he fell. Then how did you get these pictures?"

Mark stiffened. Containing his anger, he replied in slow, measured tones:

"The cinemem's assembly can be wrecked, but the diamond indium memory units are indestructible. I picked them out of a pile of twisted fragments and put them in my pocket."

"Splendid! They're numbered, and you could have turned them in on the Moon as soon as you landed!"

"Oh, Uncle! Of course I could have! But I forgot to. I was too upset over Alik's accident. I simply reported that the equipment had been smashed. Look, if it weren't for those damn formulas, it could never occur to anyone to accuse me of . . . pulling a hoax. OK, so I forgot to turn in the memory unit of the wrecked cinemem. Is that a sin? God, if only I'd known what that unit contained. I'd never have forgotten to turn it in. But I thought the only thing of interest aboard was the results of the Reichian experiment. And the cinemem had nothing to do with them. It was really a vicious circle of ridiculous coincidences. Shubenko was right. We've got to keep our mouths shut!"

"So, keep it shut! Who's forcing you to talk?"

"Uncle! How can you say that? You know very well I can't remain silent after seeing something like that. Neither could Alik. Nor you. But the main thing is that no one can help me. The most extraordinary, most fantastic fact in the entire history of the world, and not a single formal proof! Don't think I'm giving up so easily. Oh, no, I'm going to put up one helluva fight! I won't leave a stone unturned until I get to the bottom of this. I just feel rotten that things had to turn out this way."

"Listen, Mark. I understand and I'll try to help you. I have one lead. True, it may come to nothing. In that case we'll wait until Vrevsky's better. He'll confirm that he broke the equipment in flight."

"That won't help," Mark threw up his hands. "He'll say he broke it. So what? How about the memory unit I didn't turn in! Who knows how I could have tampered with it all the time I've been back?"

"Shame on you! Do you really think someone's going to suspect you of that?"

"Uncle, look at the facts! The facts, Uncle! Only a madman would accept these Earth formulas brought here from another stellar system! Yes, only a madman. If only we had some other proof. . . . Certainly no one would dare insult a scientist by casting suspicion on him. But this is a totally different case! It's impossible to accept this stuff. You've got to have impeccable proof."

"Yes, Mark, this is a very difficult situation. In any case you must turn in the memory unit and include the formula in your report to the Academy. You've no choice. Whether or not they'll believe you is entirely another matter. In the meantime, you know what we'll do? We'll go to my office at the university."

"What for?"

"I have excellent projection equipment. We'll run off your reels."

"I remember every detail on them and can rattle them off to you right now."

"Never mind. I want to see every bit of it for myself. Let's go!"

First a bright band of light appeared on the screen. It was narrow and continuous, like a string. Then it began to widen and separate into strands, like a rope.

Kranovsky saw the inner surface of a gigantic cylinder. But only for an instant. He managed to distinguish the contours of an enormous, absurd-looking machine. The relic of an age when molecular and atomic electronics had yet to be born. The science of atomic structure was in its early infancy then; neither quantum generators nor semiconductors existed; and Landau had only begun his work on the theory of Helium II's superfluidity.

Suddenly a pair of hands flashed on the screen! Enormous masculine hands. Slender, nervous fingers with barely perceptible fuzz. They were smoothing out rumpled sheets of paper that had been ripped from a notebook. Kranovsky had already seen these pages on the prints Mark had shown him. He recognized the jerky, hastily written hand of the invisible author of the mysterious formula—a variant of the unified field theory.

The scribbled, rumpled sheets quivered on the screen. Then, like mirrors reflecting the sun, they lit up, and a flame flared somewhere inside the metal reptile. Bursting from the machine like an elastic whip, it danced in lightninglike rings and spirals along the cylindrical walls. Then everything vanished.

Now only the gloom of endless space and the unfamiliar contours of distant galaxies remained on the screen.

Kranovsky was shaken and bewildered. What he had seen stunned as well as elated him—a normal reaction for any scientist suddenly confronted with the Unknown. But he was no closer to a solution. In a split second he had seen so much, yet was still completely in the dark.

Kranovsky appreciated his nephew's silence. "Too many impressions for one day!" he thought. "Don't overdo it, old man. Remember, you're close to eighty."

He must go home. In the morning he would fly to London.

For the nth time Kranovsky turned over the sheet of crude paper carefully. Traces of paste and plaster on the back of the circular indicated that it had once been fastened to a wall. It was an echo from the past, from a period of incredible barbarism; but it was also a tribute to great courage.

The printer's ink was smeared in places. The years had darkened and blurred the man's face. Beneath the stains and blemishes left by time, Kranovsky thought he could make out a high receding forehead, sunken cheeks, and intelligent, attentive eyes.

In large print below the photograph was a five digit number: 10,000. Then, in finer print: "Ten thousand Reichmarks reward for information on the whereabouts of Martin Rille. His real name is Victor Mandelblat, Doctor of Physics. He is wanted by the Imperial Security Department."

Kranovsky translated it from Danish with difficulty.

There was also a notebook, in German, which appeared to be a diary. Its pages were brittle and yellowed. Here and there were the faded traces of ink and pencil. Initially it had received great care, then it became a relic, and as time passed it was forgotten. For many years it lay buried beneath stacks of folders and manuscripts. It was passed down to Professor Cronford by a distant Danish ancestor who had worked with the great Neils Bohr.

When Kranovsky had arrived in London in search of this notebook, Cronford was puzzled by his request. After giving it some thought, he shook his head skeptically and went into his archives. Kranovsky began to despair of ever seeing him again. But Cronford finally returned, gesturing helplessly: he knew nothing about the existence of a notebook.

Further inquiry indicated that the notebook had last passed through someone's hands at the beginning of the last century when the newly created Central Information Depository had conducted a complete inventory of documents in all major archives and personal libraries.

Were it not for a thorough search into every nook and cranny by

Cronford's niece, it is doubtful that Kranovsky would ever have held this unique human document in his hands.

At last I'm in Copenhagen! Am I dreaming? Or is everything I've left behind on the other side of the border a dream? An endless nightmare?

I lead a quiet, comfortable existence here. In the morning I drink excellent coffee topped with whipped cream. Although I no longer have to glance over my shoulder to see if I'm being followed, I can't shake the habit of turning often to study reflections in shop windows. My sense organs are hypersensitive. I remember how in Hamburg, in 1929, I could catch the sound of a coin dropping hundreds of steps away, even on a foggy or rainy day. I was starving then—but one gets used to hunger more quickly than shadowing.

Oh, you nation of militant idiots! How the gall in me rises when, obeying a powerful reflex, I am forced to look around me on the streets. God, I was so damn blind. When Einstein refused to return to Germany, I pricked up my ears, but. . . . The great man repeated his silent warning to me when he refused membership in the Prussian Academy. Even then I couldn't think things through to their logical conclusion.

Books were burned in public. Screaming frenziedly, the Brown Shirts tramped through the streets at night with their torches. But the first time I heard the idiotic words of their song, I merely laughed.

> When grenades burst apart,
> Joy thunders in my heart.

I just couldn't take them seriously. Who can take degenerates seriously? I remember one evening at the Heisenbergs'. They had come to Berlin for a few days. Laue, the Jordans, Born, old Futsstoss, quiet, intelligent Otto Hahn, and some other physicist. A red lamp shade cast sunset shadows on a dazzling white tablecloth. Tea steamed cozily. The cherry jam looked almost black, the sugar bluish. For some reason a deep melancholy pervaded the atmosphere. There are evenings when you feel the future opening up before you for a momentary glimpse. This was such an evening. I went out on the balcony. The night rustled softly, and the stars and the lights from Luna Park twinkled gayly. The Tiergarten's foliage looked deep blue, like thunder clouds fallen from the skies.

Some sort of premonition haunted and oppressed me: I felt I had only to concentrate hard, and I would see into the future; I would understand at last where we were heading. But I was afraid, perhaps because a terrifying answer was already smoldering in my unconscious.

Below me, probably on the second floor, someone was playing records. A crystal-clear, stirring female voice drifted through the tender night.

> I whispered a song, replying to the rustling in the night,
> And through it, sparkling, flowed love's immortal light.

God, how beautiful! Flows and sparkles, sparkles and flows. Like the Milky Way. Like a woodland stream on a moonlit night. Love's immortal light. Yes, everything will pass; everything will end. The streams of light flooding Unter-den-Linden and Luna Park are vanishing into infinity. But even light ages on its journey. As it tears through the invisible paths of gravitational fields it turns red and dies out somewhere near the boundaries of the universe. But the light of love is immortal. Its particles are invisible; its field cannot be quantized; but without it we cannot live. Without it life would become an absurd farce or a rational absurdity.

The song ended. Like a pale blue pearl the moon rolled out from behind the Reichstag dome. I returned to the room. A single step thrust me from a world of silence and halftones into a bright, irritating world of tea grown cold and the bland wares of professorial wit.

I studied my friends, as it were, from the side: quiet and genial Werner Heisenberg, who faintly resembles Winston Churchill, understands everything, but doesn't take everything to heart. Pascal Jordan, who looks like a priest from an El Greco painting, is convinced that the origin of the universe is unknowable and does not believe that universal constants are absolute. I'm afraid he won't understand me. Who knows—maybe we're all merely subjective ideas to him. What meaning can Hilter have for a man who rejects even the reality of the galaxies? Yes, he's a courageous man and can take failure. But its not the sort of courage one would care to adopt as a model. There is the courage of a fighter and the courage of a swashbuckler. In the eyes of a crowd even a coward can appear courageous.

The world is dying with us! How often Pascal repeats these words. But is such a world worth much? Should one bother fighting for it? To lose it would be no great loss; we take away with us only some insignificant part of the world, only a glimmer of a sparkling immortal light. When we come into this world we immediately acquire a right to everything: the sun, books, love, pain, and grief. While we are alive we are responsible for everything.

A spoon tinkled softly in a glass. Venerable Max von Laue squeezed a piece of lemon into his tea. The dark amber turned pale. I sat down next to Otto. He turned to me at once and, after patting his short stubby mustache with a napkin, was ready to listen.

"Otto!" I said softly, leaning toward him. "How is all this going to end?"

Hahn linked his long, slender fingers in a helpless gesture. The pulsing veins on his high forehead stood out sharply.

"The general feeling is that this situation can't continue much longer. They'll come to their senses. Hitler has come to power and will gradually calm down his riffraff. He doesn't need them anymore and will try to get rid of them. That's what many people think."

"But what do you think, Otto? What do you *really* think?"

"In any case the Nazis will lose the next election. The man on the street will no longer play the fool. It doesn't concern physicists at all. They are politicians; we are scientists. Governments come and go, but the business of physics goes on."

"What kind of physics, Otto?"

"What do you mean *what kind?*" Otto looked at me with consternation.

Poor Otto! A great, tireless worker, but a talented blind mole.

"I'm asking you, Otto, what kind of physics do you have in mind? Aryan or non-Aryan?"

Otto still didn't understand, so I spelled it out:

"My dear Otto! I shall probably not return to my alma mater. There's no room for me anymore at the Kaiser Wilhelm Institute."

"You're joking! They wouldn't dare! Old Nernst's favorite assistant!"

"They could do it to old Nernst, too. Even Archimedes."

"Has it really gotten that bad there?"

"The last time I was at the Institute all hell had broken loose. That pair of unscrupulous—"

"Lenard and Stark?"

"The very ones. A fat-faced, fat-necked district party official barged into the Institute. He had a whole gang with him from the Party's district office. They snooped everywhere, poking their Aryan noses into everything, handing out advice and instructions to the staff, and scaring the hell out of them. Then they called a meeting. When everyone had assembled, the Party leader marched around the room, pointing at portraits and demanding: 'Who's this? Who's that?' He ordered the immediate removal of Roentgen's portrait; ordered the Kaiser's shifted above the doorway and Hitler's hung in its place."

Suddenly the ladies shushed me. "Keep it down, for God's sake! Someone might hear you. Don't forget the times you're living in."

Werner shut the balcony door and turned on the radio. Now I could continue:

"Then the party official harangued us with a speech, spouting glib phrases from *Volkischer Beobachter* and interjecting low humor and coarse jokes. The speech was received with shameful and cowardly applause. The official frowned. Then Lenard rose and bellowed: 'Get up! Sieg heil! Sieg heil!'

"In all fairness I must say that hardly anyone responded to Lenard. Then he took the floor. You can imagine what he said. His program was clear: German science, anti-Semitism, attacks on the theory of relativity. 'The Institute will become a bulwark against the Asiatic mind in science,' he foamed at the mouth. 'We shall set our Aryan physics against Jews, cosmopolitans, and Masons!' "

"God, how sick! What a wretched mentality!" Hahn shook his head. "A ranting mediocrity! As if there is a German physics, an English physics, a Russian physics! Science is international; it laughs at borders."

"That's not my point, Otto. Would a real physicist talk of nationalism in science? Only a nonentity would, a nobody incapable of participating in the international physics you're talking about. So now these people have created a new physics for themselves. An Aryan physics. They certainly won't have to worry about competition, believe me. Unless, of course, that Party official wants to become a Doctor of Aryan Physics. All right then, Otto, so you say this doesn't concern scientists. . . ."

"No, it doesn't. Perhaps these are only temporary excesses. . . . These things die down and —"

"Who are you trying to reassure, me or yourself?"

"Most likely, myself, my dear colleague. It's a very sad situation. Lisa Meitner also feels it's time to act."

"Specifically?"

"She's preparing to leave Germany."

"Impossible!"

"Yes, my dear colleague, without her it will be very difficult for all of us. I'm trying to persuade her not to be in such a hurry to leave. Maybe the situation will change."

"You're right. There's no need to hurry. When the time comes, we can always manage to get out."

Oh, how blind I was then! But don't think it's so easy to leave your native land. To sever all ties. However, that's no excuse. What followed surpassed our gloomiest, wildest speculations.

I have never forgotten my conversation with Hahn. Maybe because two days later the *Junkers* dropped bombs on Spain—on Teruel and Guadarrama, bombs that split the world in two. Then began an endless nightmare, a National Socialist hell. They took away my laboratory, evicted me from my apartment, forced me off streetcars. In brief, I shared the fate of hundreds of thousands of people. I was not permitted to leave the country with my passport. I had no choice but to leave illegally, and for that preparations would have to be made. First of all I would have to leave Berlin. Encounters with friends who turned the other way and pretended not to know me were more painful than anything else.

Heisenberg and Hahn interceded for me at the chancellery but, it seems, without success. The only concession they gained for me was police permission to live in Norddeich Halle, a small seaside town where a close relative of Hahn's had a summer home.

Every morning I would stroll down to the cold, pale green sea. Its seething white-capped waves would well up at the shore's edge, peak for an instant like a bubbly mass of bottle glass, then come crashing down with hissing white foam on the glittering pebbles. The wind chased the gloomy low clouds and rustled in the sand dunes; the tall grasses quivered and the pinkish, thin-barked pines swayed from side to side.

"Only a fool expects a reply." I recalled Heine's lines. But I didn't want to leave the sea, although I did not expect it to answer the questions tormenting me.

Even then I realized that we physicists must present humanity with a weapon that, like white-hot iron, would burn the brown-shirted scourge from the face of the earth. To create such a weapon, scientific thought would depart from orthodox paths. Neither superpowerful explosives, nor supertoxic gases would be the ultimate weapons of fascism's destruction. I envisioned other forces, wrenched from nature itself, unfettered, and subject to our command. The energy of the cosmos, a tremendous attractive force between the particles of atomic nuclei; the terrifying secrets of space—this is where we must look for it.

I believed, oh, how desperately I wanted to believe, that humanity would stand firm in its great battle with barbarism and obscurantism, but I could do nothing to spare it from senseless sacrifices. I no longer doubted that war was imminent. Nor did I have any illusions about my own fate. The racial laws introduced in Germany were only the beginning.

But when I reflected on the future of science, all else faded into the background. Nothing, I thought, was accidental. Galvani discovered electricity; a century passed and it became a powerful force. We have penetrated the secrets of matter, space, and time. How many years until we bend these fundamental principles of the universe to our will? I can foresee the day when our aircraft and tanks will look like toys compared to the force that physicists will have at their command.

No, I thought, next time we scientists shall not be fools. Generals and ministers will not receive the new weapon from our hands; Hitlers and Mussolinis no longer will be able to threaten the world. It is only a matter of time until we can shout to the madmen: "Stop, or we shall destroy you!"

I returned to the summer house. What a surprise to find old Futsstoss in my room. We had never been very close; and least of all would I have expected, in times like these, a visit from Professor Adrien von der Futsstoss, descendant of many generations of Prussian junkers.

When I entered, Futsstoss rose and bowed, and I responded to his greeting with restraint.

"Professor Mandelblat, I have taken the liberty to disturb you about a very important matter."

"What can I do for you, my dear colleague?"

"You must leave here at once. Don't ask questions: I am not free to give you the details. But I can tell you that delay could mean death. If you have any reason to doubt me, read this letter. It's from Professor Hahn."

He handed me an unsealed envelope and I put it in my pocket.

"I believe you, Herr Professor," I said. "But where can I go?"

"Don't worry, everything has been arranged. I've brought you papers made out for Martin Rille, the name you will assume. And a little money. On Thursday you will meet Hugo Kaspersen, the skipper of a fishing boat, near the Arnsk Lighthouse. He's my gardener's brother. A brave and decent man. He'll help you get to Denmark."

"I don't know how to thank you. This is all so sudden."

"There's nothing to thank me for. I've always done what I've considered necessary. Are you going?"

"Yes. But I do think you should take care of Lisa Meitner first. Then me. I've heard she's still in Germany."

"Don't let that worry you. You'll meet her abroad. Anything else?"

"Well, yes. You see, Herr Professor, several years ago I built a unique device in my laboratory at the Kaiser Wilhelm Institute. I have reason to fear its use for criminal purposes. Although the probability isn't great, it can't be ignored. I'd like to take it with me. Or at least I must be convinced that it is destroyed."

"That certainly complicates matters . . . very much so."

"I have an idea. There is one component. A despinator. It will fit into a briefcase easily. Of course, if there's no choice, I'll leave without it. But I'd like to do everything possible to separate it from my device. I didn't have time to do it myself. The storm troopers charged into my laboratory and threw me out on the street."

"Make a sketch of your component and its precise location in your laboratory."

I did this. Futsstoss slipped a silver cigarette case from his vest pocket, clicked the lid, and rushed off to catch a train. We agreed to postpone my departure until Tuesday. But on Futsstoss' advice I left Frau Beatrice's villa and, under the name of Martin Rille, moved to the Kaspersen home in a fishing village.

When I went to say good-bye to Frau Beatrice (Hahn's relative) she had just finished cutting chrysanthemums in her garden. I told her I was returning to Berlin. Outwardly she expressed not the slightest pleasure at the news, but I thought I heard a sigh of relief. I can fully understand her feelings. God, what terrifying, barbaric times!

A siren howled. The lighthouse blinker flashing through the haze looked like a grease stain. The engine hummed steadily. Behind the stern remained a vast, restless concentration camp: Germany. Coastal lights receded, grew fainter, and then vanished in the fog. A cold breath rose from the invisible black sea around us, mingling with the smell of engine exhaust and fish. Hugo had caught the fish yesterday and deliberately left them in the boat. Beneath the faintly gleaming piles lay my despinator, carefully wrapped in cellophane. Futsstoss had risked his life to get it, and Hugo's brother, Johann, had delivered it to me.

Hugo had bundled me up in a warm woolen scarf. A sou'wester protected me from the damp, fresh wind. Feeling so warm and relaxed, I longed to drift off into sweet slumber to the murmur of the engine.

But I was thinking about my future in Denmark. Could I construct another machine quickly and resume my interrupted work? Work, work. Always work. My father was killed on the Marne in 1915; mother died when I was still a student. I had never married. My whole life had been devoted to work, with time out only for food and sleep. But even as I slept my brain never ceased its search for new approaches and unorthodox solutions to problems. I knew no other life, nor did I want it.

Perhaps I have cheated myself.

This was my first night on an open sea. The lighthouse had vanished. Neither starlight nor moonlight could penetrate the dense layer of clouds. Now and then a deep-bluish phosphorescence flickered on the cold, watery abyss around us.

As I watched it, I remembered the fading coastal lights and the candles going out at a concert in Vienna. . . .

Haydn wrote a symphony which he named the *Farewell Symphony*. Traditionally it has been performed in candlelight.

The candles, set on music stands, were lit in an enormous high-ceilinged concert hall. The hall smelled of heated wax. The crystal chandeliers and wall lamps went out; the wavering tongues of candles quivered. The first notes filled the hall. "And in them sparkling, flowed love's immortal light." When the orchestra began the final movement, the candles were burning low. Like waves the solo and duets rolled through the hall. One by one the candles went out, and like dark phantoms the musicians left the stage: a cello and French horn, a French horn and violin, two oboes, a violin and cello. The dancing flames were dying, but the music continued, flowing as passionately and naturally as an immortal, sparkling river. Finally only two violins remained—the first and second. Together they played on, and when they extinguished their candles, the music still rang in my ears. For me it was still there. I closed my eyes; I didn't want to watch the chandeliers and wall lamps lighting up or the musicians leaving the stage. If I opened my eyes the ringing in my ears would cease.

Yes, I remembered the candles dying out in Vienna and the coastal lights fading a short while ago. But now, in my mind's eye, I saw something else. I saw atoms and their nuclei vanish in my machine; I saw elementary particles fade away.

It happened one night in my laboratory in Dalem.

The transformers were humming steadily and cheerfully. Forked lightning, deep blue and amethyst, leaped between the terminals of powerful Van de Graaff generators. In their quivering reflections electric lights grew dim.

Bare branches of trees rapped against the laboratory's enormous arched window. Streams of rain poured down its panes like cascades of cosmic showers. Peat in the fireplace blazed brightly. But I couldn't get rid of a strange shivering inside me. I warmed my hands over the fire, then massaged my chest and shoulders, but the chill wouldn't leave me. Lines from Poe came to mind:

> Ah, distinctly I remember, it was in the bleak December;
> And each separate dying ember . . ."

Like a medieval practitioner of black magic I was preparing to ask nature an impertinent, blasphemous question. What are the primary building blocks of the universe? Surely, I was not the first to ask. How often these words had been repeated by wise men beneath the deep blue sky of Hellas, in the gloom of Chaldean temples, and amid the stony deserts of Judea. But how can simple nature comprehend the complicated, obscure jargon of human beings?

I went over to the lab table and turned on the power. The galvanometer pointer began to crawl slowly. The capacitor began to store energy. Then I filled the recorder with red india ink and turned on the tape feeder. After I rotated the potentiometer's handle, I aligned "10" with the notch: the discharges would be produced by impulses—power increases after each sequence. The galvanometer pointer quivered at the last line. I switched on the induction unit and set the capacitor at peak frequency. All the equipment worked beautifully.

I held my hands over the fire for some time and then pressed them to my temples. They felt like icicles against my face. The window stared at me like an enormous turbid walleye. The machine hummed. Lightning crackled. The quaint-looking components of the chamber housing the despinator cast terrifying shadows on the white tiled walls.

I knew that time was running out. I could delay no longer. I turned on the despinator. A barely perceptible sapphire ray appeared somewhere in the depths of the massive crystal prisms. I began to rotate the tuning dial slowly.... The ray narrowed to a hairline. Then I switched on the scanning rheostat to the second gilbert range. The tiny ray disappeared, and instead I detected a blue particle burning somewhere, far, far away, like a distant star on the ninth magnitude. I had only to press a black button and the capacitor would belch forth ever increasing amounts of this enormously powerful energy. All the elementary particles in the tiny blue star would change their spin to "1." The law of conservation of spin would not be violated here. A redistribution, as it were, would occur, which I called spin degeneration. If now we discharged the capacitor's energy, the star's density would increase sharply and the diameter of the degenerate particles would approach that of the smallest particle. What would happen then? Not a soul on this earth knew. I hoped the particles would disappear and turn into some sort of fundamental field. I pressed the button. The relay clicked behind me. The capacitor dumped the first load of energy. Without budging from the eyepiece, I slowly turned the dial. The blue star assumed a barely perceptible elliptical shape. Another load of energy! The ellipse began to resemble a dumbbell. I was now somewhere on the molecular level. Of course I was not seeing an actual molecule but only a sign that we had passed to a new level, where matter was fissionable. The relay clicked again. What the devil was this? The blue star had disappeared. Had something broken down? Suddenly I felt very hot. Dropping into a black leather chair, I wiped my forehead with a handkerchief. The relay clicked again. I rushed to the eyepiece, but saw only the blackness of an autumn night. What had gone wrong?

Suddenly it dawned on me. Matter is continuous and discontinuous: a great unity of opposites. I had crossed to the molecular level, but still hadn't reached the atomic level. I would have to wait!

About an hour passed. The white mould outside my window had taken on a bluish tint. The energy rose seventeen billion times; and right then I saw my precious sapphire speck again. The dial was becoming a crude focusing system. I began to turn the vernier knob. The image continued to grow sharper and more distinct. The star bifurcated! I tried to figure out what was happening. Evidently this was the same molecule, but instead of a whole molecule, I was seeing its component parts—the atoms of some gas's diatomic molecule. Perhaps this was even the nucleus?

Suspense-filled hours dragged on. The screen was dark for three and a half hours, and I had despaired of seeing elementary particles. It was pitch-dark outside. Most likely my laboratory was the only inhabited one in the whole institute. I went over to the sink and wet my temples with cold water. I told myself that there was probably a limit beyond which man could not go. Suddenly the relay clicked, as if in reply to my thoughts. Although I had given up hope, I responded automatically: I went over to the machine and bent over the optical viewer. Again the star was burning against a black velvet background. Probably this was how the one and only guiding star had shone down from uncharted heavens to ancient mariners. I, too, had set out on a journey through "mare incognitum"; I, too, had been thrown off course and had lost all hope. But each time a tiny blue spark would flare up again and twinkle a friendly greeting. I sharpened the focus; the tiny star disintegrated into a multitude of microscopic dots. They kept fusing, flaring, and vanishing, only to pop up again and fade into nonexistence. Yes, I had seen the play of elementary particles, the changeable combination of changeable substances. They provided the relative stability of a microworld that appeared stable and eternal to us.

Then the elementary particles vanished completely: they faded out gradually, like the candles in the *Farewell Symphony*. After I had spent nine hours waiting for new sparks, Haydn's music began to ring in my ears. And, just as I had continued to hear the music after the orchestra had ceased playing, now, too, I believed that my star would flare up again.

Morning came. The fire had died out. The burned peat was coated with soft, yellowish ash. It was still raining, and cold, gray drops ran down the window. But I kept waiting. Suddenly it reappeared! I had kept my vigil.

I saw myriads of iridescent sparks. This was far beyond the threshold of elementary particles. I was seeing the subquantum universe! Perhaps it was even the precursor of matter. The ancient Greeks' *apeiron*, the primary building material of everything existent.

I was struck by the diversity of the shimmering dots. I couldn't shake off the feeling that I was seeing something very familiar to me. I photographed the spectrum, photographed the dots several times, even sketched them. Then I checked the equipment. Everything was in order. The relay clicked periodically. The capacitor was discharging oceans of energy. And only the counter, a standard electrical counter, spun madly—in reverse. My set-up supplied energy to the capacitor the instant the elementary particles disappeared.

Finally I pulled the switch and cut off the power. Collapsing in a chair I fell asleep.

The abrupt silence awakened me. The engine had stopped. Hugo was sitting beside me, carefully unscrewing the compass.

"What's the matter, Hugo?" I asked.

Hugo pressed a finger to his lips and pointed into the dark gray, foggy void. Peering into it I spied a blurred bright spot moving rapidly in the distance. Hugo signaled me to follow him into the cabin. Stooping to avoid striking the low ceiling, I climbed into a small bunk. An acetylene lamp, a tin of tobacco, and canvas mittens rested on a small folding table.

Hugo bent over and took a bottle of dark sweet beer from a box. He opened it and handed it to me. Then he picked up one for himself. After several gulps he said softly:

"Patrol. They won't notice us at night, in this fog. But it's getting light and it looks like we're going to have a bright morning. If they sight us we'll tell them that we went off course because our compass isn't working. I've unscrewed it already."

We went out on deck. How still it was. I heard nothing, but Hugo assured me that he could make out the rumble of engines.

For about an hour and a half we sat in absolute silence. Several times Hugo rose and listened. Finally he waved his hand:

"It's over! Looks like we slipped through."

He took the screwdriver from his pocket and fastened the compass back in place. Lighting his pipe, he went below to start the engine.

I felt great. The short nap on the silent sea had revived me amazingly.

Returning, Hugo announced we had about fifteen hours to go and suggested I go back to sleep. On deck or in the cabin.

"Don't you want to sleep? You must be awfully tired, Hugo."

"Who'll take over the boat?" he replied very calmly.

I went below, took off the sou'wester, pulled off my huge rubber boots, and lay down on a bunk covered with a camel's hair blanket. Outside the porthole it was still dark.

I caught myself waiting for a tiny sapphire spark to flare up. When you have absolutely nothing to do, your mind usually dips into yesterdays. The boat was rocking gently. . . .

I recalled the moment when the real meaning of my experiment had struck me. Now as then I was filled with an inexplicable horror and awe. Again, dreams drew me into the past.

When I suddenly realized what the distribution of the glittering subquantum dots resembled, I thought I was losing my mind. I even pressed my hands to my head and closed my eyes: I felt as if something precious was contained within my skull and it would spill out if I stirred.

For some time I remained in a stupor.

I had recognized a rough picture of the distribution of galaxies in the metagalaxy.

Was this merely coincidence, or did nature resemble a dog biting its own tail?

The idea was fantastic, totally unexpected. I was dumfounded: my brain whirled in a maelstrom of guesses and questions. I tried to get a grip on myself. After all, why not, why couldn't it be?

Our concepts of space are based on man's centuries-old experience and several dozen physics formulas. It all boils down to the existence of two infinites in nature: the infinity of the microworld and the infinity of the cosmos. By applying the word "infinity" to an elementary particle and the universe, we emphasize again their dialectical unity. In "infinity" we have the common element that compels us to arrange atoms and galaxies on one straight line, from the smallest to the largest and so on, until our imagination hits a stone wall or our limited mentality rebels. Then we resort to that old, reliable symbol ∞ and, extending both ends of the line in opposite directions, we think we understand space.

Considering large and small to be opposites, we artificially separate micro infinity from macro infinity. How our talent for shoving everything into cubbyholes misleads us at times! It's so contrived. Indeed, in nature the microcosmos is continuous and present everywhere in the macrocosmos. Nature is unified and integrated. So, that means there must be a place or, perhaps, an instant in time when the two great infinites merge into one, to demonstrate again and again the universe's physical unity. A time or place? Perhaps both? What had I seen in my machine? Maybe that's precisely what I had witnessed?

I was too excited; I should have taken a break, but I didn't have a minute to lose. . . .

I got up to go to the darkroom, to develop the film. After that I wanted to process the spectrum data. Only then could I be convinced that I wasn't losing my mind.

But at that moment the door flew open and into the room burst three stormtroopers. Long-visored, cylindrical caps; brown tunics;

pistol belts; red armbands with swastikas. What happened then is hazy.

I came to on the street. My white lab coat was smeared with blood and dirt. My clothes were torn, my face battered.

I never did get an answer to the question that had excited me so much. I had hoped then to analyze all the data and write an article. One copy would have gone to *The Annals of Physics*; two to England, to Rutherford and Eddington; two to America, to Einstein and Hubble; two to Russia, to Kapitsa and Fok; and one to Denmark, to Niels Bohr.

Wow, what a storm of activity it would have kicked up! Together, we would have rushed into the narrow breach accidentally left by nature. Before God would have had a chance to turn around, half a dozen physicists would have been settled in his innermost chamber, calmly working out their formulas.

Now I had only myself to rely on. All I could do was ponder the results of my experiment; I could check my surprising conclusions only from a purely philosophical viewpoint.

And so, nature resembled a dog biting its own tail. There was neither a microworld, a macroworld, nor the still larger metagalaxy. We invented it as a convenient tool, to simplify our understanding of a unified physical world.

Einstein proved the relativistic nature of our laws. Even such a dimension as length depends on velocity. Stoney expressed the idea of minimal spatial distance and minimal time: there is neither space nor time in space-time cells less than 10^{-45} centimeters long and where intervals measure less than 10^{-35} seconds. At least in our understanding. This is the elementary four-dimensional space-time volume projected by Stoney, Ambartzumian, and Ivanenko. It means the universe is not infinite in the direction of diminution. But what about enlargement?

We have Friedman's closed model of the universe. But is that definitive? Perhaps not only are the dimensions of space relative, but the principles governing the comparisons of these dimensions. We say that a kilogram is larger than a gram and an atom is smaller than a star. To us this seems very natural. But we don't say that an electron is larger than a photon only because it can emit photons. And, in general, to what limits are our concepts "larger" and "smaller" correct and applicable: is A greater than B because A consists of B? Perhaps there exist boundaries in respect to diminution and enlargement beyond which the concepts *larger* and *smaller* defy comparison. These comparative concepts are absent there; yet in the world we know we cannot function without them. We can say that the galaxy is larger than a photon, but no longer do we have the right to compare a subquantum particle with the metagalaxy!

Hooray! I think I finally found the answer. But I must tread cautiously: above all I must not be diverted or let my thoughts slip away. . . . So, between the time the elementary particles in my machine had vanished and the metagalaxy appeared, had I seen a world where the concepts *larger* and *smaller* were inapplicable? That interval was precisely the point where the dog bit its own tail! The soldering joint of a great ring . . . a ring, yes, a ring, and not a straight line. A ring whose both ends reached into the infinity of the universe and the infinity of the microworld. How right were those of my colleagues who maintained that nature was arranged far more simply than we had always believed. Yes, simpler and more cunningly. Let's try, I thought, to express all this mathematically. Thus we have Dirac's equation. If the wave function . . .

[Here several pages had been torn from the notebook.]

I am rushing to finish these notes. Not knowing why or for whom I am writing them frightens me more than anything else. Occasionally my mind wanders and images of loved ones rise before my eyes. I find myself telling my dear, ailing mother about the vicissitudes of my life. I must tell her how I managed all these years and what I thought about. But, as if afraid to distress her, I speak more of my hopes than my suffering. Then, when the faces of friends confront me in my reverie, I am reminded of my duty, and the pages are quickly covered with tensors and virials. I even toss off sketches of the machine, calculate parameters of the process, and determine optimum conditions. And then . . . I tear out the pages and burn them on my glass-topped desk, turning the brittle, shriveled lumps into black powder. With my handkerchief I wipe clean the brownish oily stain, similar to the trace left by mustard gas.

Sometimes I think about people like Hugo and Johann, or the workers, so calm and full of inner strength, at *Burmeister and Wein,* Copenhagen's largest shipyard. Disaster is spreading over the entire world like wildfire and will take many victims with it: the innocent as well as the guilty; Schicklgruber and his gang; and perhaps the maelstrom of history will suck in those who saw but remained silent, those who knew but did not resist. Maybe I or my colleagues will perish and not a single physicist will survive to live in that . . . that new world. And we shall be compelled to start from scratch again, avoiding all the old pitfalls.

I think about the simple and humble working people as my heirs. Having just destroyed pages of formulas, I am writing about myself for those who face the task of discovering what may disappear together with me. I argue with myself, get carried away, and lose the thread of my thoughts. When I hit a dead end, I grab onto my formulas, like a life buoy, only to burn still another page with my cigarette lighter.

So I'm writing rapidly and incoherently. My handwriting is large and the lines slant downward. When I meditate, I love to doodle, sketch female heads. Consequently, there aren't too many pages left in this thick notebook. I've probably written very little. In fact I've been at it for the past four days. I rise early, drink coffee from a large earthenware mug, eat two succulent, pink ham sandwiches, a small piece of chocolate, and a bit of marvelous cheese from a small cardboard container. Then I get my notebook and write without a break until dinnertime.

I dine in a charming, expensive little restaurant in peaceful suburban Hellerup. Shaded streets, high stone fences with wicket gates. Imposing bronze nameplates. Stern-looking villas that appear to be utterly uninhabited. Here the clatter of hoofs is heard more often than the whirring of tires. As I walk I glance over my shoulder frequently.

For dinner at the restaurant I usually have lamprey and shrimp, a bit of Russian caviar, and excellent beefsteak, English style—very rare. For dessert, Finnish cheese, soft as cream.

After dinner I stroll along the quiet, clean streets again.

I live near a port, a bustling, noisy place: chains screech, ships and sea gulls shriek, cables groan, and the swiveling platforms of cranes grate and grind. The water is always covered by a grimy, iridescent, oily film.

But when night falls, the water is transformed: it looks so deep, so dark, like a black mirror with varicolored snakes dancing on its surface. Mostly gold, some red and green, and very rarely, violet ones.

I climb five stories of a sooty six-storied house, to my little apartment. A large square room with a balcony, a white-tiled kitchen and bathroom. The kitchen is my all-purpose room where I prepare and eat breakfast, write and listen to the radio. I use the large room only for sleeping.

I open the English lock, hang my hat on the hat rack and go to the kitchen. I sit down at the table covered with blue and white flowered oilcloth and start to write. I write until late evening, without lighting my lamp, until the twilight of "white nights" sets in.

I am hurrying. It's possible that I won't have a minute to spare tomorrow. Never have I driven myself as I do here, in Denmark. I can't manage to catch up with the clock. The days, weeks, and months whiz by.

I received some money from Germany, from Dirac and de Broglie. Bohr also managed to squeeze a small sum from the Danish Academy. In general I have enough. I am speeding up the installation of a new machine. One of Niels's students had a splendid suggestion—that the ferrocapacitor be replaced by a gigantic Leyden jar whose outer surface would be the walls of a cylindrical laboratory. Energy would be discharged directly on the despinator's silver shaft. This would increase the device's resolving power considerably. I figured that if we placed a thin layer of Rochelle salt on a quartz plate, the dielectric constant [crossed out] . . . and potential well can be described by a circular integral with the limits of the exponent . . . [several pages torn out]

How I had dreamed of getting to Copenhagen! I am very familiar with Scandinavian literature and music, but it was the terse descriptions in Niels's letters that helped me visualize this great, foggy city.

The university, the academy, the majestic stock exchange,

Thorvaldsen Museum, and Rosenberg Castle's marvelous sandstone decorations: all this I had seen long before my arrival in Denmark. But I had never imagined that the morning mist above the sea and the remote hazy disk on the horizon could be so beautiful. For a long time I looked back at my invisible homeland to which I would never return. Train ferries were steaming in and out of port, and I kept watching the waves merge with the sky.

At the harbor the workers were stacking crates of oranges, rolling barrels of herring, and loading coal. Ripples lapped against the red sides of ships overgrown with mussels. Dark heaps washed in by the surf rotted near shore. Glassy water fleas hopped about, and sea gulls rocked on the water.

Over there somewhere other harbors were bustling too. Varnemunde and Hamburg.

Lisa Meitner had told me that Hahn and Strassman had split the uranium atom. Besides the fragments of fission, free neutrons had been liberated.

Lisa studied the kinetics of the process and believes that the reaction will become a chain reaction. I think she's right. Einstein probably erred, and it is possible to build an atomic bomb. The first alarming signs have appeared: Germany has prohibited the sale of Czechoslovakian uranium; the Nazis have gotten their paws on heavy water reserves. For a long time I wondered why they needed it. Evidently they are looking for a substitute in order to increase the probability of the neutrons' absorption by the nuclei. Apparently a great deal of progress has been made. I must hurry.

I smell danger, the acrid odor of gunpowder. Will they dare attack Denmark, too?

Bohr has barely managed to pack the most essential items into his roomy crocodile leather briefcase. Sitting in his laboratory, we endured those tense final minutes in silence. A car was supposed to pick him up and take him to Kastrup Airport. From there he would cross the ocean. He tried to persuade me to go with him. But I couldn't. It was physically impossible. There was so much to do, though I realized the experiment must be postponed until times were better. Would they ever come?

I must continue my work until the end. No matter what the cost.

Hitler has attacked Denmark and Norway. Soon they will be here. Maybe they are here already. For the past two days I've seen those cold-blooded mugs everywhere. Rain capes, ruddy chins, eyes staring past me into the distance like manikins. How familiar all this is! But I shall try to complete the experiment on time. I must!

Bohr was calm and cheerful.

"I'll be back soon!" he assured me.

I said nothing.

"I'll even leave something as security." Bohr rose to his towering height, crossed over to the lab table, pulled out a drawer and removed a small black suede box. Opening it, he held it out to me.

It was the Nobel medals of Franck and Laue, given to him for safekeeping.

Then he went over to the exhaust hood, took down a vessel, several bottles with fitted corks, and a calibrated funnel. Opening the bottle, he began to prepare some sort of mixture. I moved closer and read the labels.

So, that was it! Niels was mixing a solution known for its all-destroying action. *Aqua regia.* What the devil did he need it for?

The medals covered with bubbles. At first they bounced slowly on its surface, then faster and faster. The vessel began to seethe with hydrogen bubbles.

"Everything will dissolve immediately!" said Bohr cheerfully. Squinting, he half-turned to me to watch my reaction.

"Then what?" I tried to break the silence.

"Then what? I'll return here, to my lab. I'll electrolyze the contents of this vessel, precipitate the gold and have new medals stamped. Eh?!"

He looked at me, waiting for a response. I felt like crying. . . . Who cared about medals? . . . God, would we at least see each other again? . . . .

Farewell, Niels . . . Farewell!*

---

*Bohr did not manage to leave Denmark this time. He had to return but did not find Mandelblat. After a while resistance fighters ferried Bohr and his son Auge to Sweden. From there they were flown to England in the bombardier's compartment of a bomber. (Professor Kranovsky's note).

They are here. If only I can finish.... Seconds are precious. I'll give this notebook to the old porter. Why him? He cried when the little old Citroën drove Bohr away. Besides, there's no one else. When this scourge passes, everything I've put down here will be necessary and vital. Most important is the idea; even without me others will work out the rest of it little by little. I would like to leave at least the equation of a universal field, but I am afraid to. These days formulas are being cadged all too quickly. You can't work fast; you need plenty of time. Long years of struggle lie ahead. And who knows where my notebook will eventually turn up? Besides, can one man, no matter what he gives humanity, change the course of history? I believe in universal reason, in a sacred, unquenchable spark. The people will win. I, too, was with them in an hour of great struggle. But I shall not live to see their victory. I am dying, believing that victory will come. Now I shall tear out all the pages of formulas that I have not yet burned. If my experiment succeeds, I shall destroy them before I die. If it doesn't, they will perish with me. Thank you, dear old Futsstoss! Thank you, Hugo! No matter what happens the human spirit will survive. Farewell!

The entire page had been written in pencil. It could be read only under ultraviolet light. There was nothing more in the notebook.

Kranovsky got a pile of frelon paper and wrote the ending to this amazing story in a large firm hand.

"The facts end at this point. The trail ends above Domysl's unstable surface. But I say this with a certain hesitancy. Perhaps that is why I feel the need to add a few more details. A rigorous scientist might criticize me for it. But recent events have compelled me to review many judgments and opinions. I have revised my attitude toward those infallible, hackneyed truths on which our concepts of the world are based. I do not wish to draw any conclusions; I do not want to decide anything prematurely. What is needed here is careful, meticulous study, rather than hasty, rash conclusions.

"But I shall not digress. What else can we add to the accepted facts?

"Vrevsky returned to Earth after his illness and visited Mark and me. After seeing a picture of Mandelblat he claimed that he had seen his face in that instantaneous flash of brilliant light. This admission could be very significant or almost worthless. If Alik hadn't been aware of the latest stories coming from the news media; if he had known nothing about the formulas and notebooks, then. . . . But we must accept the facts as they are.

"I can list two or three secondary details, but I'm afraid of appearing biased. I shall await new data for the confirmation or rejection of a brilliant hypothesis.

"A few words about the formulas. They were subjected to comprehensive computer analysis and serious study at the mathematical Institute. Its scientists are inclined to believe that the sliding matrix $\dfrac{dR_1}{dR_2}$ described the shortest crossing between microworld and macroworld.

Mandelblat may have found the simplest path to the metagalaxy. And this path begins in the subquantum world. Everything indicates that the scientist, in his last experiment, succeeded in creating a single spinor field around himself and, after leaping across the criteria of dimension, landed in some sort of tunnel (that we know nothing about), in a space-time multiformity.

"Moving outside the time and space we know, a cluster of energy, which had burst into the cosmos long ago, accidentally encountered a stellar flight near Pale Neptune. . . .

"However, I think I'm beginning to fantasize, something completely alien to me.

"I remember Mandelblat's startling comparison of the universe with a dog biting its own tail. Mark was irritated and puzzled by it. He even began to doubt that a true classical scientist could say a thing like that. I fear that it is getting increasingly difficult for our young people to understand the past. I, for one, can still picture that brilliant galaxy of great physicists and indefatigable wags who changed the face of the world so powerfully.

"It's been a long time since anyone has smiled at the phrase *atomic pile*, although this 'strict' physics term was Fermi's own witty label. Sir Joseph John Thomson, the great English physicist, called his model of the atom *plum pudding*. And the explanation someone offered for nonconservation of parity was that God was a lefty. But a little humor never interfered with science's great advances.

"Fantasy spiced with humor is, after all, the most precious thing in the world. Of that I am certain.

"Lately I've been giving a great deal of thought to this episode. Not to the Nazis' behavior when they heard the explosion in the laboratory. Mark is sure they charged in and, finding no one, rushed around searching for the inventor of this superpowerful weapon. Not finding a trace of this mysteriously elusive *political criminal*, they printed a poster about a reward, which the old porter tore down and preserved carefully. It is possible that everything happened according to my version. Perhaps not. Any version based on pure logic is very relative.

"One point is indisputable. You can put a man in prison, lock him up in a steel cage, or throw him behind barbed wire, but you cannot take away his freedom. Thought cannot be shackled or destroyed: it will always find a way."

The Friar of Chikola

VADIM SHEFNER

DEAR FELLOW COUNTRYMEN and Fellow Dwellers on Earth!

I consider it my duty to inform you that friendly visitors from another planet are expected to land in the vicinity of Deciduousova Village on 17 May at 0519 hours local time.

All citizens and scientific organizations are requested to render all possible assistance to these guests from outer space and to mobilize all available transport for the delivery of all existing supplies of grade AA eggs to the landing site before their arrival.

The aforementioned guests are preparing for their second visit to Earth. Their first visit escaped the notice of the general public; only the inhabitants of the small resort village of Deciduousova were aware of it.

I am appending an explanatory note to this message in order to substantiate the latter statement and thereby avoid being called a charlatan or madman. Since I am not a writer, I request your forbearance with my awkward literary efforts. I am now retired, and was formerly employed as a registration inspector of the urban pet population. Only dire necessity and deep concern for the welfare of the inhabitants of this planet have compelled me to pick up my pen and undertake the presentation of the following facts.

1

Ten years ago, in the course of my normal duties, I had to visit an apartment on Vasily Island. The tenants in this communal apartment had complained about a chap by the name of Nikolai Dormidontovich. After he had gotten his room in an exchange deal, he brought with him, besides his furniture and personal belongings, a bunch of chickens and roosters. Live ones! The tenants complained that this collection of fowl disturbed their rest.

As I climbed to the fifth floor where this chap lived, I was struck by the unusual number of cats on the stairs. At the door of the apartment alone, I counted no less than nine! When the door opened, some of them tried to sneak into the apartment, but the tenant who had opened the door for me foiled them. He told me that the tenants had known no peace since the day Dormidontovich had moved in; all the neighborhood cats kept a twenty-four hour vigil on the staircase in anticipation of booty.

The foyer reeked like a chicken coop, and the tenants clustering around me bombarded me with complaints about the chickens and roosters Dormidontovich was raising in his room. Their clucking and crowing were making their lives miserable. To make matters worse Dormidontovich occasionally let his feathered friends leave the room for exercise, and then the roosters pranced brazenly through the corridor while the hens and their broods gathered in the communal kitchen or bathroom.

For all that, Dormidontovich's neighbors hadn't a bad word to say about him personally, even calling him a harmless fellow. He wasn't raising chickens for sale, didn't eat chicken, and wasn't making a kopeck's profit from poultry breeding. From time to time he would tearfully slaughter several chickens in the bathroom and give them away to his fellow tenants. If, they said, we could allot Dormidontovich space in the courtyard for a chicken coop, so he could get the birds out of his room, everybody would be satisfied.

I told them that poultry breeding in the city was illegal and a chicken coop in the courtyard was out of the question. Then I asked to be shown to Dormidontovich's room. As I followed the tenants through the corridor, the odor grew stronger and stronger.

Without the slightest show of resistance Dormidontovich let me into his room; but the roosters and hens raised an awful ruckus when I stepped through the door.

Scarcely any light filtered through the dirty windows although it was still early in the day. When Dormidontovich turned on the light, I saw before me a short man with huge spectacles. His head was covered by a rubberized hood, his jacket by an oilskin slicker. These protected him from chicken droppings which rained down every now and then from the perches lining the walls. Below the perches were sheds, knocked together from slabs; these sheltered laying hens. The furniture for the room's human inhabitant consisted of a cupboard, table, chair, and a bed covered with oilcloth. Hens, roosters, and chicks were everywhere, sitting or parading around the room. I counted forty-eight mature birds!

I explained to Dormidontovich very politely that chickens could not be kept in living quarters, and I recommended the liquidation of his poultry population.

He replied that he was raising chickens purely for scientific reasons and could not give them up. But he would try to move from this apartment as soon as possible. As he spoke tears rolled down his cheeks. Then he said that I seemed to be a serious and attentive person. Would I, he asked, stay for half an hour and listen to a brief account of his life and scientific research.

I agreed. After wiping the chair with a newspaper and draping a piece of canvas over me to protect my suit, he began his story.

2

Nikolai Dormidontovich was born in 1902 in the family of a minor St. Petersburg official. They were poor, and chicken was a special treat reserved for important holidays. On one such occasion, as his mother had served him and his sister chicken legs, it occurred to the youngster that if a chicken had four legs, each member of the family could have one: mother, father, sister, and himself. But nature's failure to endow a chicken with more than two legs struck him as grossly unjust and made a deep impression on the sensitive boy. Thus, in his early years a brilliant idea was born: mankind must have a strain of four-legged chickens! He was so excited by this brainstorm that he swore never again to taste the meat of a two-legged chicken.

Later he was expelled from high school for a composition entitled "The Four-Legged Chicken—Mankind's Future Friend." In it he presented a logical case for a strain of four-legged chickens. Unfortunately his teachers took it as a malicious insult to science.

Following his expulsion from high school Nikolai sold his textbooks, school uniform, and some household articles and with the money bought four hens, a rooster, and a self-teaching text on hypnosis. He built a chicken coop in the attic and spent whole days trying to hypnotize the hens and rooster, hoping to impress on their avian brains the need to produce four-legged offspring. The whole family was so distraught by Nikolai's scientific passion that his father finally cursed him and kicked him out of the house for good.

But all that happened a long time ago, and much of major and minor importance had transpired in the world since then. Dormidontovich had lived in many cities and gone through many jobs. He had worked as a longshoreman, hypnotist, postman, book peddler, substitute physical education teacher, mountain guide, train conductor, draftsman, janitor, and at many other jobs. But wherever he lived, he continued to pursue his goal, no matter how impossible conditions were. Naturally, this created problems and forced him to change his residence and profession frequently. In marriage he was just as unlucky. After living with him for two months his wife issued an ultimatum: "Take your choice—me or your lousy chickens." A true martyr to the cause of science, he would not abandon his idea. His wife slammed the door behind her and left him forever.

Recently, as he approached retirement, he returned, with difficulty, to the city of his birth. But even here fate compelled him to wander from apartment to apartment. His life was a hard one. Nights he worked as a warehouse guard; days he looked after his birds.

Denying himself everything, he gave his birds the finest feed, even supplementing it with various medicines and substances calculated to shift the genes from two-legged to four-legged ones. But so far he had been unsuccessful.

The confession of this dedicated but unrecognized scientist made a deep impression on me. Upon leaving, I wished him speedy success with his bold, constructive idea.

3

A month later a petition arrived from the tenants of another apartment where Dormidontovich had settled. As part of my job I had to visit him again.

As I climbed the stairs I counted seventeen cats! The tenants greeted me with the same complaints about hens and roosters as I'd heard from his old neighbors.

This time, without any assistance, I followed the scent straight to Dormidontovich's room, where I was welcomed like a good friend. Although the living area was smaller than before, the bird population wasn't. The self-taught scientist appealed to me to exert my influence on the tenants to stop submitting complaints about him. He was sick and tired of moving from place to place. I replied that his constructive idea had caught my fancy; and I gave him my address in case he might want to visit me and spend an evening chatting about the future of science.

Then I passed into the foyer where I tried to convince the tenants of the benefits a four-legged chicken would offer mankind. Unfortunately they didn't see things my way; in fact they even cut me short in the middle of my piece. And the very next day they sent me a sharply worded complaint. Called on the carpet for an explanation, I made a brief speech to my boss in which I offered my high opinion of Dormidontovich's scientific goal. My efforts were coldly received, and before long I became the victim of petty sniping. It culminated in my early involuntary retirement on pension.

This happened at the beginning of June, so I decided to rent an inexpensive room in the country for the summer season. Just then I received a letter from Dormidontovich in which he informed me that fate had taken a sharp turn for the better. His childless older sister had passed away recently without leaving direct heirs. Legal authorities had found him and granted him possession of the deceased's winterized dacha and lot in the village of Deciduousova. He had already taken possession and launched a full-scale scientific effort. Further, he told me that he liked me and would be happy to rent me an attic room for a small sum if I cared to live in the country.

A week later I went to Deciduousova. En route I learned that the village consisted of only eight houses and was pretty far from the station. It was very tranquil and secluded and attracted dachniks who sought peace and quiet. For this seclusion they paid through the nose, and their landlords' ruthlessness was legendary among the inhabitants of neighboring villages.

After hiking twelve kilometers from the station, I reached Deciduousova. I recognized my friend's house at once by the flock of hens and roosters wandering about the yard. Nikolai greeted me warmly, but informed me directly that he had already rented out the attic. Science, he said, required money, and since one of the dachniks had offered him an attractive sum, he couldn't possibly refuse it. However, he had worked out a deal with Madame Moneybagova, a dacha owner who lived two doors away, and she had reserved a wing of the main house for me. I must confess that this arrangement delighted me. Of course, it would have been flattering to my ego to live in the home of my friend, that great devotee of science. But, the abundance of hens and roosters had its negative side too.

Nikolai's summer tenants hadn't arrived yet, and all three rooms had been turned over to his birds. Perches had been nailed up everywhere, and even the piano had been put in the service of science. Nikolai stored fresh eggs inside it, and from time to time played it with one finger, hoping the musical sounds would steer the genes in the right direction.

From my friend's house I headed directly for Madame Moneybagova's where, for a rather low rent, I arranged to reside in the wing. Actually it was no more than a cubicle in a shed with a flat plywood roof. Dachniks had already settled into seven other identical cubicles. The main house itself was also jam-packed from the basement to the attic; and even the well-shelter in the yard sheltered a vacationing family.

A few days later I moved into my summer quarters. Despite the lack of a few standard amenities, I liked the little settlement and spent five peaceful summers there.

4

For five years this luminary of science made no progress. Nikolai suffered physical as well as psychological hardships because his poultry population kept increasing and required a great deal of money for feed and various chemical preparations. Rents from his dachniks were his only source of income for the chickens' upkeep, but the interests of his chickens and his dachniks didn't always coincide. All winter the chickens lived peacefully in the house, but at the onset of summer, the scientist had to move his winged friends to a shed in the yard, and, after giving the house a good scrub-down, opened it to his dachniks. Unfortunately, the chickens couldn't accept their temporary exile and kept returning to their native dwelling, and the roosters pecked the tenants from time to time. Besides, the birds always congregated in the yard next to the communal trivet where the dachniks prepared their meals. They upset pots and pans and were constantly underfoot. The victims conducted a running battle with the birds, occasionally taking the offensive. This uninterrupted warfare between the chickens and summer residents proved very disturbing to my friend. He had many a chat with his tenants, trying to point out the importance of developing a four-legged chicken. Moreover, he treated his tenants daily to free tranquilizers. Despite all the concern he demonstrated for their welfare, his tenants would see the summer through and then depart, never again to return to his dacha. Each spring he had to recruit new contingents.

To fulfill his dream, Nikolai spared no expense. Often he fed his birds canned meats in the hope that the flesh of quadrupeds would alter the chickens' genes from two-legged to four-legged ones. Sometimes he would hike twelve kilometers to the station to buy a beefsteak at the cafeteria. The steaks were pretty thin, but tough enough to require an axe to chop them up. He also fed his feathered friends everything from raisins to soap, plus vitamins from A to Z.

He even painted two full-sized portraits of a four-legged rooster and a four-legged hen. They were framed and hung in the yard half a meter above the ground, so the image of the ideal chicken would always be within the visual field of his two-legged birds. For science he gave his all, and frequently he would pull galoshes over his hands and feet and struggle around the yard on all fours, hoping, by example, to coax his biped nurslings to steer their genes onto a quadruped course.

But all his efforts were in vain. I began to notice that my friend was growing increasingly depressed.

5

In 1966 I returned to Deciduousova in April to savor the charms that only early spring can offer. Since none of the summer people had arrived yet, I enjoyed the stillness of nature and the deserted community.

On Sunday, May 16, at 1600 hours, after returning from a stroll, I lay down to rest on the folding bed in my cubicle. But the fascinating conversation I overheard minutes later left me wide awake. Doughkov, a neighbor of my landlady, dropped in and told her that he'd had a strange dream. As he walked along the seashore, he ran into a couple of mermaids sitting on the beach stark naked. They were selling canned black caviar at cost price. When he approached them, they leaped into the water. And that was that. He was so dumfounded, he woke up at once.

Madame Moneybagova declared at once that the dream was prophetic: the mermaids and the caviar were merely a curtain raiser to some imminent momentous event.

And what do you think?! No sooner had she finished her analysis, when into the yard dashed Lyuska, her little granddaughter, a preschooler.

"Grandma, look at the flower some foreigners gave me!"

"Foreigners?! What foreigners?" asked Doughkov sternly. "Never had any in these parts."

"On the other side of Nyush's Hill. They got here in two big round things. Kostya Fatsov went to pick flowers, and there they were, right in the meadow."

"Send Kostya here right away!" said Moneybagova. "Leave the flower here. If people see it, they'll start talking."

The little girl ran to fetch Kostya, while Moneybagova and Doughkov began to speculate about the youngster's story. Either the child had mixed up something or had lied. The road to Nyush's Hill cut through the settlement and ended at the hill. People once used it as a throughway to reach their plots for firewood, so the foreigners would have had to pass through the settlement to get to the other side of the hill.

My eyes wandered to the windowsill, to the flower Lyuska had brought. It was a snowdrop, but about fifty times larger than an ordinary one. A shiver ran down my spine.

Meanwhile the little girl had returned with Kostya, a lad of about twelve.

"Kostya, what kind of foreigners did you see by Nyush's Hill?" asked Madame Moneybagova.

"Lyuska's got it all wrong. Those weren't foreigners," replied Kostya. "They're from another planet. From Mars."

"Martians? Oh, my God! We need them like a hole in the head," exclaimed Madame Moneybagova. "We live here peacefully, mind our own business—and this is what we get for it? Martians!? If the dachniks find out what's going on in our woods, they won't come within a hundred kilometers of Deciduousova."

"You're right. We could be left without tenants." Doughkov was alarmed. "The dachniks come here for a nice peaceful vacation, and what happens? All of a sudden some crazy Martians show up.... But maybe they're not Martians?" He turned to Kostya hopefully.

"I know what I'm talking about!" Kostya was insulted. "I've been reading science fiction since I was a little kid. Sure they couldn't tell me intelligibly where they came from. But I could see they came from Mars. How could I tell? Well, first of all, they were obviously representatives of a civilization in the solar system. And, according to the laws of interplanetary convergence, conditions on Mars in the past were equivalent to conditions on Earth. Secondly, they were obviously humanoid types of the 'man-woman' category. This was visually confirmed by secondary sex characteristics."

"That's the limit! Secondary sexual characteristics we need in our woods?!" shrieked Madame Moneybagova. "The dachniks expect mushrooms and berries—so what do they get all of a sudden? Martians! Ghosts! All kinds of specters! We must call the police at once!"

"God forbid! We don't need the authorities messing in this business," declared Doughkov. "If the story gets around, it's goodbye tenants. We've got to keep this quiet, and meanwhile maybe those Martians will leave. Don't breathe a word to your dachnik! By the way, where is he now?"

"Probably hanging around with that friend of his, the chicken nut."

"Remember now, not a word to your tenant or that chicken freak."

"Lyusenka, darling, run to every house and tell all the grownups to come here right away," said Madame Moneybagova. "We must talk this over with them. Hurry!"

The other five landlords appeared and decided to keep secret the arrival of the Martians. If the strangers lingered more than a week, they would be asked to leave as quickly as possible. Lyuska was ordered to keep her mouth shut and was promised a whole chocolate cake as a reward. Kostya was told that he had tonsilitis and was kept home from school for a week. He was forbidden to visit the Martians for three days; after that he could check to see if they were preparing to depart.

No sooner had the conversation died down, than I tiptoed from my cubicle and hastened to Nikolai's house.

6

When I arrived, my friend was sitting on the porch, opening a bottle of Stolichnaya. A couple of empties stood next to it. But don't get the idea that he was an alcoholic. In his whole life he had never touched a drop of liquor. It was science that had driven him to vodka. Having fed his chickens everything conceivable without getting anywhere, he decided to make a last ditch effort with the most powerful means at his command.

On the ground before him sat a low trough from which the chickens usually drank water. Now he was pouring vodka into it. Several birds that had already tasted the stuff staggered around the yard. The hens cackled senselessly and the roosters shrieked and started fights.

I told my friend about the Martians.

"Great news!" he exclaimed. "Just imagine what it might do for my dream of producing a quadruped chicken. We must go to them at once." He shoved a bottle of vodka into my pocket. "We must bring our guests gifts. You, as a respected pensioner, can give them this bottle of vodka. But I, as a representative of science, should give them something more valuable and science oriented."

He went into the house and returned with a shopping bag and a small clay statuette. One of his tenants, an amateur sculptor, had modeled it for him. The piece, about thirty centimeters high, was the spitting image of Nikolai from head to foot. The scientist's outstretched hand held a tiny four-legged chick. With a pin the sculptor had scratched the following words on its small pedestal:

THIS MONUMENT HAS BEEN ERECTED TO
NIKOLAI DORMIDONTOVICH
FRIAR OF CHIKOLA
POULTRY BREEDER
TRAILBLAZER

My friend placed the statue in the shopping bag, and just as we were leaving the yard, we spied Sneakya, the cat, with a chick dangling from his mouth.

"Aha, that's what we ought to bring the Martians," said Nikolai. "They probably don't have cats, and this graceful specimen should delight them. Sneakya steals a chick a day, but I have borne this cross patiently. You see, this cat belonged to my dear late sister, and was passed on to me. But now, for the sake of strengthening interplanetary bonds, I shall give him to the visitors. Perhaps up there he may realize he is Earth's sole representative and will reform his ways."

We waited until Sneakya finished his chicken dinner, then got a sack from the shed and stuffed him into it. Groggy from his recent feast, he offered no resistance.

7

From the top of Nyush's Hill we saw two vessels lying on the ground near the edge of the swamp. They were shaped like the tanks on milk trucks. But these were larger—about the length of a railway car and as tall as a two-story house. One tank was pale blue, the other pink, and both were solidly welded.

Strange-looking machines and equipment stood at the foot of the hill, in a dry meadow surrounded by young pine trees. Living creatures moved about near them.

The closer we approached the visitors' camp, the more sure I became that these figures strongly resembled human beings. At still closer range I could distinguish their clothing—so like ours. The men wore trousers, the women skirts of average length and blouses. When we had almost reached the edge of their encampment, I noticed that the women were very pretty and the men well built, but not overly muscular. The only difference I could see between the space visitors and ourselves was a letter on their foreheads. Each man bore a light blue letter; each woman a different letter, and in pink. But in no way did this mar their appearance.

At the edge of the meadow we greeted them with a loud "Hello!" and the visitors waved their hands in a friendly manner. A serious middle-aged man came up to us and led us to the center of the meadow.

"Pardon me, you are from Mars, aren't you?" I asked. "A local youngster told us you were."

"He was mistaken," replied the Spaceling. "We're certainly not from Mars. No life there. Our world is Htrae, a mirror-image point in the Universe."

A massive table surrounded by chairs stood in the middle of the meadow. We were invited to sit down, but since the visitors remained standing, so did we. They looked at us warmly and made no attempt to interrogate us. Nikolai was too immersed in his scientific fantasies to engage in conversation, so I broke the ice. Slipping the bottle from my pocket, I deposited it on the table and presented it as my personal gift to them. Following a brief, simple explanation of its use and its invigorating effect on the body if ingested in moderation, I told them a little about myself. Then I introduced my friend to them, describing him as one of science's great martyrs.

When I finished my piece, Nikolai set his portrait-in-sculpture on the table and made a little speech. This small statue, he said, would remind our new friends on Htrae of the Earthling in whose brain the idea of producing quadruped chickens was born. This idea, he added, had always intrigued Earthlings. Thus, for example, Eugene Schwartz spoke of a magician in whose shed a four-legged chick was spontaneously hatched. In fact, during the nineteenth century skilled Byelorussian craftswomen occasionally embroidered four-legged roosters on towels. And in Africa, he told them, rock carvings were found on which some unknown artist had portrayed a living creature resembling a four-legged chicken. But, concluded Nikolai, the time had come to create a real genus of quadruped chickens!

I opened the sack and dumped a groggy cat onto the table. The Spacelings looked at this worthy representative of terrestrial fauna with interest and sympathy. Following several impassioned remarks about the benefits of cats, Nikolai announced that he was presenting this specimen to them on behalf of his fellow Earthlings. And he begged them to bestow affection and care on it. He warned them quite frankly that the cat was a chicken thief but would certainly reform its ways in its new environment.

The expedition's leader replied. First of all he apologized for his scanty knowledge of Earth language; they had only begun to study it yesterday, when they switched on all their receiving systems for this purpose. Their Earth landing was unscheduled; they had been homeward bound from another planet when aluminoglycogen leaked into the plasmatron of one of the tanks. Now the problem had been corrected and they were awaiting instructions from above (he pointed skyward) for the exact departure time.

He thanked us most sincerely for the valuable gifts but added that they could not accept the vodka because alcoholic beverages were strictly prohibited on their journey. Unfortunately, they could not take the statue of the worthy scientist with them because the cargo weight in their tanks had been calculated with such precision that the slightest increase would throw the interpolation defrosters off balance. And the cat, which appeared to have utterly delighted them, could not be transported because of a strict rule which forbade them to remove any living creature from another planet without its written permission.

At this point I took the liberty of interrupting the speaker to explain that we Earthlings treated animals differently; sportsmen had left our woodlands bare of wildlife.

When their leader asked if we had any more questions, I wondered why they had come here in two tanks. One, he explained, was for men; the other, more comfortably equipped, for women. As for the letters on their foreheads, and the different symbols for males and females, he offered the following explanation.

In olden days their women wore skirts and long hair; men wore trousers and short hair. Then, in the course of their historical development, an irrational but, fortunately, short-lived deviation occurred: women began wearing trousers and super-short hairdos; men grew long hair and wore blouses and beads. It was so hard to distinguish the sexes that all sorts of misunderstandings developed. Then, with the agreement of both sexes, sex identification letters on foreheads were introduced. When reason prevailed once more and women returned to their skirts and men to their short haircuts, it was decided to retain the forehead symbols. The letters were particularly useful because they glowed in the dark. A gentleman would always know when to make way for the "fair sex."

"Pardon me," I said, "but does that mean that as soon as a child is born you slap a letter on its forehead?"

"Oh, no," replied the Spaceling. "We're born with them. We've manipulated the genes so the letters are passed on as a genetic trait."

"Hallelujah!" Nikolai was overcome with joy. "You . . . you actually possess the secret of gene transformation? Now, my dear friends, it is your duty to help mankind, and me too, of course, create a four-legged chicken." When Nikolai finished this emotional outburst the leader introduced him at once to an attractive middle-aged Spacewoman, a specialist in genetic retraining.

Slipping a little book with tables from her pocket, she glanced into it and then explained:

"You can transform a biped chicken into a quadruped by mutational manipulation of the egg. Apply isomorphic radial vibrations. However, this requires four tons, ten kilograms, and five grams of time. Unfortunately we're waiting for a signal to take off. Hurry home and bring us some eggs. Ah yes, I forgot to tell you that we use our metrical weight system to measure time. So, by your Earth calculations the operation will take eleven hours, thirty-two minutes, and nine seconds."

Grabbing the sack and stuffing his cat into it so it wouldn't get lost in the woods, Nikolai ordered me to stand watch near our guests. Should they receive a lift-off signal too soon, I was to persuade them to delay their departure. With that he sprinted home.

I sat down by the table and began to observe the perfect teamwork of the Spacelings as they bustled around their equipment and supplies. Before long I dozed off, but my dreams were interrupted by short blasts from some device. All the Spacelings clustered around it and listened to the blasts. Their leader came over to me and said they had received the signal to depart in four tons, eleven kilograms. Therefore, they could conduct "Operation Quadruped" only if the Earth scientist returned in time. If he arrived late, the operation would have to be postponed for six Earth years. In six years the Htrae astronauts would visit Earth again in order to establish scientific contacts. And they would land at the same site.

<h2 style="text-align:center">8</h2>

Several hours later Nikolai appeared on the hillside among the heather and juniper. He ran, clutching a sack in his outstretched hands. Obviously it was loaded with eggs.

Suddenly everyone gasped. Horrors! Tripping on a stump, the venerable scientist crashed down with all his weight on his bundle of dreams.

In a flash he was up and running again, shouting something in a sobbing voice. His suit was splattered with whites and yolks, and a crushed mass of eggs oozed from the sack. When he reached the meadow, the sympathetic Spacelings and I crowded around him. By some miracle three out of fifty eggs had survived. My friend was led up to some sort of apparatus and instantly his suit and sack were spanking clean.

Picking up the three surviving eggs, the genetic retraining specialist went over to a complex machine. She pressed several buttons, and a broad blue light beam leaped out. When she placed the eggs on it, they didn't fall but began to rotate gently on the beam. A cone of greenish light appeared above the beam and, jingling softly, began to spin around its own axis.

"This will continue for a long time. Since it's now a kilogram, that is, your supper hour," announced the genetic specialist, "we'd like you to dine with us."

Everyone except one Spacegirl sat down around the table. I had mentioned earlier that the table was very massive. It rested on six tripods that were constructed of some dark metal; and the tabletop's smooth surface was made of a green substance. A cable ran from the table along the ground to a complex machine.

The Spacewaitress brought a tiny box to the table and asked us politely to remove the statue. But she said nothing about the bottle of vodka. Opening the box, she took out a miniature bread loaf, the size of a child's little finger, and placed it in the middle of the table. Then, before each of us she set out three tiny plates and miniature teaspoons, knives, and forks. From a toy-sized thermos she poured soup; then she served each of us a fish as puny as a sardine and topped it with sauce. Apples no larger than strawberries, and some other miniature fruits and vegetables were placed in the middle of the table.

"You poor things," I thought to myself, "you're certainly hard up. Any old alley cat eats a lot better than you do."

The Spacewaitress asked me to take elbows off the table and then crossed over to the machine connected to the cable. After she pulled a lever she turned a handle marked with an arrow. I glanced at the table and was stupefied. The midget bread loaf began to expand before my eyes. The plates and their contents did the same. Two or three minutes after the girl had turned off the machine, a huge appetizing loaf of bread graced the table. The rest of the vittles and dishes enlarged enormously. The Lilliputian fish ended up the size of a good carp; the tiny berries became huge succulent fruits as large as an average watermelon. And my half liter, retaining only its original shape, swelled into a gigantic bottle, enough vodka to fill five buckets! Naturally that posed a problem: how would I get it home?

Supper turned out to be a delicious, nutritious affair. During the meal Nikolai asked the leader how this miraculous enlargement was done.

"With a quantowavemitrophonic astrogenerator descalerator. For short, a scalerator," replied the leader. "We have a large population on our planet. To feed everyone we raise miniature fruits and vegetables, breed mini-fish, and then enlarge everything with a scalerator. Generally, we produce all things and objects of daily use as minis and then scale them up to the size we need. However, it is illegal to subject intelligent creatures, warm-blooded animals, and birds to scaleration because it's inhumane. Valuable works of art aren't tampered with either."

When everything had been consumed, the Spacelings helped me hoist the bottle from the table. Switching on the machine, the girl shrunk the dishes and silverware to their original size and cleared them away.

Nikolai was anxious to try out the scalerator, to put it to a practical test. Picking up his statue, he set it on the table and made a brief speech to the Spacelings. He declared that his lifelong dream of creating a quadruped chicken was about to be realized. Therefore, he felt he deserved greater recognition than this puny sculpture represented; he deserved a huge monument which he would like to erect in his own yard during his lifetime. So, he appealed to his respected hosts to produce a two and a half-meter scaleration of this statuette.

The leader replied that the respected scientist's request would be fulfilled. But, he added, clay was not a durable material. They could transform the clay into any metal. Gold, for example.

"But I wouldn't want a gold statue," protested Nikolai. "I would deserve gold only if, in addition to conceiving the idea of quadrupeds, I carried it through to fruition. However, for the technical realization of my idea I am compelled to turn to you for assistance. Therefore a bronze, rather than a gold statue, would be more appropriate."

At a sign from his chief, a young Spaceling carried the statuette to a cupboard. He touched a button and a drawer slid open. The object was placed in the drawer which then slid back into the cupboard. Three minutes later it opened again to reveal a fully bronzed statuette.

It was placed on the table, and the machine was switched on. In a few minutes a grand monument rose before us. An automated fork-lift rolled up to the table, grasped the statue gently and set it on the ground. Deeply moved, the scientist stood beside his huge monument and caressed it. Tears of joy ran down his cheeks. Meanwhile it was growing dark, and pink and blue letters began to glow on the visitors' foreheads.

At daybreak the geneticist handed Nikolai three irradiated eggs. Thanking her warmly, he wrapped them in soft moss and gently placed them in the sack.

The hour of departure arrived. The tanks' hatches opened automatically and the guests, linking arms, circled in a farewell round dance, a customary ritual they performed when leaving foreign planets. Then they waved good-bye and headed for their tanks. Their machines, all self-propelled, followed them. Soon the hatches slammed shut, and the tanks lifted smoothly off the ground. For several seconds they hovered above the meadow, then rose steeply into the sky and disappeared from sight.

The two of us were alone together. My friend stood beside his statue, I beside my bottle, and before us both loomed the problem of transporting these gigantic objects. In view of the monument's enormous weight, Nikolai decided to leave it here for the time being.

But I decided to deliver the bottle to the settlement right away. From some branches and my belt I fashioned a dragging device, and we headed for home. Nikolai walked ahead, carrying the sack; I trudged behind, dragging the bottle.

Since my friend's lot was the last one in the settlement, I stashed the bottle in his shed. That way I wouldn't stir the envy of the other dacha owners and set tongues wagging.

9

Nikolai assigned the task of hatching the three eggs to his most reliable and diligent brooder. After selecting a comfortable corner for her, he observed her tirelessly and supplied her with the finest feed. And to create optimum conditions for the development of his future nurslings, he decided not to take in summer tenants this year.

Two weeks passed. Then three. Would they be quadrupeds? Day and night Nikolai thought of nothing else. No rest, no sleep. I tried to stay with him as much as possible; my presence had a soothing effect on him. During the final three days I never left his plot of land. Actually, my friend forbade me to enter the house; he was afraid I might disturb the hen. So I slept in the shed on a pile of firewood, beside my bottle. Every now and then I took a nip to calm my nerves.

On the twenty-first day, the morning of June 7, Nikolai tugged at my leg to awaken me.

"Hallelujah!" he shouted. "It worked! Go take a look at my four-legged chick."

"Rooster or hen?"

"Hen! A four-legged hen!"

He entered the house but wouldn't let me in, fearing a misstep might crush his firstborn. As I stood in the yard and looked through the window, first I saw Nikolai, sitting cross-legged on a chair; then I spied the chick. It pattered briskly along the floor on its four tiny feet.

Suddenly my heart skipped a beat. Apparently my friend hadn't shut the door completely; Sneakya had stolen after him into the room and was preparing for a lightning leap, a mortal threat to the quadruped creation. When he noticed the cat, he froze in horror, not knowing how to avoid imminent diaster. Then, in a flash, the cat, seeing that the chick had four, not two legs, bristled in terror and shot out of the room.

"As you can see, the chick is vigorous and healthy," said my friend as he went inside. "Now we shall await the arrival into the world of her future four-legged beau."

An hour later two quadruped henchicks were scooting around the room.

"H'm, looks bad." My friend tried to suppress the tremor in his voice. "If the third chick isn't a rooster, the quadruped genus is kaput. But according to the law of probability we can expect a rooster this time."

To myself I recalled the lines of some poet:

> If you throw all your eggs into the probability basket,
> You're bound to find your dreams in a casket.

Unfortunately, the poet turned out to be right. The third chick hatched in an hour. Another henchick.

My friend's grief was indescribable. In vain I tried to console him, assuring him that the Spacelings would return in six years; then he

could create all the four-legged chickens and roosters his heart
desired. But he just sat there in utter despair, the tears rolling down
his cheeks.

10

Summer passed, but Nikolai still could not recover from the blow.
He neglected his household, and the two-legged hens and roosters
ran wild, wandering all over the place. The cat lost whatever
conscience it ever had and trained itself to consume two chicks a day.
But it was scared as hell of the quadruped hens. The two-legged
chickens shunned them too, and even the boldest roosters were
terrified of them. When the quadrupeds filed out into the settlement's
street, dogs cruised around them warily, and little kids began to cry.
It wasn't long before all three quadrupeds disappeared forever.
Rumor had it that the dachniks renting the well-shelter in Madame
Moneybagova's yard secretly caught and ate them.

In late autumn Nikolai Dormidontovich's body was found on the
meadow where the Spacelings had landed in the spring. It lay at the
foot of the monument.

11

Now the dacha belongs to Nikolai's widow. She had left her
scientist-husband at one time, but since the divorce had never been
registered, lawyers found her and turned the property over to her.
With a vengeance she destroyed every cultural vestige of her late
husband. She consumed all the hens and roosters mercilessly. The
historic chicken coop was removed, and the two portraits hanging in
the yard are lying in a dusty attic.

As for the monument on the meadow, it collapsed a long time
ago because of its weight and the unstable ground. Tourists broke off
and carted away the four-legged hen in the scientist's hand. And in
order to send the rents in this vacation spot skyrocketing, the dacha
owners started a rumor among the dachniks that the statue was a
very ancient one brought here from Greece during the reign of
Catherine II.

In conclusion may I appeal to you to extend yourselves in preparing for the Spacelings' forthcoming visit to Earth. And, above all, to have on hand for their arrival a sufficient quantity of grade AA eggs.

A
Provincial's Wings

VADIM SHEFNER

Introduction

Now THAT EVERY MAN ON THE STREET has a pair of wings and knows
that he can fly off in them at a moment's notice, their popularity on
Earth has undergone a decline. On our planet, their primary users
are romantic lovers and village mail carriers in outlying districts,
who need them to traverse the spring muds.

There are few men left who still remember the difficulties faced by
Alex Possibile in inventing those wings, in maneuvering his invention past innumerable barriers, and in engendering the general
aviazation of humankind.

This, dear Reader, is what I would like to remind you about.

Some Clarifying Points

I feel I should warn the Reader that my article does not presume
to discover any new Americas and that it (the article) is in the nature
of a compilation. It does not pretend to particular originality either
in the area of information presented or in the manner of its presentation. Wings are an eternal theme, like love. People have
dreamed of them since the most distant times. On the wall paintings

of ancient caves we find, together with other pictures, the image of a man soaring on wings. Greek mythology has Daedalus constructing a pair of wings for individual flight. The Bible, the Apocrypha, and religious literature in general, of all times and all nations, are full of references to flying beings both positive (angels) and negative (evil spirits, demons). The theme of wings fills painting, sculpture, music, cinema, science fiction, and even folklore ("If I had wings, no one would ask me could I fly . . .").

Serious literary figures—for example, Anatole France in *The Revolt of the Angels* and Mark Twain in *Captain Stormfield's Visit to Heaven* did not find the theme foreign. And there's no point in even talking about poetry—from ancient times right up to the present day there have been an immeasurable number of poems written about wings.

Even in the era of aviation and flights into the cosmos, man's interest in wings as such did not diminish, and the dream of a personal set of wings did not vanish. How many pilots and passengers, stepping onto terra firma after a dizzying flight from Leningrad to Vladivostok, could refrain from tender envy at the sight of the swallows flying over the airfield?

It is paradoxical that for all gliders, blimps, airplanes, helicopters, and rockets, man continued to dream about flying with his own wings. In his dreams he continued to see himself flying—not in the cabin of a jetliner, and not in the cabin of a rocketship, but simply flying, soaring like a bird.

However, there weren't any wings.

There were myths about wings, and stories about wings, and narrative and lyrical verse, all about wings. But no one, at any time or in any place had ever run into an ordinary human being flying in them.

Documentation

And so it was until Alex Possibile constructed a pair of wings and flew in them. (Cf. Patent No. 756617-PS, supplemental doc. No. 1899457KM, "Individual, Detachable, Fluttering Human Wings for Directed Aerial Flight.")

The Childhood of Alex Possibile

Alex Possibile was born in Siberia in the village of Horse-and-Cart (now the village of Possibility). The village was a fairly large one, with a post office-telegraph and a high school.

Alex lost his father at an early age; his mother worked as the village mail carrier. Every morning at the post office she would pick up a sack of letters, newspapers, and similar printed matter and set out for the surrounding villages. During the spring and autumn muds it was far from easy to walk along the road, and some small villages, located along the swampy taiga, were cut off altogether. On such days Seraphima would return home with a sack full of undelivered letters and bitterly complain about the bad roads.

"Was there really no way at all to deliver the letters?" the sympathetic little boy would question her.

"No way at all. At least, without a caterpillar tractor or a pair of wings."

"And you're not allowed to have wings?"

"Only angels are allowed to have wings," Seraphima would answer. This should not lead one to the conclusion that she was religious. She was simply using a vivid image to express to the child the utter impossibility of delivering the mail in the given set of conditions.

When Alex grew older, he often replaced his mother in her hikes to outlying villages. Because of this he missed a lot of school—a fact that his teachers let pass without a murmur. He was a very good student—even, according to some people, an abnormally good one. As a fifth grader he already knew several branches of higher mathematics studied in the Academy of Sciences, and when, during his final examinations, he was allowed to make up his own question, he provided a proof for the unfamiliar theorem of Sandestrome the Younger, till then considered unprovable.

His successes in school did not make Alex arrogant or callous. He was kind to his comrades and always ready to lend a hand to people in trouble, even when this involved some danger. He was kind to animals as well. If he ever found a wounded bird, or a fledgling fallen from the nest, he'd always take it home and look after it. Not all the birds flew away once they'd regained their health, and some of them stayed nearby, accompanying Alex on his hikes to the taiga villages. During the day, there was always a falcon flying overhead, and no sooner would Alex step out of his cottage at night than a gray owl would appear. The owl would fly in front of him, now swooping down to his feet, now soaring noiselessly aloft.

And each spring and fall, during the migrations, a swan would fly off from its flock just long enough to inscribe a few welcoming circles above his roof: a long time back, Alex had found it, wounded, on the river bank and nursed it back to health in his own cottage.

The Fateful Night

When he finished school, Alex decided to go to Leningrad and apply to the Aviation Institute. He had already sent his papers to them. The summer that year was unusually wet, and one day Seraphima, returned home with a sack full of undelivered letters, newspapers, and money orders. She was supposed to have delivered them to the village of Far Omshar, but she couldn't make it there. The road to Far Omshar went through the taiga and the mossy swamps.

Since, on this occasion, the printed matter in the sack included a telegram, Alex decided to make the trip to Omshar himself, although he'd never been there before. At first his mother tried to talk him out of it, but he convinced her that he'd be careful. He grabbed the sack, threw on a canvas raincoat, and set off.

Hardly had he reached the path when the falcon, as usual, caught up with him. The falcon's wings shone wetly from the rain. Every so often he would gain altitude, look over the road, and dive back down.

Next the owl joined up with him. The owl's flight was uneven and somewhat awkward: in daylight, as is well known, owls see poorly, and this was a middle-aged owl too. The owl plunked itself down on Alex's shoulder and just stayed there.

"Well, old lady, you were the only one missing," he said, and stroked the bird on her wet back. "And what made you leave your hiding place in the daytime? You never did that before."

Soon Alex turned off the main road and went onto a forest path, and from the forest path to another trail still narrower. Everything was covered with water, but the visibility was good. The falcon gained altitude again, then dove back down and flew home. Alex understood that he was on the right road and that until dark nothing bad would happen to him.

At nightfall, Alex reached the moss-covered swamp, with its low hummocks and strands of dwarf birch. Here he lost the road. He began to stumble, wandering off first to the right, then to the left. The swamp muck squished underfoot. Then in the darkness it seemed to him that he'd come to a familiar spot, and he quickly strode off to the place where, according to his calculations, he should find the road.

At this point the owl gave him a rather painful, angry peck in the shoulder. Then she started flying around him, nearly grazing his face with her wings and not allowing him to move forward. He understood that the bird had sensed that something was amiss, and that he would have to spend the night where he was. He sat down on a wet hummock and dozed off. From time to time he would wake up and hear the owl angrily rustling her wings. When dawn came she was no longer there—she had gone home to sleep.

Now, in daylight, Alex saw that if he had gone another ten steps in the darkness he would have fallen into a quagmire, a "window," as they were called. The "windows" were grown over with thick grass, and even in the daytime not every traveler could distinguish them from an ordinary harmless glade.

Soon he found the road, and with no further difficulties arrived at Far Omshar, where he distributed the mail. The telegram he handed to Ekaterina Rainbowe, who turned out to be nothing more than a Katya, a girl about a year younger than Alex. The telegram advised Katya that she had been accepted to vet school as a correspondence student.

The news made Katya very happy, and Alex was no less happy

looking at her. She was wearing a black skirt and a plaid blouse, which suited her very well. The blouse was green with black, and it was fastened with green plastic buttons.

"What were you just thinking about?" Katya asked suddenly.

"Nothing," answered Alex. "Your buttons look edible."

"Is that good or bad?"

"It's neither good nor bad," answered Alex. "But I like it."

"That's strange," said Katya. "It's really strange. I always thought these buttons looked edible too, but nobody else ever said anything about it to me."

"Now you'll be getting your assignments through the mail," Alex said. "Even if the roads are bad, I'll make sure they reach you."

"Thanks," said Katya. "That will be wonderful. It's just too bad that the first-year course includes chemistry."

"Don't you like chemistry?" asked Alex, surprised.

"Even worse," answered Katya. "You see that big aspen over there? Do you like it?"

"Well, I see it. It looks like a good tree. Can you hear the leaves rustling?"

"And what if you came here on a dark night, and I pointed you in that direction, and asked, 'Do you like that aspen?' You would say, 'It rustles, but I don't know what it looks like.' That's what chemistry is like for me."

"I'll help you," said Alex.

"That would be great," said Katya. "I've always been so afraid of it that in chemistry class at school I used to write poetry, to take some of the fear away. Here's what I wrote once:

> Today on the gully's northern end,
> Where the windswept willow loomed
> In the sun, in the snow, and the snow-wet land,
> A single flower bloomed.
>
> It rose through the snow and dried-up grass,
> And it drank in light and air
> As the fog of the morning whirled and passed
> Around its petal hair.

I could have plucked it easily,
But it stood so alone in the snow,
Awaiting spring so dauntlessly
That I had to let it go.

Then she said, "I know that wasn't very good. But it was only for me. In the summer, we swim in the river, and sometimes I go by myself to the forest lake; it's about two miles from here. I can swim there, and dive, and nobody is around to watch me. I like that very much. And it's the same way with poetry."

The night he spent in the swamp and the acquaintance with Katya that followed affected Alex in a way that might, at first glance, seem a bit odd. As soon as he got home, he wrote to the Aviation Institute to demand the return of his papers. And not long after, he set off for the nearest Administrative Center, where he enrolled in a course for postal workers.

Many people were surprised and have remained surprised up to the present day. Why should a person of such evident talents pick such a modest and less than lucrative career? According to some observers, it was his desire to be near Katya. Others believe that he didn't want to leave his mother, who was approaching retirement and often got sick. Still a third school of thought holds that during the night he passed in the forest waiting for the dawn, Alex didn't sleep at all, but sat up thinking about wings for humankind. And so clearly could he picture them to himself that he no longer felt like wasting his time in the Institute, preferring, so the theory goes, to get right down to work.

However, some late entries in the diaries of Alex Possibile show clearly that the thought of wings had not yet occurred to him at this point. He wrote: "In those days I hadn't yet thought about wings. But I had a feeling, which I could term foreknowledge. I knew that I had to discover something and that my future discovery was somewhere nearby."

No Wings as Yet

Upon completing his course, Alex Possibile was sent to his native village, where he took the post of assistant post office clerk. The post was opened because of the recent retirement of his predecessor.

In Horse-and-Cart, people were amazed that such an intelligent
person should choose such a dead-end profession. They even poked
fun at him—although always in a kindhearted way. The girls, for
example, made up the following ditty, which was performed several
times on the stage of the village club:

> Boys as smart as we are pretty
> Used to study in the city.
> But why go to an institute
> When you can have a postal route?

As you can see, there's nothing really offensive about it. It should
even be noted that some parties got rather a kick out of seeing the
talented young man set off on such a modest path in his native village.
Whenever Alex was asked if he really didn't want to go to the city to
study, or spend some time traveling around the wide world, he
wouldn't answer. But, as we know now, it was during this period that
he made the following entry in his diary: "It is my belief that close
contemplation of a quadratic meter of field or meadow, when the
observer is in a state of spiritual calm, provides the consciousness
with a greater sense of space and the fullness of life than thou-
sand-mile journeys by train or plane and multiple changes in
domicile. Every person carries his own space within him."

However, Alex was far from being such an obstinate stay-at-home.
When he heard that Moscow was to host an international tournament in computer chess, where human players vied for the best
score against the latest model machine, he asked his boss for a leave
and set off for the capital. As a preparatory measure, he got out a
teach-yourself book on how to play chess, and went through a couple
of rounds with the local champion, the check-out clerk, Peter
Birukov.

The rules for the international tournament were as follows: first
prize went to the player who tied with the machine: second prize to
the player who managed to get through at least thirty moves before
succumbing. There was no talk about winning, as it was believed that
beating the computer was impossible. Alex, however, tied the first of
his three rounds and won the next two outright.

Alex took his rather considerable winnings and bought a whole

crate of books on the most varied branches of human thought, not to
mention presents for his mother and fellow villagers. For Katya he
bought a very expensive electronic dog. The dog was about the size
of a Pomeranian and could run, jump, and bark. With that its
repertoire ended, and to make matters worse, it soon broke. In the
interests of honesty it must be said that although Alex loved to give
presents, he wasn't very good at choosing them. All of his
purchases—discounting only the books and tools—were remarkable
for their impracticality and utter uselessness.

On his return to Horse-and-Cart Alex resumed his duties at the
post office. On days when the load was particularly heavy, before
holidays, and also whenever the weather was bad, he himself would
carry the mail to the outlying villages. And we will not hide the fact
that he got his greatest pleasure from carrying letters and newspapers to the village of Far Omshar.

So passed two years.

Wings as Such

One spring day, the first day of his vacation, Alex Possibile stopped
in at the village club. There on the bulletin board, along with the
usual topical commentary, was a drawing by the local artist Andrew
Prokushev. The drawing showed a young man with a sack on his
back; the sack was overflowing with newspapers and letters. The
young man himself was on a bicycle, or, to put it more precisely, was
falling down together with the bicycle, since there was no way for
him to ride it: the bicycle was stuck to its hubs in mud.

Below the drawing was a little poem, written by the young
mailman, Nicholas Taraev:

> I just don't have the strength it takes
> To keep from falling on my face.
> For all the load a mailman brings
> He really needs not wheels but wings.

Eyewitnesses say that upon reading this four-liner, Alex Possibile
froze for an instant and then hurried toward the exit. Some say that
he also hit himself on the forehead and muttered some ancient Greek
word.

Following that, he disappeared for three days. When the neighbors asked his mother what on earth had happened to him, why he was nowhere to be seen, the latter shook her head, grief-stricken, and said, "He's writing, he's making some sort of diagrams; at night he doesn't sleep. I don't know what to do with him."

Soon after, Alex took a trip to Moscow. In five days he returned. His mother told the neighbors that he'd brought back wires and cans of things and little pieces of metal and some other objects whose purpose was incomprehensible to her.

He hitched a ride to the Administrative Center, where he bought canvas, nylon fishing line, and a lot of tubes of airplane glue.

A day later, Alex went to see the local carpenter, Michael Tabaneev, and asked him for some dry boards and slats. The latter gladly gave him all he needed but expressed some interest in what Alex had in mind to do with it.

"I'm going to knock some wings together," answered Possibile.

"Want to join up with the birds?" laughed the good-natured carpenter. "Well, why not, it's not such a bad idea. When you turn into a bird, just bring me a bottle of something in your beak."

"My pleasure."

The same day, Alex set off for Far Omshar. He told Katya about his plans to construct a pair of wings.

Katya heard him out and lapsed into thought.

"What's on your mind?" asked Alex. "Don't you believe that man can fly?"

"Yes, I do," said Katya meekly. "But even if nothing comes of it, for me you'll always be the same as ever."

Then Alex hugged and kissed her, and the next day they went to the Marriage Bureau and from there to Horse-and-Cart—and Katya moved into Alex's house. Thus, the single affair of the heart in Possibile's life was firmly and finally resolved. In this respect everything worked out for him, and he and Katya lived happily together. I must confess that when I began work on this chapter, I was sorely tempted to dramatize at least a little bit the romantic sufferings of Alex and Katya. But I kept myself in check, because I consider it my duty to stick to the facts.

Alex and Katya began spending whole days in the shed, where Alex had set up a small workshop. Alex assembled the slats, planing them down and glueing them together, and Katya, working around a cardboard pattern, cut the canvas with a pair of huge scissors. Then she sewed it with a heavy needle, using fishing line in place of thread.

Still, there was so much work to do that Alex got in touch with the kids from the model-airplane club at the local school. They turned out to be good workers—in fact, it was impossible to make them leave the shed. But they made an impossible racket, arguing with one another about the best way to tie knots, and for this reason Alex's mother was not overly pleased with them. But the help of the boys freed Alex from many hours of busywork, permitting him to spend time on the auxiliary electronic apparatus, which was intended to make flying absolutely safe.

And then the wings were ready.

Katya got specially dressed in warm-up pants and a pretty blouse, and Alex clad himself in his only suit, strapping the wings to his arms. The model-airplane enthusiasts came also. They were dressed in their usual clothes, but all of them were washed and combed, which hardly happened every day.

"Are you going to come watch the experiment?" Alex asked his mother.

"I don't want to get involved in your monkey business," Seraphima answered severely. "You'd be better off working on something serious."

Then everyone except her headed out to the pasture. Alex Possibile strode ahead in his fancy suit with the wings strapped to his arms, and Katya followed in her plaid blouse with the edible buttons. After Katya came the boys. The day was superb, but in fact that didn't make any difference—the wings were designed for all weather.

At that hour there weren't any cows in the pasture. There weren't any people nearby, and there weren't even any birds singing. Only the falcon, as always, found Alex and flew in silent circles around him.

The experimenters were also silent because the moment of truth had arrived.

"Uncle Alex is going to take off now, but no one's very happy about it," said the littlest of the model-airplane boys.

Nobody answered him.

"Well, I'm taking off." Alex took a last look at Katya and ran to the center of the pasture, spreading his wings as he went. Then he tore free from the earth and flew off.

Further Developments

Alex made a few small circles around the center of the pasture, then headed off in a beeline toward an old cherry tree at the edge of the field near a brook. The falcon flew along next to him. The bird did not appear at all astonished at the flight of a human being.

Gaining altitude, Alex cleared the top of the tree, then fell into a nose dive. Suddenly, the falcon flew out in front of him, screeching a warning. Alex made a sharp turn—had he gone any further he would have pierced his right wing on a hard, dry branch and crashed to the ground. Now, thanks to the bird, he was safe. But the falcon had gotten crushed between the branch and the wing. Silently it fell into the brook, and the current carried it away. Its feet were pressed to its body as though it were flying. But birds also hold their feet that way at the moment of death.

For a long time Alex flew above the brook, accompanying the dead falcon. The bird was carried along over the pale green duckweed, over the rusty tins and crushed pots with holes in them, and worn-out rubber boots that lay at the bottom. Further on, the bed of the brook turned to clay, and the shore was pitted with holes—here people gathered clay for their stoves. Then the brook widened; there was a whirlpool. The falcon disappeared into its depths.

Alex climbed higher and took some steep turns, so the rush of wind coming at his face might dry his tears. He couldn't wipe them with his hands—after all, he had his wings on.

Then he returned to Katya and the boys.

"I killed the falcon, it was an accident" he said to Katya, taking off his wings. On the edge of the right wing was a small red spot.

"That's so sad," said Katya. "And today of all days. . . ."

"Now you try it," said Alex.

Katya put on the wings and took a few turns above the pasture. Then the oldest of the model-airplane enthusiasts was permitted to try it. This was the tenth-grader Mitya Dobryshev.

"Well, how did you like it?" Katya asked him when he landed.

"I liked it fine," said Mitya. "But it's better in a TU-104. When me and my Dad went to Kiev in a TU-104—now, that was something!"

"And I flew in an IL-18," said the littlest of the model-airplane boys. "Boy, was that fun!"

The boys ran back to the village and Alex and Katya remained behind by themselves. As before, there was nobody around. The wind picking up from the northeast, blew dust from the airstrip across the pasture.

"Well Katya, let's go home," said Alex. "The test is over. Are you happy?"

"I'm happy," answered Katya. "But for some reason I thought I'd be happier."

"So did I," said Alex. "You know, when I was flying it was very nice, but not at all the way it happens in dreams. Isn't it true that by giving people wings I've deprived them of the dream of wings?"

"You've done a very important thing," Katya comforted him. "People never had wings before, and now they do."

"Yes, now they do."

And both of them slowly set off for home.

About an hour and a half later, Alex took some money, tied a shopping bag around his neck, put on the wings, and flew to the country store. The country store was rather far from his home. Alex didn't fly over the streets but kept to the backyards, so as not to attract unnecessary attention. When he landed at the store the midday break had just ended, and there still weren't any customers. He was the first. Auntie Sveta, the store manager, was sitting on the porch.

"Welcome to the flier," she smiled. "The boys already told me that you'd put together a set of wings. How much of a load can they carry? Besides yourself, what can you take up with you?"

"Not a whole lot," answered Alex. "Five or six pounds."

"On the small side," Auntie Sveta shook her head. "You won't get rich on it. How about the speed?"

"Faster than if you went on foot. But not a lot faster. About ten miles an hour."

"Nothing to write home about. Now take my nephew, he got himself a motorcycle, he can do sixty miles an hour on the highway. And if he has a drink first, he says, he can do seventy."

Alex made his purchase and flew to the carpenter. The latter was sitting by the window. He had already had a few to celebrate the good weather, and Alex's arrival delighted him.

"Well, good for you, pal! You really knocked a set of wings together! And brought me a bottle of something in your beak!"

Then he felt the wings and asked to try them out.

"I'm sorry, but I can't let you try them right now," said Alex. "It looks like you're a little drunk, and these wings have electrobionic brakes. A person in an inebriated state can't take off in them. So he can't fall down and break his bones."

"Incredible!" exclaimed the carpenter. "That's a smart head you've got there! And what's the ceiling?"

"About two hundred yards."

"Yup," drawled the carpenter, "with a ceiling like that you could hit your head against something. . . . But don't get upset, you've got yourself a really important invention there."

As we know now, it was on that very evening that Alex Possibile made the following entry in his diary: "Even discounting my sadness over the falcon, there's no sense of great happiness. Perhaps happiness is just a form of energy, and there is no such thing as an inexhaustible source of energy. A lot of happiness is expended on the very expectation of happiness—and then when we reach our goal, a lot of it is already lost."

Further on he writes: "I feel like a man who has long sought a treasure and finally found it. Yes, I unearthed the trunk with the sign

NEW SOVIET SCIENCE FICTION

on it, 'Here's where the money is.' I broke into the trunk, and there, indeed, was the money. But it wasn't pieces of gold. Alas, it was nothing but paper notes, which have long since lost their value, been replaced by other currencies. I couldn't give them to people—nobody needs them. They'd only please collectors (who, of course, are people too.) The treasure was found too late."

The Belated Marksman

As we now know from the memoirs of contemporaries, the invention of wings caused no great stir in the epicenter of discovery—the village of Horse-and-Cart. This is totally comprehensible. The villagers thought of Alex Possibile as one of their own: a slightly whacky kid who never would amount to much. His invention, for them, was just a harmless (and useless) outgrowth of his eccentricity.

But as time passed—though Alex made no effort to advertise his wings—rumors about them began to spread, moving from his native village to the neighboring villages and from there to the neighboring towns and cities. And the farther the rumors spread, the more their content succumbed to videotransformation. In a few days, a legend began circulating about a flying man who filched a carton of kvass from the County Co-op and carried it off under his wings. According to another variant, the said flying man was not a man at all, but a morally degenerate interplanetary paratrooper who came straight from a flying saucer and was not after alcohol but hard cash. There were other variants as well, some of them even stranger. All the rumors, however, had one point in common: each one of them named the precise location of these marvelous events—the village of Horse-and-Cart.

Thus, it was not long before the local paper of a certain town not far from Horse-and-Cart dispatched its roving correspondent, Leonid Gravedigger, to look into the matter and publish an account that would put an end to the false conjectures.

There was a time when Leonid Gravedigger was on the staff of one of the central papers. For some reason, however, he was fired and came to work for the local gazette under consideration. The local editor was much taken with the freshness of Gravedigger's style. Gravedigger, for example, would never use the word "oil," referring instead to "our black gold." In place of "cotton," he wrote "our white gold" and in place of the vulgar word "pelts," he employed the expressive image, "our soft gold." Furthermore, although he had always lived in urban centers, he was considered a specialist in agricultural affairs, and occasionally even composed poems and songs on agricultural themes. In his poetry he chose for some reason to imitate the works of the prerevolutionary poetess Mirra Loxvitsky. As proof of this, we need only cite his "Agricultural Bacchanal":

> Shepherd Mephrodich! Milkmaid Masha!
> The bells of the harvest have rung!
> Let us drink to our wheat crop, Mephrodich and Masha,
> To phosphates and nitrates and dung!
>
> Let us all raise our glasses to various factors,
> To our sheep with their soft golden fleece,
> To combines and tractors and compost compactors,
> To the eggs of our quick-laying geese.

Since Horse-and-Cart was a village located in an agricultural region, it was Gravedigger who was sent to have a look around. In two days' time the newspaper published his account, which was entitled "A Look at Those Wings in Broad Daylight." It began as follows:

As we gather in more and more soft gold, ever-widening the spread of fertilizer across our fields and pulling off a whole lot of other enterprises and activities, we must not forget certain dark spots in our midst. The dark spots of dark individuals.

A certain A. Possibile has withdrawn from the friendly collective of post office workers, abandoning any concern he may have felt for the prompt delivery of mail to the village proletariat. His apparent justification involved a harebrained scheme to fly on wings.

These counter-scientific flights, unsupported by the arguments and deductions of scholarly research, inevitably lead us to the conclusion that A. Possibile wishes to hold himself apart from the rest of the Horse-and-Cart proletariat, using his position to inspire the masses to belief in religiously oriented propaganda.

There was a whole lot more along the same lines. The article ended with an exclamation: "Wouldn't you agree that citizen Possibile has been winging it long enough?"

The appearance of the negative article soon had its positive effect. After all, had Gravedigger written something laudatory, it probably would have gone unnoticed. A positive account doesn't demand any response; a negative one does. The article under question was immediately brought up at a meeting of the regional postal workers' association, where it was denounced as third-hand information and a distortion of the facts. A letter with numerous signatures was sent off to one of the central newspapers. Soon a correspondent from the capital arrived in Horse-and-Cart, and three days later his newspaper published a small but weighty dispatch under the heading "Wings—A Reprise." The subject of the dispatch was a provincial inventor who, after constructing a set of wings for use by mail carriers, was cruelly slandered in the local press. The local journalist L. Gravedigger had obviously failed to understand the essence of the matter. Instead of extending his moral support to Inventor A. Possibile, he subjected him to a series of absurd objections in a technically illiterate article.

Soon after, the illustrious journalist, Nina Antithesis, arrived in Horse-and-Cart. In a knowledgeable and sympathetic article, she informed the reading public about Alex Possibile and his invention. The article was called "A Village Daedalus."

Horse-and-Cart soon heralded the arrival of correspondents, photographers, reporters, television cameramen, and filmmakers.

The representative of the widely read popular science magazine *Technology for Everyone* convinced Alex to send his blueprints and a technical description of his work to the Patent Bureau. Alex followed the friendly advice and soon received a patent.

Soon after, Alex Possibile made his second pair of wings. These he brought to the post office so the mail carriers could make use of them. The wings turned out to be fully justified. The autumn rains began, and the roads to a few of the outlying villages became impassable, but the delivery of mail continued without a hitch. The mail carrier setting out for a far-off village took the wings along and flew over the muddy roads and swamps. From time to time the wings were used by doctors and even by lecturers giving talks in the provinces. The wings were kept on a special shelf in the post office, ready for use. They were called "emergency wings."

The next time he stopped by the village club, Alex saw a new drawing of Andrew Prokushev on the bulletin board. This drawing also showed a village mail carrier. He was flying away on his wings, and strapped to his neck was a sack with letters and newspapers sticking out of it. Below the drawing was a little poem by a village poet already known to the reader:

> Above the taiga green I fly,
> I see a ditch and go right by
> Because in my job as a postman, I
> 've been given a pair of wings.

It must, however, be noted that Alex's mother, setting off on her mail route, never made use of the wings. Indeed, she soon retired.

Katya rarely used the wings after the test period was concluded and even regarded them with a secret fear. It wasn't that she was afraid of falling and hurting herself—not at all. Simply she was endlessly distressed by the tiny dark red stain on the right wing.

And even Alex Possibile himself rarely used the wings. His character changed slightly, and he was often morose. The following notation from his diaries relates to this period: "In essence, the formula for the fluttering wing is so simple that only pure chance prevented its discovery in the last century. I do not feel at all like a hero. I feel like an inexperienced but self-confident marksman who accidentally hit a bull's-eye. The target is riddled with shots that just missed, and it's clear that the marksmen were experienced and true but simply had bad luck. The marksmen died long ago, but the target remained, and I came along and hit a bull's-eye. But the target was theirs! I am a belated marksman."

On the Road

Now a lot of letters came addressed to Alex Possibile. His co-workers, joshing with him, declared that he'd gotten a job at the post office in order to receive his mail without, so to speak, getting up from his desk. In their letters people asked if the wings would soon be ready for mass production, and how much they would cost, and a lot of other questions.

All this brought Alex to the thought that it was time to raise the question of the mass production of wings, so that industry would be able to meet the growing demand for them. After talking the matter over with Katya, he took some time off without pay and set off for the capital. Katya accompanied him to the nearest city, where he got on a train. He had with him a small suitcase and the wings in a case sewn out of waterproof material. Katya had sewn it herself.

Three people were already sitting in the compartment. They were on their way, as it turned out, to a congress of overage inventors. Their names have not come down to us, so for the sake of convenience I will call them Brown Hair, Red Hair, and Old Boy.

Seeing the case, Brown Hair asked Alex what was in it.

"Fluttering wings for individual flight," answered Alex.

"Who needs wings these days!" exclaimed Brown Hair. "As if there weren't enough airplanes around. I know what needs inventing and what doesn't need inventing. I invented an anti-alcoholic box for safekeeping cash. I'd like to register it under the trade name "Sesame—don't open." With these words, Brown Hair got out a small iron trunk from under the seat. On the trunk was a small poem transcribed in green oil paint by what was obviously the hand of the inventor:

My wife's been good to me all year.
Our expenses are down by half.
This anti-alcoholic box here
Keeps us from our cash.

You can read my pride right on my face.
I love my new creation.
This box here just can't be replaced.
It keeps us from temptation.

"But what's the point of the box?" asked Alex.

"This here anti-alcoholic box is meant for the safekeeping of money," answered Brown Hair. "When you get your pay, you put a part of it in the box, the part you want to use for something in the future, and the rest you use for your daily expenses. If you start drinking, and you want to get some money out of the box to buy another bottle, it won't open no matter how you twist the key. I've rigged up this unit that locks automatically as soon as it picks up the scent of alcohol. Even if you're sober, as long as someone who's been drinking is standing no more than three yards away, the box won't open. It follows that if a drunken pal of yours stops by and tries to borrow some money from you, nothing will come of his efforts and you're guaranteed against loss. But if your wife (let us assume that she doesn't drink) should suddenly need money for something, she can open the box at anytime with the key which you have of course given her. So thanks to the box, you will have peace and harmony at home."

"But what if I'm a bachelor and I don't drink, then the box becomes useless, doesn't it?"

"Not at all!" answered the inventor. "A nondrinker can use the box as a piggy bank. Let's assume you want to save up for a motorcycle. Every time you get your pay you put some part of it in the box and leave the rest for daily expenses. Then every day you buy yourself a fifth of vodka and, naturally, drink it. In this way the sum of money in the box is guaranteed safe from your touch."

"But you can turn into an alcoholic that way," Alex observed.

"That's already a personal matter," answered Brown Hair in a dissatisfied tone. "It's the novelty that's important."

"And what's your invention?" asked Alex, turning to Red Hair.

Red Hair silently pulled a small package out of his pocket. He unwrapped it and revealed something faintly resembling a fuse. However, this fuse was constructed entirely of metal.

"A Lifetime Fuse!" announced Red Hair. "I've already written up an advertisement for it." He smoothed out the wrapping and read, or rather, sang the following to the tune of the old song "Oh Those Hills of Gold":

> Never letting up my steam
> I've now fulfilled your long-held dream.
> This little fuse I've put together
> Will change your life now for the better.
>
> You'll be very glad you bought it
> Once your circuits all have shorted.
> Your house will go, the wiring too
> But the fuse will be like new.

At this point Red Hair switched to prose.

"You put in this fuse and forget about it—it's never going to blow. Turn on all your appliances—it won't mean a thing! Your wiring will go, the appliances will go, the house will burn down—nothing's going to happen to that fuse. Just imagine the money that will be saved on a world-wide scale."

"Wait a minute," said Alex, astonished. "After all, that's the whole idea behind a fuse—that under certain conditions it's going to blow. That's their purpose."

"It's clear, young man, that you don't understand the first thing about inventions," interrupted Old Boy. "As long as there's a new idea involved, the invention is worthwhile. Now, I—"

"What did you invent?" Alex asked him.

"I haven't invented anything—I've made a discovery. I've created a Longevity Mixture—Gevit-Mix for short. If you take it once a year on your birthday, you're guaranteed indefatigable health and a long life. You'll live till a hundred and fifty."

The Old Boy stuck his hand under the table and pulled out a huge bottle filled with a dark liquid. A piece of paper was attached to the neck of the bottle in the manner of a pharmaceutical label, only much bigger. On one side appeared the following, traced out in the wavering handwriting of an old man:

Any person can prepare "Gevit-Mix" at home, bringing happiness to himself and his loved ones.

INGREDIENTS

1. Table Salt
2. Fixing Salts (from photographic supply house)
3. Sugar
4. Cologne
5. Kerosene
6. Denatured Alcohol
7. Blue Ink
8. Detergent
9. Garlic Juice
10. Vinegar
11. Liquid Ammonia
12. Bedbug Spray
13. Furniture Polish
14. Table Mustard
15. Castor Oil
16. Nail Polish
17. Pickle Juice
18. Cod Liver Oil

Mix, Shake, and Let Stand

On the other side of the paper was a poem, copied out in the same hand:

> Take five quarts of "Gevit-Mix"
> And gulp it down.
> You'll be stronger than an ox,
> The best in town.
>
> No viruses can cross your path,
> No women either.
> The grave may call but you just laugh,
> You're free forever.

"Excuse me," said the astonished Alex, "but you've got five quarts written there. Are you sure it's not a mistake?"

"No, it's not a mistake," answered Old Boy. "You have to take precisely that amount—not an ounce more, not an ounce less. Then Gevit-Mix will work as indicated."

"Excuse me for the indelicacy," said Alex. "But judging by the way you look, I assume you haven't yet tried it."

"No, I haven't been able to get a whole five quarts down," answered Old Boy. "But I've been training myself on beer, every day. I can already go through four bottles of beer without stopping. My old lady isn't happy about it, and we sometimes even come to blows, but I haven't given up training. In about three years I'll be up to ten bottles—and finally the day will come when I'll be able to take the needed dose of Gevit-Mix in place of the beer. Then my personal example will point the path to a healthy, long life. . . . It's true that first I have to break the nausea barrier. And I'm still not sure how to do it."

"What do you mean by the term 'nausea barrier?'" asked Alex.

"Unfortunately," said Old Boy, sadly lowering his head, "unfortunately, even in the smallest doses, my mixture brings about an irrepressible attack of the heaves."

The next morning Alex's three companions got off the train and he continued on by himself. It was during this time that he recorded the meeting with the three overage inventors in his diary. Writing of the first, he draws a parallel between the braking mechanisms used in the anti-alcoholic box and those he used in the wings. Further on, he comes to the conclusion that the inventor, whom we have called Brown Hair, may have been working for the wrong ends, but you couldn't deny his clever technical solution. In general, Alex characterized him as a pragmatist up a blind alley. Here he expressed the opinion that in addition to willpower, there must also be the power of no willpower, and that people have to come to terms with this too.

The second inventor Alex simply characterized as an idiot.

His comments on the third ran as follows: "Is he an unhappy man?

No, a happy one! He possesses the greatness of a true discoverer. In two years he'll die of dropsy, but in dying he'll be sure that if he only had another year he could bring happiness to all mankind. His path is erroneous, laughable, absurd; but the goal is wise, noble, and contemporary. He is the antipode, the negative sign, the reverse side of the coin, someday there'll be the profile of the inventor of a real elixir."

There follows something crossed out by the author's own hand, and below that the following poem, written by Alex Possibile on that very train:

> Today I'd lift my wings in flight
> To see anew
> That world of turrets, rooftops, trees,
> My sparrow's view.
>
> But mankind reaches for the stars,
> And such is fate
> That my great gift, my gift of wings,
> Has come too late.
>
> My dream, so bright and unexpected,
> Falls apart.
> The melancholy of reflection
> Fills my heart.

Seventeen Departments and BOSHI

Alex Possibile got off at the noisy railway station and set out in search of lodging. He soon found himself a room in a cheap hotel. With that taken care of, he began looking for some government department that might be interested in mass-producing his wings. Jumping ahead a bit, I might note that efforts cost him ten days.

His first stop was at GPATP (General Post and Telegraph Planning). Here they already knew about the wings and believed that they were important and necessary and would be of great help to provincial mail carriers. Unfortunately, the GPATP workshops were overloaded as it was, and Alex was advised to try his luck at GASP (General Athletic and Sports Planning).

GASP was also aware of the invention and gave Alex a warm welcome. But they didn't want to get involved in the production end of it, since wings did not come under GASP's jurisdiction. There was, after all, no such sport.

"But if we get the wings into production, then people will take up flying as a sport," objected Alex.

"As soon as people take up flying as a sport, come right to us," they answered. "Then we'll get your wings into production. In the meantime, you'd be best off going to GFFP."

At GFFP (General Forest Fire Prevention), they were also aware of the invention. But the wings would really not be much help in fighting forest fires—the carrying capacity was too low. When necessary, the fire fighters made use of helicopters, and considered themselves fully justified.

Alex made the rounds of a few more departments, and then tried the military. Here he got a very warm reception.

"We're very well aware of your invention," said a young colonel. "We were the first ones to find out about it, and we have the greatest respect for you. But we aren't going to ask you to work with us, as your wings have no military significance. Had you invented them in a different age, they would have been priceless, but now we have infinitely better devices for individual flight."

"Where would you suggest I take my invention, Comrade Colonel?" said Alex. "I put the question to you because you seem to me to have more common sense than anyone else I've come in contact with over the past few days."

The colonel thought for a moment.

"In addition to their mail-delivery function," he said, "your wings could be employed at sea for rescuing disaster victims from merchant or passenger ships. Of course they wouldn't be any help if the accident occurred far from shore, but in cases involving coastal waters, wings could be utilized to good advantage. Storms often leave coast guard cutters in bad repair, in which case your wings would be a great plus. In addition, even when a rescue vehicle is

present, people don't always make it to shore because of the strong
tides. In such conditions, wings could save a lot of lives. I advise you
to take your invention to the Shoreline Defense."

Alex Possibile thanked the colonel and went to Shoreline Defense.
The Shoreline people listened to his arguments with great interest
and agreed with him in principle, but quickly made it clear that they
had no production facilities of their own. In the end, they sent him
off to the Bureau of Standardization of Household Inventions
(BOSHI).

BOSHI turned out to be a massive institution with a host of
divisions and subdivisions. Here the wings aroused the proper
interest. But BOSHI itself could not of course produce them. It had
divisions dealing in meat grinders, washing machines, juicers,
vacuum cleaners, and table lamps, not to mention subdivisions for
soap dishes, toothbrushes, salt cellars, toilet flushing devices, and dog
leashes. None of this, however, bore any relationship to wings. There
might be some justification for bringing wings in under the category
of table fans, but the director of the table-fan division was on a
business trip.

However, BOSHI had under its jurisdiction a number of RBs
(Research Branches). It was to one of these RBs that Alex Possibile
took his wings with the object of giving them a theoretical
grounding, perfecting them, and preparing them for mass
production.

The RB Duckandgoose

The RB "Duckandgoose" was a research branch whose branch of
research was less than well defined. It had no clear ties to either
agriculture or nature conservation, although it had been founded
with an eye to some positive practical goal. Just what that goal had
been, though, nobody could remember. Over the past few years, the
entire scientific output of the research branch had come to rest on a
single intrabranch dispute between the duck and goose divisions. The
duck specialists were busy trying to prove to the goose specialists
that ducks played a far greater role in the outside world than geese
did. The goose specialists declared the opposite. Since both sides in

the dispute couched their "pros" and "contras" in proper scientific form, with footnotes and bibliographies, the argument was in the highest sense creative and scientific and allowed all parties to receive various scholarly degrees and promotions.

When Alex Possibile appeared at the branch, he could see at once that the scientists had no time for him. The goose specialists were working on a massive "Psychological and Historiographical Survey of the Technique Used by Groups of Geese in Saving the City of Rome." The duck men were working on a two-volume counterattack, the first volume of which bore the title "The Role of Ducks in the Life of Ancient Greek Society and the Reflection of This Role in the Legend of Leda and the Duck." The title page of the second volume announced "Some Notes on the Question of the Existence of Duck Populations in Several of the Planetary Systems of Alpha Duck." Alex spent some time in the halls and laboratories of both divisions, looking at the respectable scholars with their noble gray heads. Sensing a number of sidelong glances shot off in his direction, he decided that he was offensively young and had no business being there.

He was already heading for the exit, but on his way down the corridor, he saw a door with a sign on it: "Chairman, Underdepartment Wings." He decided to risk a knock—and this knock proved decisive.

In fact, in addition to the duck division and the goose division, there was an underdepartment on wings. According to the original plan, this department was to have served as the link between the two divisions, since wings are common to both ducks and geese. But the underdepartment had long since turned into a dead end. The administration used it as a collecting point for duck and goose men who had for some reason incurred their displeasure; a transfer here meant a significant slowdown in one's rise through the academic ranks. And whenever some newspaper published a story accusing the research branch of being out of touch with life or even unproductive, Director Tightsov was always able to manipulate matters so that the lumps fell on the out-of-favor underdepartment. It goes without saying that the underdepartment head, Comrade Reclinesky, was a proud man who had for years nursed a secret hatred for Tightsov.

When Alex Possibile acquainted Reclinesky with the details of his invention, Reclinesky saw that in his hands the wings could become a real trump card.

"I will personally put the finishing touches on your wings and see them into mass production," he said to Possibile. "And in order to help things along, I'm even ready to become your co-inventor. It's possible that as the work moves forward we will have to take on a few more co-inventors. I assume that will be all right with you."

"I agree," answered Alex. "So long as production starts as soon as possible."

"My first line of business is to forge a working team," said Reclinesky weightily. "First the team and then the wings."

That day, on returning to the hotel, Alex made the following entry in his diary. "I can't place much hope on Reclinesky, but it's clear there's no one else. The problem is not merely red tape (although that exists). More important is that the wings have no real technical application. In an age of rockets and jets my wings are 'undermechanized.' But looking into the future, I am not nearly so frightened by quiet failure as I am by world success, by popularity. For popularity is a sure way to complete oblivion. What is great may at times become popular. But does the popular ever become great?"

Further on we find the following: "I miss my home, I miss Katya. It may be old-fashioned, but I am not drawn to cities. I like living in Horse-and-Cart. When you live in the same place you were born, all the physical aspects of the natural world around you gradually enter into your life, take on voices, turn into advisors and friends. Man is wise, but there is also wisdom in a clump of birches by the side of the road, and in a brook that you waded across as a child. All of them can tell you something. And they ask for nothing in return."

Bulletin

Alex Possibile returned to Horse-and-Cart and took up his old life, carefully attending to his duties at the post office.

Outside the village of Horse-and-Cart other things were happening.

Although the scientific and administrative side of the project was progressing with extraordinary slowness—in fact, was not progressing at all—its private or amateur side was moving full speed ahead. A few village mail carriers decided not to wait until General Post and Telegraph started issuing wings on government funds, preferring to build their own based on diagrams published in the popular science magazines. Some lovestruck youths started making two sets at once, one for themselves and one for their beloveds. Amateur wing-builders appeared. Soon there was an All-Union Amateur Society, "Wings for Everyone."

More and more people were taking to the air.

Reclinesky's Ascension

Scientific events were underway at the RB "Duckandgoose."

Reclinesky put his underdepartment to work on the project and got busy making waves. He went everywhere announcing that his underdepartment was the only one working on a project with a future to it—that the duck and goose departments had gone up a creative blind alley. Soon an article appeared in the press on the subject of the RB "Duckandgoose." The article criticized duck men and goose men both, but the brunt of the reproach fell on Tightsov for failing to support Reclinesky's promising work. Since the BOSHI administration had long had its doubts about Tightsov's efficiency as director, the article served as the straw that broke the back of the bureaucratic camel. Tightsov was transferred to another branch and Reclinesky was named director of Duckandgoose.

Reclinesky's first act as head of the branch was to make its research interests clear. Since it had never specialized in anything in particular, there was no great astonishment when it took up the wings project. The BOSHI bigwigs were even pleased—the branch was finally doing something practical.

The duck and goose men started flying away in droves. Their scientific works were carted away to the attic where they were forgotten by everyone, but the academic ranks and professional degrees earned by these selfsame works remained. Since nobody could rescind the degrees, the departing workers were free from the threat of poverty. Reclinesky, building up his team, hired new people to take their places. The modest underdepartment grew, becoming first a full-fledged department and then, in time, giving rise to underdepartments of its own. There was an Underdepartment of Broad-Based Wing Specialists and an Underdepartment of Narrow-Based Wing Specialists; there were underdepartments for wing specialists with concentrations in economics, bionics, electronics, aesthetics, energetics, and model-building; there were water-colorists and hygienists, meteorologists, psychologists, wing-safety experts, and insurance company repairmen.

The branch newsletter also underwent reorganization and embellishment. Its editorial board was joined by a new member: the high-output poet Chameleon. It's true that despite multiple efforts, the administration refused to expand the board officially, so the poet had to be brought into the institute as a test pilot. His task was to produce no fewer than four linear meters of upbeat, singable verse per month. He began work immediately.

> On earth I suffered, felt oppressed,
> Tormented by my winglessness.
> Reclinesky! Reclinesky! Voices cry,
> You made man fly!

> The wingèd sun glows red before me.
> A sense of gratitude comes o'er me.
> Comrade Reclinesky! Voices shout,
> You've helped man out!

In hours unburdened by the necessity of fulfilling his creative duties, Chameleon wrote decadent love poems:

> Others have you loved, so why not me?
> I'm not that rotten.
> Blue weakness fills me constantly.
> By you—forgotten.

My feet I'll toward the forest point
By your directive.
Oh mightly beasts! Please let me join
Your wild collective.

Reclinesky's star was on the rise. He was heralded as the man who, having discovered the talented but nearly illiterate inventor, Alex Possible, had taken it upon himself not only to give a proper scientific grounding to the theory of individual flight on flapping wings, but also to prepare a practical model for mass production.

Gradually, people began thinking less and less about Alex Possibile and more and more about Reclinesky. He was soon awarded a chair in Wing Studies with a corresponding rise in salary. Full of his success in life, Reclinesky began to hit the bottle. He used his position to hire a young secretary by the name of Malina Taykitovskaya, in whose company, it must be said, he was soon to be seen in restaurants and other public places. In addition, he began cultivating the poet Chameleon, who now hung out in Reclinesky's house, drinking vodka and reciting his decadent love poems. The latter had a negative influence on the moral and psychological state of the host. All this taken together had such an effect that Reclinesky himself started thinking in verse.

When morning comes I drag my feet
Down to the kitchen for my treat.
And soon I'm standing right before
The white refrigerator door.
My bottle lies well-chilled within it;
I take it out—and in a minute
Lift it to my thirsting lips
And take my first redemptive sips.
The pearly moisture hits my brain
And warms it up—so without strain
I sit down at my desk to write
My monograph on human flight.

All this time, the wings that Possibile had brought to the research branch were lying in the cellar. The cellar was on the damp side, but Katya's waterproof case kept them safe from harm

The Death of the Swan

Alex and Katya lived happily together. They had a daughter whom they named Anphisa.

Alex was now working as the director of the post office. He was respected not only by his co-workers, but by all the inhabitants of Horse-and-Cart. Despite the fact that he was still very young, even older people often turned to him when they had some argument to settle.

Alex continued to get a lot of mail. In addition, many people made special trips to Horse-and-Cart to talk with him. In order to provide the visitors with some place to stay, the local authorities put up a log cabin which they called "Rest Haven." When they heard about the inn, the inhabitants of the nearest town started coming to Horse-and-Cart to spend a day or two. Then hunters started coming as well—not the kind who hunted for a living, but city types who spent six days indoors and thirsted to pass the seventh in nature, preferably with the opportunity of killing something.

That spring, as always, the swan was flying north with its flock. When it came near the village, it flew off on its own and made a few circles over Alex's house. Alex had been working in the yard; he saw the swan and waved to it. The swan made a final circle and took a sharp turn to the northeast; it was time to catch up with the flock. Then a few shots rang out from the direction of the swamp, and Alex saw the swan fall.

"They killed the swan," he said as he walked into the house.

Alex's mother shook her head and gave her son a reproachful look, as though he were guilty of something. And Katya, rocking Anphisa, started to cry.

"It's an ill omen," she whispered through her tears, "not a good one."

"It's no kind of omen at all," said Alex softly. "It's just that the swan's been killed."

Duck and Goose Matters

Around this time, readers' inquiries began appearing in the papers—why was the wing industry lagging behind? Cartoons

were published satirizing BOSHI and the research branch
"Duckandgoose." The BOSHI director sent for Reclinesky and
demanded that he deliver the wings for the mass production in the
shortest possible time.

Reclinesky assured the director that in two months' time the first
experimental models would be ready.

Indeed, blueprints for a set of revamped, creatively modernized
wings were soon ready. The research branch didn't have its own
workshops, so for the sake of efficiency, the blueprints for the right
wing, left wing, and supplementary gear were sent out to three
separate factories. The right wing went to "Lightning," a domestic
outfit producing meat grinders, coffee mills, guitar strings, and shoe
accessories. The left wing went to "Dawn," which turned out
dumbbells, metal cigar cases, and fishing tackle in addition to mouse
traps and tin funeral wreaths. The supplementary gear was left for
BOSHI's auto repair shop.

A seven-meter diving board, of the type seen at sporting events,
was constructed in the institute yard. The problem was that flight on
the modernized wings could only be achieved from a height. Following that, invitations were printed up and sent to the BOSHI
hierarchy and the press. Two weeks before the test flight, the RB
newsletter published the following song, composed by the poet
Chameleon:

> Oh thou wings, thou wings entrusted
> To my care,
> Thou fliest so swiftly, like some swallow
> Way up there.
>
> Cross field and forest dost thou speed.
> How brisk thy flight is,
> So that our branch's glorious deed
> To heaven rises.
>
> We have perfected thy pure flight.
> We have refined thee.
> So thank we now our leader bright,
> Comrade Reclinesky.

The song was sung in chorus by the entire staff of the research branch, and its author, by way of encouragement, was permitted to publish one of his decadent love poems in the forthcoming edition of the newsletter:

> One day a blue-collar worker I knew was visited by a Muse,
> So he began to write some verse to which he was not used:
> Oh, Liudmilla, how unhappy I am!
> You killed me without a knife,
> You went down to the river with another man,
> Now you'll never be my wife.
> I'll go to the green forest,
> I'll find me a maple tree
> I'll find me a strong, high-quality branch,
> And that'll be the last of me.
> I have a string, I have some soap,
> Oh farewell Liudmiller!
> The beasts of the forest weep for me,
> They know you were my killer.

Guests from the Research Branch

Since Alex Possibile was still considered a co-inventor of the wings, it was awkward for Reclinesky not to invite him to the test of the first experimental model. People might take it the wrong way. So it was that Reclinesky, knowing that Possibile disliked long journeys, sent two colleagues to Horse-and-Cart to convince him to make the trip. The two colleagues had another task as well—to provide Possibile with the text of the speech he was to memorize and deliver after the experiment was over. The speech was prepared by the poet Chameleon under the direction of Reclinesky himself. It was in prose alternating with verse:

Trembling with joy, I would like to express my gratitude to the leading light of wing studies, Comrade Reclinesky, as well as to my eighteen fine co-inventors for creatively rethinking my modest project and preparing the wings for mass production.

Thanks to thee, thanks, oh Reclinesky,
The boonies are jumping with joy.
Your wings are so fine even I see
I'm glad I was in your employ.

Soon both colleagues—the secretary, Malina Taykitovskaya, and the wing-aesthete, Victor Squaretsin—arrived in the district center where they hired a chauffeur-driven car on expense account funds. By evening they were in Horse-and-Cart. They went to see Possibile, and the latter agreed to make the trip. The guests were not in Alex's house for any length of time, as they preferred to wait for him in the car.

While Alex was getting his things together, Taykitovskaya and Squaretsin started talking about him. They talked right in front of the chauffeur, whom they dismissed as a country bumpkin. The chauffeur, however, remembered everything.

"Did you see, they didn't even have a breakfront," said Taykitovskaya. "And they call him an inventor! And did you get a load of how the old lady was looking at us—another minute and she'd spit in your eye. They don't appreciate cultured people here."

"Yeah, they live like animals," Squaretsin agreed. "It's true that they've got a lot of books, but books don't cost a lot these days, so that's nothing to be surprised at. But I took a walk around the yard and looked into the shed. I thought it was a garage, and what do you think they had in there—a cow. Unbelievable. A cow instead of a car. And he calls himself an inventor . . . although his wife's not at all bad looking."

"But did you notice how she was dressed? Right back in the eighteenth century! And she's already got herself a baby. And that Possibile is a boor. When you told him that you were one of his co-inventors, he acted like he didn't even give a damn. It's not even worth talking to someone like that."

"I can't understand why they call him an inventor," said Squaretsin. "He's nothing more than a kid, and look where he's living. And what nerve, to refuse to make a speech expressing his thanks. What are we going to say to Reclinesky?"

"You know, it wouldn't be such a bad idea for the two of us to go off without him," said Taykitovskaya thoughtfully. "We can pass the word around the RB that their backwoods genius upped and died, as a result of which he forfeited his creative initiative, isolating himself in a narrow world of unprofessional interests. Not a bad way of putting it, huh?"

"Not bad at all, but unfortunately it's impossible, we could really get flack from it," said the careful Squaretsin. "But what kind of bird is sitting on the fence there?" He got out his elegant hardwood walking stick ("Love Me and I'll Love You, A Souvenir from Sochi") and left the car. One shot rang out, and then another. And then Squaretsin dragged the dead owl into the car.

"My hunter's trophy! Is this ever a backwoods—they've got wild birds sitting on the fence. I'll whack it one with my stick."

"Terrific! A real man!" exulted Taykitovskaya.

"You've killed a pet owl," said the chauffeur severely. "That's Alex's pet owl, and no one here has ever touched it."

"What can we do now?" quavered the frightened Squaretsin. "He's liable to use his fists."

At this point Alex Possibile appeared. He didn't start any fights, but merely took the dead owl and went off somewhere into the darkness. Then he returned, got into the car, and rode the whole way in silence.

Reclinesky's Fall

The day arrived for the triumphant testing of the experimental model wings.

The morning was sunny. Numerous guests sat in the courtyard on chairs that had been removed from institute halls and specially set up for the purpose. Reclinesky and Alex Possibile were accommodated in two wide armchairs; the other eighteen co-inventors had to make do with three large couches. The courtyard was wired for sound, and to make sure that the guests seated in the last rows remained informed of what was happening, Victor Squaretsin directed a running commentary into his hand-held microphone.

On top of the diving board stood the pale poet Chameleon—he was, after all, officially listed as a test pilot and the time had come for him to fulfill his role.

The wings, however, were not yet ready—the suppliers were late. In order to distract the viewers from worrisome thoughts, the scientific staff provided two renditions of one of Chameleon's songs. The first time they sang it fast, and the second time they dragged it out. Then Reclinesky himself made a speech. He reminded everyone that dating from the most ancient times, from the dimmest sources of civilization's past, man had dreamed of an individual flying apparatus. And now, on the basis of wings developed by the provincial genius Anthony Possibile—wings which were, needless to say, embryonic in form and lacking a firm scientific foundation—the research branch had succeeded in producing a first-class model.

The guests didn't notice that he had referred to Possibile as Anthony, and if they had, they didn't say anything about it.

When he had finished his speech, a truck drove into the courtyard. It was carrying the right wing, manufactured under the auspices of "Lightning." Soon after, a second truck appeared with the left wing, constructed in the workshops of "Dawn." The wings were hauled up to the top of the diving board by means of a crane, after which two research associates—the wing safety expert and the chief maintenance man—started to load them onto the poet Chameleon. Unfortunately, some of the parts that were supposed to fit together didn't, since "Lightning" and "Dawn" used nuts of slightly different sizes. They had to call a fitter.

In the meantime, there arrived a third truck carrying the motor. According to the specifications of Duckandgoose, the wings were not to be operated by muscle-power, as was the case with Possibile's rough version, but by a motor. It was also hauled up to the top of the diving board.

Finally, the poet-test pilot was ready for flight. The fitter and both research associates climbed down, leaving Chameleon alone on the diving board. There was, however, no take-off.

Reclinesky motioned to Taykitovskaya and asked her to climb up and ask the test pilot what was keeping him. She returned at once and informed Reclinesky in an undertone: "He won't fly without straw. 'Let them put some straw down,' he says, 'or I'm not going anywhere.' That's what he said."

Fortunately, not far from the research branch "Duckandgoose" was the research branch "Hay and Straw." The latter provided three truckloads of straw, which were duly spread below the diving board.

But Chameleon still hesitated. He stood there, gazing mournfully below, his face reddening from the weight of the wings and the supplementary gear.

The test pilot had on a pair of wings quite different from the ones that Possibile had put together in his time. Each one of the eighteen co-inventors had had a creative hand in their improvement, as a result of which nothing at all remained of Possibile's invention.

Indeed, the creatively redeveloped wings were of another order entirely. As Possibile had made them, they resembled the wings of a swan, while in their new variant they were closer to those of a bat. Possibile had made his wings from whatever he had at hand—some wooden planks and canvas; the wings of the research branch "Duckandgoose" were made out of steel (according to the demands of the wing safety expert) and then gilded (according to the demands of the wing-aesthete). In Possibile's version, the auxiliary gear was almost weightless and barely noticeable; in the new version, the back of the individual preparing for flight (in the given instance, the back of the poet Chameleon) was saddled with a powerful motor. Two connecting rods led from the motor to the wings. Since the motor needed fuel, a ten-liter tank was constructed to fit on that part of the human anatomy where the legs are attached to the back. A hose led from the tank to the motor. On his heels, the test pilot wore something resembling spurs, connected to the motor by steel lines. In order to start the motor, the pilot had to give a kick with his right foot, and in order to turn it off, he gave a kick with his left.

Victor Squaretsin, in his role of radio announcer, was going out of his skin trying to fill the unscheduled pauses in the program. He chattered away nonstop while Chameleon was being outfitted in the wings and later when the straw was being laid. But toward the end, the exhausted Victor started repeating himself, and it became obvious that he no longer knew what to talk about.

The situation was becoming embarrassing. The poet-test pilot was standing on the diving board and clearly didn't feel like going anywhere. With a look of despair he stared into the faces of his audience, seeking support. Finally his glance met up with that of Reclinesky, and the latter raised his hand to chest level and made a fist. Then Chameleon closed his eyes, tiptoed out to the edge of the board and gave a kick.

The motor let out a wild roar. Flames shot out from behind the back of the test pilot, mixing in with clouds of blue-gray smoke. Something screeched, knocked, and started to whine. As the panic-stricken audience made for the exit, kicking over chairs, Chameleon rose into the air at an angle, then overturned and hung upside down in space. A moment later the motor stalled and the poet fell down on the straw, soaked with gasoline and blood. Those few people, Possibile included, who had not succumbed to panic, rushed over and relieved him of his armor. Fortunately, the poet was only bruised, and if there was a lot of blood, its single source was a broken nose.

The next day, the research branch got the news that the scandalous failure with the wings had attracted attention on a level far higher than that of the BOSHI administration. A day after that, it became common knowledge that Reclinesky had been removed. His replacement was a man from a different institution entirely—the well-known aviation builder Staunchov. The new director was given broad authority with the right to take action over BOSHI's head.

The newsletter which appeared on the following day was entirely devoted to the unmasking of Reclinesky by various research associates. Taykitovskaya, for example, wrote a short note to the effect that Reclinesky had never been a scientist at all, but had bribed his way into the institute after a stint as assistant recreational director on a sight-seeing boat, where he had been responsible for putting together the music program.

Also included in the newsletter was the latest effort of the poet Chameleon:

The cognac on your breath comes at us
Every day.
Reclinesky you've misused your status,
Now you'll pay.

We've got your number, parasite,
We know your game.
The dimming of our glorious light
Has you to blame.

Your wretched deeds inspire me
To righteous wrath.
It's clear that both of us can't be
On one true path.

Our path is pure, our path is bright,
So you—get lost.
Staunchov will lead us on to flight
At any cost!

Bulletin

Comrade Staunchov arrived at the research branch "Duckandgoose" to take charge of affairs. On the same day he went to the hotel where Alex Possibile was staying. The latter was already packing his suitcase, getting ready for his journey back to Horse-and-Cart. Staunchov asked him to put off the trip for a short time and drove him to the institute. Here, on Staunchov's orders, Possibile's blueprints had been retrieved from the archives, and his wings carried up from the cellar. They were still in flying condition, since the case that Katya had sewn from waterproof material had protected them from the dampness.

The two men took the wings, went into the courtyard, and took turns flying around in them. The eighteen co-inventors, faces pressed against the windows, looked on with astonishment and some dissatisfaction at what they felt to be a frivolous undertaking.

Possibile's wings were given over to production, and the inventor was financially recompensed. He was even offered an academic rank, which some vestige of provincial fear caused him to decline posthaste, and he soon took off for Horse-and-Cart.

Staunchov got the wing production under way and then went back to his Aircraft Construction Bureau. An order soon arrived closing the research branch "Duckandgoose" on grounds of inutility. The building was given to a kindergarten.

Initially the wings were produced by a small factory, but eventually a huge plant had to be constructed to take care of the demand. Possibile's wings had captured the market not only at home but in the west and throughout the whole world. They were cheap and flew irreproachably. The time had come for the general aviazation of humankind.

Then the interest in wings started to fall. They simply went too slowly for the hurried pace of the era. The new demand for speed was satisfied by the sale of inexpensive jet attachments which fitted into a suitcase and increased the speed of the wings up to six hundred miles an hour.

As has already been noted, primary users of wings on our planet at the present time are romantically inclined lovers and aging village mail carriers who don't trust jet technology.

Conclusion

Alex Possibile returned to Horse-and-Cart. On the occasion of his return, Katya took a whole day's leave from the village veterinary clinic where she worked. She put on her old blouse with the edible buttons. Alex had always liked that blouse very much.

"Well, you've won," she said to him. "Your wings have been accepted. Are you glad?"

"I'm glad to be back home," answered Alex. "There's too much noise in the city, too many problems. . . . Tell me how things are at the post office. There have't been any complaints about nondelivery of mail?"

From that day on, Alex never said another word about wings, and never worked on any new inventions, although he continued to order and read a lot of books. Judging from his diary notations of the period, he felt that his invention would not have been possible were it not for Katya and the night he spent in the taiga swamp before he met her. His remarks about wings are, however, extremely rare, and all of them express in some form the motif of the belated marksman—that is, his conviction that his wings had appeared in the world too late to serve humanity to the extent that they would have had they been invented earlier.

Alex took his duties as head of the post office very seriously, and had things running so smoothly that his branch won several district and even regional prizes. When he eventually retired, his farewell dinner was attended not only by his co-workers, but by practically the entire populace of Horse-and-Cart.

Alex lived for another five years after his retirement. He was burdened by inactivity. During the autumn muds he'd often appear at the post office outfitted in a raincoat and rubber boots, ready to carry mail to the outlying villages. He never took his wings, with or without the new jet attachments, preferring to go on foot.

After one of those hikes he fell ill and took to bed. Very good doctors were called in to see him, but they could do nothing. He lost consciousnes and lay in a coma for two weeks. But then one evening he woke up, and Katya was amazed to see how clear his eyes were. It seemed as though he was getting better.

"I just saw the swan," he said to Katya. "The swan is making circles over our house. . . . Go wave to him, because I can't."

So as not to hurt his feeelings, Katya went out into the yard. The floods had come to an end, and a snowstorm was howling. Blowing snow was piling up on the rooftop and then sliding off, as though someone was trying without success to build a white tent there. Through her tears, Katya almost thought that there really was a white bird circling over the house. She waved to it. The bird made one more circle, then whirled away into the darkness and was lost.

Katya went back inside, walked over to the water pump, and spent a long time washing her eyes in cold water, so that Alex wouldn't see that she'd been crying. Then she sat down beside him.

"You're right, it was a white bird. A swan. But isn't that a bad sign?"

"It's neither a bad sign nor a good one," said Alex. "It's time for us to say good-bye."

Katya took Alex's hand.

"Do you see anything?" she asked.

"I'm walking along a road in the forest, and there's a falcon flying before me, and an owl sitting on my shoulder. It's getting dark."

"But where are you going?"

"It looks like the road to Far Omshar."

"Are you having a hard time?" asked Katya.

"It's getting dark very fast. And the falcon left me."

"Why did you shudder?"

"That's the owl leaving her perch on my shoulder. There she is flying ahead and showing me the way."

For a long time he said nothing.

"Can you hear me?" asked Katya.

"Yes."

"What's happening now?"

"It's gotten dark. But the owl is still flying before me."

Alex Possibile is buried in a quiet village graveyard two kilometers from the village of Horse-and-Cart (the present-day Possibility). Katya outlived him by two weeks. Their graves lie next to one another, united by a single slab of local gray sandstone. Carved into the stone is a sketch of wings, and below it a few verses by a local poet:

> They walk along a different road,
> The light of dawn before them.
> The birds sing in a different mode,
> But still they're singing for them.
>
> Time passes swiftly as we sleep,
> No judgments will distress us.
> The grasses over us will creep
> And cities' sounds caress us.
>
> In years gone by we'd meet the dawn
> And hear the birds' bright chorus.
> And though the logic may be wrong,
> Death has no meaning for us.

Near the grave, not too high up, is a pole with a bird feeder. The village children and even the adults keep it filled with food, so that there are always a lot of birds around, especially during the winter frosts. In the summertime, there are always wreaths and bouquets of forest flowers.

Documentation

The first flowers brought to Earth from another planet were laid on the graves of Alex Possibile and his wife.

This took place seventeen years after their deaths, when the multistage cosmic expedition returned from Venus, where a research station had been set up and plans laid for populating the planet. It turned out that for Venetian atmospheric conditions, Possibile's wings were the most effective and safest form of individual transport.

At the present time, wings have become the most popular means of locomotion on Venus, as a result of which the demand for them has been rising constantly.

[This story translated by Alice Stone
Nakhimovsky and Alexander Nakhimovsky.]